T.M.

The Apotheosis of Porthos.

THE THREE
MUSKETEERS

ALEXANDRE DUMAS

VOL. I

ILLUSTRATED BY F. C. TILNEY

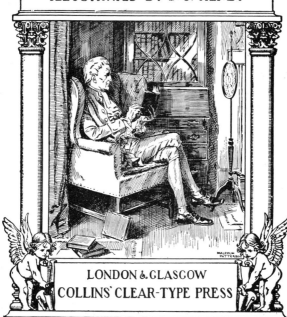

LONDON & GLASGOW
COLLINS' CLEAR-TYPE PRESS

CONTENTS.

VOLUME I.

CONTENTS.

AUTHOR'S PREFACE.

It is about a year ago, that in making researches in the Bibliotheque Nationale for my History of Louis the Fourteenth, I by chance met with the Memoirs of Monsieur d'Artagnan, printed by Peter the Red at Amsterdam—as the principal works of that period, when authors could not adhere to the truth without running the risk of the Bastile, generally were. The title attracted my notice; I took the Memoirs home, with the permission of the librarian, and actually devoured them.

It is not my intention here to make analysis of this curious work, but to satisfy myself by referring such of my readers to the work itself as appreciate the pictures of those times. They will there discover portraits traced by the hand of a master; and although these sketches are mostly drawn on the doors of a barrack, or the walls of an inn, they will not find them less true than those likenesses of Louis XIII., of Anne of Austria, of Richelieu, Mazarin, and the majority of the courtiers of that age, drawn by M. Anguetil.

But, as every one knows, that which strikes the eccentric mind of the poet, does not always make an impression on the great mass of readers. So, whilst admiring (as all others doubtless will do) the details which we have described, the thing which strikes us most, is one which certainly had not attracted the attention of any other person. D'Artagnan relates, that on his first visit to M. de Treville, Captain of the Royal Musketeers, he met three young men in the ante-chamber,

serving in the illustrious corps into which he solicited the
honour of being admitted, and bearing the names of
Athos, Porthos, and Aramis.

We confess that these foreign names struck us much,
and we suspected that they were feigned appellations,
by which d'Artagnan had perhaps concealed the names
of illustrious persons; if, perchance, the bearers of them
had not themselves chosen them, when, through caprice,
discontent, or lack of fortune, they had donned the simple
coat of a Musketeer.   Therefore we could not rest satisfied
till we had found in contemporary literature some trace
of the extraordinary titles which had so forcibly excited
our curiosity.   The mere catalogue of the books we read
to gain this end would fill a whole chapter, which would
perhaps be very instructive, but certainly far from
amusing, to our readers.   We will, therefore, content
ourselves with saying, that at the very moment when,
discouraged by such fruitless investigations, we were
about to abandon our researches, we at last, guided by
the counsels of our illustrious and learned friend, Paulin
Pâris, discovered a manuscript folio, numbered 4772, or
4773, we forget which, having for its title—

THE MEMOIRS OF M. LE COMTE DE LA FERE;

RELATING TO SOME OF THE EVENTS WHICH PASSED IN FRANCE
ABOUT THE END OF THE REIGN OF LOUIS XIII.,
AND THE BEGINNING OF THE REIGN
OF LOUIS XIV.

Our pleasure may be guessed, when, in turning over
this manuscript, our last hope, we found at the twentieth
page the name of Athos; at the twenty-first, the name of
Aramis; at the twenty-seventh, the name of Porthos.

The discovery of a manuscript entirely unknown, at a period when historical knowledge was raised to such a high pitch, appeared to be almost a miracle. We therefore quickly requested permission to print it, that we might one day introduce ourselves to the Academy of Inscriptions and Belles Lettres with the goods of others, if we do not happen (as is very probable) to enter the French Academy on our own merits.

This permission was most graciously accorded; which we here declare, to give a public contradiction to those malevolent persons who pretend that government is not inclined to indulge authors.

We offer to-day the first part of this valuable manuscript to our readers, restoring to it the title which suits it, and promising, if (as we doubt not) this should meet with the success it merits, to publish immediately the second.

In the meantime, as the godfather is a second father, we invite our readers to look to *us*, and not to the Comte de la Fere, for his amusement or his ennui.

this discovery of a manuscript, entirely unknown, at
a period when it could throw so new a light on such
a high place appeared to be almost a duty. We
thought it quite right, and permission to print it, that
each might one day have the enjoyment of the features
of its versions, and in his Letters with the goods of
others; that it not become not so very profitable to enter
the French Academy in our own bounds.

This permission was most graciously accorded by M.
——, the desire to hire a public acquaintance as
an ordinary person, who pretend that government is not
any boon to make its labors.

We offer to day the first part of this valuable manuscript,
in our next year to complete it. For the which, until it had
remaining. If less we doubt not, this should meet with the
success. If it will, to publish immediately the second
part in the discussion as here collected, as of a second labour,
we invite our readers to look to the case not for the coming
of its Part, for his enlistment of his cause.

The Three Musketeers.

CHAPTER I.

THE THREE PRESENTS OF M. D'ARTAGNAN, THE FATHER.

ON the first Monday of the month of April, 1625, the small town of Meung, the birthplace of the author of the "Romance of the Rose," appeared to be in a state of revolution, as complete as if the Huguenots were come to make a second siege of La Rochelle. Many of the townsmen, observing the flight along the high street, of women who left their children to squall at the doorsteps, hastened to don their armour, and, fortifying their courage, which was inclined to fail, with a musket or a partisan, proceeded towards the inn of the Jolly Miller, to which a vast and accumulating mob was hastening with intense curiosity.

At that period alarms were frequent, and few days passed without some bourg or other registering in its archives an event of this description. There were the nobles, who made war on each other; there was the king, who made war on the cardinal; there was the Spaniard, who made war on the king; then, besides these wars, concealed or overt, secret or public, there were bandits, mendicants, Huguenots, wolves, and lacqueys, who made war on the whole world. The townsmen always armed themselves against the bandits, the wolves, and the lacqueys; frequently against the nobles and the Huguenots; sometimes against the king; but never against the cardinal or the Spaniard. From this custom, therefore, it arose, that on the aforesaid first Monday in the month of April, 1625, the burghers, hearing a noise, and seeing neither the yellow and red flag, nor the livery of the Duke of Richelieu, rushed towards the inn of the Jolly Miller. Having reached it, every one could see and understand the cause of this alarm. A young man—

But let us trace his portrait with one stroke of the pen. Fancy to yourself Don Quixote at eighteen—Don Quixote peeled, without his coat of mail or greaves—Don Quixote clothed in a woollen doublet, whose blue colour was changed to an *undyable* shade, a shade between the lees of wine and a cerulean blue. The countenance long and brown; the cheek-bones high, denoting acuteness; the muscles of the jaw enormously developed—an infallible mark by which a Gascon may be recognised, even without the cap, and our youth wore a cap, adorned with a sort of feather; the eye full and intelligent; the nose hooked, but finely formed; the whole figure too large for a youth, yet too small for an adult; an inexperienced eye would have taken him for the son of a farmer on a journey, had it not been for the long sword, which, hanging from a leathern belt, banged against the heels of its owner whilst he was walking, and against the rough coat of his steed when he was mounted;—for our youth had a steed, and this steed was at the same time so remarkable as to attract observation. It was a Beaunese sheltie, of about twelve or fourteen years of age, yellow as an orange, without any hair on its tail, but abundance of galls on its legs, and which, whilst carrying its head lower than its knees, making the application of a martingale unnecessary, yet managed gallantly its eight leagues a day. Unfortunately, these useful qualities of the steed were so well concealed under its strange coat and eccentric gait, that at a time when every one knew something of horses, the apparition of the aforesaid sheltie at Meung, which it had entered about a quarter of an hour before, by the gate of Beaugency, produced a somewhat unfavourable sensation or impression, which extended even to its master. And this impression was the more painful to young d'Artagnan (for that was the name of the Don Quixote of this second Rozinante), that he could not conceal from himself the ridiculous light in which he, albeit so good a horseman, was placed by such a steed. He had, therefore, sighed deeply when he accepted the gift from M. d'Artagnan, his father: he knew that such a beast was worth about twenty francs. It is true that the words which accompanied the present were above price.

"My son," said the Gascon gentleman, in that pure Beaunese patois or dialect, which Henry IV. could never entirely shake off—"my son, this horse was born in the paternal homestead about thirteen years ago, and has remained in it ever since, which ought to make you regard it with affection. Never sell it; let it die honourably of old age, and in tranquillity; and should you make a campaign with it, take as much care of it as you would of an old servant. At the court, if you should ever have the honour to be presented—an honour, however, to which your long line of noble ancestors entitles you—support with dignity the name of gentleman, which has been honourably borne by your ancestors, for the sake of you and yours, for more than 500 years. Never submit quietly to the slightest indignity, except it proceed from the cardinal or the king. It is by his courage—mark this well—it is by his courage alone, that a gentleman makes his way nowadays. Whoever hesitates one moment, lets perhaps that chance escape him, which fortune, for that moment alone, has offered him. You are young, and ought to be brave, for two reasons: the first, because you are a Gascon; the second, because you are my son. Have no fear of many imbroglios, and look about for adventures. You have been taught to handle the sword; you have muscles of iron, a wrist like steel; fight whenever you can, the more so because duels are forbidden, and consequently it requires twice as much courage to fight. I have to give you but fifteen crowns, my son, besides the horse, and the advice which you have heard. Your mother will add to them the recipe for a certain balsam, which she received from a Bohemian woman, and which has the miraculous power of curing every wound

which has fallen short of the heart. Take advantage of
all, and live long and happily. I have only one word
more to add, and it is the offer of an example : not my
own, for I have never been at court ; I have only served in
the religious wars as a volunteer. I wish to speak to you
of M. de Treville, once my neighbour, who has had the
honour of playing, whilst a boy, with our king, Louis
XIII., whom God preserve. Sometimes their play turned
to battles, and in these battles the king did not always
conquer ; yet his conquests by M. de Treville imbued him
with a great deal of esteem and friendship for him.
Afterwards, M. de Treville fought other battles ; indeed,
merely during his journey to Paris, he fought five times ;
from the death of the late monarch, to the majority of the
young king, he has fought seven times, without reckoning
campaigns and sieges ; and since that majority till now,
perhaps a hundred times ! And yet, in spite of edicts,
ordinances, and writs, behold him now captain of the
Musketeers ; that is, chief of a legion of Cæsars, upon
whom the king mainly depends, and who are feared by
the cardinal, who, as every one knows, is not easily
alarmed. Moreover, M. de Treville gains ten thousand
crowns a year, and therefore is a man of consequence.
He began the world as you do. Go to him with this
letter, and let your conduct be regulated by him, that you
may meet with the same results."

Hereupon M. d'Artagnan, the father, girded his own
sword upon his son, tenderly kissed him on either cheek,
and gave him his blessing. Leaving the paternal
chamber, the young man found his mother waiting with
the famous recipe, which, from the advice he had just
received, it seemed very probable that he would require
to use pretty often. The adieus were longer and more
tender on this side than on the other ; not but that M.
d'Artagnan loved his son, who was his only child, but
that M. d'Artagnan was a man who would have considered
it unworthy of himself to give way to any sentiment ;
whilst Madame d'Artagnan was a woman, and, what is

more, a mother.   She wept much; and, to the credit of
M. d'Artagnan the younger, we may as well say that,
whatever efforts he made to remain firm, as became the
future Musketeer, nature gained the day, and he shed
many tears, some of which he had great difficulty in
concealing.

Our youth took his way the same day, furnished with
the three paternal gifts, which were, as we have said, the
fifteen crowns, the steed, and the letter to M. de Treville.
As may be well imagined, the advice was thrown into the
bargain.   With such a *vade mecum*, d'Artagnan found
himself, morally and physically, the counterpart of the
hero of Cervantes, to whom we so happily compared him,
when our duty as his historian obliged us to draw his
portrait.   Don Quixote took windmills for giants, and
sheep for armies; d'Artagnan considered every smile an
insult, and even a look a provocation.   Therefore, his fist
was doubled from Tarbes to Meung; and, from one cause
or another, his hand was on the pommel of his sword
ten times a day.   However, the fist did not descend upon
any jaw, nor did the sword leave its scabbard.   It was
not that the unlucky yellow sheltie did not excite many a
smile on the countenances of passers-by; but as beside
the said yellow sheltie clashed a sword of respectable
length, and above the sword glistened an eye rather stern
than fierce, the wayfarers repressed their mirth, or, if
their mirth surpassed their prudence, they took care only
to laugh on one side of their faces, like the ancient
masques.   D'Artagnan, therefore, remained dignified and
uninterrupted in his susceptibility, even to this fatal town
of Meung.   But there, when he dismounted at the door
of the Jolly Miller, without any one, either landlord,
waiter, or hostler, coming to hold the stirrup of his horse,
d'Artagnan perceived at the open window of a room,
on the ground-floor, a gentleman of distinguished air and
handsome figure, although with a countenance slightly
grim, conversing with two persons who appeared to listen
to him with deference.   D'Artagnan naturally thought,

according to his usual custom, that they were talking
about him, and listened accordingly. This time, however, he was partly correct: *he* was not the subject of
conversation, but his horse was. The gentleman appeared
to be enumerating to his hearers all his qualities; and
since, as I have said, his hearers appeared to pay him
great deference, they every moment laughed heartily.

Now, since even the slightest smile was sufficient to
rouse the anger of our youth, we may well imagine what
effect such unbounded mirth was likely to produce upon
him. Nevertheless, d'Artagnan wished first to examine
the countenance of the impertinent fellow who thus
laughed at him. He therefore fixed his stern look upon
the stranger, and saw a man from forty to forty-five years
of age, with eyes black and piercing, complexion pale,
nose strongly-marked, and moustache black and carefully
trimmed. He was attired in a violet-coloured doublet
and breeches, with points of the same colour, with no
other ornament than the sleeves through which the shirt
passed. This doublet and these breeches, though new,
displayed divers wrinkles and creases, as if they had been
for some time packed up in a portmanteau. D'Artagnan
made these observations with the rapidity of a most
minute observer, and doubtless with an instinct which told
him that this unknown was to have a vast influence on
his future life.

At the very moment that d'Artagnan fixed his eyes
upon the gentleman with the violet doublet, that
individual made one of his wisest and most profound
remarks upon the Beaunese sheltie. His two auditors
roared with laughter, and he himself, contrary to his
usual custom, permitted a sort of sickly smile to wander
over his countenance. This time there was no room for
doubt. D'Artagnan was really insulted. Being convinced of this, he pulled his cap over his eyes, and trying
to imitate the courtly airs which he had seen among
some chance Gascon nobility in their provincial visits, he
placed one hand on the guard of his sword, and the other

on his hip. Unfortunately, the nearer he advanced, the more angry he grew, so that instead of the high and dignified language which he had prepared as the prelude to his challenge, he found nothing at the tip of his tongue but a rough personality, which he accompanied with a furious gesture.

"Hollo, sir!" he cried; "you, sir, who hide yourself behind the shutter — yes, you! tell me what you are laughing at, and we will laugh together."

The gentleman slowly turned his eyes from the steed to his rider, as if it required some time to comprehend that these strange reproaches were addressed to himself; then, when he could no longer doubt it, he slightly knit his brows, and, after a pretty long pause, with an accent of irony and insolence impossible to describe, answered d'Artagnan, "I am not speaking to you, sir."

"But *I* am speaking to you," cried the young man, exasperated by this mixture of insolence and good manners—this polite contempt.

The unknown regarded him yet a moment with a slight smile, and then leaving the window, slowly sauntered out of the inn, and stationed himself opposite the horse, at two paces from d'Artagnan. His calm face and jeering aspect redoubled the mirth of his companions, who still remained at the window. D'Artagnan, seeing him come out, drew his sword a foot out of its scabbard.

"This horse decidedly *is*, or rather *has* been, a butter-cup," continued the unknown, pursuing his remarks, and addressing his auditors at the window, without appearing to notice the exasperation of d'Artagnan, who, nevertheless, swelled and strutted between them; "it is of a colour," he continued, "well known in botany, but as yet very rare amongst horses."

"A man may laugh at a horse, who would not dare to laugh at its master," cried the disciple of Treville with fury.

"I do not often laugh, sir," answered the unknown, "as you may yourself discover by the expression of my countenance; but yet I mean to preserve the right of laughing when I please."

"And I," roared out d'Artagnan, "do not permit any one to laugh when I do *not* please."

"Really, sir!" continued the unknown, more quietly than ever; "well, that is sound sense;" and turning on his heel, he essayed to re-enter the inn by the front door, opposite which d'Artagnan, on arriving, had observed a horse ready saddled.

But d'Artagnan was not the man to let any one who had had the insolence to mock him thus escape; he therefore drew his sword and pursued him, exclaiming, "Turn, turn, Master Jester, that I may not strike you behind!"

"Strike me!" said the other, quickly turning round, and regarding the youth with as much astonishment as contempt, "go along with you, my dear boy; you are mad." Then, in a low voice, as if he were speaking to himself, he added, "It is annoying: what a prize for his majesty, who is everywhere seeking fire-eaters to recruit his guards."

He had scarcely finished, when d'Artagnan made such a furious thrust at him, that, had he not jumped back briskly, it is probable the jest would have been his last. Perceiving now, however, that the affair was *beyond* a joke, the unknown drew his sword, saluted his adversary, and gravely put himself on guard; but at the same moment his two auditors, accompanied by the host, fell pell-mell upon d'Artagnan, with sticks, shovels, and tongs. This caused such a complete diversion of the attack, that, whilst d'Artagnan himself turned to face this shower of blows, his opponent put up his sword with the same calm as before, and, from an actor, became a spectator of the combat—a character which he supported with the same imperturbability, yet all the time muttering, "Plague upon these Gascons! Put him on his orange-coloured horse, and let him go."

"Not before I have slain you, you coward!" cried

d'Artagnan, all the time making the best resistance he could, and not yielding one step to his three opponents, who showered their blows upon him.

"Yet another gasconade!" murmured the gentleman; "upon my word these Gascons are incorrigible; keep up the dance, since he actually wishes it; when he is tired he will say that he has had enough."

But the stranger did not yet know with what a stubborn personage he had to deal. D'Artagnan was not the man ever to sue for quarter. The contest therefore continued for some moments longer, until at last, completely worn out, d'Artagnan dropped his sword, which was broken in two by a blow from a stick, while at the same instant another blow, which cut open his forehead, stretched him on the ground almost senseless.

It was now that all the burghers hastened to the scene of action. Fearing a disturbance, the landlord, assisted by his servants, carried the wounded man into the kitchen, where some care was given him. As for the stranger, he returned to the window, and viewed the crowd with evident marks of impatience, seeming rather annoyed at their refusal to go away.

"Well, how is that madman now?" said he, turning, and addressing the host, who came to inquire in what state his guest was.

"Is your excellency safe and well?" demanded the host.

"Yes, perfectly so, mine host; but I wish to know what is become of this youth."

"He is better," replied the host; "but he was quite senseless."

"Indeed!" said the gentleman.

"But before he quite lost his senses, he rallied all his strength to challenge and defy you," added the landlord.

"Well, this young fellow is the very devil himself," said the gentleman.

"Oh, no, your excellency, oh, no," replied the host, with a contemptuous grin, "he is not the devil, for while he was senseless we rummaged his outfit, and in his bundle we found but one shirt, and in his pocket only twelve crowns, which fact, however, did not prevent his saying, just before he fainted, that, had this happened in Paris, you should quickly have repented it, but as it has taken place here you will not have to repent it until later."

"Therefore," coolly observed the stranger, "he doubtless is a prince of the blood in disguise."

"I give you this information, sir," said the host, "that you may keep yourself on your guard."

"And did he not name any one in his anger?"

"Yes, he slapped his pocket, and said, 'We shall see what M. de Treville will say to this insult offered to his *protégé.*'"

"M. de Treville?" said the unknown, becoming more attentive; "he slapped his pocket, and mentioned the name of M. de Treville?—Let us see, my good host: whilst this young man was senseless, you did not fail, I am sure, to examine that pocket: what did it contain?"

"A letter, addressed to M. de Treville, captain of the Musketeers."

"Really?"

"Just as I have the honour to tell your excellency," said the host.

The latter, who had no great penetration, did not remark the expression which these words brought upon the countenance of the stranger, who now left the window-sill, on which his elbow had rested, and frowned like a man disturbed all of a sudden.

"The devil!" muttered he between his teeth; "could Treville have sent this Gascon? He is very young; but a thrust of a sword is a thrust of a sword, whatever may be the age of him that gives it, and one distrusts a boy less than an oldster; a slight obstacle is sufficient to thwart a project." And the stranger fell into a reverie which lasted some minutes. "Come, mine host," at length he said, "will you not rid me of this madman? I cannot conscientiously kill him, and yet," he added with a menacing air, "he much annoys me. Where is he?"

"In my wife's chamber, on the first storey, where they are dressing his wounds."

"Are his clothes and his bag with him? Has he taken off his doublet?"

"On the contrary, they are below in the kitchen," said the host; "but since this young madman annoys you——"

"Doubtless; he causes a disturbance in your inn, which no respectable people can bear. Go to your room, make out my bill, and give orders to my servants."

"What, sir, must you be off?"

"Yes. I ordered you to saddle my horse; have I not been obeyed?"

"Yes; and your excellency may see your horse standing under the grand entrance, quite ready for the road."

"Very well; then do as I have ordered."

"Heyday!" said the host to himself; "can he be afraid of this young boy?" But a commanding look from the stranger cut him short; he humbly bowed, and left the apartment.

"My lady must not see this strange fellow," said the stranger; "as she is already late, she must soon pass. I had better mount my horse and go to meet her. If I could only just learn the contents of that letter addressed to Treville." And thus muttering, the unknown descended to the kitchen.

In the meantime, the landlord, who doubted not that this youth's presence drove the stranger from his inn, had gone to his wife's chamber, and found that d'Artagnan had regained consciousness. Then, whilst he made him comprehend that the police might be severe on him for having attacked a great lord (for, according to the host's idea, the stranger could be nothing less than a great lord), he persuaded him, in spite of his weakness, to resume his journey.

D'Artagnan, half stunned, without doublet, his head

completely bandaged, arose, and, pushed out by the host, began to descend the stairs; but on reaching the kitchen, the first object he saw was his opponent, who was quietly talking at the door of a heavy carriage, drawn by two large Norman horses. The person with whom he conversed was a woman of from twenty to twenty-two years of age, whose head appeared, through the window of the carriage, like a picture in a frame. We have already said how rapidly d'Artagnan caught the expression of a countenance; he saw, therefore, at the first glance, that the lady was young and attractive. Now, this beauty was the more striking to him, as it was completely different from that of his own southern country. She was a pale, fair person, with long curling hair falling on her shoulders, large blue languishing eyes, rosy lips, and alabaster hands. She conversed with the unknown with great vivacity.

"So, his eminence commands me——" said she.

"To return immediately to England, and apprise him, with all speed, whether the duke has left London," said the unknown.

"And as to my other instructions?" demanded the fair traveller.

"They are enclosed in this box, which you will not open until you are on the other side of the Channel."

"Good; and you? What are you going to do?"

"I return to Paris."

"Without chastising this insolent boy?" demanded the lady.

The unknown was about to reply, but ere he could do so, d'Artagnan, who had heard every word, rushed to the doorway. "It is that insolent boy," he cried, "who chastises others, and I hope that this time he who deserves chastisement will not escape him."

"Will not escape him?" echoed the unknown, knitting his brows.

"No, in the presence of a woman you would hesitate to fly, I presume."

"Consider," said the lady, seeing the gentleman place his hand to his sword, "consider that the slightest delay might ruin all."

"You are right," said the gentleman; "you go your way, and I will go mine;" and, saluting the lady with a bow, he got into the saddle, whilst the coachman whipped his horses. The lady and gentleman therefore went off at a gallop towards the opposite ends of the street.

"Hollo! your bill!" shouted mine host, whose affection for the traveller was changed to the most profound contempt when he saw him departing without paying.

"Pay, rascal," cried the traveller, as he galloped off, to his valet, who threw three or four pieces of silver at the feet of the landlord, and set off at full speed the way his master went.

"Oh, coward! wretch! false-hearted gentleman!" cried d'Artagnan, rushing after the valet. But he was still too feeble from his wounds to bear such an effort. Scarcely had he gone ten paces, before his ears tingled, a vertigo seized him, a cloud passed before his eyes, and he fell down in the street, with a final cry of "Coward! coward! coward!"

"He is a sad coward verily," murmured the host, who now, approaching d'Artagnan, endeavoured to soothe him by this flattery, as the heron in the fable her friend the snail.

"Yes, a sad coward," murmured d'Artagnan; but *she* is beautiful."

"Who is she?" said the landlord.

"My lady!" murmured d'Artagnan, and again fainted away.

"Never mind," said the host; "although I have lost two, at any rate I have secured this one, whom I am sure of keeping for some days; at all events, I shall gain eleven crowns."

It must be borne in mind that eleven crowns was the exact sum which remained in d'Artagnan's purse; and the host had reckoned upon eleven days' illness, at a crown a day. On this point, however, he reckoned without his guest. The following day d'Artagnan left his couch, went down to the kitchen, and, besides certain ingredients, the names of which have not descended to posterity, demanded some wine, oil, and rosemary, which, with his mother's recipe in his hand, he compounded into a salve, wherewith he anointed his numerous wounds, renewing his plasters himself, and not allowing the interposition of any leech.

Thanks, no doubt, to the Bohemian salve, and perhaps also to the absence of the leech, d'Artagnan found himself on foot in the evening, and almost cured by the next day. But at the moment he was paying for this wine, oil, and rosemary, the sole expense he had incurred (for he had been completely abstinent, whilst, on the contrary, if one believed the hostler, the yellow horse had eaten three times as many oats as one would have supposed possible from his size), d'Artagnan found nothing in his pocket but his little purse, with its eleven crowns. As for the letter to M. de Treville, that was gone. The young man began by looking very patiently for this letter, turning out and rummaging his pockets and fobs twenty times, rummaging his valise again and again, and opening and shutting his purse; but when he was quite convinced that the letter was not to be found, he gave full vent to another fit of rage in a manner which was like to make necessary a second decoction of wine and spiced oil. For, upon beholding this young scatter-brain raging, and threatening to destroy everything in his establishment, if the letter were not found, the host had already seized upon a spit, his wife upon the handle of a broom, and the servants upon the same weapons they had wielded the evening before.

"My letter of introduction!" cried d'Artagnan, "my letter of introduction! or, by St. Denis, I will spit you all like so many ortolans."

One circumstance prevented the youth from accomplishing his threat, which was, that his sword, as we have said,

had unfortunately been broken in two in the first struggle
—a mischance he had entirely forgotten; consequently,
when d'Artagnan went to draw it in earnest, he found
himself armed only with the stump, about eight or ten
inches long, which the host had carefully thrust into the
scabbard. As for the rest of the blade, the cook had
adroitly set it aside for a larding-pin. And yet it is
probable that this deception would not have stopped our
fiery youth, had not the host reflected that the demand
which his guest made was perfectly just.

"But after all," said he, lowering his spit, "where is this
letter?"

"Yes, where is this letter?" roared d'Artagnan; "and
let me tell you that this lettter is for M. de Treville, and
that it must be found, otherwise M. de Treville will know
to have it found—I'll answer for it!"

This threat completely frightened mine host. Next to
the king and the cardinal, M. de Treville was the man
whose name was most frequently in the mouths of the
military, and indeed of the citizens. There was, certainly,
Father Joseph; but *his* name was never mentioned except
in an undertone; so great was the terror which his gray
eminence, as the familiar of the cardinal was called, inspired. Therefore, throwing away his spit, and ordering
his wife to do the same with her broom-handle, and the
servants with their weapons, he himself set the example
by commencing a diligent search for the letter.

"Did this letter contain anything valuable?" said he,
after some moments of fruitless search.

"I should rather think it did," cried the Gascon, who
calculated on the letter to make its way at court; "it
contained my fortune."

"Were they bills on the Bank of Spain?" demanded
the host, much disturbed.

"Bills on the private treasury of his majesty!" replied
d'Artagnan, who, calculating on entering the king's service
through this letter of introduction, thought he might,
without lying, make this somewhat rash reply.

"The devil!" exclaimed the host, at his wit's end.

"But it is of no consequence," continued d'Artagnan, with his native assurance; "the money is nothing, the letter is all I want. I had rather have lost a thousand pistoles than that!" He might as well have made it twenty thousand, but a certain youthful modesty restrained him. A sudden flash of light illumined the mind of the host, who was uttering maledictions at finding nothing.

"This letter is not lost!" he cried.

"Isn't it?" said d'Artagnan.

"No, it has been taken from you."

"Taken! and by whom?"

"By the stranger, yesterday; he went into the kitchen, where your doublet was lying; he was there for a time entirely alone; and I will lay a wager it was he who stole it from you."

"You really think so?" said d'Artagnan, only half convinced, for he knew better than anybody the strictly personal value of the letter, and saw nothing in it to excite cupidity. The fact is, that none of the servants or travellers who were there could have gained anything by the theft.

"You say, then," continued d'Artagnan, "that you suspect this impertinent gentleman?"

"I tell you that I am quite certain of it," said the host; "when I informed him that your worship was the *protégé* of M. de Treville, and that you had a letter for that illustrious noble, he appeared much disturbed, demanded where the letter was, and immediately went into the kitchen, where your doublet was lying."

"Then he is the robber," said d'Artagnan; "I will complain to M. de Treville, and he will lay my complaint before his majesty."

And he majestically drew from his pocket two crowns, which he handed to the host, who followed him, cap in hand, to the archway, where he remounted his yellow horse, which carried him without further accident to the gate of St. Antoine, at Paris. There its owner sold the animal for three crowns; which was a good price, considering that d'Artagnan had over-ridden him in the last part of the journey. The dealer to whom he sold the sheltie for these nine francs, did not conceal from the young man that he paid this exorbitant sum merely on account of the originality of his colour.

D'Artagnan therefore entered Paris on foot, carrying his small valise under his arm, and proceeded until he found a lodging suitable to his slender resources. This chamber was a sort of garret, situated in the Rue des Fossoyeurs, near the Luxembourg. Having paid the luck-penny, he took possession of his lodging, and passed the remainder of the day in sewing on his doublet and breeches sundry laces which his mother had secretly taken from a nearly new doublet of the elder M. d'Artagnan. He then repaired to the Quai de la Feraille, to procure a new blade for his sword; after which he returned to the Louvre, and learned from the first musketeer he met where M. de Treville's hotel was situated. This he ascertained to be in the Rue de Vieux Colombier; that is, in the very neighbourhood where he had himself taken up his abode; a circumstance which he construed into a happy omen of the success of his expedition.

These matters disposed of, and satisfied with the manner in which he had behaved at Meung, without remorse for the past, confident in the present, and full of hope for the future, he went to bed and slept the sleep of the brave. This sleep, still that of a rustic, lasted till nine o'clock in the morning, the hour at which he rose to repair to the hotel of this famed M. de Treville, who, according to d'Artagnan's father, was the third personage in the realm.

CHAPTER II.

THE ANTECHAMBER OF M. DE TREVILLE.

M. DE TROISVILLE, as his family was yet called in
Gascony, or M. de Treville, as he called himself in Paris,
had actually begun life like d'Artagnan; that is to say,
without being worth a sou, but with that fund of audacity,
esprit, and resolution, which makes the poorest Gascon
gentleman often inherit more in imagination than the
richest nobleman of Perigord or Berri receives in reality.
His daring and haughty courage—still more haughty in
success—at the time when blows fell thick as hail, had
raised him to the top of that difficult ladder which is
called court favour, and which he had climbed four rungs
at a time. He was the confidential friend of his king,
who, as every one knows, greatly honoured the memory
of his father, Henry IV. The father of M. de Treville
had served the latter so faithfully in his wars against the
League, that, for want of ready money—the thing that,
which, during his life, was very scarce . . . the earnest
who constantly paid his debts . . . that he never had
occasion to borrow, that is to say . . . his genius)—for
want of ready money, as we have said, he had . . .
him, after the reduction of Paris, to take for . . .
"Un lion d'or passant, sur gueules . . .
"*fidelis et fortis.*" It was a great d . . .
much profit; therefore, when . . . Henry . . .
Henry the Great died, the sol . . .
was his sword, with the arms . . . Than . . .
ever, to this double legacy, and to the nam . . .
tarnish which accompanied it, M. de Treville wa . . .
into the household of the young prince, wher . . .
such good use of his sword, and was so true to . . .
that Louis XIII., one of the best hands with the rapier
his own kingdom, used to say, that if he had a friend wh . . .
was going to fight, he would advise him to take for . . .

second, first himself, and then Treville, or even perhaps
Treville before himself. On this account Louis had a
real affection for Treville; a *royal* affection, an *egotistical*
affection, it must be allowed, but an affection nevertheless.
In those unhappy days it was an important consideration
to surround oneself with men of Treville's stamp. Many
could take for their device the epithet of "*fortis*," which
formed the second part of the motto, but very few men
could claim the epithet "*fidelis*," which formed the first
part of it. Treville was one of the few: his was one of
those rare organisations with the intelligence and obedience
of the mastiff, and a blind courage, and a ready hand,
one to whom the eye had been given only to see whether
the king was dissatisfied with any one, and the hand only
strike the offending person—a Besme, a Maurevers, a
Poltrot de Méré, a Vitry; in short, Treville only wanted
opportunity; but he watched for it, and was resolved
to seize it by the hairs if ever it came within reach
is XIII. therefore appointed Treville
musketeers, who, by their devotion, or
became what his ordinary troops were
Henry III., his Scottish guard to Louis XI. In
his respect the cardinal was not behind the king; for
when he saw the formidable picked guard with which
surrounded himself, this second, or rather this first,
wished also to have his own guard; he
the king, had his musketeers; and
's were seen selecting for their
es of France, and even from
foreign countries known for their skill as swords-
was not rare for Richelieu and the king, over
of chess in the evening, to dispute concerning
of their respective followers. Each boasted of
nent and the courage of his own; and whilst
inveighing against duels and imbroglios, they
secretly excited their respective partisans to fight, and
experienced immoderate delight, or intense chagrin, at
their respective victories or defeats. Thus at least says

the memoir of one who was concerned in some of these
defeats, and many of these victories.

Treville had seized on the weak point in his master's
character; and to this knowledge he owed the long and
constant favour of a king who has not left behind him
the reputation of having been constant in his friendships.
He paraded his musketeers before the cardinal Armand
Duplessis with an air of insolence which made the gray
moustache of his eminence curl with anger. Treville also
thoroughly understood the war of that period, when, if
you lived not at the expense of the enemy, you lived at
that of your countrymen. His soldiers formed a legion
of very devils, under no discipline but his own. Swaggering
bullies, given to wine, the king's musketeers, or rather
M. de Treville's, spread themselves through the taverns,
the public walks, and the theatres, talking loud, curling
their moustaches, jingling their swords, hustling the
guards of the cardinal when they met them, indulging,
in the open street, in a thousand jokes; sometimes killed,
but then certain of being lamented and avenged; sometimes killing, but then quite certain not to languish in
prison, since M. de Treville was always at hand to
procure their pardon and release. Therefore M. de
Treville was lauded in every tone, sung of in every key,
by these men, who adored him; yet, hang-dogs as they
were, they trembled before him as scholars before their
master, obedient to a word, and ready to meet death to
wipe away any reproach. M. de Treville had used this
powerful lever, first, for the king and his friends, and
next, for himself and his own friends. The captain of the
musketeers was, therefore, admired, feared, and loved,
which state constitutes the apogee of human affairs.

Louis XIV. absorbed all the lesser stars of his court,
by his vast brilliancy; but his father, "*Sol pluribus
impar*," imparted his personal splendour to many of his
favourites—his individual valour to each of his courtiers.
Besides the king's levee, and that of the cardinal, there
were then at Paris at least two hundred smaller ones,

fairly exclusive; and amongst these two hundred smaller levees, that of M. de Treville was one of those most frequented. From six o'clock in the morning during summer, and eight in the winter, the courtyard of his hotel, in the Rue du Vieux Colombier, resembled a camp. From fifty to sixty musketeers, who appeared to relieve each other, and to present a number always imposing, were stalking about incessantly, armed to the teeth, and ready for anything. From one end to the other of one of those long staircases, on whose space our modern civilisation would build an entire mansion, ascended and descended those petitioners who sought favours; with provincial gentlemen, eager to be enrolled; and liveried lacquers of every colour, in the act of delivering messages from their masters to M. de Treville. In the antechamber, on long circular benches, reclined the *élite*, that is, such of them as had assembled; a continual buzzing prevailed from morning till night; whilst M. de Treville, in his cabinet adjoining the antechamber, received visits, listened to complaints, gave his orders, and, like the king in his balcony at the Louvre, had only to place himself at his window to review his men and their arms.

On the day when d'Artagnan presented himself, the assembly was very imposing, especially to a provincial just arrived in Paris. It is true, this provincial was a Gascon, and at this period more especially, d'Artagnan's countrymen had the reputation of not being easily intimidated. In fact, as soon as any one had passed the threshold of the massive door, studded with long square nails, he found himself in the midst of a troop of swordsmen, who were cruising about the court, talking, quarrelling, and jesting with each other. To clear a path through these eddies, it was necessary to be an officer, a man of rank, or a pretty woman. It was, therefore, in the midst of this crowd and disorder that our youth, holding his long rapier against his slender legs, and the rim of his beaver in his hand, advanced with palpitating

heart, yet with that sort of half smile of provincial embarrassment which wishes to create a good impression.
When he had passed one group, he breathed more freely;
but he perceived that they turned to look at him, and
d'Artagnan, who to that day had invariably entertained
a pretty good opinion of himself, for the first time in his
life thought himself ridiculous. When he had reached
the staircase it was still worse; on the first step were
four musketeers, who amused themselves in the following
manner, whilst ten or a dozen of their companions waited
on the landing-place till it was their turn to have a share
in the game. One of them on a higher step, with a
naked sword in his hand, prevented, or endeavoured to
prevent, the other three from mounting the stairs; whilst
these three skirmished with him very actively with their
swords. D'Artagnan at first took these swords for foils,
and thought they were *buttoned;* but he soon found, by
certain scratches, that each weapon was as sharp as
possible, and at each of these scratches, not only the
spectators, but the actors themselves, laughed most
heartily. The one who held the higher step at that
time, kept his opponents at bay in a dexterous manner.
A circle was formed round him, the condition of the
game being, that at every hit, he who was struck
should relinquish the pastime, and surrender his turn of
reception by M. de Treville to the one who had touched
him. In five minutes three were grazed, one on the
hand, one on the chin, and another on the ear, by this
defender of the staircase, who was himself untouched—a
proof of his skill which, according to the rules of the
game, entitled him to three turns of favour. This sport
surprised our young traveller, although he did not wish
it to appear that he was astonished. He had seen in his
own province (that province where, moreover, the fiery
passions are so promptly roused) a good many provoca-
tives to duels, and yet the gasconade of these four
players appeared much stronger than any he had heard
of even in Gascony. He fancied he was transported into

that famous country of giants where Gulliver afterwards went, and was so much frightened. And yet he had not reached the end: the landing-place and antechamber still remained. On the landing-place they did not fight, but recounted histories of the fair sex; and in the antechamber, tales of the court. On the landing-place d'Artagnan blushed; in the antechamber he shuddered. But if his good manners were shocked on the landing-place, his respect for the cardinal was scandalised in the antechamber. There, to his great astonishment, he heard the policy which made all Europe tremble, openly criticised, as well as the private life of the cardinal, which so many powerful men had been punished for attempting to scrutinise. That great man, whom d'Artagnan's father had so deeply reverenced, M. de Treville and his men made their butt, deriding his bandy legs and crooked back. Some sang carols on Madame d'Aiguillon, his mistress, and Madame de Combalet, his niece; whilst others planned adventures against the pages and guards of the cardinal duke himself. All these things appeared to d'Artagnan monstrous impossibilities. Nevertheless, when the name of the king accidentally slipped out in the midst of these jokes on the cardinal, a sort of momentary gag stopped all their jeering mouths; they looked around with hesitation, and seemed to doubt the discretion of the wall of M. de Treville's cabinet. But some allusion soon brought back the conversation to his eminence. The wit was of the most brilliant kind, and none of his actions was uncommented upon. "Verily," thought d'Artagnan with terror, "these gentry will soon be put into the Bastile and hanged. Doubtless, I shall accompany them, for having heard all they have said. I shall, without doubt, be taken for an accomplice. What would my father say—he who enjoined me so strongly to respect the cardinal—if he knew that I was in the company of such reprobates?"

Of course, while d'Artagnan dared not join in the conversation, he kept his eyes and ears wide open, and every

sense on the alert, that he might lose nothing; and in
spite of the paternal advice, he found himself drawn by
his tastes and instinct, rather to praise than blame the
incredible things he heard around him.   Nevertheless,
as he was absolutely a stranger to the crowd of M. de
Treville's courtiers, and it was the first time he had been
seen there, some one came to inquire what he wanted.
At this question he humbly gave his name, relying on his
being a countryman, and requested the servant to solicit
a moment's audience of M. de Treville—a request which
the inquirer, in the tone of a protector, promised to make
at the proper time.

D'Artagnan, a little recovered from his first surprise,
had now time to study the dresses and countenances of
those around him.   In the midst of the most animated
group was a musketeer of great height, of a haughty
countenance, and so fantastical a costume as to attract
general attention.   He did not wear his uniform tunic,
which was not absolutely indispensable at that period of
less liberty, yet greater independence, but a close coat of
celestial blue, slightly faded and worn, and on this coat a
magnificent border of gold embroidery, which glittered
like scales upon a sunlit stream; a long mantle or
cloak of crimson velvet hung gracefully from his
shoulders, discovering the front alone of his splendid
belt, from which depended his enormous rapier.   This
musketeer, who had just come from guard, complained of
having caught cold, and coughed occasionally with great
affectation.   Therefore, as he averred, he had taken his
cloak; and whilst he was talking loudly over the group,
and proudly curling his moustache, every one much
admired the embroidered belt, and d'Artagnan more than
any one else.

"What would you have?" said the musketeer.   "It
is the fashion; I know very well that it is foolish, but it is
the fashion; besides, one must spend one's hereditary
property on something or other."

"Ah, Porthos!" cried one of the bystanders, "do not

try to make us believe that this lace comes from the paternal generosity : it was given you by the veiled lady with whom I met you the other Sunday, near the gate of St. Honore."

"No, upon my honour, and by the faith of a gentleman, I bought it with my own money," said he whom they called Porthos.

"Yes, as I bought this new purse with what my mistress put in the old," cried another musketeer.

"But it is true," said Porthos, "and the proof is, that I paid twelve pistoles for it."

The wonder and admiration were redoubled, though the doubt still existed.

"Is it not so, Aramis?" inquired Porthos, turning to another musketeer.

The person thus appealed to formed a perfect contrast to the one who thus questioned him, and who designated him by the name of Aramis. He was a young man, not more than twenty-two or twenty-three years of age, with a soft and ingenuous countenance, a black and mild eye, and cheeks rosy and damask as an autumnal peach ; his slender moustache marked a perfect straight line along his upper lip; his hands appeared to dread hanging down, for fear of making their veins swell; and he was continually pinching the tips of his ears, to make them preserve a delicate and transparent carnation hue. Habitually he talked little and slowly, often bowed, laughed quietly, merely showing his teeth, which were good, and of which, as of the rest of his person, he appeared to take the greatest care. He replied to his friend's question by an affirmative inclination of the head, and this affirmation appeared to settle all doubt concerning the embroidery. They therefore continued to admire it, but said no more about it ; and by a sudden change of thought, the conversation at once passed to another subject.

"What do you think of this story of Chalais's squire?" inquired another musketeer, not addressing any one in particular, but the company in general.

"And what does he say?" demanded Porthos in a conceited tone.

"He says that he found Rochefort, the tool of the cardinal, at Brussels, disguised as a Capuchin friar; and that this cursed Rochefort, thanks to his disguise, had deceived M. de Laignes, simpleton as he is."

"He *is* a simpleton," said Porthos; "but is it a fact?"

"I heard it from Aramis," answered the musketeer.

"Really!"

"Ah, you know it well enough, Porthos," said Aramis. "I told it you myself yesterday evening; do not let us talk any more about it."

"Not talk any more about it! that's your view of the matter," said Porthos; "not talk any more about it! Egad, you would make short work of it. What!, the cardinal sets a spy upon a gentleman, robs him of his correspondence through a traitor, a robber, a gallows-bird; cuts Chalais's throat through this spy, and by means of this correspondence, under the flimsy pretext that he desired to kill the king, and marry monsieur to the queen! No one knew one word of this enigma; you told us of it yesterday evening, to the great astonishment of every one; and whilst we are still all amazed at the news, you come to-day and say to us, 'Let us talk no more about it!'"

"Well, then, since it better suits your humour, let us talk about it," calmly replied Aramis.

"Were I poor Chalais's squire," cried Porthos, "this Rochefort would pass a bad minute with me!"

"And the red duke would make but short work with you," replied Aramis.

"Ah, the red duke! bravo, bravo, the red duke!" exclaimed Porthos, with an approving nod, and clapping his hands; "the *red* duke is charming! Rest assured, my dear fellow, that I will disseminate the title. What a genius he has, this Aramis! what a pity that you could not follow your vocation, my dear fellow; what an exquisite abbé you would have made!"

of his life. But going towards the antechamber, and making a sign with his hand to d'Artagnan, as if requesting permission to finish with others before he began with him, he called three times, raising his voice each time so as to run through the intermediate scale between the tone of command and that of anger —" Athos ! " — " *Porthos !*" — " ARAMIS !" The two musketeers, whose acquaintance we have already made, and who answered to the two last of these three names, immediately quitted the group of which they formed a portion, and advanced towards the cabinet, the door of which was closed immediately they had passed its threshold. Their bearing, although not quite calm, was at the same time full of dignity and submission, and their apparent indifference excited the admiration of d'Artagnan, who saw in these men a species of demi-gods, and in their chief an Olympian Jupiter, armed with all his thunders.

When the two musketeers had entered, and the door was closed behind them—when the murmuring buzz of the antechamber, to which the summons that had been given had doubtless furnished a new topic, had recommenced—when, lastly, M. de Treville had paced the whole length of his cabinet three or four times in silence, but with a frowning brow, passing each time before Porthos and Aramis, upright and mute as on parade, he suddenly stopped directly in front of them, and measuring them from top to toe with an angry look, exclaimed, " Do you know what the king said to me, and that not later than last evening ? Do you know, gentlemen ? "

" No," answered the two musketeers, after a moment's silence ; " no, sir, we do not."

" But we hope you will do us the honour of informing us," added Aramis in his most polished tone, and with the most graceful bow.

" He told me that, for the future, he should recruit his musketeers from those of the cardinal."

"From those of the cardinal! And why?" demanded Porthos with heat.

"Because he saw very well that his thin dregs required to be enlivened by some good and generous wine!"

The two musketeers blushed up to the very eyes. D'Artagnan knew not where he was, and wished himself an hundred feet below the earth.

"Yes, yes," continued M. de Treville, becoming more warm, "yes, his majesty was right; for, upon my honour, the musketeers cut but a sorry figure at court. Yesterday, whilst playing with the king, the cardinal recounted, with an air of condolence which much annoyed me, that on the previous day these cursed musketeers, these devils incarnate—and he dwelt on these words with an ironical accent, which annoyed me the more—these cutters and slashers—(looking at me with the eye of a tiger)—had loitered beyond closing time in a tavern in the Rue Ferou, and that a picquet of his guards (I thought he would laugh in my face) had been obliged to arrest the disturbers. 'Od's-life! you ought to know something about this. Arrest the musketeers! You were amongst them—you, sirs! do not deny it; you were recognised, and the cardinal named you. But it is all my own fault; yes, *my* fault; for I choose my own men. Look ye, Aramis! why did you ask me for a tunic, when a cassock suited you so well? Hark ye, Porthos! have you got such a splendid belt, only to hang to it a sword of straw? And Athos——I do not see Athos; where is *he?*"

"Sir," answered Aramis, in a melancholy tone, "he is ill, very ill."

"Ill! very ill, say you? and of what disorder?"

"We fear it is the small-pox," answered Porthos, anxious to put in a word; "and this would be very distressing, since it would certainly spoil his face."

"The small-pox! This is a marvellous story you are telling me, Porthos! Ill of small-pox at his age! No, no; but doubtless he is wounded, perhaps killed. Ah!

if I were certain of this! Zounds, gentlemen, I do not understand why you haunt such loose places, why you quarrel in the streets, and play with the sword in the crossways; and I do not wish you to afford mirth for the cardinal's guards, who are brave men, quiet, and skilful, who never throw themselves open to an arrest, and who, moreover, would not allow themselves to be arrested, not they! I am sure they would rather die than be arrested or escape! It is you who fly! who scamper away! A fine thing for the royal musketeers, indeed!"

Porthos and Aramis shook with rage. They could have strangled M. de Treville, had they not perceived that his great affection for them was the foundation of all he said. As it was, they stamped on the carpet, bit their lips till the blood ran, and grasped the hilts of their swords with all their might.

M. de Treville's summons for Athos, Porthos, and Aramis had, as we have said, been heard outside the room; and those who remained in the antechamber had concluded, from the sound of his voice, that he was in a towering rage. Ten curious heads, therefore, rested against the tapestry, and grew pale with anger, for their ears, glued to the door, lost not one word of what was said, whilst they rapidly repeated the taunting language of their captain to all who were in the antechamber. In an instant the whole hotel, from the door of the cabinet to the outer gate, was in a state of commotion.

"So! the musketeers of the king allow themselves to be arrested by the guards of the cardinal!" continued M. de Treville, not less excited within than were his soldiers without, but jerking out and mincing his words, and plunging them, as one may say, one by one, like poniards, into the bosoms of his auditors. "So, six of his excellency's guards arrest six of his majesty's musketeers! Sangdieu! I have taken my resolve. I will go hence to the Louvre, where I shall tender to the king my resignation as captain of the musketeers, and demand a lieutenancy in the cardinal's guards; and if I fail in this, mortdieu, I will turn abbé!"

At these words the murmurs without broke out into a regular explosion; nothing but oaths and curses were everywhere heard. "Morbleu!" "Sangdieu!" and "Death to all the devils!" resounded through the hotel. D'Artagnan hastily glanced around the cabinet in search of some tapestry behind which he might hide himself, and failing in this, felt an almost uncontrollable desire to get under the table.

"Well, captain," said Porthos, almost beside himself, "the truth is, we were six against six, but were unawares set upon, and before we had time to draw our swords, two of our party fell dead, and Athos was so grievously wounded as to be scarcely in better plight. You know him well, captain; twice he endeavoured to rise, and twice he fell back; and yet we did not yield ourselves up. No, we were dragged away by force; but escaped on the road. As for Athos, they believed him dead, so quietly left him on the field of battle, not thinking he was worth carrying away. That is the truth. Zounds! captain, one cannot gain every battle; even the great Pompey lost that of Pharsalia; and Francis, who, I have heard, was as brave as most men, lost the battle of Pavia."

"And I can assure you that I killed one fellow with his own sword," said Aramis, "for mine broke at the first parry. Killed or poniarded him, as you please!"

"I did not know these circumstances," said M. de Treville, in a somewhat milder tone; "from what I now learn, the cardinal must have exaggerated."

"But I beseech you, sir—" said Aramis, who, seeing his captain more calm, ventured to hazard a request— "I beseech you, sir, do not say that Athos is wounded; he would be in despair if it came to the king's ears; and as the wound is very severe, having, after passing through the shoulder, penetrated the chest, it is not impossible——"

At this moment the door opened, and a noble and beautiful face, but frightfully pale, appeared.

"Athos!" exclaimed both the gentlemen.

"Athos!" repeated M. de Treville himself.

"You inquired for me," said Athos, to M. de Treville, in a perfectly calm but feeble voice. "My comrades informed me that you commanded my presence, and I hastened to obey you; here I am, sir; what do you require me for?" And with these words the musketeer, perfectly arrayed, and girded as usual, entered the cabinet with a firm step.

M. de Treville, touched to the heart by this proof of endurance, rushed towards him. "I was just going to tell these gentlemen," added he, "that I forbid my musketeers to expose their lives unnecessarily; for brave men are dear to the king, and his majesty knows that his musketeers are the bravest on the earth. Your hand, Athos!" And without waiting till he responded to this proof of affection, M. de Treville seized his hand, and pressed it with much warmth, and without observing that Athos, notwithstanding his command over himself, uttered a cry of pain, and became even more pale than before, if it were possible.

In spite of the secrecy which had been observed respecting it, the severe wound which Athos had received was well known to his comrades, and his unlooked-for arrival had produced a great sensation amongst them. The door of the cabinet had, since his entrance, remained ajar; and, as two or three heads were, in the warmth of the general feeling, thrust through the opening of the tapestry, a simultaneous burst of applause followed the last words of their captain. M. de Treville would, doubtless, have sternly and instantly checked this infraction of the laws of propriety; but at the moment he suddenly felt the hand of Athos grasp his own, and, on looking at him, perceived that he was fainting. He had rallied all his powers to struggle against his pain during the interview; but he could now no longer sustain it, and fell senseless upon the carpet.

"A surgeon!" cried M. de Treville; "mine — or, rather, the king's — a surgeon! or my brave Athos will die!" At these exclamations of M. de Treville, every one rushed into the cabinet, and before he could stop them, pressed round the wounded man. But this eagerness would have been useless, had not the surgeon been found in the hotel. Forcing his way through the spectators, he approached Athos, who was still insensible; and as the pressure of the crowd occasioned him much inconvenience, he directed as the first step of all, that the guardsman should be instantly conveyed into an adjoining apartment. M. de Treville immediately opened a door, and pointed out the way to Porthos and Aramis, who bore off their comrade in their arms.

The cabinet of M. de Treville, that place usually deemed sacred, became for the moment an adjunct to the antechamber, and one in which every one discoursed, talked loud, swore, and consigned the cardinal and all his guards to the infernal regions. In a few moments Porthos and Aramis re-entered, having left M. de Treville and the surgeon with the wounded man. At length M. de Treville himself followed, and announced that Athos had recovered his senses; whilst the surgeon declared that there was nothing in his situation to alarm his friends, his weakness being occasioned entirely by the loss of blood.

Upon a signal from M. de Treville, every one now retired except d'Artagnan, who did not abandon his audience, but, with true Gascon tenacity, held his ground. When all the intruders had left the room, and the door was again closed, M. de Treville turned round, and found himself alone with the young man. The event which had just taken place had in some measure disarranged the previous train of his ideas; and he therefore now inquired what this persevering visitor required. D'Artagnan repeated his name; and M. de Treville, recalling the past and present, instantly became aware of his situation.

"Pardon," said he smiling, "pardon, my dear country-man, but I had entirely forgotten you. What do you want? A captain is merely the father of a family, but burdened with a heavier responsibility than an ordinary parent; for soldiers are great children; but, as I maintain, it is my duty to see that the orders of the king, and more especially those of the cardinal, are carefully executed."

D'Artagnan could not repress a smile; and this smile satisfied M. de Treville that he was not dealing with a fool. Therefore he came at once to the point, and, at the same time, changed the subject.

"I have loved your father," said he; "what can I do for his son? Tell me quickly, for my time is not my own."

"Sir," said d'Artagnan, "in quitting Tarbes, and coming here, I wished to ask from you, as a memorial of the friendship which you have not forgotten, the uniform of a musketeer; but from what I have seen during these last two hours, I more fully comprehend the extreme importance of the favour, and tremble lest I may not be deemed a fit recipient."

"It is truly a great favour, young man," said M. de Treville; "but it cannot be so far above you as you believe, or, at least, seem to believe. However, a decision his majesty has provided for this case; and I regret to inform you, that no one is received among the musketeers who has not passed the ordeal of some campaigns, per-formed certain brilliant actions, or served for two years in some less favoured regiment than our own."

D'Artagnan bowed in silence, but at the same time feeling more eager to don the uniform of the musketeers, since that object could only be obtained with great difficulty.

"But," continued M. de Treville, fixing his piercing look upon his countryman, as if he wished to penetrate the inmost recesses of his heart, "but for the sake of my ancient friend, your father, I wish to do something for you. Young man, we cadets of Bearn are not in general overburdened with wealth, and I fear that matters are not much improved in this respect since I left the province. Your purse, therefore, can scarce be as full as it was."

D'Artagnan drew himself up with a proud air, which seemed to say, " I ask charity of none."

" It is well, young man, it is very well; I understand your feelings. I came to Paris myself with only four crowns in my pocket, and I would have fought any one who had dared to dispute my ability to purchase the Louvre."

D'Artagnan assumed a still prouder air. Thanks to the sale of his horse, he began the world with four crowns more than M. de Treville.

" I should say, therefore, that however large may be the sum you really possess, you ought to preserve it. In the meantime you must perfect yourself in all those accomplishments which become a gentleman, and I will this day write a letter to the director of the Royal Academy, who will receive you to-morrow without any fee. Do not refuse this trifling favour. Gentlemen of the highest rank and wealth often solicit without being able to obtain it, the same gift. You will there learn to ride, to fence, and to dance; you will form a circle in good society; and from time to time you must personally apprise me of your progress, and let me know if I can do anything for you."

D'Artagnan, ignorant as he was of the manners of high society, felt the coldness of this reception.

" Alas, sir," said he, " I now deeply feel the want of the letter of introduction which my father gave me for you."

" I am, in truth, somewhat surprised," replied M. de Treville, " that you should have undertaken so long a journey without that viaticum, so essential to every Bearnese."

" I had one, sir, and a good one—thank God!" cried d'Artagnan, " but was perfidiously robbed of it;" and with a degree of warmth and an air of truth which charmed M. de Treville, he recounted his adventure at Meung, accurately describing his unknown adversary.

"It was very strange," said M. de Treville musingly. "You spoke of me openly, did you?"

"Yes, sir, I certainly committed that imprudence; but such a name as yours served me as a shield on my journey; therefore you can guess if I frequently covered myself with it or no!"

It was an age of flattery, and M. de Treville loved the incense as well as a king or a cardinal. He could not help smiling, therefore, with evident satisfaction; but this smile soon passed away, and returning to the adventure at Meung, he continued—

"Tell me, had not this gentleman a slight scar on the cheek?"

"Yes, as if left by a pistol-ball."

"Was he not a man of commanding air?"

"Yes."

"Of a tall figure?"

"Yes."

"With an olivine complexion?"

"Yes, yes, that is he: but do you know this man, sir? Ah! if I ever meet him—and I will find him, I swear to you, even were he in hell ——"

"He attended a woman did he not?" continued M. de Treville.

"At least he departed after he had conversed a moment with the one he had attended."

"Do you not know the subject of their conversation?"

"He gave her a box, which he said contained her instructions, and desired her not to open it until she arrived in London."

"Was this woman an Englishwoman?"

"He called her 'my lady.'"

"It is he," murmured Treville: "it must be; I thought he was at Brussels."

"Oh, sir," exclaimed d'Artagnan, "if you know this

man, tell me who and whence he is, and I will hold you
absolved even of your promise to admit me amongst the
musketeers; for before and above everything else, I long
to avenge myself."

"Beware, young man," said M. de Treville. "Should
you perceive this man walking on the one side of the
street, instead of seeking your revenge, proceed yourself
on the opposite side; precipitate not yourself against
such a rock, upon which you will assuredly be shattered
like glass."

"That fear will not deter me, should I ever meet him,"
said d'Artagnan.

"In the meantime, do not seek him," replied Treville.
"If you take my advice——"

But all at once M. de Treville paused, as if struck by a
sudden suspicion: the deadly hatred which the young
traveller so openly avowed for this man who had deprived
him of his father's letter—which was in itself a very
improbable circumstance—might not this apparent enmity
conceal some perfidy? Was not this young man sent by
his eminence? Did not he come to lay a trap for him?
Was not this pretended d'Artagnan an emissary of the
cardinal, whom the latter sought to introduce into his
house, and whom he wished to place near him to worm
himself into his confidence, and afterwards to betray him,
as was often done in similar cases? He looked more
earnestly at d'Artagnan than at first, and was but slightly
reassured by the appearance of that countenance, beaming
with acute talent and affected humility. "I know very
well that he is a Gascon," thought he; "but he is just as
likely to be one for the cardinal as for me. Yet I will
try him further."

"Young man," said he slowly, "as the son of mine
ancient friend—for I consider the history of this lost letter
as true—I wish, in order to compensate for the coolness
which you perceived in my first reception, to reveal to
you the secrets of our politics. The king and the cardinal
are the best of friends; their apparent disputes are merely

to deceive fools; and I do not wish that my countryman, a handsome cavalier, a brave youth, formed to rise in the world, should be the dupe of all these pretences, and, like a simpleton, rush headlong into the snare which has made awful examples of so many others. Rest assured, that I am entirely devoted to these two all-powerful masters, and that all my serious proceedings can never have any other object in view than the service of the king, and of the cardinal, who is one of the most illustrious geniuses that France has ever produced. Now, young man, regulate your conduct by this; and should you, through your family or connections, or even your instincts, bear the slightest hostility towards the cardinal, such as you may have seen burst forth occasionally amongst our nobility, take your leave, and quit me. I can assist you in a thousand ways, without attaching you to my own person. At all events, I hope my frankness will make you my friend, for you are the first young man to whom I have as yet spoken in this manner."

Treville ceased speaking, but he thought to himself, "If the cardinal has really sent me this young fox, he would not surely fail—he who knows how much I loathe him—to tell his spy that the best way of paying court to me, is to rail at himself. Therefore, in spite of my protestations, the cunning fellow will doubtless say that he holds his eminence in detestation."

The result, however, was far different from M. de Treville's anticipations. D'Artagnan replied, with the utmost simplicity, "Sir, I am come to Paris with sentiments and intentions exactly similar to those you have just expressed. My father charged me to obey no one but the king, the cardinal, and yourself, whom he considers the three greatest men in France." D'Artagnan, it will be perceived, added M. de Treville to the two others, but he considered that this addition would do no harm. "Hence," he continued, "I have the greatest veneration for the cardinal, and the most profound respect for his actions. It is, therefore, so much the better for me, sir, if, as you say, you speak frankly to me, since you will then do me the honour to esteem this similarity of opinions; but if, on the contrary, as may be very natural, you entertain any feelings of distrust respecting me, so much the worse, as I shall then feel that I am ruined by speaking the truth. But in any case, you will at least honour me with your esteem, which I value more than anything else."

M. de Treville was astonished. So much penetration, and yet so much candour, excited his admiration, although they failed in wholly removing his doubts. The more superior this youth was to other young men, the more formidable a traitor would he make. Nevertheless, he grasped d'Artagnan's hand, and said to him, "You are an honest fellow; but at present I can only do for you what I have promised. In the meantime, my hotel shall always be open to you; so that, having access to me at all times, and being ready to take advantage of every opportunity, you will probably hereafter obtain what you desire."

"That is to say," replied d'Artagnan, "that you will wait till I have become worthy of it. Very well," he added, with Gascon familiarity; "rest assured that you will not have to wait long;" and he bowed to retire, as if the future lay with himself.

"But wait a moment," said M. de Treville, stopping him; "I promised you a letter to the director of the Academy. Are you too proud to accept it, my little gentleman?"

"No, sir," replied d'Artagnan; "and I will answer for it that the same fate that overtook my father's letter shall not occur to this, which I will take good care shall reach its destination; and woe be to him who shall attempt to deprive me of it."

M. de Treville smiled at this gasconade, and leaving his young countryman in the embrasure of the window, where they had been talking, sat down to write the promised letter of introduction. In the meantime, d'Artagnan, who had nothing better to do, beat a march on the window, looking at the musketeers, who followed each other, and watching them rounding the corner of the street. M. de Treville, having written the letter and sealed it, approached the young man to give it to him; but at the very moment when d'Artagnan held out his hand to receive it, M. de Treville was astonished to perceive his *protégé* spring up, redden with anger, and rush out of the cabinet, exclaiming—

"'Od's-blood! he shall not escape me this time!"

"And who is he?" demanded M. de Treville.

"It is *he*—the robber!" replied d'Artagnan. "Oh, what a traitor!"—and he vanished.

"Deuce take the madman!" murmured M. de Treville, "unless it is, after all, a clever mode of giving me the slip, seeing that he has failed in his attempts."

CHAPTER IV.

THE SHOULDER OF ATHOS, THE BELT OF PORTHOS, AND THE HANDKERCHIEF OF ARAMIS.

D'ARTAGNAN, quite furious, had passed through the antechamber in three bounds, and reached the staircase, which he was about to descend by four steps at a time, when he suddenly ran full butt against a musketeer, who was leaving M. de Treville's suite of rooms by a private door, and butting his shoulder, made him utter a cry, or rather a howl. "Excuse me," said d'Artagnan, trying to continue his course; "excuse me; I am in a great hurry."

But he had hardly descended the first step, before a hand of iron seized him by the scarf and stopped him. "You are in a hurry!" exclaimed the musketeer, as pale as a sheet, "and under this pretext you dash against me. You say, 'Excuse me,' and think that is sufficient. But it is not so, my young man. Do you imagine, because you heard M. de Treville address us somewhat bluntly to-day that any one may speak to us as *he* speaks? Undeceive yourself, comrade : you are not M. de Treville?"

"Upon my word—" said d'Artagnan, seeing that it was Athos, who, after the treatment of the surgeon, was now returning to his apartments—"upon my word, I did not run against you on purpose; and not having done it on purpose, I said, 'Excuse me.' It appears to me, therefore, quite sufficient. Nevertheless, I repeat —and this time perhaps it *is* an excess of courtesy—that, upon my honour, I am in a hurry, a confounded hurry : loose me, therefore, I beseech you, and permit me to go about my business."

"Sir," said Athos, releasing him, "you are by no means polite ; it is evident that you come from a distance."

D'Artagnan had already descended three or four steps, but at the remark of Athos, he stopped short. "Sir," said he, "from whatever distance I may come, I assure you that you are not the individual to give me a lesson in good manners."

"Perhaps I am," replied Athos.

"Ah! would that I were not in such a hurry," exclaimed d'Artagnan, "and that I were not running after some one!"

"Monsieur in a hurry! you will find me without running; do you understand?"

"And where, may it please you?"

"Near the Carmes-Deschaux."

"At what hour?"

"About twelve o'clock."

"Very well, I will be there."

"Take care that you do not make me wait too long," said Athos, "for I tell you plainly, at a quarter past twelve, it is I that will run after you, and cut off your ears as you go!"

"Good!" exclaimed d'Artagnan; "but I will take special care to be there at ten minutes before twelve."

And he commenced running again as if possessed by devils, hoping still to catch the unknown, whose slow pace could not yet have carried him beyond his reach.   But at the corner of the street Porthos was talking with one of the soldiers on guard, and between these two there was just space enough for a man to pass.   D'Artagnan fancied that this space was sufficient for him, and he shot forward to rush like an arrow between the two.   He had not, however, made allowance for the wind, which, whilst he was passing, actually bellied out the enormous cloak of Porthos, into which he fairly plunged.   Doubtless Porthos had cogent reasons for not abandoning this most essential portion of his dress; and therefore, instead of letting go the corner which he held, he drew it more closely towards him, so that d'Artagnan found himself rolled up in the velvet, by a rotatory motion which is clearly explained by the obstinate resistance of Porthos.

D'Artagnan, hearing the musketeer swear, wished to escape from under the cloak, which completely blinded him, and sought for an outlet from the folds.   Above all things he feared that he had injured the freshness of the magnificent belt, of which we have heard so much; but on recovering his powers of vision he found his nose jammed between the shoulders of Porthos; that is, exactly on the belt.   Alas! like the majority of the fine things of this world, which are only made for outward show, the belt was of gold in front, and of simple leather behind.   In fact, Porthos, proud as he was, being unable to afford a belt entirely of gold, had procured one of which the half at least was of that metal.   And this may perhaps account for the cold under which Porthos had avowed himself as suffering, and the consequent need of the cloak.

" 'Od's-boddikins!" cried Porthos, making every effort to free himself from d'Artagnan, who kept poking his nose into his back; "you are mad to throw yourself in this manner upon people."

"Excuse me," said d'Artagnan, reappearing from beneath the shoulder of the giant, "but I was in a hurry; I am running after some one——"

"Do you shut your eyes when you run?" demanded Porthos.

"No," answered d'Artagnan, somewhat piqued, "no; and, thanks to my eyes, I can see what others do not see."

Whether Porthos understood him or not, he yet gave way to his anger. "Sir," said he, "you will get yourself chastised, if you thus rub against the musketeers."

"Chastised, sir!" said d'Artagnan; "your expression is harsh."

"It is such as becomes a man who is accustomed to face his enemies."

"Ah, by St. Denis," replied d'Artagnan, "I know well that you would not turn your back upon yours!" and the young man, delighted with his joke, marched off, laughing outrageously.

Porthos foamed with anger, and was hastening after him; but d'Artagnan turned and said—

"By and by, by and by, when you are without your cloak."

"At one o'clock, then, behind the Luxembourg," shouted Porthos.

"Very well, at one o'clock," answered d'Artagnan, as he turned into the street adjoining.

But neither in the street which he had just traversed, nor in that down which he looked, did he see any one. Slowly as the stranger had walked, he had disappeared. Perhaps he had entered some house. D'Artagnan inquired after him of every one he met; he even went down to the ferry, returned by the Rue de Seine and La Croix Rouge, but no one, actually no one, was to be seen. This pursuit, however, was so far serviceable to him, that, as the perspiration bathed his forehead, his heart grew cool, and he then began to reflect on the events which had just transpired. They were numerous and inauspicious. It was scarcely eleven o'clock, and already the morning had brought with it the loss of M. de Treville's favour, since he must have deemed the mode in which d'Artagnan left him extremely abrupt; besides this, he had picked up good duels, with two men, each of them capable of slaying three d'Artagnans; and, lastly, these duels were with musketeers, with two of those very men whom he esteemed so highly as to rank them in his mind and heart above all the world. The Fates were against him; sure of being killed by Athos, it is clear our youth did not care much about Porthos. However, as hope is the last thing which is extinguished in man's heart, he began to hope he might survive — it might be, to be sure, with some terrible wounds; and, under the impression that he should survive, he gave himself the following rebukes as a guard for the future:—"What a hare-brained fellow I am! What a booby! This brave and unlucky Athos was wounded on the shoulder, against which I must therefore run full butt like a ram. The only thing which surprises me is, that he did not kill me at once. He would have been justified in doing so, for the pain I caused him must have been excruciating. As for Porthos—oh! as for Porthos, upon my word, it is even more droll." And in spite of all his efforts to restrain himself, the youth began to laugh, at the same time looking round lest this solitary merriment, which to those who might see him must appear without cause, should offend any one passing. "As to Porthos," he continued, "it is more droll; but I am not the less a miserable giddy-pate, to throw myself thus upon people, without saying 'take care.' And, besides, does any one look under a person's cloak to search for what no one supposes to be there? He would doubtless have pardoned me, had I not spoken to him of that cursed belt. It was, it is true, only by insinuation—yes, but a neat insinuation. I'faith a pretty business! Foolish Gascon that I am—a pretty kettle of fish I shall make. Come, my friend, d'Artagnan," he continued, addressing himself with all the amenity to which he thought himself entitled; "should you escape, which is not very probable, you must practise courtesy for the future; hereafter every one must admire you, and must quote you as a model. To be obliging and polite is not to be cowardly. Observe Aramis: he is softness and grace personified. And yet did any one ever pretend to say that Aramis was a coward? No; and for the future I will in all points make him my model. Ah! singular enough, here he is."

D'Artagnan, thus walking and soliloquising, had arrived within a few paces of the hotel d'Aiguillon, and before this hotel he perceived Aramis talking gaily with three gentlemen of the king's guards. On the other hand, although Aramis perceived d'Artagnan, he had not forgotten that it was before this young man that M. de Treville had given way to passion, and a witness of the reproaches that the musketeers had received was by no means agreeable to him. He therefore pretended not to see him; but d'Artagnan, full of his new-formed plans of conciliation and courtesy, approached the four young men, making them a profound obeisance, accompanied by a gracious smile. Aramis bowed slightly, but did not smile. Silence fell upon the group. D'Artagnan had acuteness enough to perceive that he was an intruder; but he was not sufficiently skilled in the ways of polite society to withdraw himself dexterously from a false position, such as is generally that of a man who joins those he scarcely knows, and intrudes himself into a conversation in which he has no interest. He therefore sought within himself for some means of retreat which might be the least awkward, when he suddenly perceived that Aramis had dropped his handkerchief, and, inadvertently no doubt, had put his foot upon it. The moment appeared to be favourable for repairing his ill-timed intrusion; he therefore stooped down with the most graceful air imaginable, drew the handkerchief from under the musketeer's foot, notwithstanding the efforts he made to retain it there, saying, as he presented it to Aramis, " I believe, sir, this is a handkerchief which you would be sorry to lose."

The handkerchief was, in fact, richly embroidered, and had a coronet and arms in one of its corners. Aramis blushed excessively, and snatched, rather than took, the handkerchief from the hands of the Gascon.

" Ah! ah!" said one of the guards, " will you still insist, most discreet Aramis, that you are on bad terms with Madame de Bois Tracy, when that gracious lady condescends to lend you her handkerchief?"

Aramis threw such a glance at d'Artagnan, as makes a man understand that he has gained a mortal enemy. Then, resuming his soft air, "You guess wrong, comrades," said he; "this handkerchief is not mine, and I know not why this gentleman has had the fancy to give it to me, rather than to one of you; and as a proof of what I say, here is my own in my pocket." So saying, he drew from his pocket his own handkerchief, a very handsome one, of fine cambric, although cambric at that time was very dear; but it was without embroidery, without arms, and adorned with a simple cipher, that of its owner.

This time d'Artagnan was silent. He had discovered his mistake. But the friends of Aramis would not allow themselves to be convinced by his denial; and one of them, addressing the young musketeer with an affected air of solemnity, said—

" If the fact is as you assert, my dear Aramis, I shall be compelled to demand possession of the handkerchief, de Bois Tracy being, as you are aware, one of my most intimate friends, and I should not wish any one to display his wife's property by way of a trophy."

" You make this demand with a bad grace," replied Aramis; " and on this ground alone, even were I to admit its justice fundamentally, I should still refuse compliance with your request."

"The fact is," modestly observed d'Artagnan, "I did not *see* the handkerchief fall from the pocket of M. Aramis; he had his foot upon it, however, and hence my reason for supposing that it belonged to him."

"And you were mistaken, sir," coldly replied Aramis, not very grateful for the apology. Then, turning to the guardsman who had avowed himself the friend of de Bois Tracy, he added, "Besides, on reflection, my worthy comrade, I am the friend of de Bois Tracy as well as yourself, and this handkerchief, strictly speaking, might have come from your pocket as well as from mine."

"No, upon my honour," said the musketeer.

"You swear by your honour, and I pledge my word; therefore one of us must evidently lie. But come, Monterau, let us do something better than indulge in counter assertions and denials: let each of us take half."

"Of the handkerchief?"

"Yes."

"Perfectly fair," cried the other two guardsmen; "decidedly the judgment of Solomon. Aramis, you are certainly cram-full of wisdom!" exclaimed the young men, indulging in hearty laughter; and the affair, as may be imagined, was thus deprived of further import-ance. Immediately afterwards the conversation ceased, and the friends separated, with a cordial shaking of hands, the three guardsmen going one way, and Aramis another.

"Now is my opportunity for making my peace with this gentleman," mentally ejaculated d'Artagnan, who had kept somewhat aloof during the latter part of the conversation, and who now, impelled by this good feeling, approached Aramis, who was departing without taking any further notice of him.

"I hope, sir, that you will excuse me," said he, addressing Aramis.

"Sir," rejoined the latter, "you must permit me to

remark, that you have not acted in this affair as a man of good breeding ought to have done."

"What inference, sir, am I to draw from your remark?"

"Why, sir, I take it for granted that you are not a fool; and that, although coming from Gascony, you must be well aware that no one walks upon pocket-handkerchiefs without sufficient reason for so doing. Zounds, sir, Paris is not paved with cambric!"

"You do me injustice, sir, in thus endeavouring to mortify me," said d'Artagnan, in whom the inherent love of quarrelling began to operate much more forcibly than his previous pacific intentions. "I am a Gascon, it is true; and, as you do not require to be informed, the Gascons are not very long-suffering; therefore, when they have once apologised, even should it be for some imprudence, they consider that they have done one half more than they ought to do."

"What I have said to you, sir," retorted Aramis, "is not for the purpose of seeking a quarrel with you. Thank God! I am no bully; and being a musketeer only temporarily, I never fight except when I am compelled, and then with the utmost reluctance. This, however, is a serious affair, for a lady here is compromised by you."

"Say rather by us," cried d'Artagnan.

"Why did you perpetrate such a stupid blunder as to give me this handkerchief?"

"Why were you so stupid as to let it fall?"

"I have declared, and I repeat, sir, that this handkerchief did not come from my pocket."

"Well, then, you have twice lied; for I myself saw it fall from your pocket."

"Ah, is this the tone you choose to assume, Sir Gascon? Well, I must teach you how to behave better."

"And I will send you back to your missal, M. Abbé; so draw, if you please, this instant?"

"No, I thank you, my fine fellow; not here, at any

rate. Do you not perceive that we are opposite the hotel d'Aiguillon, which is full of the cardinal's creatures. In fact, who can say that it is not his eminence who has commissioned you to procure my head for him. Now, as it happens that I entertain what may appear to you a ridiculous affection for my head, provided it remains tolerably firm on my shoulders, I wish, before parting with it, to kill you. But keep yourself quite easy on that score; I will kill you at leisure, in a retired and secret spot, where you may not be able to boast of your death to any one."

"I am quite agreeable," replied d'Artagnan; "but do not be puffed up; and here, take away your hand-kerchief, whether it belongs to you or not; probably you may have tears to dry."

"Spoken like a true Gascon, sir," said Aramis.

"Yes; but that is no reason why you should delay our little affair, unless, indeed, you are influenced by more prudential motives."

"I know well that prudence, although indispensable to churchmen, is a virtue unknown to the musketeers," replied Aramis, "and being, as I have informed you, only a soldier temporarily, I am resolved to remain prudent. At two o'clock I shall have the honour of awaiting you at the hotel of M. de Treville, whence I will conduct you to a more convenient spot."

The two young men then bowed to each other, and parted. Aramis proceeded towards the Luxembourg; whilst D'Artagnan, finding that the time approached, took the road to the Carmes Deschaux, all the while inwardly ejaculating—"Positively, I cannot escape! but at all events, if I am killed, it will be by a musketeer."

CHAPTER V.

THE KING'S MUSKETEERS AND THE CARDINAL'S GUARDS.

D'ARTAGNAN was friendless in Paris. He therefore went to meet Athos without being provided with a second, having made up his mind to be satisfied with those which accompanied his adversary. Besides, he fully intended to offer the brave musketeer all suitable apologies, but, at the same time, to betray nothing having the slightest appearance of timidity or weakness. He also feared such a result from this duel as may be naturally anticipated in an affair of the kind, where a young and vigorous man fights with an opponent who is wounded and enfeebled; and in which, should the former be vanquished, the triumph of his opponent is doubled; whilst, should the former prove the conqueror, he is not only accused of being brave at small risk, but even his courage is regarded as extremely doubtful. Moreover, unless we have been unsuccessful in our attempt to portray the true character of our adventurer, the reader must have already remarked, that d'Artagnan was no common type. Therefore, although he could not divest himself of the idea that his death was inevitable, he had by no means resolved quietly to resign himself to his fate with that patience which another less courageous than himself might perhaps have displayed in such a case. He pondered upon the different characters of those with whom he was about to engage, and at length began to obtain a clearer view of his situation. By means of the sincere apology which he contemplated, he hoped to conciliate Athos, whose aristocratic air and austere manner quite delighted him. Then he flattered himself that he might intimidate Porthos by the adventure of the belt, whose story, if he were not instantaneously killed, he might relate to every one, so as to overwhelm him with ridicule. Lastly, as regarded the quiet Aramis, he entertained very slight apprehensions; for, supposing that he should survive to fight him, he entertained no doubt of his ability to make short work of him, or, at all events, by wounding him in the face (as Cæsar recommended his men to do with Pompey's soldiers), to spoil for ever that beauty of which he was so vain. In fine, d'Artagnan now brought into action those principles of unconquerable and steady resolve which the counsels of his father had implanted in his heart—counsels which, as we know, had instructed him to submit to nothing like indignity unless it proceeded from the king, the cardinal, or M. de Treville.

Full of these ideas, he sped as if on wings towards the convent des Carmes Deschaux — a building without windows, adjoining a chapel of ease of the Pré-aux-Clercs, and surrounded by dry meadows, which generally served as a rendezvous for those combatants who had no time to lose. As d'Artagnan came in sight of the small open space in front of the convent, it struck the hour of noon, and Athos had already been about five minutes on the ground. He was therefore as punctual as the Samaritan woman, and the most rigorous casuist in the laws of duelling could have found nothing to censure.

Athos, who continued to suffer severely from his wound, although it had again been dressed by M. de Treville's surgeon, had seated himself on a large stone, where he awaited his adversary with that air of calmness and dignity which never forsook him. As d'Artagnan approached, he arose, and politely advanced some steps to meet him; whilst d'Artagnan, on his part, went towards his antagonist bowing until his plume touched the ground.

"Sir," said Athos, "I expected two of my friends who are to act as my seconds, but they are not yet arrived. I am surprised that they should be so late, as they are generally punctual!"

"I have no second, sir," said d'Artagnan; "I only arrived in Paris yesterday; consequently I am unknown to any one here except M. de Treville, to whom I was introduced by my father, who has the honour to claim his friendship."

Athos mused for an instant, and then said: "So M. de Treville is your only acquaintance?"

"Yes, sir, I know no one but him."

"Oh, then," continued Athos *sotto voce*, "if I should kill you, I shall acquire the reputation of a child-eater."

"Not entirely so, sir," answered d'Artagnan, with a bow which was not devoid of dignity, "not quite so: since you do me the honour to draw your sword against me whilst suffering from a wound which must occasion you great inconvenience."

"Inconvenience! Upon my honour I assure you that you hurt me confoundedly. But I will use my left hand, as I usually do under such circumstances. Yet do not imagine that by this means I do you a favour, as I fight equally well with either hand. Indeed, it will rather be a disadvantage to you, a left-handed man being a very trying opponent to one who is not used to it. I regret, therefore, that I did not apprise you sooner of this circumstance."

"Really, sir," said d'Artagnan, again bowing, "you are so very courteous that I cannot be sufficiently grateful."

"You overwhelm me," replied Athos, with the air of a well-bred man; "if it be not disagreeable to you, pray let us converse upon some other subject. Ah! how you did hurt me! how my shoulder still burns!"

"Would you permit me——?" said d'Artagnan, somewhat timidly.

"To do what, sir?" inquired Athos.

"I have a salve which is quite a panacea for wounds—a salve which my mother gave me, and which I have tried upon myself with success."

"And what of it?" continued Athos.

"Why, sir, I am certain that in less than three days this salve would cure you; and at the end of that time, when your cure is completed, it would be a great honour for me to cross swords with you."

D'Artagnan uttered these words with a simplicity which did honour to his courtesy, without in the slightest degree detracting from his courage.

"By my faith!" exclaimed Athos, "this is a proposition which much pleases me; not that I should think of accepting it; but it savours of the perfect knight, and it was thus that, in the days of Charlemagne, those brave men, whom every man of honour should make his model, spoke. Unfortunately, however, we do not live in the times of the great emperor, but in those of the cardinal; and three days hence, however well we might preserve our secret, it would be known that we were going to fight, and we should be prevented. But," he added, with some impatience, "these seconds are laggards."

"If you are in haste, sir," said d'Artagnan, with the same simplicity that had the moment before characterised his proposition to put off the duel for three days—"if you are in haste, and should wish to dispose of me at once, dispense with the seconds, I beseech you."

"This speech of yours pleases me still more," said Athos, gracefully bowing to d'Artagnan, "it does not seem that of a man who lacks either head or heart. I admire men of your stamp, and, if we are spared, I shall hereafter have sincere pleasure in your acquaintance. Meantime, let us wait for these gentlemen, I pray you. I have plenty of time, and it will be more according to rule. Ah! see, here comes one of them."

And as he spoke, the gigantic form of Porthos was seen at the end of the Rue de Vaugirard.

"What!" exclaimed d'Artagnan, "is M. Porthos one of your seconds!"

"Yes, have you any objection to him?"

"Oh, certainly not!"

"And here is the other."

D'Artagnan looked in the direction indicated by Athos, and beheld Aramis.

"What!" cried he, in a tone of yet greater astonishment, "is M. Aramis the other of your seconds?"

"Certainly; are you not aware that one is rarely seen without the other, and that amongst the musketeers and guards, at court and in the town, we are known as Athos, Porthos, and Aramis, or the three inseparables? But as you come from Dax or Pau——"

"From Tarbes," said d'Artagnan.

"You may very naturally be ignorant of all this."

"Really, gentlemen," said d'Artagnan, "you are well named; and should my adventure become known, it will at least prove that like draws to like."

In the meantime Porthos approached, shook hands with Athos, and turning towards d'Artagnan, seemed lost in astonishment. We may mention, in passing, that he had changed his belt, and laid aside his cloak.

"It is with this gentleman that I am about to fight," said Athos, pointing towards d'Artagnan, and at the same time saluting him.

"And I also am going to fight him," replied Porthos.

"But not till one o'clock," interrupted d'Artagnan.

"And I also—it is with him that *I* am to fight," said Aramis, who had arrived on the ground, just after Porthos.

"Our appointment, however, is for two o'clock," replied d'Artagnan, with the same coolness.

"But what are you going to fight about, Athos?" demanded Aramis.

"Upon my faith, I do not well know, except that he hurt my shoulder."

"And you, Porthos?"

"I fight because I fight," replied Porthos colouring.

Athos, whom nothing escaped, perceived a slight smile curling the lips of the Gascon.

"We had a dispute about dress," said d'Artagnan.

"And you, Aramis?" demanded Athos.

"Me? I fight on account of a theological dispute," answered Aramis, making a sign to d'Artagnan that he wished him to conceal the true cause of their duel.

C

"Really!" said Athos, who observed d'Artagnan smile again.

"Yes, a point of St. Augustine, on which we could not agree," said the Gascon.

"Decidedly he is a man of spirit," murmured Athos.

"And now that you are all arrived, gentlemen," said d'Artagnan, "permit me to offer my apologies."

A frown passed over the brow of Athos, a haughty smile glided over the lips of Porthos, and a negative sign was the reply of Aramis.

"You do not rightly understand me, gentlemen," said d'Artagnan, elevating his head, on which a sunbeam played, gilding its fine and manly lines. "I wish to apologise because it is improbable that I shall be able to pay my debt to all three; for M. Athos has the right to kill me first, which greatly decreases the value of your bill, M. Porthos, whilst it renders yours, M. Aramis, of scarcely the slightest value. Therefore, gentlemen, on that account alone, I again repeat my offer of apology. And now upon your guard!"

And with the most gallant and fearless mien he drew his sword. His blood was fairly roused, and at that moment he would have drawn his sword against all the musketeers in the kingdom with as little hesitation as he then did against Athos, Porthos, and Aramis.

It was a quarter past twelve, the sun was at its meridian, and the situation chosen for the rencounter was exposed to its fierce heat.

"It is very hot," said Athos, drawing his sword, "and yet I cannot take off my doublet, for just now I perceived that my wound bled, and I fear to distress this gentleman by showing him blood which he has not drawn from me himself."

"True, sir," replied d'Artagnan, "but I assure you that, whether drawn by myself or by any other person, I shall always see with regret the blood of so brave a gentleman; I will therefore follow your example, and fight in my doublet."

"Come," said Porthos, "a truce to these compliments. Remember that we also await our turn."

"Speak for yourself only, Porthos, when you choose to be so rude," interposed Aramis. "As for me, I consider the courtesies which have passed between these gentlemen as worthy of men of the highest honour."

"When you please, sir," said Athos, placing himself on his guard.

"I was at your service," said d'Artagnan, crossing his sword.

But the two rapiers had scarcely met, when a party of the cardinal's guards, commanded by M. de Jussac, appeared at the corner of the convent.

"The cardinal's guards!" exclaimed Porthos and Aramis at the same moment. "Sheathe swords— gentlemen—sheathe swords!"

But it was too late. The combatants had been seen in a position which left no doubt of their intentions.

"Hollo!" cried Jussac, advancing towards them, and giving a signal to his men to do the same. "Hollo, musketeers! What, fighting here? And the edicts— are they forgotten, eh?"

"You are extremely generous, gentlemen of the guards," said Athos, in a tone of the most bitter animosity, for Jussac had been one of the aggressors on the night before last. "If we saw you fighting, I promise you that we should not prevent it; therefore let us alone, and you will enjoy the spectacle without any of the pain."

"Gentlemen," answered Jussac, "it is with regret I declare that what you request is impossible. Duty must take precedence of everything else. Sheathe, therefore, if you please, and follow us."

"Sir," said Aramis, parodying Jussac's manner, "if it depended upon ourselves, we should accept your polite invitation with the utmost pleasure; but unfortunately the thing is impossible. M. de Treville has forbidden it. Move on, therefore; it is the best thing you can do."

This mockery exasperated Jussac. "We will charge you," said he, "if you disobey."

"They are five," said Athos in a low voice, "and we are only three; we shall he beaten again, and we must die here; for I positively swear that I will not again appear before the captain a vanquished man."

Athos, Porthos, and Aramis closed up to each other, whilst Jussac drew up his men. This moment of delay sufficed for d'Artagnan to form his resolution. It was one of those moments weighed with a man's whole destiny; it was a choice between the king and the cardinal, and this choice, once made, must be adhered to. To fight was to disobey the law, to risk his head, and, by one blow, to make an enemy of a minister more powerful than the king himself. All this the young man plainly perceived, and we must do him the justice to declare that he did not hesitate a single instant.

"Gentlemen," said he, "you must allow me to correct one thing which you have said. You affirmed that you were but three; but it appears to me that there are four of us."

"You are not one of us," said Porthos.

"True," replied d'Artagnan, "I have not the dress, but I have the heart and soul of a musketeer; I feel it, sir, and it impels me along, as it were, by force."

"Hark ye, young man!" cried Jussac, who doubtless, from d'Artagnan's gestures and the expression of his countenance, had divined his intentions; "you may retire; we permit you; save your skin, and that quickly."

But d'Artagnan moved not a step.

"You are unquestionably a man of spirit," said Athos, pressing the young man's hand.

"Come, come; decide, decide!" exclaimed Jussac.

"We must make up our minds," said Porthos and Aramis.

"You are truly generous," said Athos to d'Artagnan.

But all three thought of d'Artagnan's youth, and feared his inexperience.

"We are but three, and one of us wounded, exclusive of this boy," remarked Athos; "and yet it will be said that we were four men."

"Ay, but to retreat!" said Porthos.

"It is difficult," said Athos.

"Quite impossible!" said Aramis.

D'Artagnan comprehended the cause of their irresolution. "Gentlemen," said he, "only try me, and I pledge you my honour that I will not leave this spot except as a conqueror."

"What is your name, my fine fellow?" said Athos.

"D'Artagnan, sir."

"Well, then, Athos, Porthos, Aramis, and d'Artagnan, forward!" exclaimed Athos.

"So, you have made up your minds, gentlemen?" cried Jussac for the third time.

"Quite so," replied Athos.

"And what is your resolve?" demanded Jussac.

"We are about to have the honour of charging you," replied Aramis, raising his hat with one hand, and drawing his sword with the other.

"Ah! you resist!" cried Jussac.

"Mortdieu! Does that surprise you?"

And the nine combatants rushed upon each other with a fury which did not, however, exclude a kind of method. Athos took Cahusac, one of the cardinal's favourites; Porthos selected Biscarrat; and Aramis found himself opposed to two adversaries. As for d'Artagnan, he sprang towards Jussac himself.

The heart of the young Gascon throbbed violently, not with fear, but with eagerness. He fought with the fury of an enraged tiger, turning round his adversary, and every moment changing his guard and position. Jussac, as we have before said, was a most skilful and experienced swordsman; nevertheless, he found the utmost difficulty

in defending himself against his adversary, who, active
and nimble, perpetually deviated from all the received
rules of fencing, attacking on all sides at once, and yet at
the same time guarding himself like one who had the
greatest respect in the world for his own person.   At
length the struggle was brought to a conclusion by
Jussac's rashness.   Furious at being thus held at bay by
one whom he regarded as a mere boy, he became less
cautious, and committed various indiscretions ; whilst
d'Artagnan, who, although deficient in practice, had a
profound knowledge of the theory of the art, redoubled
his agility.   Jussac, eager to dispatch him, made a
tremendous lunge, at the same time breaking ground ;
but d'Artagnan parried the thrust, and whilst Jussac
recovered himself, he glided like a serpent under his
weapon, and passed his sword through his body ; Jussac
fell heavily on the ground.

D'Artagnan now cast a rapid and anxious glance over
the field of battle.   Aramis had already killed one of his
adversaries, but the other pressed him sharply.   He was,
however, in very good trim, and could well defend himself.   Biscarrat and Porthos had both received wounds,
Porthos in the arm, and his adversary in the thigh ; but
as neither of these wounds was severe, they only fought
the more fiercely.   Athos, wounded afresh by Cahusac,
looked more and more pale, but did not yield an inch ;
he had merely changed hands, and fought with his left.
According to the laws of duelling at that period,
d'Artagnan was at liberty to assist any one of his
companions ; and whilst he sought to ascertain which of
them most required his aid, he caught a glance from
Athos, which served instead of speech.   Athos would
have died sooner than call for assistance ; but his
look plainly denoted how much he required support.
D'Artagnan at once comprehended his meaning, and
with a single bound he fell on Cahusac's flank, exclaiming,
"Turn, sir guardsman, or I kill you !"

Cahusac did turn, just as Athos, whom his extreme

courage had alone sustained, sunk upon one knee.
"Hollo, young man!" exclaimed Athos, "do not kill
him, I beseech you; I have an old affair to settle with
him when I am cured. Disarm him only; deprive him
of his sword—that's it—good, very good!"

This exclamation escaped Athos on perceiving the
sword of Cahusac flying from his hand a distance of
twenty paces. D'Artagnan and Cahusac both rushed
forward to secure the weapon; but d'Artagnan being the
most active, reached it first, and placed his foot upon it.
Cahusac then went to the guardsman killed by Aramis,
seized his rapier, and was returning to d'Artagnan; but
on his way he encountered Athos, who during this
momentary pause had recovered his breath, and fearing
that d'Artagnan might kill his opponent, wished to renew
the contest. D'Artagnan perceived that he would offend
Athos if he did not permit him to have his own way;
and in a few minutes Cahusac fell pierced in the throat.
At the same moment Aramis placed the point of his
sword at the breast of his fallen adversary, and compelled
him to sue for mercy.

Porthos and Biscarrat alone remained fighting. Porthos,
whilst fighting, indulged himself in a thousand fantastic
jests and humours, asking Biscarrat what time of day it
was, and congratulating him on the company his brother
had just obtained in the regiment of Navarre. This
jesting, however, gained him no advantage; for Biscarrat
was one of those indomitable spirits who die, but do not
surrender. It was time, however, to stop the fight, as the
guard might arrive, and arrest all the combatants, whether
wounded or not, whether royalists or cardinalists. Athos,
Aramis, and d'Artagnan, therefore, surrounded Biscarrat,
and summoned him to surrender. Although alone against
all four, and with a wound which had passed through his
thigh, Biscarrat refused to yield; but Jussac, raising himself on his elbow, requested him to desist. Biscarrat,
however, like d'Artagnan, was a Gascon: he therefore
only laughed, and pretended not to hear; and finding

time, between the parries, to point with his sword to the
ground at his feet—

"Here," said he, "will Biscarrat die, the sole survivor
of those that were with him."

"But they are four—four against one!" cried Jussac;
"yield, I command you!"

"Ah, if you command me, it is another thing," said
Biscarrat; "you are my commander, and I must obey."

And suddenly springing backwards, he broke his sword
across his knee, in order that he might not give it up,
threw the pieces over the wall of the convent; and then,
crossing his arms, he whistled a cardinalist air.

Bravery is always respected, even in an enemy. The
musketeers saluted Biscarrat with their swords, and
returned them to their scabbards. D'Artagnan did the
same; and then, assisted by Biscarrat, the only one who
remained on his legs, he carried Jussac, Cahusac, and
that one of the adversaries of Aramis who was only
wounded, under the porch of the convent. The fourth,
as we have said, was dead. They then rang the bell,
and confiscating four out of the five swords, they set
off, intoxicated with joy, towards M. de Treville's hotel.
They proceeded arm in arm, occupying the whole breadth
of the street; and as they detained every musketeer they
met, the march soon became like a triumphal procession.
D'Artagnan's heart was in a delirium of exultation, as he
marched between Athos and Porthos.

"If I am not yet a musketeer," said he to his new
friends, whilst passing the threshold of M. de Treville's
hotel, "I am at least next door to one.   Is it not so?"

CHAPTER VI.

HIS MAJESTY KING LOUIS THE THIRTEENTH.

THE affair made a great noise. M. de Treville strongly censured his musketeers in public; but privately they heard only his congratulations. As, however, it was essential that no time should be lost in gaining the king, M. de Treville hastened to the Louvre. But he was too late; the king was closeted with the cardinal, and M. de Treville was informed that his majesty was engaged, and could not then see any one. In the evening, M. de Treville returned. The king was at play, and was winning; and his majesty, being very covetous, was in an excellent humour. Therefore, as soon as he saw M. de Treville, he exclaimed—

"Come here, my captain, that I may chide you. Are you aware that his eminence came to complain to me of your musketeers, and with so much emotion as to be indisposed? Well, really, these musketeers of yours are perfect devils—thorough hang-dogs!"

"No, sire," replied M. de Treville, who at the first glance saw the turn the affair was likely to take. "No, on the contrary, they are good creatures, gentle as lambs, and who, I am confident, have only one wish, that their swords should never leave their scabbards except in time of war. But what are they to do? The guards of the cardinal are continually seeking opportunities of quarrelling with them; and, for the honour of the regiment, the poor young men are obliged to defend themselves."

"Hark ye, M. de Treville," said the king; "hark ye! Is this a religious fraternity—these men of yours—that you are speaking of? Truly, my dear captain, I am half inclined to deprive you of your command, and bestow it upon Mademoiselle de Chemerault, to whom I have promised an abbey. Do not suppose, however, that I give implicit credence to this simple story of yours. I am called Louis the Just, M. de Treville; and soon, very soon, we shall see——"

"And it is because I confide in that justice, sire, that I shall calmly and patiently await your majesty's good pleasure."

"Wait then, sir, wait then," said the king, "and it will not be long."

In fact, at that moment the chances of the game turned against the king, who began to lose what he had before gained. Therefore he was not sorry to find an excuse (to use an expression of the gaming table, of which we confess we know not the origin) for making Charlemagne. The king therefore rose, and putting into his pocket the money which was before him, and most of which he had won——

"La Vieuville," said he, "take my place. I must talk with M. de Treville on an affair of importance. Ah! I had eighty louis before me: lay down the same sum, that those who have lost may not want their revenge. Justice above all things!"

Then turning towards M. de Treville, and walking with him towards a recess in one of the windows——

"Well, sir," continued he, "you affirm that it is the guards of his eminence who seek quarrels with your musketeers?"

"Yes, sire; invariably."

"Well, and how did this affair happen? Relate the facts; for you know, my dear captain, a judge must hear both parties."

"Oh! by my faith, in the most simple and natural manner: three of my best soldiers, whom your majesty knows by name, and whose services you have often appreciated, and who, I can assure your majesty, are wholly devoted to your service—three of my best soldiers, Athos, Porthos, and Aramis, had made a party of pleasure with a young Gascon, a volunteer, whom I had introduced to them the same morning. The party was to be held at St. Germain's, I believe; and the rendezvous was fixed at Carmes-Deschaux, when it was interrupted by de Jussac, Cahusac, Biscarrat, and two other musketeers of the cardinal, who doubtless did not assemble there in such force without some intention in opposition to the edicts."

"Ah! you give me ground for a conjecture," said the king; "doubtless they came there to have an affair of honour."

"I do not accuse them, sire, but I leave your majesty to judge what five armed men could be doing in a spot so retired as is the neighbourhood of the convent."

"Very true, Treville; yes, you are right."

"But, when they saw my musketeers, they changed their intentions, and forgot their individual and personal hatred, to indulge their enmity towards our corps; for your majesty well knows that the musketeers, who are wholly for the king, and nothing but the king, are the natural enemies of the guards, who are for the cardinal alone."

"Yes, Treville," said the king sorrowfully; "and it is a sad thing, believe me, thus to see two parties in France —two royal heads, as it were, under one crown. But this must be brought to an end. You say, then, that the guards sought a difference with the musketeers?"

"I say it is probable that this was the case, but I do not swear to it, sire. Your majesty well knows how difficult it is to discover the truth, unless, indeed, one were gifted with that admirable penetration which has caused Louis XIII. to be named *the Just.*"

"There again you are right, Treville. But your musketeers were not alone; there was a boy with them."

"Yes, sire, and a wounded man; so that three of the king's musketeers, of whom one was wounded, and this boy, not only made head against five of the most formidable of the cardinal's guards, but even bore four of them to the earth."

"Why, it is a complete victory!" exclaimed the king, radiant with joy—"a most complete victory!"

"Yes, sire, as complete as that of the bridge of Cé."

"Four men—of whom one was wounded, and another a boy—do you say?"

"A stripling; but who behaved so nobly on this occasion, tbat I shall take the liberty of recommending him to your majesty."

"What is his name?"

"D'Artagnan, sire; he is the son of one of my oldest friends—the son of a man who was engaged in the Partizan war on the side of the king your father, of glorious memory."

"And you say this youth acquitted himself bravely? Tell me all about it, Treville, for you know how I love to hear of war and combats."

And the king placed himself in an attentive posture, at the same time twirling his moustache in a military manner.

"Sire," replied M. de Treville, "as I have already told you, M. d'Artagnan is almost a child; and as he has not the honour of being a musketeer, he was in plain clothes. The cardinal's guards, perceiving his youth and also that he was a civilian, invited him to retire before they commenced their assault."

"Thus we may clearly perceive, Treville," interrupted the king, "that it was the guards who began the attack."

"Most assuredly, sire, there cannot be a doubt on the subject. They therefore warned him to retire; but he replied that as he was at heart a musketeer, and wholly devoted to his majesty, he should remain with the musketeers."

"Brave youth!" murmured the king.

"And he did remain with them; and in him your majesty has the resolute and valiant champion who gave Jussac that terrific sword thrust which has so much enraged the cardinal."

"He who wounded Jussac?" exclaimed the king. "He—a boy! Treville, it is impossible!"

"It is as I have the honour to inform your majesty."

"Jussac! one of the best duellists in the realm!"

"Yes, sire; but he has now found his master."

"Treville, I must see this young man," said Louis; "I must see him; and if I can do anything—— However, we will think about that."

"When will your majesty condescend to receive him?"

"To-morrow, at twelve, Treville."

"Shall I bring him alone?"

"No, bring the other three. I wish to thank them all at the same time. Men so brave are rare, Treville, and such devotion ought to be rewarded."

"At twelve, sire, we will be at the Louvre."

"By the private staircase, Treville—by the private staircase; it is unnecessary to let the cardinal know it."

"Yes, sire."

"You understand, Treville; an edict is always an edict; at all events, fighting is forbidden by the law."

"But this combat," said Treville, "is altogether different from the common duels: it was a sudden brawl; and the proof of it is, that there were five of the cardinal's guards against three of the musketeers and M. d'Artagnan."

"It is quite true," said the king; "yet, nevertheless, Treville, come by the private staircase."

Treville smiled; but conceiving that he had already secured an important advantage, by thus inducing the pupil to rebel against his master, he respectfully saluted the king, and, with his permission, made his retiral.

The same evening the three musketeers were apprised of the honour intended for them. As they had long known the king, they were not much enchanted by the news; but d'Artagnan, with his Gascon imagination, saw in it his future fortunes, and passed the night amid golden dreams. By eight in the morning he was with Athos, whom he found dressed, and ready to go out.

As they were not to see the king until twelve o'clock, and Athos had engaged to meet Porthos and Aramis at a tennis-court, near the Luxembourg stables, to play a match of tennis, he invited d'Artagnan to join them. Although ignorant of the game, which he had never played, d'Artagnan accepted the invitation, not knowing how otherwise to dispose of his time in the interval. Porthos and Aramis were already there, knocking the balls about. Athos, who was very skilful in all athletic games, went to one side with d'Artagnan, and challenged them. But at the first movement which he made, although he played with his left hand, he found that his wound was too fresh to permit such an exertion. D'Artagnan, therefore, remained alone; and as he declared that he was too unskilful to play a regular game, they only sent the balls about, without counting the points. One of these balls, however, driven by the Herculean hand of Porthos, passed so near d'Artagnan as to satisfy him that, had it hit him full in the face, instead of going on one side, his royal audience would have been lost, as, in all probability, he would thereby have been rendered unfit to be presented to the king. Now, since, in his Gascon imagination, all his fortune depended upon this audience, he politely saluted Porthos and Aramis, declaring that he would not renew the game until he was up to their standard, and then took his station near the ropes and the gallery.

Unfortunately for d'Artagnan, amongst the spectators there was one of the cardinal's guards, who was irritated by the previous night's defeat of his companions, and had resolved to take the first opportunity of avenging it. He now believed that this opportunity had arrived, and addressing a bystander—

"It is no wonder," said he, "that this young man is afraid of the ball; he is, doubtless, a musketeer recruit."

D'Artagnan turned as if bitten by a serpent, and looked fiercely at the guardsman who had uttered this insolent remark.

"I'faith," continued the latter, proudly curling his moustache, "you may look at me as much as you please, my little gentleman. What I have said, I mean."

" And since what you have said explains itself," replied d'Artagnan, in a low voice, " I will thank you to follow me."

" Ah! indeed! and when, pray?" said the guardsman, with the same air of mockery.

" Immediately, if you please."

" Doubtless you know who I am?"

" I have not the slightest idea; and, what is more, I do not care."

" And yet you are wrong; for if you knew my name, perhaps you would be less courageous."

" Indeed! and pray what is your name?" said d'Artagnan.

" Bernajoux, at your service."

" Well, M. Bernajoux," replied d'Artagnan with the utmost tranquillity, " I shall await you at the gate."

" Proceed, sir; I will follow you."

" But do not be in too great haste, sir," said d'Artagnan, "lest it should be perceived that we go out together; for, considering how we are about to be engaged, you must be aware that too many witnesses might prove inconvenient."

" There is some sense in that," replied the guardsman, much surprised that his name had not produced a greater effect on the young man.

The name of Bernajoux was indeed known to every one, except d'Artagnan; for he was one of those who constantly figured in the daily brawls which all the edicts of the king and the cardinal could not suppress.

Porthos and Aramis were so much occupied by their game, and Athos was watching them so attentively, that they did not even perceive the departure of their young companion, who, as he had promised, waited a moment at the door for his opponent. In fact, d'Artagnan had no time to lose, considering the expected audience, which was fixed for twelve o'clock. He therefore cast his eyes around, and seeing that there was no one in the street—

"Faith, sir," said he to his adversary, "although your name is Bernajoux, it is very fortunate for you that you have to deal with a musketeer recruit only. However, be content: I will do my best. On your guard, sir!"

"But," said he whom d'Artagnan thus addressed, "it appears to me this place is badly chosen, and that we should be better behind the abbey of St. Germain, or in the Pré-aux-Clercs."

"True enough," replied d'Artagnan, "but, unfortunately, my time is precious, as I have an important engagement precisely at twelve; therefore draw, sir, draw!"

Bernajoux was not the man to wait the repetition of such a compliment. In an instant, therefore, his sword glittered in his hand, and he rushed upon his adversary, whom, on account of his extreme youth, he hoped to intimidate.

But d'Artagnan had served his apprenticeship the evening before, and now fresh, and elated with his victory, as well as inflamed with hopes of future favour, he was fully resolved not to recede an inch. The two swords were therefore engaged, even to the guard; and as d'Artagnan kept his ground firmly, his adversary was obliged to retreat a single step. By this movement Bernajoux's sword deviated from "opposition," and d'Artagnan, seizing the opportunity, made a lunge which wounded his adversary in the shoulder. He immediately stepped back one pace, and raised his sword; but Bernajoux, declaring that it was nothing, made a blind thrust at d'Artagnan, and impaled himself upon his sword. Nevertheless, as Bernajoux neither fell, nor declared himself vanquished, but merely retreated towards the hotel of M. de la Tremouille, in whose service he had a relative, d'Artagnan, ignorant of the severity of his adversary's wound, pressed him closely, and doubtless would have despatched him by a third thrust, had not the clash of the rapiers reached the tennis-court, from which now rushed, sword in hand, two of the guardsman's friends (who had heard him exchange words with d'Artagnan), and fell upon the conqueror. But Athos, Porthos, and Aramis, now also joined the fray; and at the moment when the two guardsmen attacked their young comrade, forced them to turn. At that instant Bernajoux fell; and as the guards were then only two against four, they began to cry out—"To our aid! hotel de la Tremouille!" At this cry, all the inmates of the hotel rushed out, and fell upon the four friends; who, on their side, exclaimed—"Help, musketeers!"

The latter cry was very common; for it was known that the musketeers hated the cardinal, and they were beloved for the very hatred they bore towards his eminence. Hence, in those quarrels, the guards of all the other regiments, excepting those actually belonging to the Red Duke, as Aramis had designated the cardinal, generally sided with the king's musketeers. Of three guardsmen, who were passing, of the company of M. des Essarts, two came to the assistance of the four friends, whilst the third ran to the hotel of M. de Treville, crying, "Help! musketeers, help!" As usual, M. de Treville's hotel was full of soldiers, who ran to the assistance of their comrades, and the battle became general. But the superiority of force was with the musketeers; and the cardinal's guards, with M. de la Tremouille's people, retired into the hotel, the doors of which they secured in time to exclude their opponents. As for the wounded man, he had been carried away at first, and, as we have said, in very bad plight.

Excitement amongst the musketeers and their allies was at its height, and they deliberated whether they should not set fire to the hotel, to punish the insolence of M. de la Tremouille's retainers, who had presumed to charge the king's musketeers. The proposition had been made and received with enthusiasm, when fortunately it struck eleven o'clock; and d'Artagnan and his companions, remembering their audience, and not wishing a feat so daring to be performed without their aid, succeeded in quelling the commotion; they therefore contented themselves with throwing some stones at the door, and then left the place. Besides, those whom they regarded as their leaders had just left them to proceed towards the hotel of M. de Treville, who, already aware of this fresh insult, awaited their arrival.

"Quick, to the Louvre!" said he; "to the Louvre, without losing one moment; and let us endeavour to see the king before the cardinal prejudices him. We will narrate the affair as a consequence of that of yesterday, and the two will be disposed of together."

M. de Treville, accompanied by the four young men, hastened towards the Louvre; but, to the great surprise of the captain of the musketeers, he was informed that the king had gone to the chase in the forest of St. Germain. M. de Treville caused this intelligence to be twice repeated, and each time his companions observed his countenance become darker.

"Had his majesty formed the intention of hunting, yesterday?" demanded he.

"No, your excellency," replied the valet. "The master of the hounds came this morning to announce that he had roused a stag; at first the king said he would not go, but subsequently he could not resist the pleasure which the chase promised him, and he set out after dinner."

"And has the king seen the cardinal?" demanded M. de Treville.

"In all probability," replied the valet, "for this morning I saw the horses harnessed to the cardinal's carriage; I inquired where it was going, and was told to St. Germain."

"We are anticipated," said M. de Treville. "I shall see the king this evening; but, as for you, I would not counsel you at present to attempt it."

The advice was too reasonable; especially as that of a man who knew the king too well, to be opposed by the young men. M. de Treville therefore requested them to return to their respective homes, and await his orders.

On reaching his hotel, it occurred to M. de Treville that it would be prudent to be in advance with his complaint. He therefore despatched a letter to M. de la Tremouille, requesting him to dismiss from his house the cardinal's guards ; and, further, to reprimand his own people for charging the musketeers. M. de la Tremouille, however, being already prejudiced by his equerry, whose relative Bernajoux was, replied that neither M. de Treville nor his musketeers had a right to complain, but, on the contrary, he himself ; the musketeers having not only attacked and wounded his people, but also threatened to burn his mansion. Now, as a dispute between two such great men might last a long time, each being likely to adhere obstinately to his opinion, M. de Treville thought of an expedient to bring it to a close ; and this was to go himself to M. de la Tremouille. He therefore repaired to his hotel, and caused himself to be announced.

The two noblemen saluted each other politely, for, although they were not friends, they yet esteemed each other. They were both brave and honourable men; and as M. de la Tremouille was a protestant, and therefore rarely saw the king, he intrigued on no side, and had contracted few prejudices in his social relations. On the present occasion, however, his reception of his visitor, though polite, was colder than usual.

" Sir," said M. de Treville, " we each believe that we have cause of complaint against the other, and I am now here to see if we cannot together clear up the matter."

" Most willingly," replied M. de la Tremouille, " but I tell you beforehand that I have full information, and am satisfied all the blame rests with your musketeers."

" You are too just a man, sir, and too reasonable," observed M. de Treville, " not to accept the proposition I shall now make to you."

" Proceed, sir ; I will hear it."

" How is M. Bernajoux, the relative of your equerry?"

"Why, sir," replied Tremouille, " he is very ill indeed. Besides the wound which he received in the arm, and which is not dangerous, he has also received another, which has passed through his lungs; so that the physician gives but a poor account of him."

"But does the wounded man retain his senses?" inquired Treville.

"Perfectly."

"Can he speak?"

"With difficulty; but still he *can* speak."

"Well, then, sir, let us interview him. Let us adjure him in the name of that God before whom, perhaps, he is about to appear, to tell the truth. I will acknowledge him as the judge, even in his own cause; and I will abide by his explanation."

M. de la Tremouille reflected for a moment, and as it would have been difficult to conceive a more reasonable proposition, he agreed to it.

They therefore proceeded together to the chamber of the wounded man, who, when he saw them enter his apartment, endeavoured to raise himself in bed; but being too feeble, and, exhausted by the effort, he fell back, almost insensible.

M. de la Tremouille approached his bed, and by the application of some smelling-salts, restored him to consciousness. Then, in order to avoid any future imputation of having influenced the guardsman, M. de la Tremouille invited M. de Treville to question him himself.

The result was as M. de Treville had foreseen. Lingering as he was between life and death, Bernajoux had not the slightest idea of concealing the truth, and therefore gave a true narration of the occurrence. This was all that M. de Treville required; so wishing Bernajoux a speedy recovery, he took leave of M. de la Tremouille; and having regained his own hotel, he immediately summoned the four friends to dine with him.

M. de Treville received the best company; but, of course, all were anti-cardinalists. It may be readily imagined, therefore, that the conversation turned upon the two defeats which the cardinal's guards had sustained; and as d'Artagnan had been the hero of the last two days, he received all the congratulations; which Athos, Porthos, and Aramis yielded to him with pleasure, not only as true comrades, but as men who had had their turn too often not to let him have his.

About six o'clock, M. de Treville announced his intention of proceeding to the Louvre; but, as the original hour of audience was past, instead of obtaining admission by the private staircase, he placed himself in the antechamber, with the four young men. The king was not yet returned from the chase; but our friends had scarcely waited half an hour amongst the crowd of courtiers, before the doors were opened, and his majesty was announced.

This announcement caused d'Artagnan to shudder with emotion. The important moment was arrived upon which, in all probability, his future fate depended. His eyes, therefore, were fixed with intense anxiety on the door through which the king was about to enter.

Louis XIII. appeared, followed by his attendants. He was attired in his hunting-dress, still covered with dust; he was heavily booted; and in his hand he held his riding-whip. At the first glance, d'Artagnan perceived that the king was in a violent rage. This humour, though distinctly visible in his majesty's features, did not prevent the courtiers from ranging themselves along the sides of the room; and as, in the royal antechamber, it is better to be seen by an irritable and angry eye, than not to be seen at all, the three musketeers did not hesitate to step forward, although d'Artagnan, on his part, concealed himself behind them as much as possible. Yet though Athos, Porthos, and Aramis were personally known to the king, he passed on as if he had never seen them before, without either looking at or addressing them. But when his eyes rested for a moment upon M. de Treville, the latter met them with so much firmness, that the king turned aside his gaze, and, muttering to himself, entered his apartment.

"The aspects are unfavourable," said Athos smiling; "we shall not be knighted this time."

"Wait here ten minutes," said M. de Treville, "and if I do not return to you in that time, proceed to my hotel, as it will be useless for you to wait longer for me."

The young men waited ten minutes, a quarter of an hour, even twenty minutes; and then, finding that M. de Treville did not return, they departed, very uneasy with the turn things were taking.

M. de Treville, who had boldly entered the royal cabinet, found his majesty in a very bad humour; he was seated in an arm-chair, venting his irritation by striking his boots with the handle of his whip. This, however, M. de Treville did no appear to notice, but with the utmost composure he inquired after his majesty's health.

"Bad, very bad," replied the king. "I am dull and dispirited."

This was, in fact, the worst malady of Louis XIII., who often withdrew to a window with one of his courtiers, saying to him, "Come, sir, let us be bored together."

"I regret to find your majesty thus," said M. de Treville. "Have you not, then, enjoyed the pleasure of the chase?"

"A fine pleasure, truly! By my faith, all goes to ruin, and I know not whether it is the game that is no longer so swift a-foot, or the dogs that have no noses. We roused a stag of ten tines; we ran him for six hours; and when we were on the point of taking him, and just as Saint Simon was about to place his horn to his mouth, to sound the 'mort'—*crac*, all the pack went off on the wrong scent, in pursuit of a brocket. You will thus see that I must now renounce the chase with hounds, as I have already relinquished it with falcons. Ah! I am a most unhappy king, M. de Treville; I had only one ger-falcon remaining, and he died yesterday."

"Truly, sire, I can estimate your misfortune; it is, indeed, very great; but there are yet, I believe, a goodly number of falcons, hawks, and tercels, remaining."

"But who is to train them? The falconers are all gone; and I alone now preserve the true art of venery. With me, all will be lost, and the game will hereafter be taken by snares, pitfalls, and traps. Oh! had I only leisure to instruct scholars! But then there is the cardinal, who never leaves me any leisure, and who is ever talking to me of Spain, of Austria, and of England! But apropos of the cardinal, I am very angry with you, M. de Treville."

The latter had anticipated this turn of the conversation. From his long and intimate knowledge of the king, he was well aware that complaints of this nature were only a sort of prelude, as it were, to arouse his majesty's courage to the proper pitch, which he had on this occasion attained.

"In what have I had the misfortune to offend your majesty?" inquired M. de Treville, feigning the utmost astonishment.

"Is it thus that you discharge your office, sir?" continued the king, answering one question by another; "was it for this that I created you captain of my musketeers—that they should assassinate a man, excite a whole neighbourhood, and threaten to burn all Paris, without your saying a word to me on the subject? However," added the king, "without doubt you have come here to accuse yourself, and, having committed all the rioters to safe custody, inform me that justice has been satisfied."

"Sire," said M. de Treville, with the utmost composure, "I am, on the contrary, come to demand justice."

"And against whom?" exclaimed the king.

"Against calumniators!" replied M. de Treville.

"Ah! this is something quite new," rejoined the king. "Do you pretend to say that your three confounded musketeers, and your Bearnese recruit, did not rush like madmen on poor Bernajoux, and so ill-treat him, that he is probably now dying? Do you also pretend to say, that they did not lay siege to the hotel of the Duke de la Tremouille, and that they did not propose to burn it—

which, during a period of war, would have been of little
consequence, seeing it is merely a nest of Huguenots, but
which, nevertheless, in time of peace, is a bad example.
Say, are you about to deny these matters?"

"And who has related to your majesty all this fine
story?" quietly demanded M. de Treville.

"Who has related to me this fine story, sir? Who
should it be, pray, but he who watches whilst I sleep;
who labours whilst I amuse myself; who manages everything within and without the realm; in Europe, as well as
in France?"

"Your majesty no doubt means God," said M. de
Treville, "for I know no other being who can be so far
above your majesty."

"No, sir; I speak of the pillar of the state; of my only
servant—of my only friend—of the cardinal."

"His eminence is not his holiness, sire!"

"What do you mean by that, sir?"

"That it is only the pope who is infallible; the
infallibility which he possesses does not extend to
cardinals."

"You would say, then," said the king, "that he
deceives me; you would say that he betrays me?"

"No, sire," said M. de Treville, "but I say that he
deceives himself; I say, that he has been deceived; I
say, that he has hastily accused his majesty's musketeers,
towards whom he is unjust; and that he has not drawn
his information from authentic sources."

"The accusation comes from M. de la Tremouille—
from the duke himself. What say you to that?" asked
the king.

"I might say that he is too deeply interested in the
question, to be an impartial witness; but, far from doing
that, sire, I, knowing the duke for a loyal gentleman,
willingly refer to him, but on one condition."

"And what is that?" said the king.

"It is that your majesty will send for him; will
question him, but by yourself, face to face, without

witnesses; and that I may see your majesty as soon as you have parted from the duke."

"Ay, marry, indeed!" said the king; "and you will be judged by what the duke may say?"

"Yes, sire."

"You will accept his judgment?"

"Without hesitation!" replied Treville.

"And you will submit to the reparations he may require?"

"Entirely!"

"La Chesnaye!" exclaimed the king, "La Chesnaye, let some one go immediately to inquire for M. de la Tremouille. I wish to speak with him this evening."

"Your majesty gives me your word that you will not speak with any one between M. de la Tremouille and myself?" asked Treville.

"With no one, on the word of a gentleman!" replied the king.

"To-morrow, then, sire?"

"To-morrow, sir."

"At what hour will it please your majesty?"

"At any hour you desire!"

"But in coming too early in the morning, I fear I may wake your majesty!"

"Wake me! Do I sleep? I never sleep now, sir! I may dream sometimes; nothing more. So come as early as you like, at seven o'clock if you choose; but I will not spare you, if your musketeers are in fault!"

"If my musketeers are guilty, sire, the guilty shall be delivered up to your majesty to await your pleasure. Does your majesty require anything else? You have but to speak, and you shall be obeyed!"

"No, sir, no! It is not without reason that I have been named Louis the Just. Farewell, then, till to-morrow, sir! Farewell!"

"May God preserve your majesty till then!"

However little the king might sleep, M. de Treville slept even less. He had told the three musketeers and their comrade, to be with him at half-past six in the morning; and he took them with him without telling them anything, or making them any promise; confessing to them that their favour, as well as his own, was not worth more than the chances of a cast of dice.

He left them at the foot of the staircase. If the king remained angry with them, they were to go away unnoticed; but, if his majesty consented to receive them, they would be ready at a call.

On entering the king's antechamber, M. de Treville found Chesnaye there, who informed him that M. de la Tremouille could not be found the evening before, and returned too late to be presented at the Louvre; that he had, in fact, but just arrived, and was now with the king.

This circumstance much pleased M. de Treville, who was certain that nothing could come between M. de la Tremouille's deposition, and his own audience. Scarcely, indeed, had ten minutes elapsed, before the door of the king's cabinet opened, and de Treville saw M. de la Tremouille come out. The duke immediately said to him,

"M. de Treville, his majesty sent for me; to inquire into the affair that happened yesterday morning at my hotel. I have told him the truth, that the fault lay with my people, and that I was ready to make you my excuses. As I have met you, will you now receive them, and do me the favour always to consider me as one of your friends!"

"Sir," said M. de Treville, "I was so convinced of your loyalty, that I did not wish for any other defender with his majesty than yourself. I see that I did not deceive myself; and I thank you that there is still one man in France, of whom I may say what I have said of you, without danger, deception, or mistake."

"It is well! it is well!" said the king, who had heard all these compliments. "Only tell him, Treville, since he wishes for your friendship, that I also wish for his, but that he neglects me; that it is just three years since I have seen him; and that he only comes to a levee when invited. Tell him this for me; for those are the kind of things which a king cannot say for himself!"

"Thanks, sire! thanks!" exclaimed the duke. "But let me assure your majesty that it is not those whom you see every day (I do not refer to M. de Treville) who are the most devoted to you."

"Ah! you heard what I said! So much the better, duke! so much the better!" said the king, advancing to the door. "Ah! it is you, Treville! where are your musketeers? I commanded you the day before yesterday to bring them! Why are they not here?"

"They are below, sire, and with your permission, Chesnaye will call them up."

"Yes, yes! let them come directly; it will soon be eight o'clock, and at nine I have an appointment. Go, duke! and, above all things, forget not to return. Come in, Treville!"

The duke bowed and departed. The moment that he opened the door, the three musketeers and d'Artagnan, conducted by Chesnaye, appeared at the top of the stairs.

"Come, my brave fellows!" said the king, "I must scold you!"

The musketeers approached, with obeisances, d'Artagnan following behind.

"What! the devil!" continued the king, "seven of his eminence's guards regularly doubled up by you four in two days! It is too many, gentlemen; it is too many: at this rate, his eminence will have to renew his regiment in three weeks, and I shall have to enforce the edicts in their full rigour. I say nothing of one by chance; but seven in two days, I repeat it, are too many, a great deal too many!"

"But your majesty perceives that they have come in sorrow and repentance, to excuse themselves."

"In sorrow and repentance! hum!" said the king. "I do not put much trust in their hypocritical faces.

There is, above all, a Gascon face in the background there! Come here, you, sir!"

D'Artagnan, who comprehended that the compliment was addressed to him, approached his majesty with a desperately desponding look.

"What! you told me it was a young man! But this is a mere boy, M. de Treville, quite a boy. Did he give that terrible wound to Jussac?"

"Yes! And those two beautiful sword thrusts to Bernajoux," said M. de Treville.

"Really!"

"Without reckoning," said Athos, "that if he had not rescued me from the hands of Biscarrat, I should certainly not have had the honour of paying my very humble reverence to your majesty."

"Why, M. de Treville, this Bearnese must be the very devil. Ventre saint-gris, as the king, my sire, would have said, at this rate many doublets must be riddled, and lots of swords broken. Now, the Gascons are always poor, are they not?"

"Sire, I must say that they have found no mines of gold in their mountains, though the Almighty owed them that recompense for the manner in which they supported the cause of your father."

"Which is to say, is it not, Treville, that it was the Gascons who made me king, as I am my father's son? Well, let it be so; I will not contradict it. La Chesnaye, go and see if, by rummaging my pockets, you can find forty pistoles; and if you find them, bring them to me. And now let me hear, young man, with your hand on your heart, how this affair happened?"

D'Artagnan told all the circumstances of the adventure; how, not being able to sleep, from the expectation of seeing his majesty, he went to his friend's house three hours before the time of the audience; how they went together to the tennis-court! and how, on account of the fear he betrayed of being struck upon his face by a ball, he had been rallied by Bernajoux, who had narrowly escaped paying for this raillery with his life; and M. de Tremouille, who was innocent, with the loss of his hotel.

"It is exactly so," murmured the king; "yes, it is exactly as the duke recounted the affair. Poor cardinal! Seven men in two days, and seven of his most valued soldiers, too! But this is sufficient, gentlemen; do you understand? You have taken your revenge for the Rue Ferou, and more than enough. You ought now to be satisfied."

"So we are, if your majesty is," said Treville.

"Yes! I am," replied the king; and taking a handful of gold from the hand of Chesnaye, and putting it into d'Artagnan's, he added, "there is a proof of my satisfaction."

At this period, the independent notions which are now current were not yet in fashion. A gentleman received money from the king's hand, without being humiliated. D'Artagnan, therefore, put the forty pistoles into his pocket, without any other ceremony than that of warmly thanking his majesty for the gift.

"There," said the king, examining his watch, "now that it is half-past eight, retire. I have told you that I have an appointment at nine. Thanks for your devotion, gentlemen! I may rely upon it, may I not?"

"Oh! sire!" replied the four at once, "we will allow ourselves to be cut in pieces in your defence!"

"Well! well! But it will be much better to remain whole, and you will be far more useful to me in that state. Treville," added the king, in a low voice, as the others retired, "as you have no commission vacant in the musketeers, and as we have decided that it should be necessary to pass a certain probation before entering that corps, place this young man in your brother-in-law, M. des Essarts', company of guards. Ah! I quite enjoy the thought of the grimace that the cardinal will make: he will be furious; but I do not care, I am quite right this time."

The king bowed to Treville, and the latter joined his musketeers, whom he found sharing the forty pistoles which his majesty had given d'Artagnan.

The cardinal was in reality as furious as his master had anticipated—so furious, in fact, that for eight days he took no hand at the king's card-table. But this did not prevent the king from putting on the most charming face, and asking, every time he met him, in a most insinuating tone—

"Well! M. le Cardinal! how is your poor Bernajoux? and your poor Jussac?"

CHAPTER VII.

THE DOMESTIC MANNERS OF THE MUSKETEERS.

WHEN d'Artagnan had left the Louvre, and had consulted his friends what he ought to do with his portion of the forty pistoles, Athos advised him to order a good dinner, and Porthos and Aramis to hire a lackey.

The dinner was accomplished on the same day; and the lackey waited at table. The dinner had been ordered by Athos; and the lackey, who had been provided by Porthos, was a Picard, whom the glorious musketeer had enlisted, on that very day, for that occasion, whilst he was sauntering about on the bridge of Latournelle, spitting into the stream. Porthos pretended that this occupation was a proof of a meditative organization, and had hired him without any other testimonial. The magnificent appearance of the gentleman, on whose account he had been hired, seduced Planchet, for that was the name of the Picard. He had, indeed, been slightly disappointed when he found, on his arrival, that the situation he expected was already held by a brother lackey of the name of Mousqueton; and when Porthos told him that his *ménage*, though on a large scale, did not admit of two servants, and that he must therefore wait on d'Artagnan. But when he attended at the dinner which his master gave, and saw him, when paying, draw from his pocket a handful of gold, he believed his fortune made, and thanked Heaven that he had fallen into the possession of such a Crœsus. In that opinion he remained until the feast was ended, and he had made up for his long abstinence by an attack upon the remnants. But, on making his master's bed, the visions of Planchet all vanished. There was only that one bed in the chambers, which consisted merely of an anteroom and bedroom. Planchet slept upon a coverlet, with which d'Artagnan from that time forward dispensed, taken from d'Artagnan's bed.

Athos, on his part, had a valet, whom he had drilled to his service in a manner peculiar to himself, and whom he called Grimaud. He was very taciturn, this worthy signor—we mean Athos, not his man. For the four or five years that he had lived in the closest intimacy with his companions, Porthos and Aramis, these two had often seen him smile, but never remembered to have heard him laugh. His words were brief and expressive; saying what he wished them to express, but no more; he employed no ornaments or embellishments whatever. Although Athos was scarcely thirty, and was possessed of great personal and mental attractions, no one ever knew him to have had a mistress. He never spoke of the female sex; and although he did not prevent such conversation from others, it was evident, from bitter and misogynous remarks, that it was disagreeable to him. His reserve, austerity, and silence, made him almost an old man, and he had therefore accustomed Grimaud, that he might not interrupt his habits, to obey a simple gesture, or even a motion of his lips. He never addressed him orally but in extreme cases. Sometimes Grimaud, who feared his master like fire, but at the same time was greatly attached to him, believed he understood him perfectly, rushed forward to execute his orders, and did something directly contrary to what was wanted. Then Athos shrugged his shoulders, and, in cold blood, belaboured him soundly. On such days he spoke a little.

Porthos, as is easy to see, had a character diametrically opposed to that of Athos: he not only spoke a great deal, but in a loud voice. It must be owned, to do him justice, that it was of little consequence to him, whether any one attended to him or not; he talked for the mere pleasure of speaking, or of hearing himself talk; and talked, too, of everything but the sciences, which he never alluded to but to express the inveterate hatred he had from his infancy entertained towards savants. He had not such an aristocratic air as Athos, and the sense of his inferiority on that point had, at the commencement of their connection, made him often unjust towards that gentleman, whom he endeavoured to surpass by the splendour of his dress. But, in his simple uniform coat, merely, and by the manner in which he carried himself, Athos took at once the rank to which he was entitled, and sent the foppish Porthos back to the second place. Porthos consoled himself by making M. de Treville's antechamber, and the guard-room of the Louvre, ring with the account of his conquests —a subject upon which Athos never spoke—and boasted of none lower than a foreign princess, who was deeply enamoured of him.

An old proverb says, "Like master like man." Let us then pass from the valet of Athos, to the valet of Porthos, from Grimaud to Mousqueton. Mousqueton was a Norman, whose pacific name of Boniface, his master had changed to the much more sonorous and warlike one of Mousqueton. He had entered Porthos' service on the sole payment of dress, board, and lodging, but in a sumptuous manner; and he only demanded two hours a day to provide for his other wants. Porthos had accepted the bargain, and things went on wonderfully well. He had old doublets and cloaks cut up and turned in a manner that made Mousqueton cut a very good figure.

As to Aramis, whose character we believe we have sufficiently explained, and which, as well as those of his comrades, we shall more fully develop hereafter his lackey was named Bazin. Thanks to the hopes which his master entertained of some day taking orders, he was always dressed in black, as became a churchman's servant. He was of the province of Berri; thirty-five or forty years of age; mild, peaceable, and fat; and passed his leisure in reading devotional treatises. He was dexterous in preparing a dinner for two; of excellent quality, though of few dishes. In all else he was dumb, blind, deaf, and of approved fidelity.

Now that we know, at least superficially, the masters and the men, let us turn to their habitations.

Athos dwelt in the Rue Ferou, at two paces from the Luxembourg. His habitation, or lodging, consisted of two small rooms in a very neatly-furnished house, whose mistress was still young and pretty, but ogled him in vain. Some few fragments of long-departed splendour adorned the walls of this modest lodging; such as a richly-mounted sword, which looked of the age of Francis I., and of which the handle alone, encrusted with precious stones, might be worth about two hundred pistoles. Nevertheless, Athos, even in moments of the greatest distress, could never be persuaded to dispose of or to pawn it. This sword had long excited the envy of Porthos, who would willingly have given ten years of his life for the possession of it.

One day when, as he said, he had an appointment with a duchess, he endeavoured to borrow it of Athos. But his friend, without saying a word, emptied his pockets of all his money and trinkets, purses, points, and gold chains, and offered them all to Porthos; but as for the sword, so he said, it was fixed to its place, and must only leave it when its master quitted the lodging. Besides this sword, he had the portrait of a nobleman, of the time of Henry III., dressed with great elegance, and adorned with the order of the Saint-Esprit; and this portrait had some slight resemblance to Athos, a certain family likeness, which denoted that this great noble, a royal knight, was his ancestor. Lastly, a box of splendid jewellery-work, with the same arms as the sword and portrait, completed a mantel decoration, which clashed fearfully with the furniture. Athos always carried the key of this box; but one day he opened it before Porthos, and Porthos could bear witness that it contained only letters and papers; love-letters, and family records, no doubt.

Porthos inhabited a lodging of vast size, and of most sumptuous appearance, in the Rue du Vieux Colombier. Every time Porthos passed the windows of this house, at one of which Mousqueton always appeared in splendid livery, he raised his head and his hand, saying, " Behold my habitation ! " But no one ever found him at home, nor did he ever ask any one in; and it was therefore impossible ·to form an idea of the reality of those riches which this sumptuous appearance promised.

As for Aramis, he dwelt in a small apartment, comprising a drawing-room, a dining-room, and a sleeping chamber, which were situate on the ground-floor, and had access to a small garden, fresh, green, shady, and quite impenetrable to the eyes of the surrounding neighbourhood.

We have already had occasion to know how d'Artagnan was lodged, and have already formed an acquaintance with his lackey, Master Planchet.

D'Artagnan, who was naturally very curious, as men of talent generally are, made every effort to find out who Athos, Porthos, and Aramis really were ; for, under one of those assumed appellations, each of these young men concealed his real name.

It was evident they were of good origin, too, particularly Athos, who might be known as a nobleman at a league's distance. He therefore tried from Porthos to get some information concerning Athos and Aramis ; and assailed Aramis, to find out something concerning Porthos.

Unfortunately, Porthos knew no more of the life of his silent comrade than that which has been told. It was said that he had met with great misfortunes of the heart, and that a terrible treachery had for ever poisoned the happiness of this gallant man. What this treachery was, no one knew.

As for Porthos, except his real name, with which M. de Treville alone was acquainted, as well as with those of his two comrades also, his life was easily discovered. Vain and indiscreet, he was as easily seen through as crystal. The only thing which could mislead the investigator would have been a belief in all the good which he announced of himself.

As for Aramis, with the appearance of entire openness he was enveloped in mystery. He replied but little to the questions put to him about others, and entirely eluded those which related to himself. One day d'Artagnan, having questioned him a long time about Porthos, and having learned the report of his love affair with a princess, wished to ascertain something of a similar nature as regarded himself.

"And you, my dear companion," said he, " I have an opinion that you are familiar with coats of arms: witness a certain handkerchief."

Aramis was not angry this time, but he put on a most modest air, and said, affectedly : " My dear fellow, do not forget that I wish to enter the church, and that I fly from all worldly things. That handkerchief was not a love-token for me, but was left by mistake at my house by one of my friends. I was obliged to take it for fear of compromising him, and his mistress. As for myself, I am, like Athos, indifferent to these affairs."

" But what the devil ! you are not an abbé, but a musketeer ! " exclaimed d'Artagnan.

"A musketeer, my dear fellow, for a time, as the cardinal says; a musketeer by accident, but a churchman at heart, believe me. Athos and Porthos have foisted me in, to occupy my time. I had, at the moment I was going to be ordained, a slight difficulty with—— But that does not much interest you, and I take up your valuable time."

"On the contrary," said d'Artagnan; "it interests me much, and I have at present actually nothing to do."

"Yes, but I have my breviary to say," replied Aramis, "then some verses to compose, which Madame d'Aiguillon has requested of me; then I must go into the Rue St. Honoré, to buy some rouge for Madame de Chevreuse; so you see, my dear friend, that though you are not in a hurry, I am;" and Aramis, tenderly pressing his young companion's hand, took leave of him.

D'Artagnan could not, with all his pains, learn any more of his three new friends; he therefore determined to believe all that was at present said of their past life, and hope for better and more full information from the future. In the meantime, he considered Athos an Achilles, Porthos an Ajax, and Aramis a Joseph!

The days of the four young men passed happily on. Athos played, and always with ill-luck; yet he never borrowed a sou of his friends, although he lent to them when he could. And, when he played on credit, he always awoke his creditor at six in the morning to pay him the debt of the evening before. Porthos had his humours: one day, if he gained, he was insolent and splendid; and when he lost, he disappeared entirely for a time, and then came back, wan and thin, but with his pockets stored with coin. As for Aramis, he never played; he was the worst musketeer, and the most unpleasant guest possible. He always wanted to study; even in the middle of dinner, when all expected him to spend two or three hours in the midst of the wine and company, out came his watch, and he would say—rising with a graceful smile, and taking leave of the company—that he must consult a casuist with whom he had an appointment.

Planchet, d'Artagnan's válet, nobly supported his good fortune. He received thirty sous a day; and, during a month, entered the lodgings gay as a chaffinch, and affable to his master. When the wind of adversity began to blow on the household of the Rue des Fossoyeurs — that is to say, when Louis XIII.'s forty pistoles were eaten up, or nearly so — he began to utter complaints which d'Artagnan found very nauseous, Porthos indelicate, and Aramis ridiculous. On this account, Athos advised d'Artagnan to dismiss the rascal; Porthos wished him to thrash him first; and Aramis declared that a master should never listen to anything but his servant's compliments.

"It is very easy for you to talk," replied d'Artagnan; "for you, Athos, who live mutely with Grimaud, and forbid him to speak; and, consequently, can never hear anything unpleasant from him; for you Porthos, who live magnificently, and are a sort of demigod to your valet, Mousqueton; for you, in fine, Aramis, who, being always engaged in thought, make your servant Bazin, who is a mild, religious man, respect you; but I—who am without stability or resources—I, who am neither musketeer nor guardsman—what can I do to inspire Planchet with affection, terror, or respect?"

"The thing is weighty," answered the three friends; "the discipline of your establishment is in the balance. With valets, as with women, it is necessary to prove master at once, if you wish to keep them with you; let us therefore reflect!"

D'Artagnan reflected, and resolved to thrash Planchet provisionally, which was executed as conscientiously as he acted in all other affairs. Then, after having drubbed him soundly, he forbade him to quit his service without permission. "For," said he, "the future cannot be unfavourable to me; I have an infallible expectation of better times, and your fortune is therefore made if you remain with me. Yes! I am too good a master to let your prospects be sacrificed, by giving you the notice you demand."

This manner of proceeding gave the musketeers great respect for d'Artagnan's policy; and Planchet was seized with equal admiration, and spoke no more of leaving him.

The lives of the four young men were now passed alike. D'Artagnan, who had formed no habits whatever, as he had but just arrived from the provinces and fallen into the midst of a world entirely new to him, immediately assumed those of his friends.

They rose at eight in the winter, and at six in the summer; and went to take the countersign, and see what was doing at M. de Treville's. D'Artagnan, though he was not a musketeer, performed the duties of one with great punctuality. He was always on guard, as he always accompanied that one of his friends whose turn it chanced to be. Every one at the hotel knew him, and regarded him as a comrade. M. de Treville, who, at the first glance took his measure, and had a sincere affection for him, did not cease to recommend him to the king.

The three musketeers had, on their parts, a great affection for their young companion. The friendship which united these four men, and the necessity of seeing each other three or four times a day, whether the affair were one of honour or of pleasure, made them run after each other like shadows; and they were always to be seen seeking each other, from the Luxembourg to the Place de Saint Sulpice, or from the Rue du Vieux Colombier to the Luxembourg.

In the meantime, the promises of M. de Treville were fulfilled. One fine day, the king commanded M. the Chevalier des Essarts to take d'Artagnan, as a recruit, into his company of guards. It was not without a sigh that d'Artagnan put on the uniform, which he would have exchanged for that of the musketeers at the cost of ten years of his existence. But M. de Treville promised him that favour after a cadetship of two years; a cadetship which, however, might be abridged, if he should find an opportunity of distinguishing himself by some brilliant action. D'Artagnan retired with this promise, and entered on his service the next day.

Then it was that Athos, Porthos, and Aramis, mounted guard, in turn, with d'Artagnan, when the duty came to him. The company of M. des Essarts, therefore, on the day that it received the youthful Gascon, received four men, in the place of one!

CHAPTER VIII.

THE COURT INTRIGUE.

NEVERTHELESS, the forty pistoles of Louis XIII., like everything else in this world, after having had a beginning, had also an end; and, after the end, our four companions fell into difficulties. Athos, at first, supported the association from his own private funds; to him succeeded Porthos, and, thanks to one of his occasional disappearances, he supplied the necessities of his friends for about fifteen days. Lastly, came the turn of Aramis, who performed his part with a good grace, on the strength of a few pistoles, procured, as he asserted, by the sale of some of his theological books. After all these resources were exhausted, they had recourse to M. de Treville, who made some advances of pay; but these could not go very far with our musketeers, who had had advances already; while the young guardsman had as yet no pay due. When they were at last almost destitute, they mustered, as a last resource, about eight or ten pistoles, which Porthos staked at play; but, being in ill-luck, he lost not only them, but twenty-five more, for which he gave his word of honour. Their difficulties thus became transformed to actual bankruptcy; and the four half-starved soldiers, followed by their lackeys, were seen running about the promenades and guard-rooms, picking up dinners wherever they could find them; for whilst in prosperity they had, by Aramis's advice, sown repasts right and left, in order that they might reap some in the season of adversity. Athos received four invitations, and every time took his three friends and their lackeys with him; Porthos had six chances, of which, also, they all took advantage; but Aramis had eight, for he, as may be seen, was a man who made but little noise over a good deal of work. As for d'Artagnan, who scarcely knew any one in the capital, he only found a breakfast on chocolate at the house of a Gascon priest, and one dinner with a cornet of the guards. He took his little army with him to the priest—whose two months' stock of provisions it mercilessly consumed—and to the cornet's, who gave them quite a banquet; but, as Planchet observed, however much we may devour, it still makes only a single meal.

D'Artagnan, therefore, was somewhat humbled at returning only one meal and a half for the feasts which Athos, Porthos, and Aramis had procured him. He thought himself a burden to the clique; forgetting, in his youthful sincerity, that he had supported that clique throughout a whole month. It was by this reflection that his ardent mind was set to work. He conceived that this coalition of four brave, enterprising, and active young men, ought to have some nobler aim than idle walks, fencing lessons, and more or less amusing jests. In fact, four such men as they—so devoted to each other, with their purses or their lives; so ready to support each other without surrendering an inch; executing, either singly or together, the common resolutions; menacing the four cardinal points at one time, or concentrating their united efforts on some single focus—ought inevitably, either secretly or openly, either by mine or trench, by stratagem or force, to find a way to what they had in view, however well defended or however distant that object might be. The only thing that surprised d'Artagnan was, that this capacity had never yet occurred to his companions. He himself now thought of it seriously, racking his brain to find a direction for his

individual power four times multiplied, with which he
felt assured that he might, as with the lever which
Archimedes sought, succeed in moving the world.—But
his meditations were disturbed by a gentle knock at the
door.

D'Artagnan roused Planchet, and told him to see who
was there. But from this phrase of *rousing Planchet*, it
must not be supposed that it was night. No! it was four
in the afternoon; but two hours had elapsed since
Planchet, on coming to ask his master for some dinner,
had been answered—

"He who sleeps, dines!"

And Planchet was having dinner on this economical fare.

A man of plain and simple appearance, who had
a bourgeois air, was introduced.

Planchet would have liked, by way of dessert, to hear
the conversation; but the man declared to d'Artagnan
that what he had to say being urgent and confidential,
he would wish to be alone with him. D'Artagnan
therefore dismissed Planchet, and begged his visitor to be
seated.

There was a momentary silence, during which the
two men regarded one another inquisitively, after which
d'Artagnan bowed as a signal of attention.

"I have heard M. d'Artagnan mentioned as a very
brave young man," said the citizen, "and this it is that
has determined me to confide a secret to him."

"Speak, sir, speak!" exclaimed d'Artagnan, who
instinctively suspected something profitable.

The citizen paused; and then continued—"I have a
wife, who is seamstress to the queen, and who is not without wit or beauty. I was induced to marry her, three
years ago, though she had but a small dowry, because M.
de la Porte, the queen's cloak-bearer, is her godfather and
patron."

"Well, sir?" demanded d'Artagnan.

"Well, sir," replied the citizen, "she was abducted
yesterday morning, as she left her workroom."

"And by whom has she been abducted?" inquired d'Artagnan.

"I do not know positively, sir," said the other; "but I suspect a certain person."

"And who is this person whom you suspect?"

"One who has for a long time pursued her."

"The deuce he has!"

"But, allow me to tell you, sir, that there is less of love than of policy in all this."

"Less of love than of policy!" exclaimed d'Artagnan, with an air of profound reflection; "and whom do you suspect?"

"I scarcely know whether I ought to mention names."

"Sir," said d'Artagnan, "permit me to observe, that I have absolutely demanded nothing from you; it is *you* who have come to *me;* it is you who told me that you had a secret to confide to me; do then as you please; there is yet time to draw back."

"No, sir, you have the air of an honourable man, and I can trust you. I believe it is in consequence of no love affair of her own that my wife has been entrapped, but because of an amour of a lady of far more exalted station than her own!"

"Ah, ah! can it be on account of some amour of Madame de Bois Tracy?" asked d'Artagnan; who wished to appear familiar with Court circles.

"Higher, sir, higher!"

"Of Madame d'Aiguillon?"

"Higher yet!" said the citizen.

"Of Madame de Chevreuse?"

"Higher still!—much higher!"

"Of the——"

And here d'Artagnan paused.

"Yes!" answered the frightened citizen, in such a low voice as scarcely to be audible.

"And who is the other party?" said d'Artagnan.

"Who can it be, if not the Duke of ——?" replied the mercer.

"With the Duke of —— ? "

"Yes, sir," replied the citizen, in a still lower tone.

"But how do you know all this ? "

"How do I know it ? " said the mercer.

"Yes! How do you know it? You must tell me all or nothing, you understand," said d'Artagnan.

"I know it from my wife, sir—from my wife herself."

"And from whom does she know it ? "

"From M. de la Porte. Did I not tell you that she is his god-daughter? Well! M. de la Porte, who is the confidential agent of the queen, had placed her near her majesty, that the poor thing—abandoned as she is by the king, watched as she is by the cardinal, and betrayed as she is by all—might at any rate have some one in whom she could confide."

"Ah, ah! I begin to understand," said d'Artagnan.

"Now, sir, my wife came home four days ago. One of the conditions of our marriage was, that she should come and see me twice a week; for, as I have the honour to inform you, she is my love as well as my wife. Well, sir, she came to inform me, in confidence, that the queen is at the present time in great alarm."

"Really ? " said d'Artagnan.

"Yes! the cardinal, as it appears, spies upon her and persecutes her more than ever; he cannot pardon her the episode of the Sarabande—you know the story of the Sarabande, sir ? "

"Egad! I should think I do!" replied d'Artagnan; who knew nothing at all about it, but would not for the world appear ignorant.

"So that it is no longer hatred now, but revenge!" said the citizen.

"Really!" replied d'Artagnan.

"And the queen believes——"

"Well! what does the queen believe ? "

"She believes that they have forged a letter in her name to the Duke of Buckingham."

"In her majesty's name ? "

"Yes, to entice him to Paris; and when they have got him here, to lead him into some snare."

"The deuce! But your wife, my dear sir—what is her part in all this?"

"They know her devotion to the queen, and want to separate her from her mistress; and either to intimidate her into betraying her majesty's secrets, or seduce her into serving as a spy upon her."

"It seems probable!" said d'Artagnan; "but, do you know her abductor?"

"I have told you that I believe I know him!"

"His name?"

"I have not an idea what it is; all I know is that he is a creature of the cardinal—the minister's tool."

"But you know him by sight?"

"Yes; my wife pointed him out one day."

"Has he any mark by which he may he recognised?"

"Yes, certainly; he is a man of aristocratic appearance, and has a dark skin, a tawny complexion, piercing eyes, white teeth, and a scar on his forehead."

"A scar on his forehead!" cried d'Artagnan; "and with white teeth, piercing eyes, dark complexion, and proud air—it is my man of Meung!"

"Your man, do you say?"

"Yes, yes!" said d'Artagnan; "but that has nothing to do with this affair. Yet I mistake! It has, on the contrary, a great deal to do with it; for if your man is mine also, I shall at one blow perform two acts of revenge.—But where can I meet with him?"

"I have not the slightest idea."

"Have you no clue to his abode?"

"None whatever. One day, when I accompanied my wife to the Louvre, he came out as she entered, and she pointed him out to me."

"Plague on it!" murmured d'Artagnan; "this is all very vague. But how did you hear of the abduction of your wife?"

"From M. de la Porte."

"Did he tell you the details?"

"He knew none."

"You have got no information from other quarters?"

"Yes, I have received——"

"What?"

"But I know not whether I should inform you."

"You return to your hesitation; but permit me to observe, that you have now advanced too far to recede."

"I do not draw back," exclaimed the citizen, accompanying the assurance with an oath, to support his courage; besides, on the honour of Bonancieux——"

"Then your name is Bonancieux?" interrupted d'Artagnan.

"Yes, that is my name."

"You say, on the honour of Bonancieux! Pardon this interruption, but the name appears not to be unknown to me."

"It is very possible, sir, for I am your landlord."

"Ah, ah!" said d'Artagnan, half rising, "ah, you are my landlord?"

"Yes, sir, yes; and as for the three months that you have been in my house (diverted, no doubt, by your great and splendid occupations), you have forgotten to pay me my rent, and as, likewise, I have not once asked you for payment, I thought that you would have some regard on account of my delicacy in that respect."

"Why, I have no alternative, my dear M. Bonancieux," answered d'Artagnan, "believe me, I am grateful for such a proceeding, and shall, as I have said, be most happy if I can be of use in any way."

"I believe you, I believe you," interrupted the citizen; "and as I said, on the honour of Bonancieux, I have confidence in you."

"Then go on with your account."

The citizen drew a paper from his pocket, and gave it to d'Artagnan.

"A letter!" exclaimed the young man.

"Which I received this morning."

D'Artagnan opened it, and, as the light commenced to wane, he approached the window, followed by Bonancieux.

"Do not seek for your wife," read d'Artagnan: "she will be returned to you when she is no longer required. If you make a single attempt to discover her, you are lost!"

"Well, this is pretty positive!" continued d'Artagnan; "but, after all, it is only a threat."

"Yes, but this threat frightens me, sir: I am not at all warlike, and I fear the Bastile."

"Humph!" said d'Artagnan, "I do not like the Bastile any more than you do; if it was only a sword thrust, now, it would be of no consequence!"

"And yet I had depended much on your assistance."

"Quite right!"

"Seeing you always surrounded by musketeers of haughty carriage, and perceiving that those musketeers belonged to M. de Treville, and, consequently, were the enemies of the cardinal, I thought that you and your friends, whilst gaining justice for our poor queen, would be enchanted at doing his eminence an ill turn."

"Unquestionably!"

"And then I thought, that, owing me three months' rent, which I never demanded——"

"Yes, yes, you have already mentioned that reason, and I consider it excellent."

"Reckoning, moreover, that as long as you will do me the honour of remaining in my house, I should make no reference to rent——"

"Good, again!" said d'Artagnan.

"And, added to that, calculating upon offering you fifty pistoles, should you be at all distressed at this time, which I don't say for a moment——"

"Wonderfully good! You are rich, then, my dear M. Bonancieux!"

"Say, rather, in easy circumstances, sir. I have

amassed something like two or three thousand crowns a year in the linen-drapery line; and more particularly, by investing something in the last voyage of the celebrated navigator, Jean Mocquet; so that you understand, sir—— Ah! but——" exclaimed the citizen.

"What?" demanded d'Artagnan.

"What do I see there?"

"Where?"

"In the street, opposite your windows; in the opening of that entry—a man wrapped in a cloak!"

"It is he!" cried d'Artagnan and the citizen in one breath; each having at the same moment recognised his man.

"Ah! this time he shall not escape me!" exclaimed d'Artagnan, rushing out, sword in hand.

On the staircase he met Athos and Porthos, who were coming to see him. They stood apart, and he passed between them like a meteor.

"Ah, where are you running to?" cried the two musketeers.

"The man of Meung!" ejaculated d'Artagnan, as he disappeared.

D'Artagnan had more than once related to his friends his adventure with the stranger, and also the apparition of the fair traveller, to whom this man appeared to confide such an important missive. Athos was of opinion that d'Artagnan had lost the letter during the quarrel, since a gentleman, such as he had described the unknown to be, must have been incapable of theft: Porthos only saw in the affair an amorous appointment, which d'Artagnan and his yellow horse had disturbed; and Aramis had said, these kind of things being mysterious, had better not be searched into. From the few words which escaped d'Artagnan, they understood, therefore, what was his object; and concluding that he would return, after he had found his man, they proceeded to his apartment.

When they entered the room which d'Artagnan had

just quitted, they found it empty; for the landlord, fearing the consequences of the meeting and duel which he doubted not was about to take place between the young man and the stranger, had judged it most prudent to decamp.

CHAPTER IX.

D'ARTAGNAN BEGINS TO SHOW HIMSELF.

As Athos and Porthos had anticipated, d'Artagnan returned in half an hour. He had again missed his man, who had disappeared as if by enchantment. The young Gascon had run through all the neighbouring streets, sword in hand, but found no one resembling him. Whilst d'Artagnan was engaged in this pursuit, Aramis had joined his companions, so that on his return he found the re-union complete.

"Well!" exclaimed they, when they saw him enter, covered with perspiration, and furious.

"Well!" said he, throwing his sword on the bed; "this man must be the devil himself: he disappeared like a phantom, a shadow, a spectre!"

"Do you believe in apparitions?" demanded Athos and Porthos.

"I only believe in what I see; and as I have never seen an apparition, I do not believe in them."

"The Bible declares that one appeared to Saul!" said Aramis.

"Be it how it may," said d'Artagnan, "man or devil, body or shadow, illusion or reality, this man is born to be my bane; for his escape has caused us to lose a fine opportunity—one, gentlemen, by which an hundred pistoles, or more, were to be gained!"

"How is that?" asked Aramis and Porthos; but Athos, true to his principle of silence, merely interrogated d'Artagnan by a look.

"Planchet," said d'Artagnan, "go to my landlord,

M. Bonancieux, and tell him to send me half a dozen bottles of Beaugency, which is my favourite wine."

"Ah! then you have credit with your landlord?" demanded Porthos.

"Yes, from this day," said d'Artagnan; "and be assured that if the wine is bad, we will send to him for better."

"You should use, and not abuse," sententiously remarked Aramis.

"I always said that d'Artagnan had the best head of the four," said Athos; who, having delivered himself of this opinion, which d'Artagnan acknowledged by a bow, relapsed into his usual silence.

"But now let us hear what is the scheme," demanded Porthos.

"Yes," said Aramis, "confide in us, my dear friend; at least, if the honour of some lady be not compromised."

"Be easy," replied d'Artagnan, "the honour of no one shall be in danger from what I have to tell you." He then related, word for word, his intercourse with his landlord; and how the man who had carried off the worthy mercer's wife was the same with whom he had quarrelled at the Jolly Miller, at Meung.

"The thing looks well," said Athos, after he had tasted the wine like a connoisseur, and testified by an approving nod of the head that it was good; and had calculated also whether it was worth while to risk four heads for sixty or seventy pistoles.

"But, observe," said d'Artagnan, "that there is a woman in the case; a woman who is carried off, and no doubt threatened, perhaps tortured, merely on account of her fidelity to her royal mistress."

"Take care, d'Artagnan—take care," said Aramis; "in my opinion you are too interested in Madame Bonancieux. Woman was created for our destruction; and from her all our miseries arise."

Athos frowned, and bit his lip, whilst he listened to this profound opinion.

"It is not for Madame Bonancieux that I distress myself," said d'Artagnan, "but for the queen, whom the king abandons, whom the cardinal persecutes, and who sees the execution of all her truest friends in succession."

"But why will she love what we most detest—the English and the Spaniards?" asked Athos.

"Spain is her country," replied d'Artagnan, "and it is but natural that she should love the Spaniards, who are her compatriots. As to your first reproach, I never heard that she loved *the* English, but *an* Englishman."

"And truly," replied Athos, "one must confess, that that Englishman is well worthy of being loved. I never saw a man of a more noble air."

"Besides, you do not consider the perfect style in which he dresses," said Porthos. "I was at the Louvre the day he scattered his pearls, and I picked up two which sold for twenty pistoles. Do you know him, Aramis?"

"As well as you do, gentlemen; for I was one of those who arrested him in the garden at Amiens, where the queen's equerry, M. de Putange, had introduced me. I was at the seminary at that time, and the adventure appeared to me to bear hard upon the king."

"Which would not hinder me," said d'Artagnan, "from taking him by the hand, and conducting him to the queen; if it were only to enrage the cardinal. Our one eternal enemy is the cardinal; and if we could find the means of doing him some injury, I confess that I would willingly risk my life to employ them."

"And the mercer told you, d'Artagnan," said Athos, "that the queen thought they had decoyed Buckingham into France by some false information?"

"She fears so! And I am convinced," added d'Artagnan, "that the abduction of this woman, one of the queen's suite, has some connection with the circumstances of which we are speaking, and perhaps with the presence of his grace the Duke of Buckingham in Paris."

"The Gascon is full of imagination," said Porthos.

"I like to hear him talk," said Athos; "his dialect amuses me."

"Gentlemen," said Aramis, "listen!"

"Let us attend to Aramis!" exclaimed the three friends.

Yesterday, I was at the house of a learned doctor of theology whom I sometimes consult on technical difficulties."

Athos smiled.

"He lives in a retired spot, convenient to his tastes and his profession. Now, just as I was leaving his house——" Here Aramis hesitated.

"Well!" said his auditors—"just, as you were leaving his house?"

Aramis appeared to make an effort, like a man who, in the full swing of making up a story, finds himself suddenly arrested by an unforeseen obstacle; but, as the eyes of his three friends were upon him, he could not by any means draw back.

"This doctor has a niece," continued Aramis.

"Oh! he has a niece," interrupted Porthos.

"Yes, a lady of the highest morality," said Aramis.

The three friends began to laugh.

"Ah! if you either laugh or make insinuations, you shall hear no more," said Aramis.

"We are credulous as the Mahometans, and dumb as catafalks!" said Athos.

"Then I will continue," said Aramis. "This niece comes sometimes to see her uncle, and as she was there by chance yesterday at the same time that I was, I was obliged to offer to conduct her to the carriage."

"Ah! the niece of this doctor has a carriage," interrupted Porthos, whose chief fault consisted in having too long a tongue. "A desirable connection, my friend!"

"Porthos," said Aramis, "I have often intimated to you, that you are very indiscreet, and it does you no good in the eyes of gentlemen."

"Gentlemen," said d'Artagnan, who saw how the

adventure arose, "the thing is serious; let us endeavour to avoid joking. Go on, Aramis; go on."

"All of a sudden a tall, dark man, with the manners of a gentleman—like your man, d'Artagnan——"

"The same, perhaps," said the Gascon.

"It is possible!" said Aramis; "however, he approached me, accompanied by six or seven men, who followed him at about ten paces' distance, and then, in the most polite tone, said, 'My lord duke, and you, madame,' addressing the lady——"

"What! the doctor's niece?" said Porthos.

"Silence, Porthos," said Athos; "you are insupportable."

"'Please to enter that carriage, without resistance, and in silence.'"

"He took you for Buckingham?" said d'Artagnan.

"Almost certainly," said Aramis.

"But this lady?" said Porthos.

"He took her for the queen," said d'Artagnan.

"Precisely!" said Aramis.

"The Gascon is the devil!" said Athos; "nothing escapes him!"

"The fact is," said Porthos, "that Aramis is about the height, and has something of the figure, of the handsome duke; and yet one would think that the uniform of a musketeer——"

"I had on an enormous cloak."

"In the month of July! Excellent!" cried Porthos; "was the doctor afraid that you might be recognised?"

"I can conceive," said Athos, "that the spy might be deceived by the figure; but the countenance?"

"I had a large hat," replied Aramis.

"Good heavens!" exclaimed Porthos, "what extraordinary precautions for studying theology?"

"Gentlemen," said d'Artagnan, "do not let us lose our time in badinage; let us rather make inquiries, and discover the mercer's wife, who might prove a key to the intrigue."

"What! a woman of such an inferior condition! Do you think it likely, d'Artagnan?" asked Porthos, with a derisive pout.

"Have I not told you, gentlemen," said d'Artagnan, "that she is the god-daughter of la Porte, who is the confidential servant of the queen. Perhaps it is her majesty's policy to seek assistance from a source so humble. Lofty heads are visible at a distance, and the cardinal has a good eye."

"Well, then," said Porthos, "come to terms with the mercer immediately, and good terms."

"It is unnecessary," said d'Artagnan; "if he should not pay us, we shall be well enough paid from another quarter."

At this moment a noise of hasty steps was heard upon the stairs; the door opened with a crash, and the unhappy mercer rushed into the room in which this council had taken place.

"Oh, gentlemen!" he exclaimed, "save me, save me! in the name of heaven save me! There are four men come to arrest me!"

Porthos and Aramis arose.

"One moment," cried d'Artagnan, making them a sign to sheath their swords, which they had half drawn —"wait one moment; it is not courage, but diplomacy, that is necessary here!"

"Nevertheless," said Porthos, "we will not permit——"

"Give d'Artagnan a free hand," said Athos; "he is the cleverest of the party, and, for my part, I declare that I will obey him. Do what you like, d'Artagnan."

As this speech was uttered, the four guards appeared at the door of the ante-room, but seeing four musketeers standing there, with swords by their sides, they hesitated to advance any farther.

"Enter, gentlemen, enter," said d'Artagnan; "you are in my apartment, and we are all the loyal subjects of the king and cardinal."

"Then, gentlemen, you will not oppose any obstacle

to the execution of our orders?" demanded he who appeared to be the leader of the party.

"On the contrary, we would assist you were it necessary."

"What is he saying?" inquired Porthos.

"You are stupid!" said Athos. "Silence!"

"But you promised to assist me!" whispered the poor mercer.

"We cannot assist you in prison," hastily replied d'Artagnan, in an undertone; "and if we appear to defend you, we shall be arrested also."

"It seems to me, however——" said the poor man.

"Come, gentlemen, come," said d'Artagnan aloud. "I have no motive for defending this person; I saw him to-day for the first time, and on what occasion he will himself tell you. He came to demand his rent—did you not, M. Bonancieux?—Answer!"

"It is the plain truth!" cried the mercer; "but the gentleman does not add——"

"Silence about me! silence concerning my friends! silence, more especially, about the queen!" whispered d'Artagnan, "or you will destroy us all, without saving yourself.—Go, go, gentlemen, take away this man!"

So saying, d'Artagnan pushed the poor bewildered mercer into the hands of the guards, at the same time exclaiming—

"You are a rascally niggard! You come to demand money of *me*, a musketeer!—to prison with you! Gentlemen, I say again, take him to prison; and keep him under lock and key as long as possible; that will give me time to pay."

The officers overwhelmed d'Artagnan with thanks, and carried off their prey.

As they were leaving, d'Artagnan detained the leader.

"Suppose we drank to each other's health?" said he, filling two glasses with the Beaugency, for which he was indebted to the liberality of M. Bonancieux.

"It will be a great honour to me," replied the leader of the guards; "and I accept the offer with gratitude."

"Here's to you, then, M. —— You have the advantage of me, sir."

"Boisrenard."

"M. Boisrenard!"

"I drink to you, sir, but, in return, you have the advantage of me."

"D'Artagnan."

"To your health, M. d'Artagnan!"

"And, above all," said d'Artagnan, as if carried away by his enthusiasm, "to the health of the king and the cardinal."

The officer might have doubted d'Artagnan's sincerity had the wine been bad; but it was excellent, and he was satisfied.

"But what devil's own villainy have you done now?" exclaimed Porthos, when the officer had joined his companions, and the four friends found themselves alone. "For shame! Four musketeers allow a miserable creature, who implored their assistance, to be arrested in the midst of them! and, more than that, a gentleman to tipple with a bailiff!"

"Porthos," said Aramis, "Athos has already told you that you are stupid; and I am of his opinion. D'Artagnan, you are a great man; and when you are in M. de Treville's situation, I beg your interest to procure me an abbey."

"Ah! I am quite in the dark!" said Porthos. "Do you also, Athos, approve of what d'Artagnan has done?"

"Most assuredly!" said Athos. "I not only approve of it, but I congratulate him."

"And now, gentlemen," said d'Artagnan, not deigning to explain himself to Porthos—"'All for one—one for all!' this is our motto, is it not?"

"Nevertheless——" said Porthos.

"Stretch out your hand, and swear," cried Athos and Aramis at the same time.

Conquered by the example, but muttering in a low tone, Porthos stretched out his hand, and the four friends repeated with one voice the formal motto dictated by d'Artagnan—

" ' All for one ; and one for all ! ' "

" That is right. Now, retire to your homes," said d'Artagnan, as if he had never been accustomed to anything but to command others. " But," he added, " be watchful ; for remember, that from this moment we are at issue with the cardinal ! "

CHAPTER X.

A MOUSETRAP OF THE SEVENTEENTH CENTURY.

THE mousetrap is not a modern invention. As soon as societies had, in establishing themselves, instituted some kind of police, that police in its turn invented mousetraps.

As our readers are perhaps not familiar with the slang of the Rue de Jerusalem, and as it is, although we have been engaged in authorship for fifteen years, the first time that we have used the word in this signification, let us explain to them what a mousetrap is.

When an individual has been arrested, in any house whatever, on suspicion of some crime, his arrest is kept secret ; four or five men are placed in ambush in the front room of this house ; all who knock are admitted, and also locked in and detained ; and, in this manner, at the end of three or four days, they can lay their fingers on all the frequenters of the establishment.

This, reader, is a mousetrap ! and into such a one was M. Bonancieux's apartment transformed. Whoever applied there, was seized and examined by the cardinal's people. But as there was a private court leading to the first floor, which d'Artagnan occupied, his visitors were all exempt from this detention. The three musketeers, however, were, in fact, the only visitors he had ; and each of these had, by this time, commenced a separate search, but had discovered nothing. Athos had even gone so far as to question M. de Treville—a circumstance which, considering his habitual taciturnity, had greatly surprised his captain. But M. de Treville knew nothing about it; excepting that the last time he had seen either the king, the queen, and the cardinal, the cardinal was very morose, the king very uneasy, and the queen's eyes were red from watching or weeping. But this last circumstance had not attracted much of his notice, as the queen had, since her marriage, both watched and wept frequently.

Furthermore, M. de Treville strongly advised Athos to be active in the king's service, and more particularly in the queen's, and requested him to transmit the advice to his companions.

As to d'Artagnan, he did not stir out of his lodgings. He had converted his room into an observatory. From his own windows he saw everybody who came into the trap; and as he had taken up some squares from the floor, and dug up the deafening, so that nothing but a ceiling separated him from the room below, where the examinations were made, he heard all that passed between the inquisitors and the accused. The interrogatories, which were preceded by a strict search, were almost always in these terms—

"Has Madame Bonancieux entrusted you with anything for her husband or any other person?"

"Has M. Bonancieux entrusted you with anything for his wife, or any one else?"

"Has either of them made any verbal communication to you?"

"If they knew anything, they would not put such questions as these," said d'Artagnan to himself. "But what are they trying to find out? Whether the Duke of Buckingham is in Paris at present; and if he has not had, or is not about to have, an interview with the queen?"

D'Artagnan stopped at this idea, which, after all that he had heard, was not without its probability. In the meantime, however, both the mousetrap and the vigilance of d'Artagnan remained in operation.

Just as it was striking nine on the evening of the day after poor Bonancieux's arrest, and just as Athos had left d'Artagnan to go to M. de Treville's, whilst Planchet, who had not made the bed, was about to do so, there was a knocking at the street door, which was immediately opened, and shut again : it was some new prey caught in the trap.

D'Artagnan rushed towards the unpaved part of his room, and laid himself down to listen. In a short time cries were heard, and then groans, which someone endeavoured to stifle.

There was no thought of examination.

"The devil !" said d'Artagnan to himself ; "it seems to me to be a woman ; they are searching her, and she resists ; the wretches are using violence !"

In spite of his prudence, d'Artagnan had some trouble to restrain himself from interfering in the scene which was being enacted underneath.

"I tell you, gentlemen, that I am the mistress of the house; I am Madame Bonancieux. I tell you that I am a servant of the queen's !" exclaimed the unfortunate woman.

"Madame Bonancieux !" murmured d'Artagnan ; "shall I be so fortunate as to have found her whom everybody searches for in vain ? "

"You are the very person we were waiting for," replied the officers.

The voice became more and more stifled. Violent struggling made the wainscot rattle. The victim was offering all the resistance that one woman could offer against four men.

"Forgive me, gentlemen, by——" murmured the voice, which then uttered only inarticulate sounds.

"They are gagging her ! They are going to abduct

her!" ejaculated d'Artagnan, raising himself up with a bound. "My sword!—Right! it is by my side!—Planchet!"

"Sir."

"Run, and seek Athos, Porthos, and Aramis; one of the three must be at home; perhaps all. Tell them to arm themselves, and hasten here. Ah, now I remember Athos is with M. de Treville."

"But where are you going, sir?— Where *are* you going?"

"I shall get down through the window," said d'Artagnan, "that I may be there sooner. Replace the squares, sweep the floor, go out by the door, and hasten whither I have told you."

"Oh! sir, you will be killed!" cried Planchet.

"Hold your tongue, idiot!" exclaimed d'Artagnan.

Then, grasping the window-sill, he dropped from the first storey, which was fortunately not high, without giving himself even a scratch. He then went immediately and knocked at the door, muttering—

"I in my turn am going to be caught in the mousetrap; but woe betide the cats who shall deal with such a mouse!"

Scarcely had the knocker sounded beneath the young man's hand, ere the tumult ceased, and footsteps approached. The door was opened, and d'Artagnan, armed with his naked sword, sprang into the apartment of M. Bonancieux. The door, doubtless moved by a spring, closed automatically behind him.

Then might those who yet inhabited the unfortunate house of M. Bonancieux, as well as the nearest neighbours, hear loud outcries, stampings, and the clashing of swords and the continual crash of furniture. After a moment more, those who had looked from their windows to learn the cause of this surprising noise, might see the door open, and four men clothed in black, not merely go out, but fly like frightened crows, leaving on the ground, and at the corners of the house, their feathers and wings, that is to say, portions of their coats and fragments of their cloaks.

D'Artagnan had come off victorious, without much difficulty, it must be confessed; for only one of the officers was armed, and he had only gone through a form of defence. It is quite true that the other three had endeavoured to knock down the young man with chairs, stools, and crockery, but two or three scratches from the Gascon's sword had scared them. Ten minutes had sufficed for their defeat, and d'Artagnan had remained master of the field of battle.

The neighbours, who had opened their windows with the indifference habitual to the inhabitants of Paris at that season of perpetual disturbances and riots, closed them again when they saw the four men escape; their instinct told them no more was to be seen for the time. Besides, it was getting late; and then, as well as now, people went to bed early in the quarter of the Luxembourg.

When d'Artagnan was left alone with Madame Bonancieux, he turned towards her. The poor woman was reclining in an easy chair, almost senseless. D'Artagnan examined her with a rapid glance.

She was a charming woman, about twenty-two or twenty-three years of age; with blue eyes, a nose slightly turned up, beautiful teeth, and a complexion of inter-mingled rose and opal. Here, however, ended the charms which might have confounded her with a lady of high birth. Her hands were white, but not delicately formed; and her feet did not indicate a woman of quality. Fortunately, d'Artagnan was not of an age to be nice in these matters.

Whilst d'Artagnan was examining Madame Bonancieux, and had got, as we have said, to her feet, he saw on the ground a fine cambric handkerchief, which, naturally, he picked up; and, at the corner of it, he discovered the same cipher that he had seen on the handkerchief which had nearly caused him and Aramis to cut one another's

throats.   Since that time d'Artagnan had mistrusted all
coronetted handkerchiefs ; and he now put that which he
had picked up into Madame Bonancieux's pocket, without
saying a word.

At that moment Madame Bonancieux recovered her
senses.   She opened her eyes, looked around her in
affright, and saw that the room was empty, and that she
was alone with her deliverer.   She immediately held out
her hands to him, with a smile · and Madame Bonancieux
had the most charming smile in the world.

"Ah ! sir," said she, "it is you who have saved me ;
allow me to thank you ! "

"Madame," replied d'Artagnan, "I have only done
what any gentleman would have done in my situation.
You owe me no thanks."

"Yes, yes, sir, I do ; and I hope to prove to you that
this service has not been for naught.   But what did
these men, whom I at first took for robbers, want with
me ? and why is not M. Bonancieux here ? "

"Madame, these men were far more dangerous than
any robbers would have been, for they are agents of the
cardinal ; and as for your husband, M. Bonancieux,
he is not here, because he was taken yesterday to the
Bastile."

"My husband in the Bastile !" cried Madame
Bonancieux.   "Oh, my God ! what can he have done,
poor, dear man !   Why, he is innocence itself ¡ "

And something like a smile glanced across the yet
alarmed countenance of the young woman.

"As to what he has been doing, madame," said
d'Artagnan, "I believe that his only crime consists in
having at the same time the good fortune and the
misfortune of being your husband."

"Then, sir, you know ¿ "

"I know that you were carried off, madame."

"But by whom ? do you know that ? Oh, if you know,
pray tell me ! "

"By a man about forty or forty-five years of age, with

dark hair, a brown complexion, and a scar on the left temple."

"Just so, just so : but his name?"

"Ah! his name—I don't know it myself."

"And did my husband know that I had been carried off?"

"He had been informed of it by a letter sent him by the ravisher himself."

"And does he suspect," demanded Madame Bonancieux, with some confusion, "the cause of this abduction?"

"He attributes it, I believe, to some political cause."

"At first I doubted whether it was so, but now, as I think, he does; and so my dear M. Bonancieux did not mistrust me for a single instant?"

"Ah! so far from that, madame, he was too proud of your prudence and your love."

A second smile, almost imperceptible, glided over the rosy lips of the beautiful young woman.

"But," continued d'Artagnan, "how did you make your escape?"

"I profited by a moment in which I was left alone; and as I learned this morning the cause of my abduction, by the help of my sheets I got out of the window, and hurried here, where I expected to find my husband."

"To place yourself under his protection?"

"Oh, no! poor dear man! I knew that he was incapable of protecting me; but, as he might be of some service to us, I wished to put him on his guard."

"Against what?"

"Alas! that is not my secret; and I dare not tell it to you."

"Besides," said d'Artagnan—"(pardon me, madame, if, protector as I am, I remind you of prudence)—besides, I think that we are scarcely in a situation suitable for confidences. The men whom I have put to flight will return reinforced, and if they find us here, we shall be lost. I have sent to summon three of my friends, but it is uncertain whether they may be at home!"

"Yes! yes! you are right," said Madame Bonancieux, in alarm; "let us fly: let us escape!"

And seizing d'Artagnan by his arm, she eagerly drew him along.

"But whether shall we fly? where shall we escape to?" said d'Artagnan.

"Let us get away from this place first, and then, having got clear of it, we shall see."

Without taking the trouble to shut the door, the two young people hastily passed down the Rue des Fossoyeurs, crossed the Rue des Fosses Monsieur le Prince, and did not stop until they reached the Place de St. Sulpice.

"And now, what next?" inquired d'Artagnan; "and whither would you like me to conduct you?"

"I confess that I scarcely know whither," said Madame Bonancieux. "I had intended, through my husband, to intimate my escape to M. de la Porte, so that the latter might tell us exactly what has happened at the Louvre within the last three days, and whether there would be any danger in my presenting myself there."

"But I," said d'Artagnan, "can go and inform M. de la Porte."

"Undoubtedly; yet there is one difficulty. M. Bonancieux is known at the Louvre, and would be allowed to enter; whilst you, not being known, would not be admitted."

"Nonsense!" said d'Artagnan: "there is doubtless a porter at some wicket of the Louvre who is devoted to you, and who, thanks to some countersign——"

Madame Bonancieux looked earnestly at the young man.

"And if I trusted you with this countersign," said she, "would you undertake to forget it as soon as you had made use of it?"

"On my word of honour! on the faith of a gentleman!" said d'Artagnan, with that accent of truth which never can mislead.

"Well, I believe you! You look like a man of honour, and your fortune perhaps may depend on your devotion."

"I will perform, without any promises, and conscientiously, whatever I can to serve the king, and to be acceptable to the queen," said d'Artagnan; "use me, therefore, as a friend!"

"But what is to become of me in the meantime?"

"Have you no acquaintance, to whose house M. de la Porte can come for you?"

"No, I would rather not trust to any one!"

"Wait," said d'Artagnan; "we are now just by Athos's door; yes, this is the best way!"

"And who is Athos?"

"A friend of mine."

"But, if he is at home, and sees me?"

"But he is not there, and I will take away the key when I have placed you in his apartment."

"Suppose he should return?"

"He will not return; besides, if he should, he will be told that I have brought a woman here, and that she is now in his apartment."

"But don't you see this will compromise me very much?"

"What need you care! no one knows you. Besides, we are not in a position to be particular."

"Well, let us go to your friend's house, then; where does he live?"

"In the Rue Ferou—two steps from here."

"Come, then."

And the two proceeded on their way. As d'Artagnan had foreseen, Athos was not at home; so taking the key, which they were in the habit of giving to him as a friend of the musketeer, he ascended the stairs, and introduced Madame Bonancieux into the little apartment which we have already described.

"You are now at home," said he. "Lock the door inside, and do not open it to any one, unless you hear three knocks—thus;" and he tapped three times—two taps together, pretty hard, and, after a short interval, a gentler tap.

"That will do," said Madame Bonancieux; "and now let me give you my instructions."

"I am all attention."

"Present yourself at the postern of the Louvre, on the side of the Rue de l'Echelle; and ask for Germain."

"Very well; and what next?"

"He will ask you what you want; you must answer by these words — 'Tours and Brussels' — and he will immediately listen to your commands."

"And what shall I tell him to do?"

"To go and find M. de la Porte, the queen's valet-de-chambre."

"And when M. de la Porte has come?"

"You will send him to me."

"Very well. But where, and how, shall I see you again?"

"Do you feel particularly anxious to see me again?"

"Particularly."

"Well, then, leave that to my care; and be at ease."

"I rely upon your word."

"And quite right."

D'Artagnan took leave of Madame Bonancieux, with the most amorous glance that he could possibly concentrate upon her charming little person; and whilst he was descending the stairs, he heard the door behind him double locked. In two bounds he was at the Louvre; and, as he entered the small door in the Rue de l'Echelle, it struck ten; so that all the events we have just related had transpired within half an hour.

Everything happened just as Madame Bonancieux had predicted. Germain heard the watchword with a bow, and in ten minutes de la Porte was in the porter's lodge; and in two words d'Artagnan told him what had occurred, and where Madame Bonancieux was to be found. La Porte made himself certain of the address by having it

twice repeated, and then hurried away. But he had
scarcely taken ten steps, before he returned.

"Young man," said he, "let me give you some good
counsel."

"What is it?"

"You may possibly get into some trouble on account
of this affair."

"Do you think so?"

"I do! Have you any friend whose clock is slow?"

"Suppose I have?"

"Go and pay him a visit, that he may be able to bear
witness that you were in his company at half-past nine.
In law, this is what is called an *alibi*."

D'Artagnan thought the advice prudent. He therefore
took to his heels, and reached M. de Treville's; but,
instead of entering the drawing-room, with the rest of the
company, he asked to be admitted into the cabinet, and
as he was one of the habitual frequenters of the hotel, no
objection was made to this; and M. de Treville was soon
informed that his young compatriot, having something of
importance to communicate, solicited a private interview.

In five minutes M. de Treville was there, and asked
d'Artagnan what he could do for him, and to what he
was indebted for a visit at such a late hour?

"Forgive me, sir," said d'Artagnan (who had taken
advantage of the moment he was left alone, to put the
clock back three quarters of an hour), "but I thought, as
it was only twenty-five minutes past nine, it was not yet
too late to wait upon you."

"Twenty-five minutes past nine!" exclaimed M. de
Treville, looking at the clock, "it is impossible!"

"Look for yourself, sir," said d'Artagnan, "the clock
shows it."

"You are right," replied M. de Treville: "I should
have thought it was later. But what can I do for you?"

Then d'Artagnan entered into a long story about the
queen; expressing all the fears that he entertained upon
her majesty's account, and recounting all that he had

heard about the cardinal's designs against Buckingham; and this with a degree of tranquillity and consistency by which M. de Treville was the more readily duped, inasmuch as he had himself, as we have already said, remarked that something fresh was stirring between the cardinal, the king, and the queen.

Just as the clock was striking ten, d'Artagnan arose, and took his leave of M. de Treville, who thanked him for his information, expressed on him an incessant earnestness in the service of the king and queen, and returned to his saloon.

But d'Artagnan remembered, at the bottom of the stairs, that he had forgotten his cane; he therefore hastened up again, re-entered the cabinet, and with one touch of his finger put the clock to its right time, so that it might not be seen the next day to have been wrong: then, satisfied that he had a witness there to prove his *alibi*, he again descended the stairs, and soon found himself in the street.

CHAPTER XI.

THE INTRIGUE BECOMES CONFUSED.

WHEN his visit to M de Treville was ended, d'Artagnan took, in pensive mood, the longest road to return to his own home.

But what were the meditations which thus led him from his way; contemplating, with successive sighs and smiles, the stars that glittered in the sky.

Alas! he was intent on Madame Bonancieux. To an apprentice musketeer, the charms of that young person raised her almost into an ideal of love. Pretty, mysterious, and initiated into all the court secrets, which reflected so much charming seriousness over her seductive features, he supposed her, also, to be not wholly unimpassioned, which is an irresistible attraction to novices in these engagements of the heart. He felt, moreover, that he had delivered her from the hands of miscreants who wished to search and maltreat her; and this important service had prepossessed her with a sentiment of gratitude towards him, which might easily be made to take a character of greater tenderness.

So rapidly do our dreams travel on imagination's wings, that d'Artagnan already fancied himself accosted by some messenger from Madame Bonancieux, handing to him an appointment for an interview, or a diamond or a chain of gold. We have already intimated that the young cavaliers were not then ashamed of accepting presents from their king; and we may add, that, in those times of easy morality, they were not more scrupulous in respect of their mistresses, and that these latter almost always conferred upon them some precious and durable memorials, as though they were endeavouring to overcome the instability of their sentiments by the solidity of gifts.

Men did not then blush at owing their advancement to women; and we might refer to many amongst the heroes of that age of gallantry, who would neither have won their spurs at first, nor their battles afterwards, but for the better or worse furnished purse which some mistress had suspended at their saddle-bow.

Now, d'Artagnan possessed nothing. His provincial hesitation—that superficial varnish, and ephemeral bloom, that down on the peach—had evaporated in the storm of somewhat unorthodox advice which the three musketeers had given to their friend. According to the curious customs of the time, he had come to look upon himself as being just as much engaged in a campaign whilst he was at Paris, as though he had been in Flanders. Spaniard there, woman here: yet, in either case, there was an enemy to overcome, and contributions to raise.

But let us not disguise that the young Gascon was, at present, influenced by a nobler and more disinterested feeling. The mercer had confessed to him that he was rich; and it was easy to infer that, with a simpleton like

Bonancieux, the wife would be the keeper of the purse. But nothing of this kind had contributed to that sentiment which the sight of Madame Bonancieux had inspired, and selfishness had been almost disregarded in the dawning love which had arisen from his interview. We say almost —for the assurance that a young, lovely, charming and witty woman is rich also, has a tendency, not to diminish, but rather to corroborate, this growth of sentiment. In easy circumstances, there are a crowd of aristocratic cares and caprices which accord well with beauty. A white and fine stocking, a silken dress, a lace kerchief, a pretty little shoe, a becoming ribband, do not make an ugly woman pretty, but they make a pretty woman irresistible; whilst her hands, moreover, are sure to be the gainers by her wealth; for the hands—in women, especially—must remain idle to be beautiful.

Now, as the reader very well knows—for we have made no secret of the state of his finances—d'Artagnan was not a man of large fortune. It is true that he quite expected to become so, at some future time; but the date which he had himself fixed on for that happy transformation, was as yet far distant. In the meantime, what sorrow would it be to see the woman whom one idolizes sighing for the thousand trifles in which so much of the happiness of womankind consists, and to be unable to procure them for her. But when the woman is rich, although the lover is poor, the gifts which he cannot present, she can provide for herself; and then, although it may most frequently be with the husband's money that these enjoyments are obtained, it is not commonly to this husband that the gratitude is shown.

Thus disposed to become the most passionate of admirers, d'Artagnan had not ceased to be a devoted friend. In the midst of his more tender feelings towards the mercer's wife, he was not forgetful of his companions. The pretty Madame Bonancieux was the very woman to take on an excursion to the plain of Saint Denis, or the fair at St. Germain, in company with Athos, Porthos, and

Aramis, to whom he should be so proud to show his charming conquest. And then — as d'Artagnan had happened to remark of late—after a long walk one gets hungry; and they would have some of those pleasant little dinners, during which one touches on this side the hand of a friend, on that the foot of a mistress. Finally, in moments of emergency, in great extremities, might it not be his happiness to be the saviour of his friends?

But what of M. Bonancieux, whom d'Artagnan had given over to the keeping of the officers; disowning him aloud, whilst, in a whisper, he assured him of his care? We must confess to our readers, that d'Artagnan had never thought of him at all; or, if he did think of him, it was merely to congratulate himself, that he was very well where he was, wherever that might be. Love is the most selfish of all our passions.

Nevertheless, let our readers take comfort: though d'Artagnan forgets his landlord, or pretends to forget him, under the excuse of not knowing where he has been taken, we have not forgotten him, and do know where he is. But, for the present, let us act like the amorous Gascon. As for the worthy mercer, we will return to him by and by.

D'Artagnan, whilst meditating on his future love, and conversing with the night, and smiling on the stars, proceeded along the Rue de Cherche Midi, or Chasse Midi, as it was then called. Being in Aramis's neighbourhood, he thought he might as well pay him a visit, to explain why he had sent Planchet with the invitation to come immediately to the mousetrap.

If Planchet had found Aramis at home, the latter had probably hastened to the Rue des Fossoyeurs, and, finding nobody there but his other two friends, perhaps, they would all have been in ignorance of what the summons meant. This dilemma needed some explanation; or, at least, so said d'Artagnan aloud.

But, in his inner soul, he thought that this call would

give him an opportunity of talking of the pretty Madame Bonancieux, with whom his mind, if not his heart, was already quite occupied. It is not in regard to a first love that we must look for discretion. The joy with which such a love is attended is so exuberant, that it must overflow, or it would suffocate us.

For the last two hours Paris had been dark and nearly deserted. Eleven o'clock was striking from all the clocks of the Faubourg St. Germain; the time was mild, and d'Artagnan was passing down a small street situated on the ground where the Rue d'Assas now stands, where the air was redolent of odours which were borne on the wind along the Rue de Vaugiraud, from gardens that the evening dews and the gentle gales refreshed. Afar off, though deadened by substantial shutters, was heard the revelry of the wine shops which were scattered over the flat quarters. Having reached the end of this street, d'Artagnan turned to the left. The house where Aramis lived was situated between the Rue Cassette and the Rue Servandoni.

D'Artagnan had already passed by the Rue Cassette, and could just perceive the door of his friend's house, embosomed amidst sycamores and clematis, when he saw something like a shadow which came out of the Rue Servandoni. This something was enveloped in a cloak, and d'Artagnan at first thought that it was a man; but from the smallness of its size, the irresolution of its manner, and its impeded step, he soon became convinced that it must be a woman. And, moreover, this woman, as though she was uncertain of the house she sought for, lifted up her eyes to examine, stopped, turned back, and then retraced her steps. D'Artagnan was at a loss.

"Suppose I should go and proffer my services!" thought he. "By her manner it is evident that she is young, and perhaps she is pretty. Oh, yes! But then a a woman who runs about the streets at this hour, seldom goes out except to meet her lover. Plague! if I should interrupt an appointment, it would be but a bad kind of introduction."

The young woman, however, still came forward, counting the windows and the houses. This was not indeed a long or difficult operation. There were but three hotels in that part of the street, and but two windows looking upon the thoroughfare; of which one was that of a pavilion, parallel to the pavilion of Aramis, and the other that of Aramis himself.

"By Jove!" said d'Artagnan to himself, as he suddenly remembered the theologian's niece—"by Jove! it would be droll if this wandering dove is looking for my friend's house. But, upon my soul, it seems very like it. Ah, my dear Aramis! I will be satisfied about it once and for all."

Making himself as small as possible, d'Artagnan concealed himself in the most obscure part of the street, near a stone bench placed at the back of a niche.

The young woman continued to advance; for, besides the lightness of her step which had betrayed her, a slight, small cough had also denoted a gentle voice. D'Artagnan concluded that this cough was a signal.

Nevertheless, whether this cough had been answered by some corresponding signal which had ended the uncertainties of her nocturnal search, or whether, without any such external aid, she perceived herself to have found her journey's end, the lady advanced resolutely, and knocked three times, at equal intervals, and with a bent finger, on the shutter of Aramis's window.

"It is really at Aramis's house," muttered d'Artagnan. "Ah, Mr. Hypocrite! I catch you studying theology!"

Scarcely had the three taps been given, before the inner casement opened, and a light appeared.

"Ah, ah!" said the listener, "not at the door, but the window! Ah! ah! the visit was expected. Come, the shutter will be opened presently, and the lady will get in by escalade. Good!"

But, to his great astonishment, the shutter continued

closed; and, what was more, the light, which had
flashed for an instant, disappeared, and all became
dark again.

D'Artagnan thought that this could not last, and
continued to watch with all his eyes and ears. He was
right; in a few seconds, two knocks were heard from
the inside; and when the young woman of the street
answered by one knock, the shutter opened.

It may be judged if d'Artagnan did not look and
listen eagerly.

Unfortunately, the light had been removed into some
other room; but the eyes of the young man were
accustomed to the darkness. Besides, it is said that
the eyes of Gascons, like those of cats, have the
faculty of seeing in the night.

D'Artagnan was able, therefore, to see the young
woman take from her pocket something white, which
she unfolded quickly, and which took the form of a
pocket handkerchief, and she then drew the attention
of the person she addressed to the corner of the object
she unfolded.

This reminded d'Artagnan of the handkerchief he
had found at the feet of Madame Bonancieux, which,
also, had recalled to his recollection the one that he had
drawn from under the foot of Aramis.

What the deuce, then, could this handkerchief mean?

Situated as he was, d'Artagnan could not see the
countenance of Aramis—we say Aramis, because the
young man had no doubt that it was his friend who
was conversing from the inside with the lady on the
outside. His curiosity, therefore, overcame his prudence;
and, profiting by the earnest attention which the sight
of the handkerchief excited in the two persons whom we
have described, he left his place of concealment, and,
quickly as lightning, yet with cautious step, placed
himself near a corner of the wall, from which his eye
could completely overlook the inside of Aramis's
apartment.

On reaching this spot, he was scarcely able to restrain an exclamation of surprise It was not Aramis who was conferring with the midnight visitor, but a woman. D'Artagnan could just discern enough to recognise the general aspect of her vesture, but not to distinguish her features. At that moment the woman in the room drew a handkerchief from her own pocket, and exchanged it for the one which had been shown to her. A few words were then pronounced by the two women, the shutter was closed, and the woman in the street returned, and, lowering the hood of her cloak, passed within four paces of d'Artagnan. But her precaution had been taken too late; he had already recognised Madame Bonancieux.

Madame Bonancieux! The suspicion had already crossed his mind when he saw her take the handkerchief from her pocket; but what probability was there that Madame Bonancieux, who had sent for M. de la Porte, in order that he might conduct her to the Louvre, should be coursing through the streets of Paris at half-past eleven at night, at the hazard of being carried off a second time? It must unquestionably be on some important affair; and what affair is of importance to a woman of twenty-five, but love?

But was it on her own account, or that of some other person, that she exposed herself to this risk? This was the inward doubt of the young man, whom the demon of jealousy was now tormenting, as though he had been an acknowledged lover. To satisfy himself as to where Madame Bonancieux was going, there was, in fact, one very simple way, which was to follow her. So simple, indeed, did this course appear, that d'Artagnan adopted it naturally, and as it were by instinct.

But, at the sight of the young man who moved from the wall, like a statue escaping from its alcove, and at the sound of his steps behind her, Madame Bonancieux uttered a faint scream, and fled.

D'Artagnan ran after her. It was no great difficulty

for him to catch a woman encumbered by a large cloak. He overtook her, in fact, before she had gone a third of the length of the street. The poor woman was exhausted, not by fatigue, but terror; and when d'Artagnan put his hand upon her shoulder, she sunk upon one knee, exclaiming in a suffocated voice—

"I will die before you learn anything."

D'Artagnan raised her up, by placing his arm round her waist, but, perceiving by her weight that she was upon the point of fainting, he hastened to encourage her by protestations of devotion. These protestations were of no avail against Madame Bonancieux, for they may easily be made with the most mischievous intentions in the world; but the voice was everything. The young woman thought that she recognised that voice. She opened her eyes, threw one glance upon the man who had so frightened her, and, seeing that it was d'Artagnan, gave utterance to a cry of joy.

"Oh! it is you, it is you," said she. "God be thanked!"

"Yes, it is I," said d'Artagnan, "whom God has sent to guard you."

"And was it with this intent that you followed me," asked the young woman, with a smile full of coquetry; for all her fears had vanished, and her love of badinage had resumed its ascendancy, on the instant that she recognised a friend in him whom she had dreaded as a foe.

"No," replied d'Artagnan. "No, I confess that it is chance which put me on your track. I saw a woman knocking at the window of one of my friends."

"Of one of your friends!" interrupted Madame Bonancieux.

"Yes, certainly! Aramis is one of my intimates."

"Aramis! who is he?"

"Come, now, do you pretend to tell me that you do not know Aramis?"

"It is the first time that I ever heard his name."

"Then it is the first time that you have visited this house?"

"Yes, indeed!"

"And you did not know that a young man occupied it?"

"No."

"A musketeer?"

"By no means."

"Then it was not him that you came to look for?"

"Most assuredly not! Besides, you must have plainly seem that the person whom I talked to was a woman."

"That is true; but then this woman is one of Aramis's friends!"

"I know nothing about that."

"Why, she lodges at his house."

"That is not my affair."

"But who is she?"

"Oh! that is not my secret."

"My dear Madame Bonancieux, you are very charming, but you are at the same time the most mysterious creature."

"Is that to my loss?"

"No; on the contrary, it lends you enchantment!"

"As that is the case, give me your arm."

"With great pleasure; what now?"

"Now take care of me."

"Where to?"

"Where I am going."

"But where may that be?"

"You will see, since you will leave me at the door."

"May I wait for you there?"

"That would be useless."

"Then you will return alone?"

"Possibly."

"But the person who will accompany you afterwards —will it be a man or a woman?"

"I do not know yet."

"But I will find it out."

"And how so?"

"I will wait to see you come out."

"In that case, adieu!"

"But, why?"

"I do not want you!"

"But you claimed my protection."

"I claimed the assistance of a gentleman, and not the vigilance of a spy."

"You are severe."

"How would you call those who follow people who don't want them?"

"Indiscreet!"

"The term is too mild!"

"Come, madame, I see that one must obey you."

"Why deprive yourself of the merit of doing so at once?"

"Is there none in my repentance?"

"But do you sincerely repent?"

"I don't know that myself. But I do know that I promise to do just what you wish, if you will let me accompany you where you are going."

"And you will leave me afterwards?"

"Yes."

"Without awaiting my exit?"

"Certainly."

"On your word of honour?"

"On the word of a gentleman!"

"Then take my arm, and let us get on."

D'Artagnan offered his arm, which Madame Bonancieux, half laughing and half trembling, accepted, and they reached the top of the Rue de la Harpe; but the young woman appeared to hesitate there, as she had hesitated before at the Rue Vaugirard. Nevertheless, by certain marks, she appeared to recognise a door, which she approached.

"Now, sir," said she, "it is here that my business calls me. I return you a thousand thanks for your good company, which has saved me from all the dangers to which I should have been exposed alone; but the time is now come for you to keep your word. You must leave me here."

" And will you be exposed to no danger in returning?"

"I shall only have to fear robbers."

"Is that nothing?"

"What could they take from me? I have not a farthing in my possession!"

"You forget that beautiful embroidered handkerchief, with the arms on it."

"Which?"

"That which I found at your feet, and replaced in your pocket."

"Silence! Silence! you imprudent man! Would you ruin me?"

"You see now that there is still some danger, since one word makes you tremble, and you confess that if this word was heard you would be ruined. Come now, madame," continued d'Artagnan, seizing her hand, "be more generous; put some confidence in me; have you not read in my eyes that my heart is full of sympathy and devotion?"

"Yes," said Madame Bonancieux; "and do but ask me for my own secrets, and I will trust you with them all; but those of others are a different matter."

"Very well!" replied d'Artagnan, "then I will find them out. Since these secrets have an influence on your life, it is necessary that they should become mine also."

"Have a care!" exclaimed the young woman, in a tone of seriousness which made d'Artagnan shudder involuntarily. "Oh! do not interfere in anything that concerns me; do not seek to aid me in any of my undertakings;—avoid them, I beseech you, in the name of the interest that you feel for me, and in the name of that service which you rendered to me, and which I never shall forget whilst my life lasts! Let me advise you rather to think of me no more; let my existence be obliterated from your mind; let me be to you as though you had never chanced to see me."

"Would you like Aramis to do the same, madame?" asked d'Artagnan, full of jealousy.

"This makes the second or third time that you have mentioned that name, sir, although I have already told you that I do not know the owner of it."

"You do not know the man at whose window-shutters you went to knock? Come, madame, you must think me credulous indeed!"

"Confess that it is to keep me talking here, that you have invented this tale, and this person."

"I invent nothing, madame—nothing. I am telling the exact truth!"

"And you say that one of your friends lives in that house?"

"I say it, and I repeat it for the third time—that house is inhabited by a friend of mine, and that friend is Aramis."

"All this will be explained by and by," murmured the young woman; "and now, sir, be silent."

"If you could see into my heart," said d'Artagnan, "you would discover so much curiosity, that you would have pity on me: and so much love, that you would directly satisfy my curiosity. You ought not to distrust those who love you!"

"You come quickly to love, sir," said the young woman, shaking her head.

"It is because love has come quickly on me, and for the first time; and I am no. yet twenty years of age."

The young woman stole a glance at him.

"Listen," continued d'Artagnan; "I am already on the track: three months ago I was near fighting a duel with Aramis on account of a handkerchief like that which you showed the lady who was at his house; it was on account of a handkerchief marked in the same manner, I am positive."

"Sir," said the young woman, "you really bore me, I declare, with these questions."

"But you, madame, prudent as you are, suppose you were arrested with this handkerchief upon you, and the handkerchief was seized, would you not be compromised?"

"How so? Are not the initials my own—C. B.— Constance Bonancieux?"

"Or, Camille de Bois Tracy."

"Silence, sir! Again I say, silence! Oh, since the dangers which I run do not deter you, think of those you may run yourself."

"I?"

"Yes, you. There is the danger of imprisonment and death in knowing me."

"Then I will never leave you!"

"Sir," said the young woman, in a tone of supplication, clasping her hands as she spoke; "in the name of heaven, by the honour of a soldier, by the courtesy of a gentleman, I implore you to leave me. See! it is now striking twelve, the very hour at which I am expected."

"Madame," said the young man, bowing, "I can refuse nothing solicited in those terms. Be reassured; I leave you."

"But you will not follow—will not watch me?"

"No, I shall return home immediately."

"Ah! I was convinced that you were an honourable man!" exclaimed Madame Bonancieux, offering one of her hands to him, as she placed the other on the knocker of a small door, which was well-nigh concealed in a recess.

D'Artagnan seized the hand which was offered to him, and kissed it eagerly.

"Alas!" exclaimed d'Artagnan, with that unpolished simplicity which women sometimes prefer to the delicacies of politeness, because it illuminates the depths of thought, and proves that feeling is more powerful than reason, "I wish I had never seen you!"

"Well!" said Madame Bonancieux, in a tone almost affectionate, and pressing the hand which held hers, "well! I will not say the same as you do; that which is lost to-day may not be lost for ever. Who knows whether, when I am freed from my present embarrassments, I may not satisfy your curiosity?"

"And do you make the same promise regarding my love?" asked the overjoyed d'Artagnan.

"Oh! I dare give no promises in that respect. It must depend upon the sentiments with which you may inspire me."

"But, at present, madame?"

"At present, sir, I have not got beyond gratitude."

"Alas! you are too charming; and only take advantage of my love."

"No, I take advantage of your generosity, that's all. But, believe me, with some people, nothing can be wholly lost.

"You make me the happiest of men. Oh! do not forget this evening, and this promise?"

"Be assured, I will remember everything at the right time and place. But now go; go, in heaven's name! I was expected at midnight, and am behind my time."

"By five minutes."

"But, under certain circumstances, five minutes are five ages."

"Yes! when one loves."

"Well, who has told you that this is not a love-affair?"

"It is a man who expects you!" cried d'Artagnan; "a man!"

"There, now, the discussion is about to be renewed," cried Madame Bonancieux, with a half smile, which was not altogether exempt from impatience.

"No! I am going. I trust you; I wish to have all the merit of my devotion, even if I am a fool for it! Adieu! madame, adieu."

Then, as though he felt himself too weak to relinquish

the fair hand he held but by a shock, he hastily ran off, whilst Madame Bonancieux rapped three times at the door, slowly and regularly, as she had before done at the window-shutter. At the corner of the street he turned, but the door had been opened and closed again, and the mercer's pretty wife had disappeared.

D'Artagnan proceeded on his way. He had promised Madame Bonancieux not to watch her; and, had his life depended on a knowledge of the place that she was going to, or the person who went with her, he would still have gone home, as he had promised to do. In five minutes he was in the Rue des Fossoyeurs.

"Poor Athos," said he, "he will not understand this. He will have fallen asleep waiting for me, or he will have returned home, and will have learned that there has been a woman there. A woman at *his* house! After all," continued d'Artagnan, "there certainly was one at Aramis's. All this is very strange, and I shall be extremely curious to know how it will end."

"Badly, sir, badly," replied a voice, which the young man recognised as that of Planchet, for in soliloquising aloud, in the manner of persons who are deeply occupied, he had entered the passage, at the bottom of which was his own staircase.

"How, badly! what are you saying, you fool?" said d'Artagnan, "and what has happened?"

"All sorts of misfortunes."

"What misfortunes?"

"In the first place, M. Athos is arrested."

"Arrested! Athos arrested! and what for?"

"He was found in your lodgings, and they mistook him for you."

"And by whom has he been arrested?"

"By the guard which was brought by the men in black whom you put to flight."

"Why did he not give his name? Why not say that he was not concerned in this affair?"

"He was very careful not to do that, sir. On the

contrary, he came near me and said — 'Thy master wants his liberty just now, and I do not need mine; since he knows all, and I know nothing. They will believe him to be in custody, and that will give him time; in three days I will declare who I am, and they will be obliged to let me go.'"

"Brave Athos! noble heart!" muttered d'Artagnan. "I recognise him well in that! And what did the officers do?"

"Four of them took him either to the Bastile or to Fort l'Eveque; and two remained with the men in black, rummaging everywhere, and carrying away all your papers. The other two mounted guard at the door whilst all this was doing; and at last they went away, leaving the house empty and the door open."

"And Porthos and Aramis?"

"I could not find them; they have not been."

"But they may come at any moment, for you left word that I was waiting for them."

"Yes, sir."

"Well, then, do not stir from here. If they should come, tell them what has happened, and that they must wait for me at the Pine-apple Tavern. There might be some danger here; the house may be watched. I will run to M. de Treville's, to tell him all this, and then will rejoin them there."

"Very well, sir," said Planchet.

"But you will remain? you will not be afraid," said d'Artagnan, turning back a step to encourage his lackey.

"Be easy, sir," said Planchet; "you do not know me yet. I am brave when I please to set about it; the great thing is to get me in the right mind. Besides, I come from Picardy."

"Then it is all settled," said d'Artagnan; "you will rather die than desert your post."

"Yes, sir; and I will stick at nothing to prove my attachment to you."

"Good," said d'Artagnan to himself; "it is plain that the method I have followed with this lad is decidedly a proper one. I will adopt it henceforth on every occasion."

And as fast as his legs, which were already somewhat fatigued, could carry him, he ran towards the Rue de Colombier.

M. de Treville was not at home. His company was on guard at the Louvre; and he was at the Louvre with it.

It was necessary, however, to see M. de Treville. It was important that he should be informed of these events. D'Artagnan determined, therefore, to obtain an entrance at the Louvre. His uniform, as one of M. de Essarts's guards, ought to be a passport for admission.

He therefore went down the Rue des Petits-Augustins, and along the Quai to reach the Pont-Neuf. He had half a mind to cross the ferry; but on reaching the side of the river he mechanically put his hand into his pocket, and found that he had not enough to pay the ferryman.

When he reached the top of the Rue Guénégaud, he saw two persons, whose appearance struck him, coming out of the Rue Dauphine. They were a man and a woman. The woman resembled in figure Madame Bonancieux; and the man had such a look of Aramis that he might be mistaken for him. Besides, the woman had on the black mantle which d'Artagnan still seemed to see delineated on the shutter in the Rue Vaugirard, and on the door in the Rue de la Harpe. Moreover, the man wore the uniform of the musketeers.

The hood of the woman was lowered, and the man held his handkerchief before his face. This double precaution showed that they were both anxious to escape recognition.

They went over the bridge, and this was also d'Artagnan's road, as he was going to the Louvre; he therefore followed them.

Scarcely, however, had he taken twenty steps, before he was convinced that the woman was Madame Bonancieux, and the man Aramis.

At the very instant he felt fermenting in his heart all the suspicious torments of jealousy.

He was doubly betrayed; betrayed both by his friend, and by her whom he had already loved as a mistress.

Madame Bonancieux had sworn to him that she did not know Aramis; and a quarter of an hour after she had made this oath he found her hanging on his arm.

D'Artagnan did not reflect that he had only known the mercer's pretty wife during the last three hours; that she only owed him a little gratitude for having delivered her from the men in black, who wished to carry her away; and that she had made him no promise. He looked upon himself as an outraged lover; as deceived, and laughed at; and the flush of anger passed over his face, as he resolved to ascertain the truth.

The young couple perceived that they were followed, and they increased their haste. D'Artagnan, however, had made his determination; he passed by them, and then returned towards them just as they were opposite the Samaritan, which was lighted by a lamp that threw its radiance over all that part of the bridge.

D'Artagnan stopped in front of them, and they stopped also.

"What do you want, sir?" asked the musketeer, recoiling a step, and in a foreign accent, which proved to d'Artagnan that he had at least deceived himself in one of his conjectures.

"It is not Aramis!" exclaimed d'Artagnan.

"No, sir, it is not Aramis; and as I find by your exclamation that you mistook me for another, I excuse you."

"Excuse me indeed!" said d'Artagnan.

"Yes," replied the unknown; "now let me pass on, since it is not with me that you have anything to do."

"You are right, sir," said d'Artagnan; "it is not with you that I have anything to settle, it is with the lady."

"With the lady! You do not even know her," exclaimed the stranger.

"You are mistaken, sir. I do know her."

"Ah!" said Madame Bonancieux, in a reproachful tone; "I had your word of honour as a soldier, your promise as a gentleman, and I hoped I might have trusted to them."

"And I," said d'Artagnan, in confusion, "I had your promise."

"Take my arm, madame," said the stranger, "and let us proceed."

But d'Artagnan—stunned, overwhelmed, annihilated by all that had happened—remained standing, with his arms crossed, before the musketeer and Madame Bonancieux.

The former came forward two paces, and put d'Artagnan aside with his hand.

D'Artagnan made one bound backwards, and drew his sword.

At the same moment, and with the quickness of lightning, the stranger drew his.

"In God's name, my lord!" said Madame Bonancieux, throwing herself between the combatants, and seizing their swords with both her hands—

"My lord!" cried d'Artagnan, enlightened by a sudden idea; "My lord! pardon me, sir, but can you be——"

"My Lord Duke of Buckingham!" said Madame Bonancieux, in a very low voice, "and now you may destroy us all."

"My lord—madame—pardon me; a thousand pardons; but, my lord, I loved her, and was jealous. *You* know, my lord, what it is to love! Pardon me, and tell me how I may die in your grace's cause."

"You are a brave youth," said Buckingham, offering him a hand, which d'Artagnan pressed respectfully. "You offer me your services, and I accept them.

Follow us, at the distance of twenty paces, to the Louvre, and if any one dogs our steps, kill him!"

D'Artagnan put his naked sword under his arm, let the duke and Madame Bonancieux go forward about twenty steps, and then followed them, ready to execute to the letter the instructions of the elegant and noble minister of Charles I.

But, unfortunately, the young volunteer had no opportunity of affording this proof of his devotion to the duke; and the young woman and the handsome musketeer entered the Louvre, by the wicket in the Rue de l'Echelle, without encountering any interruption.

As for d'Artagnan, he went immediately to the Pineapple, where he found Porthos and Aramis waiting for him.

But without giving them any further reason for the trouble he had caused them, he told them that he had concluded by himself the business for which he at first thought he should have wanted their assistance.

And now, carried on as we have been by our history, let us leave our three friends to return each to his own home, whilst we follow, amidst the tortuous corridors of the Louvre, the Duke of Buckingham and his guide.

CHAPTER XII.

GEORGE VILLIERS, DUKE OF BUCKINGHAM.

MADAME BONANCIEUX and the duke entered the Louvre without any difficulty; Madame Bonancieux was known to be of the household of the queen; and the duke wore the uniform of the musketeers of M. de Treville, who, as we have said, were on guard that evening. Besides, Germain was devoted to the queen, and, if anything happened, Madame Bonancieux would be accused of having introduced her lover into the Louvre—that was all! She took the blame upon herself; her reputation

would be lost, it is true; but of what value in the world
was the reputation of a mercer's little wife?

When they were once inside the court, the duke and
the young woman kept close to the wall for about twenty
paces; at the end of which Madame Bonancieux tried
a small private door, which was usually open during
the day, but closed at night. The door opened, and
they both entered, and found themselves in total darkness; but Madame Bonancieux was well acquainted
with all the turnings and twistings of this part of the
Louvre, which was appropriated to the persons of the
royal suite. She shut all the doors behind her, took the
duke by the hand and going some steps on tip-toe,
seized hold of a banister, put a foot upon the staircase,
and began to ascend it. The duke had already counted
two flights, when she turned to the left, went through
a long corridor, descended another stage, walked a few
steps forward, introduced a key into a lock, opened a
door, and pushed her companion into a room lighted
only by a night-lamp, saying to him—" Remain here,
my lord duke; some one will come immediately." Then
she went out by the same door, locking it after her, so
that the duke found himself literally a prisoner.

Yet though thus deserted, as it were, the duke, it must
be confessed, did not feel the slightest fear. One of the
prominent features of his character was the love of
adventure and romance. Brave, determined, and enterprising, it was not the first time he had risked his life in
such adventures. He had learned that this pretended
message of Anne of Austria, on the faith of which he
had come to Paris, was a snare; and, instead of returning to England, he had taken advantage of his
position, and assured the queen that he would not depart
without seeing her. The queen had at first positively
refused an interview; but, fearing lest the duke might
be guilty of some folly in his rage, she had resolved to
see him, and to entreat him to return directly; when, on
the very evening on which Madame Bonancieux was

charged to conduct him to the Louvre, that lady was
herself carried off. During two days it was not known
what had become of her, and everything continued in
suspense. But Madame Bonancieux once free, and in
communication with la Porte, affairs had resumed their
course; and she had now accomplished the perilous
enterprise, which, but for her abduction, she would have
executed three days before. Buckingham being left
alone, approached a looking-glass. The dress of a
musketeer became him wondrously. At thirty-five years
old, he was justly considered as the handsomest man,
and the most complete gentleman, of France or England.
The favourite of two kings, rich as Crœsus, all-powerful
in a realm which he disturbed and tranquillised as he
pleased, George Villiers, Duke of Buckingham, had engaged in one of those fabulous existences which remain,
throughout the course of ages, an astonishment to
posterity. Confident in himself, convinced of his power,
and satisfied that the laws which restrain other people
could not reach him, he went straight to the object he
had fixed upon, even when that object was so elevated,
and so dazzling, that it would have been madness in
another to have even glanced towards it. It was thus
that he had managed to approach the beautiful and
haughty Anne of Austria many times, and to make
her love him for his brilliant qualities.

Placing himself before the glass, the duke arrayed his
beautiful fair hair, of which the pressure of his hat had
disarranged the curls, and put his moustache in order;
and then, his heart swelling with joy; happy and elated
at having reached the moment he had so long desired,
he smiled to himself proudly and hopefully

At that moment a door concealed in the tapestry
opened, and a woman appeared. Buckingham saw the reflection in the glass; he uttered a cry; it was the queen!

Anne of Austria was at that time twenty-six or twenty-
seven years of age; that is, she was in all the glory of
her beauty. Her deportment was that of a queen, or a

goddess. Her eyes, which shone like emeralds, were perfectly beautiful, but at the same time full of gentleness and majesty. Her mouth was small and rosy; and though her under lip, like that of the princes of the house of Austria, protruded slightly beyond the other, her smile was eminently gracious, but at the same time could be profoundly haughty in its scorn. Her skin was celebrated for its velvet softness, and her hand and arm were of such surpassing beauty as to be immortalised, as incomparable, by all the poets of the time. Admirably, too, did her hair, which in her youth had been fair, but had now become chestnut, and which she wore plainly dressed, and with a great deal of powder, shade a face, on which the most rigid critic could have desired only a little less rouge, and the most fastidious sculptor only a little more delicacy in the formation of the nose.

Buckingham remained an instant perfectly dazzled. Anne of Austria never had appeared to him so beautiful even in the midst of balls, and festivals, and entertainments, as she now appeared, in her simple robe of white satin, and accompanied by Donna Estefana, the only one of her Spanish ladies who had not been driven from her by the jealousy of the king and the persecutions of the cardinal.

Anne of Austria advanced two steps; the duke threw himself at her feet, and before the queen could prevent him, had kissed the hem of her robe.

"My lord, you already know that it was not I who sent for you from England?"

"Oh! yes! madame; yes, your majesty!" exclaimed Buckingham. "I know that I have been a fool, a madman, to believe that the snow could have been animated, that the marble could grow warm; but what would you expect? The lover easily believes in love; nor has my journey been entirely in vain, since I behold you now."

"Yes," replied Anne, "but you know why, and how, I see you, my lord. I see you because, insensible to all my distress, you persist in remaining in a city where, by remaining, you risk your own life, and my honour; I see you, to tell you that everything separates us—the depths of the sea, the enmity of nations, the sanctity of vows! It is sacrilege to struggle against such things, my lord! And, lastly, I see you to tell you, that I must never see you more."

"Speak, madame—speak, queen," said Buckingham; "the softness of your voice repays the sternness of your words. You speak of sacrilege; but the sacrilege is in the separation of hearts, which God had formed for one another!"

"My lord," cried the queen, "you forget that I have never said I loved you."

"But neither have you ever said that you did not love me; and indeed, to say so, would be a proof of the greatest ingratitude on the part of your majesty. For tell me, where would you find a love like mine—a love, which neither time, nor absence, nor despair can extinguish, and which is recompensed by a riband, by a glance, a word? It is now three years, madame, since I saw you for the first time, and for three years have I adored you thus. Will you allow me to describe to you your dress on that occasion, and to tell the detail of the ornaments you wore? Mark me! I seem to see you now, seated, in the Spanish manner, upon cushions, wearing a dress of green satin, embroidered in silver and in gold, with pendant sleeves, fastened around your beautiful arms by large diamonds: you wore, also, a close ruff; and a small hat, of the same colour as your dress and adorned with a heron's plume, upon your head. Oh! thus, thus, with closed eyes do I behold you as you then were; and I open my eyes again, only to see you now, a hundred times more lovely still!"

"What folly," murmured Anne of Austria, who dared not be offended with the duke for preserving her portrait so faithfully in his heart: "what folly to nourish so useless a passion on such memories as these!"

"Alas! what would your majesty exact? I have nothing but memories; they are my happiness, my treasure, and my hope. Each meeting with you is a new jewel that I enshrine within the casket of my heart. This is the fourth of them that you have let fall, and that I have eagerly secured. Yes, in three years, madame, I have seen you only four times: the first I have already recalled to you; the second was at Madame de Chevreuse's; the third was in the gardens of Amiens."

"My Lord!" exclaimed the queen, blushing, "do not refer to that evening!"

"Oh! rather let me dwell upon it, madame, for it is the one radiant, blissful night of my existence! Does your majesty remember how lovely a night it was? The air was laden with odoriferous sweetness, and the blue sky was studded with innumerable stars. Ah! madame, I was alone with you for an instant then, and you were about to make me the confidant of your griefs—of the isolation of your life, and the deep sorrows of your heart. You were leaning on my arm—on this one, madam—and, when I bent my head towards you, I felt my face gently touched by your beautiful hair; and every time that I so felt it, I trembled through every vein. Oh! queen! queen! you know not the heavenly bliss, the joys of paradise, comprised in such a moment. Goods, fortune, glory, life, gladly would I give them all for another interview like that on such a night; for, madame, I will swear that then, at least on that night, you loved me!"

"My lord, it is possible that the influence of the place, the charm of that enchanting evening, the fascination of your looks, and the thousand circumstances which some-times concur in leading a woman onwards to her fall, may have grouped themselves around me on that fatal night; but you are not ignorant, my lord, that the queen gave succour to the weakness of the woman; and that at the first word that you presumed to say, at the first liberty that you dared to take, I summoned others to my presence there!"

"Alas! it is but too true, and any feebler love than mine would never have survived the test; but my love, madame, came out from it more ardent, and immortalised. You thought to escape from me by returning to Paris;— you believed that I should never dare to quit the treasure which my master had commanded me to guard;—but what cared I for all the treasures and all the kings upon the earth! In one week, madame, I was on my return. On that occasion, madame, you had nothing to complain of; I had risked favour, and life, to see you for a single second; I did not even touch your hand; and you forgave me when you found I was submissive and repentant."

"Yes, my lord, but you are well aware that calumny fastened even upon those follies in which I had so small a share. Prompted by the cardinal, the king felt extreme resentment. Madame de Vernet was dismissed; Putange was banished; and Madame de Chevreuse was disgraced. And do you not remember, my lord, that when you wished to return as an ambassador to France, it was his majesty himself by whom you were opposed."

"Yes! and France is about to pay with a war for that opposition. I cannot see you again, madame; well! I will take care that you shall continually hear of me. What do you suppose to have been the true aim of that expedition to Rhe, and that league which I am projecting with the Protestants? The delight of seeing you! I am well enough aware that I have no chance of reaching Paris at the head of an army; but then, this war must bring about a peace; peace will require negotiations; and those negotiations shall be made by none but me. They will no longer dare to reject me then; and I shall return to Paris, and behold you once again, and be, for an instant, happy. It is but too true that my enjoyment will have been bought by the blood of thousands of human beings; but what will their lives be to me, provided that my eyes are blessed once more by seeing you! This may be folly, madame—perhaps madness; but tell me, pray, had ever woman a more impassioned lover, had ever queen a more enthusiastic servant?"

"My lord! my lord! the witnesses you call for your

defence accuse you. These very proofs, that you would give me of your love, are themselves almost crimes!"

"But only because you do not love me, madame. Oh! if you loved me, how different would these circumstances seem, but the joy would be too great, and I should go mad. You spoke but now, madame, of Madame de Chevreuse; but, oh! how much less cruel was that lady than you are! Holland loved her, and she responded to his love."

"Madame de Chevreuse was not a queen!" murmured Anne of Austria; subdued, in spite of herself, by the expression of a passion so profound.

"And would you then love me if you were not? Oh! tell me, madame! say, that you would love me? let me believe that it is but the dignity of your rank that has come between you and me! let me believe that if you had been but Madame de Chevreuse, there might have been hope for the unhappy Buckingham! Oh! charming queen! thanks for these sweet words—a thousand, thousand thanks!"

"Alas! my lord! you have misunderstood me; I did not mean to let you infer——"

"Hush! hush!" exclaimed the duke. "Be not so cruel as to correct an error that is so full of happiness to me! You have yourself told me that I have been drawn into a snare; and I perhaps shall leave my life in it, for, strangely enough, for some time I have had presentiments of an approaching death."—And the duke smiled, with a sad, yet winning smile.

"Oh, God!" exclaimed the queen, in a tone of terror, which manifested, more fully than she might have wished, her interest in the duke.

"But I did not tell you this to alarm you, madame. No, it is even ridiculous to speak of it; and, believe me, I do not give importance to such silly dreams. But the words which you have just uttered, the hope which you almost gave me, would be a recompense for everything, even for my life!"

"Oh! but I," said Anne of Austria—"I also have had my presentiments. I dreamed that I saw you stretched upon the earth, all bloody from a wound."

"On the left side, and inflicted by a knife, was it not?" said the duke.

"Yes, my lord! it was in the left side, and by a knife. But who could have told you of my dream? I have never spoken of it but in my prayers to God."

"I ask for no more. You love me, madame! yes, you love me!"

"I love you?"

"Yes, you! Would God send to you the same dreams as to me, if you did not love me? Should we be visited by the same presentiments, if our two existences did not meet in our hearts? Yes, queen, you love me, and you weep for me!"

"Oh, my God! my God!" exclaimed the queen, "this is more than I can bear. In the name of heaven, my lord, withdraw! I know not whether I love you or not; but this I know, that I will never break my vow at the altar. Have pity on me then, and leave this kingdom. Oh! if you should be wounded in France—if you should die in France—if I could imagine that your love for me had been the cause of your death, I should never be consoled. The thought would madden me! Depart then, depart, I beseech you."

"Oh! how beautiful you are now! How devotedly I love you!" exclaimed Buckingham.

"Depart, I implore you, and return hereafter," continued the queen. "Come back as an ambassador, as a minister; come back, surrounded by your guards who will defend you, and your servants who will watch over you, and then I shall have no fear for your life, and shall have some happiness in seeing you!"

"Oh! but is it really true what you now tell me?"

"Yes."

"Give me, then, some pledge of your regard—some object which has once been yours—to satisfy me that I have not been indulging in a dream ; something that you have once worn, and that I may wear now—a ring, a necklace, or a chain !"

"And will you go if I give you what you ask ?"

"Yes !"

"Immediately ?"

"Yes !"

"You will quit France, and will return to England ?"

"Yes, I swear I will."

"Wait, then ; wait, sir."

And Anne of Austria returned to her chamber, and came back almost in an instant, holding in her hand a small casket of rosewood, with her monogram encrusted in gold.

"Here my lord, here ! keep this as a memorial of me !"

Buckingham took the casket, and again sank upon his knee.

"You promised me to go," said the queen.

"And I will keep my word ! Your hand, madame, and I leave you !"

Closing her eyes, and leaning on Donna Estefana—for she felt her strength was failing her—Anne of Austria extended her hand.

On that beautiful hand Buckingham pressed his lips passionately, and then arose.

"Before six months have passed," said he, "if I be not dead, I will see you again, if I must turn the world upside down to accomplish it."

And true to his promise, he rushed out of the room.

In the corridor he found Madame Bonancieux awaiting him ; and, with the same precaution, and the same good fortune, she led him forth out of the Louvre.

"'The cardinal's guards! Sheathe swords—gentlemen!'"

CHAPTER XIII.

MONSIEUR BONANCIEUX.

THERE was in all this affair, as might be remarked, a
person of whom, in spite of his precarious situation, we
have appeared to take very little notice. This person
was M. Bonancieux, a respectable martyr to the political
and amorous intrigues which so thoroughly entangled
themselves together in that chivalrous and gallant age.
Fortunately, as our readers may or may not remember,
we have promised not to lose sight of him.

The officers who had arrested him, conducted him at
once to the Bastile, where he had to pass, all trembling
as he was, before a company of soldiers, who were
charging their muskets.

Taken from there into a partly subterraneous gallery,
he had to endure the most brutal insults and ill-treat-
ment. The attendants saw that he was not a nobleman,
and they treated him therefore like a beggar.

In about half an hour, a registrar came to put an end
to his tortures, but not to his anxiety, by ordering that
he should be conducted to the question chamber. They
generally questioned prisoners in their own cells,
but they did not observe so much ceremony with
M. Bonancieux.

Two guards laid hold of the mercer, and made him
cross a court, and then, entering a corridor where there
were three sentinels, they opened a door and pushed
him into a low room, which only contained a table, a
chair, and a commissary. The commissary was seated
on the chair, and was engaged in writing at the table.

The two guards led the prisoner to the table, and at
a signal from the commissary, went out of earshot. The
commissary, who had till then kept his head bent down
over his papers, raised it up to see who he had before
him. This commissary was a man with a very crabbed

look ; a sharp nose ; cheeks yellow and puffed out ; small, but piercing eyes ; and with a countenance reminding one, at the same time, of a polecat and a fox. His head, supported by a long and flexible neck, was thrust out of his full black robe, and balanced itself with a motion very much like that of a turtle putting its head out of its shell.

He began by asking M. Bonancieux his christian name and surname, his age, profession, and place of abode.

The accused replied that his name was Jacques Bonancieux, that his age was 51 years, that he was a retired mercer, and lived in the Rue des Fossoyeurs, No. 11.

Instead of continuing his questions, the commissary then made him a long speech on the danger of an obscure citizen interfering in public affairs. With this exordium he combined an exposition of the power and actions of the cardinal—that incomparable minister, the conqueror of all preceding ministers, and the example for all future ministers—whom no one could oppose or thwart with impunity.

After this second part of his discourse, he fixed his hawk's eye on poor Bonancieux, and exhorted him to reflect upon the seriousness of his situation.

This the mercer had already done : he wished M. de la Porte at the devil for having put it into his head to marry his god-daughter, and cursed the hour when that god-daughter had been received into the queen's service.

The foundation of M. Bonancieux's character was profound selfishness, mingled with sordid avarice, the whole being seasoned with excessive cowardice. The love which he entertained towards his young wife was quite a secondary sentiment, and could not stand against those primary feelings which we have just enumerated.

Bonancieux, in fact, reflected on what had been said to him.

"But, Mr. Commissary," he timidly observed, "believe

me, that I know well and appreciate the incomparable merit of his eminence, by whom we have the honour of being governed."

"Really!" said the commissary, with a doubtful look; "but if this be true, how came you to be in the Bastile?"

"How I am there, or rather, why I am there," replied Bonancieux, "is what it is utterly impossible for me to tell you, seeing that I do not know myself; but most certainly it is not for having offended the cardinal, consciously, at least."

"It is certain, nevertheless, that you must have committed some crime, as you are here accused of high treason."

"Of high treason!" cried Bonancieux, confounded; "of high treason! And how can you believe that a poor mercer, who hates the Huguenots, and abhors the Spaniards, can be accused of high treason? Reflect, sir—the thing is a moral impossibility."

"M. Bonancieux," said the commissary, regarding the accused with his little eyes, as though he had the power of looking into the very depths of his heart, "M. Bonancieux, you have a wife."

"Yes, sir," replied the trembling mercer, perceiving that it was on her account that he was now about to be inculpated; "that is to say, I had one."

"What? you had one! And what have you done with her, that you have her no longer?"

"Some one has carried her off, sir!"

"Some one has taken her from you?" said the commissary. "Ah!"

Bonancieux perceived by this "ah!" that matters were getting worse and worse.

"Some one has taken her from you," resumed the commissary. "And do you know who has been guilty of this abduction?"

"I think I know."

"Who is it?"

"Remember that I affirm nothing, Mr. Commissary —I only suspect."

"Whom do you suspect? Come, don't hesitate to speak."

M. Bonancieux was in the greatest perplexity. Ought he to deny everything, or to confess? From a total denial, it might be inferred that he knew too much to admit; and, by a general confession, he might give evidence of his good faith.

He determined, therefore, to have no concealments.

"I suspect," said he, "a tall, dark man, of lofty air, who has all the appearance of a man of rank. He followed us, I think, many times, when I went to fetch my wife from the gate of the Louvre."

The commissary appeared somewhat disturbed.

"And his name?" said he.

"Oh! as to his name, I do not know it; but if I should meet him, I could recognise him amongst a thousand persons."

The brow of the commissary grew dark.

"You could recognise him amongst a thousand, you say?" continued he.

"That is to say," replied Bonancieux, who saw that he had made a false step, "that is to say——"

"You have said that you could recognise him," said the commissary; "very well, that is enough for to-day; it is necessary, before we proceed any further, that some one should be informed that you know the person who has carried off your wife."

"But I did not tell you that I knew him!" cried M. Bonancieux, in despair. "I told you, on the contrary——"

"Take away the prisoner!" exclaimed the commissary to the two guards.

"Where to?" asked the registrar.

"To a dungeon."

"To which?"

"Oh! to the first that offers, provided it be secure,"

answered the commissary, with an indifference which
filled the breast of poor Bonancieux with horror and
dismay.

"Alas! alas!" said he, "I am undone. My wife must
have committed some frightful crime; and I am supposed to be an accomplice, and shall be punished with
her. She must have said something—have confessed
that I was her confidant. A woman is such a weak
creature! A dungeon! The first that offers! that's it.
A night is soon passed; and then, to-morrow, to the
wheel, to the gibbet! Oh! my God, my God, have
pity on me!"

Without in the least attending to the lamentations of
Master Bonancieux, that were of a kind to which they
were tolerably well accustomed, the two guards took
him by the arms, and led him away, while the commissary hastily wrote a letter, for which his officer waited.

Bonancieux did not close an eye; not because his
dungeon was very uncomfortable, but because his
anxiety was very great. He sat upon his stool the
whole night, trembling at every noise; and when the
first rays of light penetrated his chamber, Aurora herself appeared to him to be dressed in funereal array.

Suddenly he heard the bolts withdrawn, and gave a
terrible start. He believed that they were coming to
conduct him to the scaffold; and, therefore, when he
saw that it was only the commissary and his attendant,
he was almost ready to embrace them.

"Your affair has become sadly complicated since
last evening, my fine fellow," said the commissary. "I
advise you to tell the whole truth, for your repentance
alone can mitigate the anger of the cardinal."

"But I am ready to tell everything," said Bonancieux; "everything, at least, that I know; question
me, I beseech you!"

"In the first place, where is your wife?"

"I have just told you that some one has carried her
off."

"Yes, but since five o'clock yesterday evening, thanks to you, she has escaped."

"My wife escaped!" cried Bonancieux; "oh! the wretch! Sir, if she has escaped, I assure you it is not my fault!"

"What were you doing, then, in the apartment of your neighbour, M. d'Artagnan, with whom you had a long conference in the course of the day?"

"Ah, yes, Mr. Commissary, yes, that is true; and I confess I was wrong in that; yes, I was in M. d Artagnan's apartments."

"And why?"

"To entreat him to assist me in finding my wife. I thought I had a right to reclaim her. I was mistaken, it appears, and I humbly beg your pardon."

"And what answer did M. d'Artagnan give?"

"M. d'Artagnan promised me his assistance; but I soon perceived that he betrayed me."

"You would mislead justice! M. d'Artagnan made an agreement with you; and in virtue of that agreement, he put to flight the officers who had arrested your wife, and has now secreted her from all our researches."

"M. d'Artagnan has hidden away my wife? Alas! what do you tell me?"

"Fortunately, M. d'Artagnan is in our power, and you shall be confronted with him."

"Ah, faith! I desire nothing better," cried M. Bonancieux. "I shall not be sorry to see the face of an acquaintance."

"Bring in M. d'Artagnan," said the commissary to the two guards.

The guards brought in Athos.

"M. d'Artagnan," said the commissary, addressing Athos, "declare what passed between you and that other gentleman."

"But," cried M. Bonancieux, "that is not M. d'Artagnan that you show me there."

"What! not M. d'Artagnan?" cried the commissary.

"By no means," answered Bonancieux.

"What *is* the gentleman's name?" demanded the commissary.

"I cannot tell you; I don't know him!" replied Bonancieux.

"What! you do not know him?"

"No."

"You have never set eyes on him?"

"Yes; but I do not know his name."

"Your name?" demanded the commissary of Athos.

"Athos!" answered the musketeer.

"But that is not the name of a man; it is the name of a mountain!" cried the unfortunate commissary, who began to get confused.

"It is my name," calmly replied Athos.

"But you said your name was d'Artagnan."

"I said so?"

"Yes, you!"

"The fact is, that they said to me—you are M. d'Artagnan. I replied—do you think so? My guards said they were sure of it. I did not wish to contradict them; besides, I might be mistaken."

"Sir! you mock the majesty of justice."

"Not at all," calmly replied Athos.

"You are M. d'Artagnan?"

"You see that you still tell me so."

"But," cried M. Bonancieux, "I tell you, Mr. Commissary, "that there is not the smallest doubt. M. d'Artagnan is my lodger, and, consequently, as he does not pay his rent, I know him only too well. M. d'Artagnan is a young man of nineteen or twenty years of age, at most, and this gentleman is at least thirty M. d'Artagnan is in the guards of M. des Essarts, and this gentleman is in the company of M. de Treville's musketeers: observe the uniform."

"By heavens! it is true!" muttered the commissary. "It is true, by God!"

At this instant the door was quickly opened, and one

of the turnkeys of the Bastile introduced a messenger, who gave the commissary a letter.

"Oh! the wretch!" exclaimed the commissary.

"What? of whom do you speak? It is not of my wife, I hope."

"On the contrary, it is of her. Your affairs are in a nice state."

"Do me the pleasure," said the exasperated mercer, "to tell me, sir, how my affairs can be made worse by what my wife does whilst I am in prison?"

"Because what she does is the consequence of an infernal plan arranged between you!"

"I swear to you, Mr. Commissary, that you are in the most profound error; that I know nothing in the world of my wife's actions; that I am completely ignorant of what she has done; and that, if she has committed follies, I renounce her, I give her the lie, and I curse her."

"And now," said Athos, "if you have no further business with me, dismiss me. Your M. Bonancieux is very tiresome."

"Take the prisoners back to their dungeons," said the commissary, pointing to Athos and Bonancieux, "and guard them more strictly than ever."

"Nevertheless," said Athos, with his usual tranquillity, "your business is with M. d'Artagnan; I do not well see how I can supply his place!"

"Do what I have ordered," cried the commissary; "and the most solitary confinement—do you hear?"

The two followed the guards, Athos shrugging his shoulders, and M. Bonancieux uttering lamentations which might have softened the heart of a tiger.

They took the mercer into the same dungeon where he had passed the night, and left him there throughout the whole day. Hour after hour did poor Bonancieux weep like a very mercer; he was not at all a man of warlike soul, as he himself told us.

About nine o'clock in the evening, just as he had made

up his mind to go to bed, he heard steps in his corridor.
These steps approached his dungeon, the door opened,
and the guards appeared.

"Follow me," said a sergeant who commanded the
guards.

"Follow you!" cried Bonancieux, "follow you at this
time of night! And where? my God!"

"Where we have orders to conduct you."

"But that is no answer."

"It is, nevertheless, the only answer you will get."

"O Lord! O Lord!" muttered the poor mercer, "now
I am lost!"

He followed, mechanically, and without resistance.

He went down the same corridor as before, crossed a
first court, then a second floor; and then, at the entrance
gate, he found a carriage surrounded by four horse
guards. They made him enter this carriage; the sergeant
placed himself at his side; the door was locked, and they
both found themselves in a moving prison.

The carriage proceeded slowly, like a funeral coach.
Through the padlocked bars the prisoner could only see
the horses and the pavement. But, like a true Parisian
as he was, Bonancieux recognised each street by its
corners, its lamps, and its signs. At the moment they
reached St. Paul, where the criminals of the Bastile were
executed, he nearly fainted, and crossed himself twice.
He thought the carriage would have stopped there; but
it went on, nevertheless. Farther on, he was seized with
great fear: it was in skirting the cemetery of St. Jean,
where the state criminals were buried. One thing alone
encouraged him, which was, that before burying them,
one generally cut off their heads; and his head was yet
upon his shoulders. But when the carriage took the road
to La Grève, and he perceived the painted roof of the
Hotel de Ville, and saw that the carriage went under its
colonnade, he thought it was all over with him, and
wished to confess himself to the sergeant; and, on the
refusal of the latter, uttered such piteous cries, that the

sergeant declared that if he continued to deafen him so, he would put a gag on him. This threat reassured him a little: if they meant to execute him at the Grève, it was scarcely worth while to gag him, as they had nearly reached the place of execution. In fact, the carriage crossed this fatal place without stopping. There was only the Croix du Trahoir, then, to fear; and the carriage took the exact road to it.

This time there was no further room for doubt. It was at the Croix du Trahoir that inferior criminals were executed. Bonancieux had flattered himself, by considering that he was worthy of St. Paul, or the place de Grève. It was at the Croix du Trahoir that his journey and his destiny would end. He could not yet see this unhappy cross, but he felt it, as it were, loom before him. When he was only about twenty paces from it, he heard a noise, and the carriage stopped. This was more than poor Bonancieux could bear: already crushed by the successive emotions he had experienced, he uttered a feeble cry, or rather groan, which might have been taken for the last sigh of a dying man, and fainted.

CHAPTER XIV.

THE MAN OF MEUNG.

THE mob that stopped the way was produced, not by the expectation of seeing a man hanged, but by the contemplation of man who was already hanging. After a moment's hindrance, the carriage proceeded on its way, passed through the crowd, went along the Rue St. Honore, and turning at the Rue des Bons Enfants, stopped at a low doorway.

When the door opened, two guards, assisted by the sergeant, received Bonancieux in their arms, and pushed him into a court; they then made him ascend a staircase, and placed him in an antechamber. All these operations were performed nearly mechanically, as far as he was concerned. He had walked as in a dream; he had seen things as through a mist; he had heard without understanding; and they might have executed him then without his making the slightest resistance, or uttering an appeal for mercy.

He remained passive on the bench, with his back resting against the wall, and his arms hanging down, on the very spot where his guards had placed him.

And yet, as, in looking around him, he saw nothing threatening, as no real danger was indicated, as the bench was comfortably stuffed, as the wall was covered with beautiful cordovan leather, and as long curtains of red damask, held by gilt brackets, hung before the windows, he became by degrees aware that his fears were exaggerated, and began to move his head from right to left, and vertically. At this motion, which no one opposed, he resumed a little courage, ventured to draw up one leg, and then the other; and, at last, supporting himself upon his hands, he raised himself on the bench, and found himself on his feet.

At this moment an officer of pleasant appearance opened a door, exchanged a few words with some person in the next room, and then, turning towards the prisoner, said—

"Is it you who are called Bonancieux?"

"Yes, sir," stammered the mercer, more dead than alive, "at your service."

"Enter!"

The officer bade the mercer precede him; and the latter, obeying without reply, entered a room where he appeared to be expected.

It was a large cabinet, the walls of which were furnished with offensive and defensive weapons—a close and suffocating room, in which there was already a fire, although it was scarcely yet the end of September. A square table, loaded with books and papers, and on which there was unrolled an immense plan of the town of Rochelle,

occupied the middle of the apartment. In front of the
chimney-piece there stood a man of middle height, with a
proud and haughty air, piercing eyes, a large forehead,
and an emaciated countenance, which was yet further
elongated by an imperial, surmounted by a pair of
moustaches.

Although this man was scarcely thirty-six or thirty-seven
years old, both imperial and moustaches were beginning
to grow gray. His appearance, except that he wore no
sword, was military; and his buff leather boots, which
were yet slightly covered with dust, pointed out that he
had been on horseback during the day.

This individual was Armand-Jean Duplessis, Cardinal
de Richelieu; not as he is represented—broken down
like an old man, suffering like a martyr, his body shattered,
his voice extinguished, buried in an enormous easy-chair,
no longer living but by the power of his genius, and no
longer supporting the struggle against Europe but by the
eternal energy of his extraordinary mind—but such as he
really was at this period; that is, a skilful and gallant
cavalier, already feeble in body, but upheld by that moral
force which made him one of the most unparalleled of
mankind, and now preparing, after sustaining the Duc de
Nevers in his duchy of Mantua, and taking Nismes,
Castres, and Elzes, to drive the English from the Isle of
Rhé, and to undertake the siege of La Rochelle.

At first sight, nothing denoted that it was the cardinal,
and it was impossible for those who were unacquainted
with his appearance to guess in whose presence they
were.

The poor mercer remained standing at the door, whilst
the eyes of the person we have been describing fixed
themselves upon him as if they would penetrate his most
secret thoughts.

"Is that this Bonancieux?" he demanded, after a
moment's pause.

"Yes, my lord!" replied the officer.

"Very well; give me those papers, and leave us."

The officer took the papers indicated, gave them to him who asked for them, bowed to the very ground, and left the room.

In these papers Bonancieux recognised his examinations at the Bastile. From time to time the man by the chimney-piece lifted his eyes from the papers, and plunged them, like two poniards, into the very heart of the poor mercer.

At the end of ten minutes' reading, and ten seconds' scrutiny of Bonancieux, he had made up his mind.

"That head has never conspired," murmured the cardinal; "but never mind, let us see." Then he said slowly, "You are accused of high treason."

"That is what they have already told me, my lord!" said Bonancieux, giving his interrogator the same title that he had heard the officer give him; "but I give you my oath, that I knew nothing about it."

The cardinal suppressed a smile.

"You have conspired with your wife, with Madame de Chevreuse, and with my Lord Duke of Buckingham."

"I admit, my lord," replied the mercer, "I have heard all those names mentioned by her."

"And on what occasion?"

"She said that the Cardinal de Richelieu had enticed the Duke of Buckingham to Paris, to destroy him and the queen."

"She said that, did she?" cried the cardinal, with great violence.

"Yes, my lord; but I told her that she was wrong in saying such a thing, and that his eminence was incapable——"

"Hold your tongue—you are a fool!" replied the cardinal.

"That is exactly what my wife said to me, my lord?"

"Do you know who carried off your wife?"

"No, my lord."

"But you had some suspicions?"

"Yes, my lord; but as these suspicions appeared to displease the commissary, I have them no longer."

"Your wife has escaped: did you know that?"

"Not at the time, my lord; I learned it, since I have been in prison, from the commissary, who is a most amiable man."

The cardinal suppressed another smile.

"Then you do not know what has become of your wife since her escape?"

"Not positively, my lord; but she has probably returned to the Louvre."

"At one o'clock this morning she had not yet returned there."

"Ah! good God! but what can have become of her?"

"Have no fear—it will soon be known; nothing escapes the cardinal; the cardinal knows everything."

"In that case, my lord, do you believe that the cardinal will tell me what has become of my wife?"

"Perhaps so; but it is necessary, first, that you should tell me all you know in relation to the connection of your wife with Madame de Chevreuse."

"But, my lord, I know nothing about it; I never saw her."

"When you went to fetch your wife from the Louvre, did she return directly to your house?"

"Scarcely ever. She had business to transact with the queen's drapers, to whom I convoyed her."

"And how many linen-drapers were there?"

"Two, my lord."

"Where do they live?"

"One in the Rue Vaugirard, and the other in the Rue de la Harpe."

"Did you accompany your wife into these houses?"

"Never, my lord. I always waited for her at the door."

"And what excuse did she make for entering alone?"

"None: she told me to wait, and I waited."

"You are a most accommodating husband, my dear M. Bonancieux," said the cardinal.

"He has called me 'my dear monsieur,'" said the mercer to himself. "'Pon my faith, things are taking a good turn."

"Should you know those doors again?"

"Yes."

"Do you know the numbers?"

"Yes."

"What are they?"

"No. 25 in the Rue Vaugirard, and No. 75 in the Rue de la Harpe."

"Good!" said the cardinal; and, taking a silver bell, he rang it.

"Go," said he in a low voice, to the officer who entered— "go and find Rochefort, and tell him to come here directly, if he is within."

"The count is already here," said the officer, "and requests an immediate audience of your eminence."

"Your eminence!" muttered Bonancieux, who knew that such was the title ordinarily given to the cardinal; "your eminence!"

"Let him come in, then, let him come in!" said Richelieu eagerly.

The officer hurried out of the room with that rapidity with which the cardinal was generally obeyed by his followers.

"Your eminence!" again muttered Bonancieux, rolling his eyes in astonishment.

Two seconds had scarcely elapsed after the officer left the room before the door opened again, and another person entered.

"It is he!" exclaimed Bonancieux.

"Who is he?" demanded the cardinal.

"He who ran away with my wife."

The cardinal rang a second time, and the officer re-appeared.

"Put this man into the hands of the two guards, and let him wait till I send for him."

"No, my lord, no, it is not he!" exclaimed Bonancieux:

"no, I was mistaken; it is another person, not at all like him.   The gentleman is an honest man."

"Take away that simpleton!" said the cardinal.

The officer took him by the arm, and led him to the antechamber, where he was met by the two guards.

The person who had last entered impatiently followed Bonancieux with his eyes till he was gone, and, when the door was closed behind him—

"They have met," he said, eagerly approaching the cardinal.

"Who?" demanded the cardinal.

"Those two."

"The queen and the duke!" cried the cardinal.

"Yes."

"And where?"

"At the Louvre!"

"Are you sure?"

"Perfectly sure!"

"Who told you of it?"

"Madame de Lannoy, who is entirely devoted to your eminence, as you well know!"

"Why did she not tell you sooner?"

"Either by chance, or by mistrust, the queen made Madame de Surgis sleep in her room, and kept it throughout the day."

"Very well; we have been beaten; let us try to have our revenge."

"Be assured that I will assist your eminence with all my soul."

"How did this happen?"

"At half-past twelve the queen was with her women."

"Where?"

"In her bed-chamber, where a pocket-handkerchief was brought her from her seamstress."

"Well?"

"The queen immediately showed great emotion; and grew pale, under her rouge."

"Well! what then?"

" Nevertheless, she arose; and, in an agitated voice said, 'ladies, wait ten minutes for me; I will return.' Then, opening the door of her alcove, she went out."

" Why did not Madame de Lannoy come and tell you directly ? "

" There was no certainty about the matter; besides, the queen had said, 'ladies, wait for me.' And Madame de Lannoy dared not disobey her majesty."

" And how long did the queen remain absent from her room ? "

" Three-quarters of an hour."

" Did none of her women accompany her ? "

" Only Donna Estefana."

" And she returned ? "

" Yes, but only to take a small rosewood casket, bearing her initials, with which she went out again directly."

" And when she came back, finally, did she bring the casket with her ? "

" No ! "

" Does Madame de Lannoy know what the casket contained ? "

" Yes ! the diamond studs which his majesty presented to the queen."

" And she came back without the casket ? "

" Yes."

" Then the opinion of Madame de Lannoy is, that she gave this casket to Buckingham ? "

" She is sure of it."

" How so ? "

"During the day, Madame de Lannoy, in her office of tire-woman to the queen, looked for this casket, appeared uneasy at not finding it, and ended by inquiring for it of the queen."

" And then the queen——"

" The queen blushed deeply, and answered that, having the evening before broken one of the studs, she had sent it to her jeweller's to be repaired."

"You must go there, and ascertain whether that is true, or not."

"I have been."

"Well, and the goldsmith——?"

"The goldsmith has heard nothing about it."

"Good! good! Rochefort, all is not lost, and perhaps —perhaps all is for the best!"

"The fact is, that I have no doubt but what the genius of your eminence——"

"May repair the errors of my agent! Is that what you mean?"

"It was just what I was about to say, if your eminence had permitted me to finish the sentence."

"Now, do you know where the Duchess de Chevreuse and the Duke of Buckingham concealed themselves?"

"No, my lord; my agents have no positive information upon that point."

"I know it myself, though."

"You! my lord?"

"Yes, or at least I have no doubt of it. They lived, the one in the Rue Vaugirard, at No. 25, and the other in the Rue de la Harpe, No. 75."

"Would your eminence wish me to arrest them both?"

"It is too late; they will be gone."

"Never mind; there is no harm in trying!"

"Take ten of my guards, and ransack the two houses."

"It shall be done, my lord!"

So saying, Rochefort rushed from the room.

When the cardinal was left alone, he remained a moment in thought, and then rang a third time.

The officer who had come before appeared again.

"Bring in the prisoner," said the cardinal.

Master Bonancieux was again brought in, and, at a sign from the cardinal, the officer withdrew.

"You have deceived me," said the cardinal, with great severity.

"I!" cried Bonancieux; "I deceive your eminence!"

"When your wife went to the Rue Vaugirard, and the Rue de la Harpe, she did not go to linen-drapers."

"Good God! To whom did she go, then?"

"She went to see the Duchess de Chevreuse, and the Duke of Buckingham."

"Yes!" said Bonancieux, with a flash of recollection; "yes, exactly so; your eminence is right. I often told my wife that it was astonishing that linen-drapers should live in such houses; in houses which had no signs; and every time I said so, my wife began to laugh. Ah! my lord!" he continued, throwing himself at the feet of his eminence, "it is plain that you are the cardinal, the great cardinal—the man of genius, whom all the world reveres!"

The cardinal, small as was the triumph to be achieved over a being so vulgar as was Bonancieux, did not the less enjoy it for a moment. Then, as if a new idea struck him, he smiled, and, stretching out his hand to the mercer—

"Rise, my friend," said he, "you are a worthy fellow."

"The cardinal has taken my hand! I have touched the hand of the great man!" exclaimed Bonancieux; "the great man has called me his friend!"

"Yes, my friend, yes," said the cardinal, in that paternal tone which he was sometimes able to assume, but which only deceived those who did not know him; "and as you have been unjustly suspected, we must make you some amends. Here, take this bag of a hundred pistoles, and forgive me."

"*I* forgive *you*, my lord!" said Bonancieux, hesitating to take the bag, from a fear that this supposed gift was only a jest. "But you were quite at liberty to have me arrested; you are quite at liberty to send me to the torture; you are quite at liberty to hang me; you are the master, and I should not have the smallest word to say against it. Forgive you, my lord! But you cannot mean that!"

"Ah! my dear M. Bonancieux, you are very generous; I see it, and I thank you. But you must take this bag, and then you will go away not very discontented—will you?"

"I go away perfectly enchanted, my lord!"

"Adieu, then; or, rather, *au revoir*; for I hope that we shall see each other again."

"As often as my lord may please; I am at your eminence's command."

"It shall be often, depend upon it; for I have found your conversation quite charming."

"Oh! my lord!"

"Farewell, till our next meeting, M. Bonancieux—till our next meeting."

Bonancieux, at a sign from the cardinal's hand, bowed to the very ground, and then backed himself out of the room. When he was in the anteroom, the cardinal heard him, in his enthusiasm, crying out, at the top of his voice: "Long live his eminence! long live the great cardinal!"

Richelieu listened with a smile to this noisy manifestation of the enthusiastic feelings of Master Bonancieux: and, when his shouts were lost in the distance: "There," he said, "is a man who would henceforth die for me!"

The cardinal then set himself to examine with great attention the map of La Rochelle, which was spread out upon the table, and to mark with a pencil the position of the famous breakwater which, eighteen months afterwards, closed the port of the besieged city.

Whilst he was most deeply occupied with these strategic meditations, the door opened, and Rochefort reappeared.

"Well!" said the cardinal, with vivacity, which proved what consequence he attached to the intelligence that he expected from the count.

"Well!" said the latter, "a young woman, between twenty-six and twenty-eight years old, and a man of about thirty-five or forty years of age, have really lodged in the houses indicated by your eminence; but the woman left last night, and the man this morning."

"It was they!" exclaimed the duke, whose eyes were fixed upon the clock: "but now," he continued, "it is too late to follow them. The duchess is at Tours, and the duke at Boulogne. It is in London that they must be overtaken."

"What are your eminence's commands?"

"Let not one word be said of what has passed. Let

the queen remain in perfect peace of mind; let her be ignorant that we know her secret; let her believe that we are hunting after some conspiracy. Send me Séguier, the keeper of the seals."

"And this man? What has your eminence done with him?"

"What man?" demanded the cardinal.

"This Bonancieux."

"I have done all that could be done with him. I have set him to spy upon his wife."

The Count de Rochefort bowed low, like a man who felt the great superiority of his master, and withdrew.

As soon as the cardinal was again alone, he seated himself once more, and wrote a letter, which he sealed with his private signet, and then rang his bell. The officer entered for the fourth time.

"Tell Vitry to come here," said the cardinal, "and order him to be ready for a journey."

In another moment the man he had sent for was standing before him, booted and spurred.

"Vitry," said he, "you must go off at once, without an instant's delay, to London. You must not stop one moment on the road, and you will give this letter to my lady. There is a cheque for two hundred pistoles; go to my treasurer, and get the money. You shall have the same sum if you return in six days, having performed my commission with success!"

The messenger, without answering one word, bowed; took the letter, and the order for two hundred pistoles, and left the room.

These were the contents of the letter—

"MY LADY,

"Be present at the first ball where you can meet the Duke of Buckingham. He will have on his doublet twelve diamond studs; get close to him, and cut off two.

"As soon as these studs are in your possession, let me know it."

CHAPTER XV.

CIVILIANS AND SOLDIERS.

On the day after these events had happened, as Athos had not returned to them, d'Artagnan and Porthos informed M. de Treville of his disappearance.

As for Aramis, he had requested leave of absence for five days, and it was said that he was at Rouen on some family affairs.

M. de Treville was the father of his soldiers. The humblest individual amongst them, from the time that he put on the uniform of the company, was as certain of his assistance and support, as M. de Treville's own brother could have been.

He went, therefore, at once to the criminal lieutenant. The officer who commanded at La Croix Rouge was sent for, and from various inquiries it was ascertained that Athos was at that time lodged at Fort l'Eveque.

Athos had been subjected to the same trials as we have seen Bonancieux exposed to.

We have witnessed the confrontation of the two prisoners. Athos, who, till then, had said nothing, from fear that d'Artagnan had not had the time he needed, from that moment declared that his name was Athos, and not d'Artagnan. He added that he knew neither M. nor Madame Bonancieux; that he had never spoken either to the one or the other; and that he had gone at about ten at night to pay a visit to his friend, M. d'Artagnan, but until that hour he had been at M. de Treville's, where he had dined. Twenty witnesses, he added, could confirm this fact, and he named many distinguished gentlemen, amongst whom was the Duc de la Tremouille.

The second commissary was as much surprised as the first, at this simple but firm declaration of the musketeer, on whom he would gladly have taken that revenge which civilians so much love to take on soldiers; but the names of Treville and la Tremouille demanded consideration.

Athos was, therefore, sent to the cardinal; but his eminence was, unfortunately, at the Louvre with the king.

It was just at this time that M. de Treville, having in vain sought Athos from the lieutenant and the governor of Fort l'Eveque, came to make an application to his majesty; to whom he had, as captain of the musketeers, the right of immediate access upon all occasions.

The prejudices of the king against the queen are well known—prejudices which were skilfully fostered by the cardinal, who, in political intrigues, had much greater fear of women than of men. One of the chief causes of this prejudice was the friendship of the queen for Madame de Chevreuse. These two women gave his eminence more uneasiness than the Spanish war, the rupture with England, and the embarrassment of the finances, all combined. He was convinced that Madame de Chevreuse served the queen, not only in political intrigues, but— what was far more vexatious to him—in amorous intrigues as well.

At the first word which the cardinal had uttered, that Madame de Chevreuse, who was exiled to Tours, and had been supposed to be in that city, had come to Paris, and had stayed there five days, escaping the police, the king became furiously enraged. At once capricious, and a false husband, Louis still wished to be distinguished as *the just* and *the chaste*. Posterity will, with difficulty, understand this character, which history explains, not by reasoning, but by facts.

But when the cardinal added that not only had Madame de Chevreuse been to Paris, but that the queen had renewed her friendship with her by means of one of those mysterious correspondences which were then called *cabals*—when he affirmed that he, the cardinal, had all but unravelled the threads of this intrigue—when, at the moment that he was about to detect in the very fact, provided with the fullest proofs, an emissary of the queen, who was in communication with the exile, a musketeer, had dared violently to interrupt the course of justice, by falling, sword in hand, upon the honest officers of the law, who had been charged to examine the whole affair with impartiality, in order to lay it before the king—Louis was no longer able to restrain himself. He took a step towards the queen's apartments, with that pale and speechless indignation, which, when it burst out, led that prince to acts of the most unfeeling cruelty.

And yet, in all this, the cardinal had not said one word concerning the Duke of Buckingham.

It was at that moment that M. de Treville entered, cool, polite, and with a manner perfectly unobjectionable.

Warned of what had taken place by the presence of the cardinal, and by the change in the king's countenance, M. de Treville felt himself as strong as Samson in the presence of the Philistines.

The king had already placed his hand upon the handle of the door; but, at the noise of M. de Treville's entrance, he turned round.

"You come in good time, sir," said his majesty; who, when his passions were thoroughly excited, never dissembled, "for I hear fine things of your musketeers."

"And I," said Treville coolly, "have fine things to tell you of your civilians."

"What is that you say?" said the king haughtily.

"I have the honour to inform your majesty," said Treville in the same tone, "that a party of lawyers, commissaries, and police agents—people very respectable in their way, but very bitter, as it appears, against the military—have presumed to arrest in a house, to drag through the public streets, and to cast into Fort l'Eveque (and all this under an order which they refuse to show me), one of my musketeers, or rather of yours, sir, of irreproachable conduct, of an almost illustrious reputation, and favourably known to your majesty—M. Athos!"

"Athos," said the king mechanically; "yes, I certainly do know that man!"

" Your majesty may remember," said M. de Treville,
" M. Athos is the musketeer who, in the vexatious duel
that you heard of, had the misfortune to wound M. de
Cahusac severely :—by the bye, my lord," continued
Treville, addressing the cardinal, " M. de Cahusac is
entirely recovered, is he not ? "

" Yes, thank you," said the cardinal, biting his lips
with anger.

" M. Athos," continued Treville, " had gone to visit
one of his friends who was from home, a young Bearnese,
a cadet in his majesty's guards, in the company of
Essarts ; but scarcely had he settled himself in his
friend's room, and taken up a book whilst waiting,
when a cloud of bailiffs and soldiers, mingled together,
laid siege to the house, and broke open several doors."

The cardinal here made the king a sign, which
signified, " It was on account of the business which I
have been telling you."

" We know all that," said the king, " for it was all
done in our service."

" And was it," asked Treville, " in your majesty's
service, also, that one of my musketeers, who was
perfectly innocent, has been seized, placed between two
guards like a criminal, and marched through the midst
of an insolent crowd, although he is a gallant man, who
has shed his blood for your majesty ten times, and is
yet ready to shed it again ? "

" Bah," said the king, somewhat shaken ; " and
was that really the way of it ? "

" M. de Treville does not say," replied the cardinal
with the greatest indifference, " that this innocent
musketeer, this gallant man, had, only one hour before,
attacked, sword in hand, four commissaries delegated
by me to collect information concerning an affair of
the greatest importance."

" I defy your eminence to prove it," cried Treville,
with true Gascon frankness, and true military bluntness,
" for, an hour before, M. Athos, who, I can assure you,

is a man of the noble origin, did me the honour, after having dined with me, of conversing in my drawing-room with the Count de Chalons and the Duc de la Tremouille."

The king looked at the cardinal.

"It is proved by a deposition," said the cardinal, in answer to the mute interrogation of the king; "and the individuals who were ill-treated have prepared what I have now the honour to present to your majesty."

"Is the affidavit of a civilian of equal value with the word of honour of a soldier?" demanded Treville fiercely.

"Come, come, Treville, be silent," said the king.

"If his eminence has any suspicions against one of my musketeers," replied Treville, "the justice of the cardinal is so well known, that I should myself demand an inquiry."

"In the house in which this attack on justice has been made," said the immovable cardinal, "there lodges, I believe, a Bearnese, a friend of the musketeer."

"Your eminence probably alludes to M. d'Artagnan?"

"I allude to a *protégé* of yours, M. de Treville."

"Yes, your eminence; precisely so."

"Do you not suspect this young man of having led M. Athos astray?'

"M. Athos—a man nearly double his own age," broke in M. de Treville. "No, sir; besides, M. d'Artagnan passed the evening at my house!"

"Ah!" said the cardinal, "everybody seems to have passed the evening at your house."

"Does his eminence doubt my word?" exclaimed Treville, his face flushed with anger.

"No, God forbid!" said the cardinal; "but, only, at what hour was he at your house?"

"Oh! as to that, I can speak with certainty to your eminence; for, as he entered, I remarked that it was half-past nine by the clock, although I had believed it to be later."

"And at what hour did he leave your hotel?"

"At half-past ten—exactly one hour after this event happened."

"But, at least, M. Athos was seized in that house, in the Rue des Fossoyeurs!" said the cardinal, who did not for a moment doubt the loyalty of M. de Treville, yet felt that victory was leaving him.

"Is it unlawful for a friend to visit a friend? or for a musketeer of my company to keep company with a guard of M. des Essarts?"

"Yes, when the house where he associates with his friend is suspected."

"This house is suspected, Treville!" said the king: "perhaps you did not know that."

"Indeed, sire, I did not know it. But, although it might be suspected, I deny that it was in that part which M. d'Artagnan inhabits; for I can assure you, sir, if I may believe what he has said, that there does not exist a more devoted servant of your majesty, or a more profound admirer of the cardinal."

"Is it not this d'Artagnan who wounded Jussac in that unfortunate encounter which took place one day near the convent des Carmes Dechaux?" demanded the king, looking at the cardinal, who coloured with spite. "And wounded Bernajoux the next day."

"Yes, sire, yes; it is the same. Your majesty has a good memory!"

"Come, what shall we decide upon?" said the king.

"That concerns your majesty more than me," answered the cardinal. "I assert his guilt."

"And I deny it," said Treville. "But his majesty has judges—let them determine on the affair."

"Exactly so," said the king, "let us refer the matter to the judges: it is their business to judge, and they shall judge it."

"Only," said Treville, "it is a sad thing, in these unhappy times in which we live, that the purest life, the most indisputable virtue, cannot secure a man from disgrace and persecution. The army will be but little satisfied, I can answer for it, at being the object of such rigorous treatment at the hands of the police."

The expression was imprudent, but Treville had thrown it out purposely. He wished for an explosion; because the mine flames out as it explodes, and the flame enlightens us.

"The police!" cried the king, taking up Treville's words. "Affairs of the police! And what do you know about them, sir? Busy yourself with your musketeers, and don't perplex my brain. It would seem, to hear you, that if a musketeer is arrested, France is imperilled. Ah! what a fuss about a musketeer! I will arrest ten, fifty, a hundred, ay, even the whole company, nor will any one utter a word!"

"The instant that they are suspected by your majesty," said Treville, "the musketeers become guilty. I am ready, therefore, to surrender my sword; for, after having accused my soldiers, I do not doubt that the cardinal will conclude by accusing me; and it is unquestionably better that I should deliver myself up as a prisoner with M. Athos, who is already arrested, and with M. d'Artagnan, who will doubtless before long be so too."

"Gascon head! will you have done?" said the king.

"Sire," said Treville, without in the least lowering his voice, "give me up my musketeer, or let him be tried!"

"He shall be tried," said the king.

"Well, so much the better; for then I shall demand your majesty's permission to plead his cause."

The king dreaded an outbreak.

"If his eminence," said he, "had not any personal motives——"

The cardinal saw which way the king was tending, and anticipated him.

"Pardon me," said he, "but the moment that the king sees in me a prejudiced judge, I retire."

"Come," said the king to M. de Treville, "do you

swear to me by my father, that M. Athos was at your house during this event, and that he had nothing to do with it ? "

" By your glorious father, and by yourself, whom I love and venerate most in the world, I swear it ! "

" You must reflect, sire," said the cardinal, " that if we thus release this prisoner, the truth cannot be discovered."

" M. Athos shall always be forthcoming," said Treville, " when it may please the lawyers to interrogate him. He will not run away. I stand surety for him."

" In reality he will not desert," said the king ; " he can always be found, as Treville says. Besides," added he, lowering his voice, and regarding the cardinal with a supplicating air, " put them in security : it is politic."

This policy of Louis XIII. made Richelieu smile.

" Give your order, sire," said he, " for you have the privilege of pardon."

" The privilege of pardon applies only to the guilty," said Treville, who wished to have the last word, " and my musketeer is innocent. It is not a pardon, therefore, that your majesty is going to grant, but justice."

" Is he at Fort l'Eveque ? " asked the king.

" Yes, sire, and in a solitary dungeon, like the worst of criminals."

" 'Od's blood ! " said the king, " what is to be done ?"

" Sign the order for his release," said the cardinal, " and all will be ended. I believe, like your majesty, that M. de Treville's security is more than sufficient."

Treville bowed respectfully, with a joy not un-mingled with fear. He would have preferred an obstinate resistance on the part of the cardinal, to this sudden concession.

The king signed the order of release, and Treville carried it away immediately.

At the moment he was going out, the cardinal gave him a friendly smile, and said to the king—

" Great harmony exists between the officers and the

soldiers of your musketeers, sire; it must be very beneficial to the service, and reflects honour on them all."

"He will play me some scurvy trick presently," thought Treville; "one never has the last word with such a man. But let me hasten, for the king may change his mind soon; and, after all, it is more difficult to put a man back into the Bastile, or Fort l'Eveque, once he has got out of it, than to keep him prisoner there when they have already caught him."

M. de Treville entered Fort l'Eveque triumphantly, and set at liberty his musketeer, who had not lost his calm indifference.

And the first time that he saw d'Artagnan, he said to him, "You have escaped well: your sword-thrust to Jussac is now paid for; that to Bernajoux still remains; but you must not be too confident."

M. de Treville had reason to distrust the cardinal, and to think that all was not ended; for scarcely had the captain of musketeers closed the door behind him before his eminence said to the king—

"Now that we are alone together, we must have some serious conversation, if it please your majesty. Sire, the Duke of Buckingham has been in Paris for five days, and left it only this morning."

CHAPTER XVI.

IN WHICH THE KEEPER OF THE SEALS, SÉGUIER, LOOKED MORE THAN ONCE AFTER THE BELL, THAT HE MIGHT RING IT AS HE HAD BEEN USED TO DO.

IT is impossible to form an idea of the impression which these few words produced on the king. He grew red and pale by turns, and the cardinal saw immediately that he had regained, by a single stroke, all the ground that he had previously lost.

"The Duke of Buckingham at Paris!" said the king; "and what has he been doing there?"

"No doubt plotting with your enemies, the Huguenots and the Spaniards.'

"No, by God, no! Plotting, rather against my honour, with Madame de Chevreuse, Madame de Longueville, and the Conde."

"Oh! sire, what an idea! The queen is too good, and, above all, loves your majesty too well."

"Woman is feeble," said the king: "and as for her loving me too well, I have my own opinion about that!"

"Nevertheless, I maintain that the Duke of Buckingham came to Paris for an entirely political object."

"And I am just as sure that he came for other purposes; but, if the queen is guilty, let her tremble!"

"After all," said the cardinal, "however unwilling I am to dwell upon a treason of this kind, your majesty, by your words, reminds me that Madame de Lannoy, whom, by your majesty's order, I have several times questioned, told me this morning that, the night before last, the queen was up very late, that this morning she was weeping very much, and that she had been writing throughout the whole day."

"That confirms it!" said the king: "writing to *him*, no doubt. Cardinal, I must have the queen's papers!"

"But how are we to get them, sire? It appears to me that neither I nor your majesty ought to undertake such an office."

"How did they proceed towards the Maréchale d'Ancre," said the king, in the most violent rage; "they first ransacked her chests, and at last searched her person."

The Maréchale d'Ancre was only the Maréchale d'Ancre, a Florentine adventuress: but the august spouse of your majesty is Anne of Austria, Queen of France; that is, one of the greatest princesses in the world."

"That only makes her the more criminal! The more

she has forgotten the high position in which she is placed, the lower has she fallen. For a long time, now, I have been determined to put an end to all these petty intrigues of politics and love. There is, also, one La Porte in her service."

"Whom I believe to be the master-spirit in all this."

"Then you think as I do—that she is deceiving me," said the king.

"I believe, and I repeat it to your majesty, that the queen plots against the king's power, but I have not said against his honour."

"And I tell you, against both. I tell you that the queen does not love me ; I tell you that she loves another ; I tell you that she loves this infamous Duke of Buckingham ! Why did not you arrest him, whilst he was in Paris ? "

"Arrest the duke ! arrest the prime minister of Charles I. Think, sire, what a commotion ! And then, if the suspicions of your majesty had any foundation, which I much doubt, what a dreadful exposure—what horrible scandal."

"But if he exposed himself to it, like a vagabond and a pilferer, he ought——"

Louis stopped, catching himself on the verge of a dreadful expression, whilst Richelieu, stretching out his neck, in vain expected the word which hung upon the king's lips.

"He ought——"

"Nothing," said the king, "nothing. But," added he, "during all the time that he was in Paris, you did not ever lose sight of him ? "

"Never, sire ! "

"Where did he reside ? '

"In the Rue de la Harpe, at No. 75."

"Where is that ? "

"Near the Luxembourg."

"And you are certain that the queen and he did not see each other ? "

" He put his naked sword under his arm, and followed.''

" I believe that the queen is too much attached to her duty, sire ! "

" But they corresponded : it is to him that the queen was writing all day ! Duke, I must have those letters."

" Sire, and yet——"

" Duke, at whatever cost, I must have them ! "

" I would observe to your majesty, however——"

" And would you also betray me, cardinal, since you thus oppose my wishes ? Are you also in league with the Spaniard, and the English ; with Madame de Chevreuse, and with the queen ? "

" Sire," replied the cardinal, with a smile, " I thought myself far removed from any such suspicion."

" But cardinal, you hear what I say : I will have these letters ! "

" There can be only one way."

" What is that ? "

" It is to charge M. de Séguier, the keeper of the seals, with this commission. The matter is wholly within his scope."

" Let him be sent for immediately."

" He must be at my house, sire. I sent for him there, and when I came to the Louvre, I left word that he should wait for me ! "

" Let him be sent for instantly ! "

" Your majesty's orders shall be executed ; but——"

" But what ? "

" But the queen may perhaps refuse to obey."

" What, my orders ? "

" Yes, if she does not know that these orders come from the king."

" Well, then, that she may have no doubt, I will convey the orders to her myself ! "

" Your majesty will not forget that I have done all I could to prevent a rupture ! "

" Yes, duke, yes ; I know that you are very indulgent, perhaps too indulgent, to the queen ; and I can tell you we must have some talk about that hereafter."

"Whenever your majesty pleases; but I shall be always happy and proud to sacrifice myself for the harmony which I should wish to see between the king and queen of France."

"Well and good, cardinal; but, in the meantime, send for the chancellor. And now I hasten to the queen."

Then, opening the door of communication, Louis entered into the corridor which led from his own apartments to those of Anne of Austria.

The queen was surrounded by her ladies, Madame de Guitaut, Madame de Sablé, Madame de Monthazon, and Madame de Guéméné. In a corner was the Spanish lady of the bed-chamber, Donna Estefana, who had accompanied her majesty from Madrid. Madame Guéméné was reading aloud, and everybody was listening to her, except the queen, who had promoted this reading that she might, under the pretence of paying attention, indulge the train of her own thoughts.

These thoughts, all gilded as they were by a dying beam of love, were not therefore the less sad. Anne of Austria—deprived of the confidence of her husband, pursued by the hatred of the cardinal, who could never pardon her repulsion of a softer sentiment, and having constantly before her eyes the case of the queen-mother whom that hatred had tormented throughout her life, although, if the memoirs of the times are to be believed, Marie de Medici had begun by granting to the cardinal the sentiment which Anne of Austria had persisted in refusing him—Anne of Austria had seen her most devoted servants, her most confidential companions, her dearest favourites, fall around her. Like those unhappy beings who are endowed with a baleful nature, she brought misfortune upon everything she touched. Her friendship was a fatal gift, which attracted persecution. Madame de Chevreuse and Madame de Vernal were banished; and La Porte did not conceal from his mistress that he was in momentary expectation of an arrest.

It was at the very instant that she was profoundly indulging in these melancholy reflections that the door opened, and the king entered.

The reader became immediately silent; the ladies arose; and all was silence.

As for the king, he made no show of politeness; only stopping before the queen.

"Madame," said he in a nervous voice, "you are about to receive a visit from the chancellor, who will make known to you certain commands with which I have charged him."

The unhappy queen, who was often threatened with divorce, with exile, and even with death, grew pale beneath her rouge, and could not restrain herself from saying—

"But why that visit, sire? What can the chancellor have to say, which your majesty could not tell me personally?"

The king turned on his heel without any answer; and almost at the same moment, the captain of the guards, M. de Guitaut, announced the presence of the chancellor.

Before the chancellor appeared, the king had already left the apartment by another door.

The chancellor entered, half smiling, and half blushing. As we shall probably fall into his company again in the course of this history, there will be no harm in our readers making acquaintance with him now.

This chancellor was a pleasant fellow. It was by des Roches le Masle, a canon of Notre-Dame, who had formerly been the cardinal's valet, that he had been recommended to his eminence, as one entirely devoted to his interests. The cardinal trusted him, and was always well served.

The following is one of the many stories which were circulated concerning him:—

After a stormy youth, he had retired into a monastery to expiate, at least for a time, the follies of his juvenile years. But, in entering into this holy place, the poor

penitent had been unable to close the door so quickly but
that the passions which he flew from could enter with
him. They worried him, in fact, unceasingly; and the
superior—to whom he had confided this disgrace, and
who wished to preserve him from it as far as he was able
—advised him, in order to drive out the diabolical
tempter, to have recourse to the bell-rope, and to pull it
with his utmost might; since, on hearing this admoni-
tory sound, the monks would understand that a brother
was beset by temptation, and the whole community
would instantly proceed to prayers.

The counsel seemed good to the future chancellor, who
exorcised the evil spirit by a large volume of prayers,
which were offered up by the monks. The devil, however, is not easily displaced, when he has once got into
garrison; and in proportion as these exorcisms were
multiplied, the temptations were increased; so that the
unceasing clamour of the bell, by day and by night,
perpetually announced the extreme need of mortifica-
tion which the penitent experienced.

The monks no longer enjoyed a moment's rest. By
day, they did nothing but go up and down the chapel
stairs; and by night, besides complines and matins,
they were obliged to jump out of their beds at least
twenty times, to prostrate themselves upon the flooring
of their cells.

It is not known whether the devil quitted his hold, or
the monks got tired out; but at the end of three months
the penitent reappeared in the world, with the reputation of being more terribly possessed by the evil spirit
than any one who had ever lived.

On leaving the convent, he entered the magistracy,
and became president in the place of his uncle. He then
joined the cardinal's party, in doing which he evinced no
small sagacity; became chancellor; served his eminence
zealously against Anne of Austria; stimulated the judge
in the business of Chalais; encouraged the efforts of
the royal forest-master, M. de Laffemas; and, finally,

invested with the fullest confidence of the cardinal, which he had so well won, he had just received that singular commission, in the execution of which he now presented himself before the queen.

The queen was standing when he entered, but as soon as she perceived him she seated herself in her easy-chair, and making a sign for her ladies to place themselves on their cushions and stools, said, in a tone of supreme haughtiness—

"What do you want, sir ; and for what object do you come here ? "

" To make, madame, in the king's name, and without abating the respect which I entertain for your majesty, an exact examination of all your papers."

" What, sir ! an examination of my papers—of mine ! Truly, it is a most disgraceful act ! "

" Deign to pardon me, madame, but in this affair I am only an instrument of the royal will. Has not his majesty but just left the room ; and did he not himself invite you to expect this visit ? "

" Search, then, sir ; I am, it seems, a criminal. Estefana, give up the keys of my tables and desks."

The chancellor went through the formality of searching throughout the room, although he well knew that it was not there that the queen would hide the important letter which she had that day written.

But when he had, at least twenty times, opened all the drawers, and shut them again, it became necessary, in spite of any hesitation he might experience, to end the business by searching the queen herself. The chancellor advanced, therefore, towards her majesty, and, with a nervous tone and manner, said—

" And now I must make the principal search."

" And what is that ? " demanded the queen, who did not, or rather would not, understand him.

" His majesty is certain that a letter has been written by you during the day ; and he knows that it has not yet been forwarded to its destination. This letter is not to be found either in your table, or your desk, and yet it must be somewhere."

"Would you dare to lay your hand upon your queen?" asked Anne of Austria, assuming all her haughtiness, and fixing on the chancellor eyes which had become almost threatening.

"I am a faithful subject of the king, madame, and everything that his majesty may order, I shall execute."

"Well, it is true!" exclaimed the queen, "and the spies of the cardinal have served him faithfully. I *have* written a letter to-day, and that letter is not gone. It is here!" and her majesty placed her beautiful hand upon her bosom.

"Give me the letter, then, madame," said the chancellor.

"I will only give it to the king, sir," said the queen.

"If his majesty had wished the letter to be handed to him, madame, he would have demanded it himself. But I repeat, it is to me that he gave the order to obtain it, and, if you did not give it up——"

"Well! what then?"

"It is me that he has ordered to take it."

"How? What can you mean?"

"That my orders go very far, madame, and that I am authorised to seek for this suspected paper, even on the person of your majesty."

"Horrible!" exclaimed the queen.

"Be more compliant, then, madame."

"This conduct is infamous in its violence! Cannot you see that, sir?"

"The king commands it! Therefore, madame, excuse me."

"I will not endure it. No! no! I will die rather!" said the queen, in whom the imperial blood of Spain and Austria revolted at the outrage.

The chancellor made a most reverential bow, but it was evident that he did not mean to recede one step in the accomplishment of his commission. Just as an executioner's man might have done in the torture-chamber, he approached Anne of Austria, from whose eyes large tears of rage were gushing.

The queen was, as we have already said, of a singular beauty. The commission, therefore, was a delicate one ; but the king had come, from very jealousy of Buckingham, to be no longer jealous of any other person.

At that moment the chancellor, Séguier, was no doubt looking out for the rope of the memorable bell ; but, not finding it, he summoned up his resolution, and moved his hand towards the place where the queen had admitted that the paper was concealed.

Anne of Austria—blanched as though it had been by the approach of death—receded for a single step. Then, supporting herself by leaning with her left hand on a table which stood behind her, she drew with her right the paper from her bosom, and presented it to the keeper of the seals.

"Here, sir, take the letter," cried the queen, in a trembling, sobbing voice ; "take it, and free me from your odious presence."

The chancellor, who was also trembling from an emotion easy to conceive, took the letter, bowed to the very ground, and withdrew.

Scarcely was the door closed upon him, before the queen fell nearly senseless into the arms of her women.

The chancellor carried the letter to the king, without having read one syllable of its contents. His majesty took it with a trembling hand, and looked for the address but, finding none, he became very pale, and opened the paper slowly. Then, seeing by the first words that it was addressed to the King of Spain, he read it very rapidly.

It was a complete plan of attack against the cardinal. The queen invited her brother and the Emperor of Austria to make a show—offended as they were by the policy of Richelieu, whose constant aim it was to humble the house of Austria—of declaring war against France, and to lay down the dismissal of the cardinal as a condition of peace; but, of love, there was not one single word in all the letter.

The king, in great delight, inquired whether the cardinal was still at the Louvre. The answer was that his eminence was in the official cabinet, awaiting his majesty's commands.

The king immediately hastened to him.

"Here, duke," said he, "you were right, and I was wrong. The whole intrigue is political, and love was not the subject of this letter. But, on the other hand, there is a good deal about you."

The cardinal took the letter, and read it with the greatest attention; and when he had reached the end, he read it a second time.

"Well, your majesty," said he, "you see how far my enemies go: they threaten you with two wars if you do not dismiss me. Truly, sire, in your place I would yield to such pressing inducements; and, on my part, I should be truly happy to retire from affairs of state."

"What are you saying, duke?"

"I say, sire, that my health fails under these excessive struggles and eternal labours. I say, that in all probability I shall be unable to support the fatigues of the siege of La Rochelle; and that it would be better for you to appoint either M. de Condé, or M. de Bassompierre, or some valiant man whose profession is to conduct a war, instead of me, a churchman, continually turned aside from my vocation to engage in affairs for which I am entirely unfit. You will be more prosperous in the interior of the kingdom, sire; and I doubt not that you will also be more triumphant abroad."

"Duke," said the king, "your irony does not deceive me. Depend upon it, that all those who are mentioned in this letter shall be punished as they deserve;—even the queen herself."

"What can your majesty mean? God forbid that the queen should be harassed upon my account! She has always believed me her enemy, sire, though your majesty can testify that I have ever taken her part warmly, even against yourself. Oh! if she betrayed your majesty's honour, it would be a very different thing, and I should be the first to say—no mercy, sire, no mercy on the guilty! Happily, there is nothing of the kind here; and your majesty has just obtained a new proof of her innocence!"

"It is true, cardinal, and you were right, as you always are; but yet the queen has none the less deserved all my anger."

"It is you, sire, who have incurred hers; and when she seriously resents your conduct, I shall not blame her. Your majesty has treated her with great severity!"

"It is thus that I will always treat my enemies, and yours, duke, however lofty they may be, and whatever risk I may incur from being severe towards them."

"The queen is my enemy, but not yours, sire; she is, on the contrary, a submissive, irreproachable, and devoted wife: permit me, then, to intercede for her with your majesty."

"Let her humble herself, then, and make the first overtures."

"On the contrary, sire, set her the example: you were wrong first, since you were suspicious of the queen."

"Make the first overtures?" said the king. "Never!"

"Sire, I beseech you!"

"Besides, how could I make overtures?"

"By doing something which you know will be agreeable to her."

"What?"

"Give a ball. You know how much the queen loves dancing, and I will answer for it that her anger will not resist such an attention."

"Cardinal, you know that I do not like these worldly pleasures."

"Her majesty will be only the more grateful to you, as she knows your antipathy to this amusement. Besides, it will enable her to wear those beautiful diamond studs which you gave her on her birthday, and with which she has not yet had any opportunity to adorn herself."

"We shall see, cardinal; we shall see." said the king, who, in his delight at finding the queen merely guilty of a fault about which he did not much care, and innocent of a crime which he greatly dreaded, was quite ready to reconcile himself with her. "We shall see; but, upon my honour, you are too indulgent."

"Sire," said the cardinal, "leave severity to ministers: indulgence is a regal virtue: make use of it, and you will reap its benefits."

Hearing the clock strike eleven, the cardinal made an obeisance, and begged permission to retire; beseeching his majesty to make his peace with the queen.

Anne of Austria, who, after the seizure of her letter, expected some reproaches, was much surprised the next day to see the king make some attempts at a reconciliation with her. The first emotion was repulsion: her pride as a woman, and her dignity as a queen, had both been so cruelly outraged, that she was unable to meet these first advances of the king. But, vanquished by the advice of her ladies, she at last appeared to be disposed to forgiveness. The king took advantage of this favourable moment to tell her that he thought of giving an immediate entertainment.

An entertainment was so rare a thing to the poor queen, that at this declaration, as the cardinal had foreseen, the last trace of her resentment vanished, if not from her heart, at any rate from her countenance. She asked on what day this entertainment was to be given; bu the king answered that, on that point, he must consult the cardinal.

Not a day elapsed, in fact, but the king asked the cardinal when it was to be; and, day by day, his eminence deferred it upon some pretext or other. Thus did ten days pass away.

On the eighth day after the scene we have described,

the cardinal received a letter with the London post-mark, and containing only these few lines—

"I have got them, but cannot leave London for want of money. Send me five hundred pistoles, and, four or five days after having received them, I shall be in Paris."

On the very day that the cardinal received this letter, the king asked the usual question.

Richelieu counted on his fingers, and said to himself in a low voice—

"'She will reach Paris,' she says, 'four or five days after the receipt of this money.' Four or five days will be required for the money to get there; four or five days for her to return; that makes ten days. Allow for contrary winds and accidents of fate, and the weakness of a woman, and let us fix it at twelve days."

"Well, duke," said the king, "have you calculated?"

"Yes, sire: this is the 20th of September; the city magistrates will give an entertainment on the 3rd of October. That will suit exactly, for you will not have the appearance of going out of your way to please the queen."

Then the cardinal added—

"By the way, sire, do not forget to tell her majesty, *the evening before the fête*, that you wish to see how the diamond studs become her."

CHAPTER XVII.

THE BONANCIEUX HOUSEHOLD.

IT was the second time that the cardinal had recalled the king's attention to these diamond studs. His majesty had been struck by this circumstance, and supposed that the recommendation concealed some mystery.

More than once had his majesty been annoyed that the cardinal's police—which, without having attained the perfection of that of modern times, was nevertheless very good—was better informed than he himself was of what was taking place in his own royal household. He hoped, therefore, to glean some information from a conversation with the queen, and then to return to the cardinal, and tell him some secret which his eminence might, or might not, be acquainted with, but whose exposition, in either case, must raise him very much in the eyes of his minister.

He went accordingly to the queen, and, in his habitual way, accosted her with threats against those by whom she was surrounded. The queen bowed her head, and allowed the torrent to pass by without reply, hoping that it would at last exhaust itself. But that was not his majesty's design. He wished for a discussion, in which some light or other might be struck out, being convinced that the cardinal had kept something back, and was springing upon him one of those terrible surprises which his eminence so well knew how to contrive. He obtained his object by perseverance in accusing.

"But," said Anne of Austria, wearied of these vague attacks, "but, sire, you do not tell me all that you have in your heart. What have I done? What crime have I committed? It is impossible that your majesty should make all this disturbance about a letter written to my brother!"

The king, being attacked in such a direct manner himself, did not know what to answer. He thought that this was the time to issue the injunction which he had been charged to make on the eve of the ball.

"Madame," said he, with dignity, "there will soon be a ball at the Hotel de Ville. I desire that, to honour our worthy magistrates, you will be present at it in state dress, and, above all, adorned by those diamond studs which I gave you on your birthday. There is my answer."

And terrible that answer was. The queen believed that his majesty knew all her secret; and that the cardinal had persuaded him to that long dissimulation of seven or eight days, which, moreover, accorded well with his own character. She became excessively pale; rested her beautiful hand, which looked then as though it were of wax, upon a bracket; and, gazing at the king with terrified eyes, answered not a word.

"You hear me, madame," said the king, who thoroughly enjoyed this embarrassment, but without guessing its cause; "you hear me?"

"Yes, sire, I hear you," stammered the queen.

"You will be present at this ball?"

"Yes."

"With your diamond studs?"

"Yes."

The paleness of the queen, if possible, increased; and the king perceived, and enjoyed it, with that cold-blooded cruelty which was one of the worst parts of his character.

"It is settled then," said he, "and that is all I had to say to you."

"But on what day will this ball take place?" asked Anne of Austria.

The king instinctively felt that he ought not to reply to this question, which the queen had put to him in an almost dying voice.

"Almost immediately, madame," said he; "but I do not exactly remember the precise date. I will ask the cardinal about it."

"It was the cardinal, then, who told you of this ball?" said the queen.

"Yes, madame," said the astonished king; "but what of that?"

"And was it he who told you to request me to appear in these studs?"

"That is to say, madame——"

"It was he, sire; it was he!"

"Well, what does it signify, whether it was the cardinal or me? Is there any crime in the request?"

" No, sire."

" Then you will appear ? "

" Yes, sire ! "

" Very well," said the king, retiring ; "very well; I shall depend upon it."

The queen curtseyed, less from etiquette, than because her knees bent under her.

His majesty departed, enchanted.

" I am lost," muttered the queen ; " lost, for the cardinal evidently knows all, and he it is who pushes forward the king, who, as yet, is in ignorance, but will soon be made acquainted with the whole. I am lost! My God ! my God ! "

She knelt down upon a cushion, and prayed, with her head buried between her palpitating arms. Her position, was, in fact, terrible. Buckingham had returned to London. Madame de Chevreuse was at Tours. More closely watched than ever, the queen felt painfully certain that one of her ladies had betrayed her, without knowing which. La Porte could not quit the Louvre. She had not a soul in the world in whom she could trust.

In the prospect of the ruin which was hanging over her, and the desolation which she experienced, the queen gave way to tears and sobs.

" Cannot I be of any service to your majesty? " said a voice, full of gentleness and pity.

The queen turned eagerly, for there could be no deception in the expression of that voice: it was the voice of a friend.

In fact, at one of those doors which opened into the queen's apartment, appeared the pretty Madame Bonancieux. She had been engaged arranging dresses and linen in a closet when the king entered, and, being unable to get out, had heard the whole of the conversation.

The queen uttered a cry on seeing herself surprised ; for, in her agitation, she did not recognise the young woman who had been given to her by La Porte.

" Oh, do not be afraid," said Madame Bonancieux,

joining her hands, and crying herself, at the queen's agony. "I am your majesty's slave, in body and in soul; and far as I am below you, inferior as my position may be, I believe that I have found a way of relieving your majesty from your difficulty!"

"You? oh, Heaven! you!" exclaimed the queen. "But let me see you, let me look you in the face. I am betrayed on all sides: may I confide in you?"

"Oh! madame!" said the young woman, falling on her knees, "oh! doubt me not. On my soul, I am ready to die for your majesty."

This exclamation came from the very depths of the heart, and it was impossible to distrust it.

"Yes," continued Madame Bonancieux, "there are traitors here; but, by the blessed name of the Virgin, I swear to you, that there is no one more devoted to your majesty than I am. Those diamond studs that the king has mentioned, you gave to the Duke of Buckingham, did you not? They were within the little rosewood casket which he carried under his arm. Am I mistaken? Is it not as I have said?"

"Oh! my God, my God!" muttered the queen, her teeth chattering with affright.

"Well, these studs," said Madame Bonancieux, "must be got back again."

"Yes, without doubt," said the queen; "but how can it be done? How can we succeed?"

"Some one must be sent to the duke."

"But who? who? None can be trusted."

"Have confidence in me, madame: do me this honour, my queen, and I will find a messenger."

"But it will be necessary to write!"

"Oh, yes, that is indispensable. But two words from your majesty's hand, and under your own private seal, will serve."

"But those two words! They will be my condemnation—divorce! exile!"

"Yes, if they fall into the wrong hands. But I will

undertake that these two words shall be delivered according to their address."

"Oh! my God! must I then entrust my life, my honour, my reputation, to your hands?"

"Yes! yes, madame, you must, and I will preserve them all."

"But how? Tell me that, at least."

"My husband has been set at liberty these two or three days. I have not yet had time to see him. He is a worthy, honest man, incapable of hatred or love. He will do what I wish: he will set out at my request, without knowing what he carries; and he will deliver your majesty's letter, without even knowing it is your majesty's, to the address which it may bear."

The queen seized the young woman's hands with a passionate impulse, looked at her as if to read the depths of her heart, and then, seeing nothing but sincerity in her beautiful eyes, kissed her tenderly.

"Do this," exclaimed she, "and you will have saved me my life and my honour!"

"Oh! do not exaggerate the service which I have the honour to render you. I have nothing to save for your majesty. You are only the victim of treacherous plots."

"It is true, it is true, my child," said the queen; "you are right."

"Give me this letter, then, madame, for time presses."

The queen ran to a small table, on which there were pens, ink, and paper, and wrote two lines, which she sealed with her own seal, and handed to Madame Bonancieux.

"And now," said the queen, "we forget one thing, which is very necessary."

"And what is that, madame?"

"Money."

Madame Bonancieux blushed.

"Yes, it is true," said she; "and I will confess to your majesty that my husband——"

"Your husband has none. Is that what you would say?" said the queen.

"Yes, he has got it, but he is very avaricious : that is his chief fault. Nevertheless, let not your majesty be uneasy; we will find means."

"And I have got none either;" (those who may read the memoirs of Madame de Motteville will not be astonished at this reply) "but wait a minute!"

The queen ran to her jewel-box.

"Here," said she; "here is a ring of great value, as I am assured. It was given me by my brother, the King of Spain; it is mine, and I may dispose of it. Take this ring, convert it into money, and let your husband set out."

"In one hour you shall be obeyed."

"You see the address," said the queen, speaking so low that she could scarcely be heard—"*To my Lord Duke of Buckingham, London.*"

"The letter shall be delivered to himself alone!"

"Generous child!" exclaimed Anne of Austria.

Madame Bonancieux kissed the queen's hand, concealed the letter in her bosom, and disappeared with the lightness of a bird.

In ten minutes she was at her own house. She had not seen her husband since his liberation, as she had told the queen, and was therefore ignorant of the change which had taken place in him regarding the cardinal— a change which his eminence's flattery and money had effected, and which had been strengthened by two or three visits from Rochefort, who had become Bonancieux's best friend, having persuaded him that the abduction of his wife had proceeded from no culpable sentiment, but was merely a political precaution.

She found M. Bonancieux alone. The poor man was with great difficulty restoring some order to his house, where he had found the furniture almost destroyed, and the chests mostly empty ;—justice not being one of the three things which King Solomon points out as leaving no traces of their course.   As for the servant-girl, she had fled on the arrest of her master.   Terror had taken such hold of the poor thing, that she never ceased walking until she had reached Burgundy, her native province.

The worthy mercer had, as soon as he reached home, announced his happy return to his wife, and she had replied by congratulations, and an assurance that the first moment she could snatch from her duties should be altogether devoted to a visit to him.

The first moment had been five days in arriving, which, in other circumstances, might have appeared rather long to Master Bonancieux; but he had ample food for reflection in the visit he had paid the cardinal, and in those which he had received from Rochefort; and it is well known that nothing makes the time pass so well as reflection.

And the reflections of Bonancieux were, besides, all of a rosy tint.   Rochefort called him his good friend, his dear Bonancieux, and did not cease to tell him that the cardinal thought very highly of him.   The mercer already saw himself on the high road to honours and fortune.

On her part, Madame Bonancieux had reflected also; but, it must be confessed, on other things than ambition. In spite of all she could do, her thoughts would turn towards that handsome young man, who was so brave, and seemed to be so full of love.   Married at eighteen, and having always lived in the midst of her husband's friends, who were but little calculated to excite the affections of one whose sentiments were more elevated than her station, Madame Bonancieux had remained insensible to all vulgar impressions.

But, at that period more particularly, the title of gentleman had great influence over the citizens; and d'Artagnan was a gentleman, and, besides, wore the uniform of the guards, which, except that of the musketeers, was the most highly appreciated by the fair sex.   He was, moreover, young, handsome, and adventurous; and he talked of love like one who loved, and is eager to be loved in return. All this was more than enough to turn a heart of twenty-three years of age; and Madame Bonancieux had just arrived at that period of her life.

The happy married couple, although they had not met for more than eight days, and during that time some grave events had happened, addressed each other with a certain pre-occupation of mind. Nevertheless, M. Bonancieux manifested sincere joy, and advanced towards his wife with open arms.

Madame Bonancieux offered her forehead to be kissed.

"Let us have a little talk," said she.

"What!" said the astonished Bonancieux.

"Yes, certainly. I have something of the greatest importance to tell you."

"Really! and I have some questions of importance to put to you. Explain to me your abduction, I beg of you."

"That is of no consequence just now," said Madame Bonancieux.

"And what is this affair of consequence, then? Is it about my imprisonment?"

"I heard of that on the same day; but, as you were guilty of no crime, as you were connected with no intrigue, and as you knew nothing that could compromise you, I only attached to that event the importance which it merited."

"You speak of it with little concern, madame," replied Bonancieux, hurt at the slight interest which his wife manifested in him. "Do you not know that I was incarcerated for one day and one night in a dungeon of the Bastile?

"A night and a day are soon passed. But let us have done with your captivity, and return to the object of my return to you."

"What! the object of your return to me! Then is it

not the desire of seeing your husband, from whom you have been separated for eight days?" demanded the mercer, cut to the quick.

"It is that first, and something else afterwards."

"Speak!"

"An affair of the very greatest importance; on which, perhaps, our future fortune may depend."

"Our fortune has a very different look since I saw you last, Madame Bonancieux; and I should not wonder if, some months hence, it should excite the envy of many."

"Yes, particularly if you will follow the instructions which I am going to give you."

"Me?"

"Yes, you. There is a good and sacred action to be performed, sir, and much money to be gained at the same time."

Madame Bonancieux knew that, in speaking to her husband of money, she attacked his weak side. But a man, even a mercer, when he has conversed ten minutes with a Cardinal Richelieu, is no longer the same man.

"Much money to be gained?" said Bonancieux, pouting.

"Yes, a great deal."

"About how much?"

"A thousand pistoles, perhaps."

"Then what you are going to ask of me is of serious consequence?"

"Yes."

"What must I do?"

"Set out immediately. I will give you a paper, which you will not let out of your own possession under any pretence whatever, and which you will deliver to the proper person."

"And where am I to go?"

"To London."

"I go to London! Come, now, you are joking. I have no business at London."

"But others have business for you there."

"Who are these others? I tell you, beforehand, I will do nothing in the dark; and I wish to know, not only to what I expose myself, but also for whom I expose myself."

"An illustrious person sends you, and an illustrious person will receive you: the recompense will surpass your desires, and this is all that I can concede you."

"Intrigues again! nothing but intrigues! Thank you, I am now somewhat distrustful of them: the cardinal has rather enlightened me on that subject."

"The cardinal," cried Madame Bonancieux; "have you seen the cardinal?"

"He sent for me," proudly answered the mercer.

"And were you imprudent enough to accept his invitation?"

"I ought to say that I had not the choice whether I would accept it or not, for I was between two guards. It is true, also, that as I did not then know his eminence, I should have been greatly delighted if I could have avoided the visit."

"And he treated you ill—he threatened you?"

"He gave me his hand and called me his friend," said Bonancieux: "his friend! do you hear, madame, I am the friend of the great cardinal?"

"Of the great cardinal!"

"But perhaps you will not allow him that title, madame?"

"I dispute nothing; but I tell you, that the favour of a minister is ephemeral; that he must be mad who attaches himself to one. There are powers above a minister's which do not rest on the caprice of one man, or the issue of one event; and it is to these powers that one ought to cleave."

"I am very sorry, madame, but I know no other power than that of the great man whom I have the honour to serve."

"You serve the cardinal?"

"Yes, madame; and, as his servant, I will not permit

you to engage in plots which compromise the safety of
the state, or to assist the intrigues of a woman who is not
French, but Spanish, in her soul. Happily, the great
cardinal is there : his vigilant eye watches and penetrates
the very depths of the heart."

Bonancieux was repeating, word for word, a sentence
he had heard from the Count de Rochefort ; but the poor
woman, who had entirely relied upon her husband, and
had, in this hope, stood surety for him to the queen, did
not the less shudder, both at the danger from which she
had just escaped, and the utter helplessness of her
present state. And yet, knowing the weakness, and,
above all, the avarice of her husband, she did not despair
of leading him into her schemes.

"Ah ! you are cardinalist, sir ! " cried she ; "ah ! you
serve the party who ill-uses your wife, and insults your
queen !"

"The interests of individuals are nothing in comparison
to the interests of the public. I am for those who serve
the state !" said Bonancieux emphatically.

This was another of Rochefort's phrases which he had
retained, and now made use of at the first opportunity.

"And do you know what the state you speak of is ?"
asked Madame Bonancieux, shrugging her shoulders.
"Be content at being a private citizen, and cling to that
side which offers you the greatest advantages."

"Ah ! ah !" said Bonancieux, striking a bag whose
goodly paunch gave out a silvery sound ; "what do you
say to this, Mistress Preacher ?"

"Where did this money come from ?"

"Can't you guess ?"

"From the cardinal ?"

"From him, and from my friend the Count de
Rochefort."

"The Count de Rochefort ! Why, that is the man
who carried me off !"

"Possibly, madame !"

"And do you accept money from such a man ?"

"Did you not tell me that this abduction was entirely political?"

"Yes: but then it was designed to make me betray my mistress—to drag from me, by tortures, confessions which might compromise the honour, and perhaps the life, of my august mistress."

"Madame," said Bonancieux, "your august mistress is a perfidious Spaniard; and the cardinal does only what is quite right."

"Sir," said the young woman, "I knew that you were cowardly, avaricious, and imbecile, but I did not know that you were infamous."

"Madame," said Bonancieux, who had never before seen his wife angry, and who recoiled before this conjugal rage; "madame, what are you saying?"

"I say that you are a wretch!" continued Madame Bonancieux, who saw that she was recovering some influence over her husband. "Ah! you are a politician! and, moreover, a cardinalist politician! Ah, you sell yourself, both body and soul, to the devil for gold!"

"No, but to the cardinal."

"No difference," cried the young woman. "He who says Richelieu, says Satan."

"Hold your tongue, madame; hold your tongue: you might be heard!"

"Yes, you are right, and I should be ashamed for any one to know your cowardice!"

"But what do you require of me, then? Let me hear!"

"I have told you that you should set off this instant for London, sir; and should loyally and truly perform the commission with which I condescend to entrust you. On this condition, I forget and forgive everything; and what is more," she added, holding out her hand, "I restore to you my affection!"

Bonancieux was a coward, and a miser; but he loved his wife and was therefore subdued.

A man of fifty cannot long be cross with a woman of

three-and-twenty.   Madame Bonancieux saw that he hesitated.

"Come," said she; "have you determined?"

"But, my dear woman, reflect a little on what you require of me. London is a long way from Paris—a very long way. And perhaps the business may involve some dangers."

"What does that signify, if you escape then?"

"Well, then," said the mercer, "listen, Madame Bonancieux. I decidedly refuse. Intrigues frighten me. I have seen the Bastile. Oh! it is frightful, that Bastile! It makes my flesh creep, only to think of it. I was threatened with the torture. Do you know what the torture is? Wedges of wood, which they drive alongside your legs till the very bones split! No, most decidedly, I will not go. Why the deuce do you not go yourself? for, really, I begin to think I must have been mistaken about you until now. I suspect that you are a man, and a very violent one too!"

"And you! you are a very woman—a miserable, stupid, soulless woman. What! you are afraid! Well, then, if you do not set out this instant, I will have you arrested by order of the queen, and clapped into that Bastile which you dread so much."

Bonancieux sunk into a deep consideration. He carefully balanced the two enmities in his brain—that of the cardinal against that of the queen: but the cardinal's preponderated enormously.

"Have me arrested by the queen!" said he; "well, I will get myself liberated through his eminence."

Madame Bonancieux saw that she had gone too far this time, and she trembled at her own rashness. She looked with terror for an instant at this stupid figure, as invincible in its obstinacy as all fools who are in fear.

"Well, then," said she, "so let it be. Perhaps, after all, you are right: a man sees further in politics than a woman does, and you more particularly, M. Bonancieux, who have chatted with the cardinal. And yet it is very hard," continued she, " that my husband, that a man on whose affection I thought I could rely, should treat me so unkindly, and not satisfy my request."

" It is because your requests may lead too far," said Bonancieux triumphantly, " that I distrust them ! "

" I renounce them, then," said the young woman, with a sigh ; " let us talk no more about them."

" If you would only tell me what I was to do in London," resumed Bonancieux, who remembered, somewhat too late, that Rochefort had advised him to worm out all his wife's secrets.

" It is unnecessary that you should know it, ' said the young woman, who was now restrained by an instinctive distrust ; " it was about a trifle such as women sigh for —about a purchase by which money might be gained."

But the more the young woman defended it, the more important did Bonancieux esteem the secret which she refused to confide to him. He determined, therefore, to go immediately to the Count de Rochefort, and tell him that the queen was seeking for a messenger to send to London.

" Pardon me, if I leave you, my dear Madame Bonancieux," said he, " but not knowing that you were coming to see me, I had made an appointment with one of my friends. I will return directly. If you will only wait half a minute for me, as soon as I have done with this friend, I will return ; and, as it begins to get late, I will accompany you to the Louvre."

" Thanks, sir," said Madame Bonancieux ; " you are not brave enough to be any protection whatever to me, and I will return alone to the Louvre."

" As you please, Madame Bonancieux," replied the ex-mercer. " Shall I see you again soon ? "

" Certainly. Next week I hope that I shall have a little liberty, and I will take advantage of it, to come and put our things in some order. They must be a good deal deranged."

"Very well ; I shall expect you. Have you any further commands for me ? "

" Me ? none in the world."

" *Au revoir*, then."

" *Au revoir*."

Bonancieux kissed his wife's hand, and hastened away.

" So," said Madame Bonancieux, when her husband had shut the street door, and she found herself alone— " so, nothing remained for that fool but to become a cardinalist ! And I, who answered for him to the queen —I who promised my poor mistress—ah ! my God ! my God ! she will take me for one of those wretches who swarm the palace, and who are placed about her as spies. Ah ! M. Bonancieux, I never loved you much, but it is worse than that now ! I hate you ; and, upon my word, you shall pay for this ! "

At the moment that she uttered these words, a knock on the ceiling made her raise her head, and a voice, which came through the floor, called out to her—

" Dear Madame Bonancieux, open the little door in the alley, and I will come down to you."

CHAPTER XVIII.

THE LOVER AND THE HUSBAND.

"Ah, madame," said d'Artagnan, as he entered the door which the young woman opened for him, " allow me to tell you that you have but a sorry husband."

" What ! have you heard our conversation ? " eagerly demanded Madame Bonancieux, looking anxiously at d'Artagnan.

" Every word of it."

" But, good God ! how could you ? "

" By a plan of my own, whereby I also heard the more animated conversation which you had with the cardinal's myrmidons."

"And what did you understand from what we said?"

"A thousand things. First, that your husband is, happily, a fool and a blockhead; I am heartily glad of this, since it gives me an opportunity of engaging myself in your service; and God knows I am willing to throw myself in the fire for you. Then, that the queen wants some brave, intelligent, and devoted man, to go to London for her. I have, at least, two of the three qualifications which you require, and here I am."

Madame Bonancieux did not answer, but her heart beat with joy, and a secret hope sparkled in her eyes.

"And what security will you give me," she demanded "if I consent to entrust you with this commission?"

"My love for you. Come, speak; command: what is there to be done?"

"My God! my God!" uttered the young woman, "ought I to confide such a secret to you, sir? You are almost a child!"

"Oh! I see, you want some one who will answer for me."

"I confess that it would give me more confidence."

"Do you know Athos?"

"No."

"Porthos?"

"No."

"Aramis?"

"No. Who are these gentlemen?"

"They belong to the king's musketeers. Do you know M. de Treville, their captain?"

"Yes, him I do know—not personally, but from having heard him mentioned to the queen as a brave and honourable gentleman."

"You would not fear that he would betray you for the cardinal?

"Certainly not."

"Well, then, reveal to him your secret, and ask him whether, however important, however precious, however terrible it may be, you may not entrust it safely to me."

"But this secret is not mine, and I must not thus disclose it."

"You were going to confide it to M. Bonancieux,' said d'Artagnan, with some sharpness.

"As one would confide a letter to a hollow tree, to the wing of a pigeon, or the collar of a dog."

"And yet you know that I love you."

"You say so."

"I am an honourable man."

"I believe it."

"I am brave."

"Oh! of that I am sure."

"Put me to the proof, then."

Madame Bonancieux looked at the young man, restrained only by a last, lingering hesitation. But there was so much ardour in his eyes, and so much persuasiveness in his voice, that she felt constrained to trust him. Besides, she was in one of those positions in which it is necessary to run great risks for the sake of great results. The queen might be as certainly lost by too much caution, as by too much confidence. We must confess, also, that the involuntary sentiment which she experienced for this young protector determined her to speak.

"Listen," said she; "I yield to your protestations and assurances; but I swear to you, before God, who hears us, that if you betray me, and my enemies let me escape, I will destroy myself, and accuse you of my death."

"And I swear to you, before God, madame," said d'Artagnan, "that if I am seized whilst performing the orders you may give me, I will die sooner than do or say anything to compromise any one."

Then the young woman confided to him the terrible secret, part of which had been by chance disclosed to him opposite the Samaritan.

This was their declaration of mutual love. D'Artagnan glowed with joy and pride. This secret which he possessed, this woman whom he loved—the confidence and the love made him a giant.

"I am off," said he. "I am off directly."

"What! you are going? And what about your regiment? your captain?"

"Upon my life, you made me forget all about them, dear Constance. Yes, you are right; I must get leave of absence."

"Another obstacle!" murmured Madame Bonancieux sorrowfully.

"Oh," said d'Artagnan, after a moment's reflection, "I shall easily manage that, never fear."

"How so?"

"I will interview M. de Treville this evening, and will request him to ask this favour for me of his brother-in-law, M. des Essarts."

"Now for another thing, said Madame Bonancieux. "And what is that?" inquired d'Artagnan, seeing that she hesitated.

"Perhaps you have got no money?"

"Take away the '*perhaps*,'" said d'Artagnan, with a smile.

"Then," said Madame Bonancieux, opening a chest, and taking from it the bag which her husband had so lovingly caressed half an hour before, "take this bag."

"That which belonged to the cardinal!" exclaimed d'Artagnan, with a hearty laugh, as, thanks to the uplifted squares, he had not lost one syllable of the conversation between the mercer and his wife.

"Yes, the cardinal's," replied Madame Bonancieux; "you see that it makes a very imposing appearance."

"Egad!" cried d'Artagnan, "it will be doubly amusing to save the queen with his eminence's money."

"You are an amiable and charming young man," said Madame Bonancieux; "and depend upon it, her majesty will not prove ungrateful."

"Oh! I am abundantly rewarded already," said d'Artagnan. "I love you, and you allow me to tell you so; and even this is more happiness than I had dared to hope for."

"Hush!" said Madame Bonancieux, starting.

"What is the matter?"

"Some one is speaking in the street."

"It is the voice——"

"Of my husband. Yes, I recognise it."

D'Artagnan ran and bolted the door.

"He shall not enter till I am gone," said he; "and when I have left, you will open the door."

"But I ought to be gone too; and the disappearance of this money—how am I to explain it, if I am here?"

"You are right—we must both go."

"Go? but how? He will see us if we go out."

"Then we must go up to my room."

"Ah!" exclaimed Madame Bonancieux, "you say that in a tone that frightens me."

Madame Bonancieux pronounced these words with tearful eyes. D'Artagnan perceived the tear, and threw himself upon his knees in deep emotion.

"On the word of a gentleman," said he, "in my room you shall be as sacred as in a temple."

"Let us go, then, my friend," said she; "I trust in that word."

D'Artagnan carefully unfastened the bolt, and both, light as shadows, glided through the inner door into the court, and, noiselessly ascending the stairs, entered d'Artagnan's chamber.

Once in his own room, the young man, for greater security, barricaded the door; and then they both went to the window, and, through a chink of the shutter, saw M. Bonancieux talking to a man in a cloak.

At the sight of the man in the cloak, d'Artagnan made a spring, and, partly drawing his sword, rushed towards the door.

It was the man of Meung.

"What are you going to do?" cried Madame Bonancieux; "you will ruin us all."

"But I have sworn to kill that man!" said d'Artagnan.

"Your life is at present consecrated, and does not belong to you. In the queen's name, I forbid you to throw yourself into any danger beyond that of the journey."

"And in your own name do you command nothing?"

"Yes, in my own name," said Madame Bonancieux, with emotion; "in my own name, I entreat you. But listen: I think they are talking about me."

D'Artagnan approached the window, and listened.

M. Bonancieux had opened his door, and finding the room empty, had returned to the man in the cloak, whom he had left for an instant alone.

"She is gone," said he; "she must have returned to the Louvre."

"You are quite sure," replied the stranger, "that she had no suspicion of your object in going out?"

"No," said Bonancieux, with much self-complacence; "she is a woman of too superficial an intellect."

"And the young guardsman—is he at home?"

"I do not think he is. As you may perceive, his shutter is closed, and there is no light in his room."

"Never mind; we had better make certain."

"How so?"

"By rapping at his door. I will ask his servant."

"Go!"

Bonancieux re-entered his room, passed through the same door which had just given egress to the two fugitives, ascended to d'Artagnan s landing-place, and knocked.

No one answered. Porthos, in order to make a display, had borrowed Planchet for that evening; and as for d'Artagnan, he was careful to give no sign of his presence.

At the moment that Bonancieux's knock resounded on the door, the two young people felt their hearts bound.

"There is no one at home," said Bonancieux.

"Let us go into your room, nevertheless; we shall be in greater privacy than at the door."

" Ah ! my God," said Madame Bonancieux, " we shall not hear any more."

" On the contrary," said d'Artagnan, " we shall hear all the better."

D'Artagnan lifted up the three or four squares which made another St. Denys's ear of his chamber, laid a piece of carpet on the floor, kneeled down upon it, and then made a sign to Madame Bonancieux to lean, as he was doing, over the aperture.

" You are sure that there is no one ? " said the stranger.

" Quite," said Bonancieux.

" And you think that your wife——"

" Is returned to the Louvre."

" Without speaking to any other person than yourself ? "

" I am sure of it."

" It is a point of the greatest importance : do you understand ? "

" Then the intelligence I have given you is of some value ? "

" Very great, my dear Bonancieux ; I would not disguise it to you."

"Then the cardinal will be satisfied with me."

" I do not doubt it."

" The great cardinal ! "

" You are quite sure that, in her conversation with you, your wife mentioned no names ? "

" I am almost sure."

" She did not mention either Madame de Chevreuse, or the Duke of Buckingham, or Madame de Vernel ? "

" No ; she merely said that she wished to send me to London, in the service of an illustrious person."

" The traitor ! " muttered Madame Bonancieux.

" Hush ! " said d'Artagnan, taking her hand, which she gave up to him without a thought.

" Never mind," said the man in the cloak ; " you are a blockhead for not pretending to accept the commission;

then you would have had the letter in your possession. The state, which is in danger, would have been saved, and you——"

"And I?"

"Well! and you—the cardinal would have given you letters of nobility."

"Did he tell you so?"

"Yes, I know that he wished to surprise you with this present."

"Be easy," replied Bonancieux, "my wife adores me, and there is plenty of time yet."

"The ninny!" whispered Madame Bonancieux.

"Be quiet!" said d'Artagnan, pressing her hand more closely.

"What! is there yet time?" said the man in the cloak.

"I shall proceed to the Louvre, ask for Madame Bonancieux, say that I have considered the affair, obtain the letter, and hasten to the cardinal."

"Well! go quickly. I will soon return, to know the result of your proceedings."

The stranger then departed.

"The wretch!" said Madame Bonancieux, referring to her husband.

"Silence!" said d'Artagnan, again pressing her hand, and this time yet more warmly.

A terrible hullaballoo interrupted the reflections of d'Artagnan and Madame Bonancieux.

It was her husband, who had just discovered the loss of his bag, and was exclaiming against the robber.

"Oh, my God!" exclaimed Madame Bonancieux: "he will awaken all the neighbourhood."

Bonancieux cried out for a long time; but, as such cries were of common occurrence, they attracted no attention in the Rue des Fossoyeurs; and as the mercer's house was, moreover, in no very good repute, finding that nobody came to his help, he went out, still uttering his outcries, which they heard gradually dying away in the direction of the Rue du Bac.

"And, now that he is gone, it is your turn to depart," said Madame Bonancieux. "Be brave, but, above all, be prudent, and remember that you serve the queen."

"The queen, and you!" exclaimed d'Artagnan. "Be assured, beautiful Constance, that I shall return worthy of her gratitude; but shall I return worthy, also, of your love?"

The young woman only replied by the glowing blush that mantled on her cheek. After a few moments, d'Artagnan went out in his turn, enveloped in a long cloak, which was cavalierly thrust backward by the sheath of his enormous sword.

Madame Bonancieux followed him with that long look of affection which woman fixes on the man she loves; but, as soon as he had turned the corner of the street, she sank upon her knees, and, joining her hands, exclaimed—

"Oh, my God! preserve the queen, and preserve me!"

CHAPTER XIX.

THE PLAN OF THE CAMPAIGN.

D'ARTAGNAN went straight to M. de Treville. He had reflected that the cardinal would, in a few minutes, be put upon his guard by that cursed stranger, who appeared to be his agent, and he very wisely thought that there was not a moment to lose.

The heart of the young man overflowed with joy. An adventure was presented to him, by which both gold and glory might be won, and which, as a first encouragement, brought him into communication with the woman he adored. This chance had thus given to him, at once, more than he had even dared to solicit from Providence.

M. de Treville was in his saloon, surrounded by his usual circle of gentlemen. D'Artagnan, who was known as an intimate of the house, went directly to his cabinet, and asked to speak to him on business of importance.

He had scarcely been there five minutes before M. de Treville entered. At the first glance, and from the joy which sparkled in d'Artagnan's eyes, the worthy captain at once perceived that some new scheme was really in his mind.

On his way there, d'Artagnan had been considering whether he should confide in M. de Treville, or merely ask for a free leave of absence for a secret expedition. But M. de Treville had always been so kind to him, was so entirely devoted to the king and queen, and so cordially hated the cardinal, that the young man determined to tell him all the affair.

"You sent for me, my young friend?" said M. de Treville.

"Yes, sir," said d'Artagnan, "and you will pardon me, I hope, for having disturbed you, when you know the importance of the occasion."

"Speak, then. I am all attention."

"It is nothing less," said d'Artagnan, speaking low, "than that the honour—and perhaps the life—of the queen is at stake."

"What are you saying," said M. de Treville, looking round, to be certain that they were alone.

"I say, sir, that chance has made me master of a secret."

"Which you will guard with your life, I hope, young man."

"But which I ought to impart to you, sir; for you alone can assist me in the mission which has just been entrusted on behalf of her majesty."

"Is this secret your own?"

"No, sir, it is the queen's."

"Are you authorised by the queen to impart it to me?"

"No, sir; for, on the contrary, the most profound secrecy is recommended."

"And why, then, are you about to betray it to me?"

"Because, as I tell you, without you I am powerless ; and I fear that you will refuse me the favour which I come to solicit, unless you know the purpose for which it is solicited."

"Keep your secret, young man, and tell me what you want."

"I wish you to obtain for me, from M. des Essarts, a leave of absence for fifteen days."

"When?"

"This very night."

"Do you leave Paris?"

"I go on a mission."

"Can you tell me where?"

"To London."

"Has any one an interest in preventing the success of your design?"

"The cardinal, I believe, would give all the world to prevent that success."

"And do you go alone?"

"Yes."

"In that case, you will not get past Bondy. It is I who tell you so, on the word of Treville."

"And why so?"

"You will be assassinated."

"I shall die doing my duty."

"But your mission will not be performed."

"That is true," said d'Artagnan.

"Believe me," said M. de Treville, "in every enterprise of this kind, there ought to be four at least, in order that one may succeed."

"Ah! sir, you are right," said d'Artagnan; "but you know Athos, Porthos, and Aramis, and you can judge whether I may employ them."

"Without imparting to them the secret, which I should rather not know?"

"We have sworn to one another, once for all, a blind confidence, and a devotion proof against all trials ; besides, you can tell them that you have the fullest confidence in me, and they will not be more incredulous than yourself."

"I can give each of them a leave of absence for fifteen days, and that is all :—to Athos, who still suffers from his wound, to go to the waters of Forges ; and to Porthos and Aramis, to follow their friend, whom they do not wish to abandon in his melancholy condition.   My sending their leave will be a proof that I authorise the expedition."

"Thank you — a thousand thanks, sir, for your goodness !"

"Go, and find them, then, immediately ; and let everything be settled this very night.   But, first, write me your request to M. des Essarts.   Perhaps you had a spy at your heels, and your visit, which is in that case already known to the cardinal, will be thus accounted for."

D'Artagnan wrote his request in due form ; and M. de Treville, as he received it from him, assured him that before two in the morning the four furloughs should be at the respective homes of the travellers.

"Have the goodness to send mine to the lodgings of Athos," said d'Artagnan.   "I should be afraid of some disagreeable encounter if I returned home again."

"Don't be uneasy.   Farewell, and a good journey to you," said M. de Treville ; "but," added he, recalling him, "apropos——"

D'Artagnan returned.

"Have you got any money ?"

D'Artagnan replied by shaking the bag which he had in his pocket.

"Have you enough ?" said M. de Treville.

"Three hundred pistoles."

"That will do : you might go to the end of the world with that."

D'Artagnan bowed to M. de Treville, and pressed the hand which he offered him with respect, mingled with gratitude.   From the time of his arrival in Paris, this excellent man had been uniformly entitled to his highest esteem: he had found him always consistent, honourable, and elevated.

His first visit was to Aramis. He had not been to his friend's lodgings since the evening when he had followed Madame Bonancieux; and, what is more, he had scarcely seen him since; but whenever he had met him he fancied that he saw a corroding sorrow stamped upon his countenance.

This evening, also, Aramis was sorrowful and dreamy. D'Artagnan put some questions to him concerning this continual melancholy; but Aramis ascribed it to a commentary on the eighteenth chapter of St. Augustin, which he was obliged to write in Latin by the following week, and which much occupied him.

When the two friends had been talking some time, a servant of M. de Treville brought a sealed packet.

"What is that?" demanded Aramis.

"The leave of absence which monsieur has demanded," replied the servant.

"Me? I have not demanded a leave."

"Hold your tongue, and take it," said d'Artagnan. "And here, my friend, here is half a pistole for your trouble; you will tell M. de Treville that M. Aramis very sincerely thanks him. Go."

The servant bowed to the ground, and left the room.

"What does all this mean?" inquired Aramis.

"Pack what you may want for a fifteen days' journey, and follow me."

"But I cannot leave Paris at present, without knowing——"

Aramis stopped himself.

"What is become of _her_? is that not it?" continued d'Artagnan.

"Whom?" resumed Aramis.

"The lady who was here—the lady with the embroidered handkerchief."

"Who told you there was a lady here?" said Aramis, becoming as pale as death.

"I saw her."

"And do you know who she is?"

"I think I have a fair idea, at least."

"Listen," said Aramis: "since you know so many things, do you know what has become of this lady?"

"I presume that she has returned to Tours."

"To Tours? Yes! that may be; you evidently know her. But how is it that she returned to Tours, without saying anything to me about it?"

"Because she was in fear of being arrested."

"Why did she not write to me?"

"Because she was afraid of compromising you."

"D'Artagnan, you give me new life!" cried Aramis. "I believed that I was despised; deceived. I was so happy to see her again! I could not believe that she had hazarded her liberty to see me; and yet for what other cause could she have returned to Paris?"

"For the same cause which this day obliges us to go to England."

"And what is that cause?" demanded Aramis.

"You shall know it some day, Aramis; but, for the present, I will imitate the discretion of *the doctor's niece.*"

Aramis smiled, for he remembered the tale he had told his friends on a certain evening.

"Well, then, since she has left Paris—and you are sure of it, d'Artagnan—nothing more detains me here, and I am ready to follow you. You say we are going——"

"To Athos, at present; and, if you wish to come, I beg you will make haste, for we have already lost too much time. *Apropos*, tell Bazin."

"Does Bazin accompany us?" inquired Aramis.

"Perhaps so. At any rate, it is better that he should follow us to Athos."

Aramis called Bazin, and after having told him to come to them at Athos's—

"Let us go, then," said he, taking his cloak, his sword, his pistols, and fruitlessly opening three or four drawers in hopes of finding a few stray pistoles. Then, when he was quite satisfied that this search was useless, he followed d'Artagnan, wondering how it was that the young guardsman knew, as well as he did, who the lady was to whom he had afforded hospitality, and knew better than he did where she was now gone.

Just as they were going out, he laid his hand on d'Artagnan's arm, and looking earnestly at him—

"You have not spoken to any one about this lady?" said he.

"To no one in the world."

"Not even to Porthos and Athos?"

"I have not breathed a word to them about it."

"That's right."

Satisfied on that important point, Aramis went on his way with d'Artagnan, and they both soon reached Athos's lodgings.

They found him holding his leave of absence in one hand, and M. de Treville's letter in the other.

"Can you explain to me," said he, "what these mean that I have just received?"

"MY DEAR ATHOS,—I very much wish, as your health absolutely requires it, that you should repose yourself for fifteen days. Go, therefore, and take the waters of Forges, or any others which may agree better with you, and get well quickly. Yours affectionately,   TREVILLE."

"Well," said d'Artagnan, "the leave and the letter mean that you must follow me."

"To the waters of Forges?"

"There or elsewhere."

"On the king's service?"

"The king's or the queen's. Are we not the servants of both?"

At this moment Porthos entered.

"Egad!" said he, "here's a curious circumstance. Since when have they granted leave to the musketeers, without their asking for it?"

"Ever since they have had friends who ask it for them," said d'Artagnan.

"Ah! ah!" said Porthos, "it appears that there is something fresh in the wind."

"Yes, we are off," said Aramis.

"To what country?" demanded Porthos.

"Upon my word, I do not know exactly," said Athos; "ask d'Artagnan."

"To London, gentlemen," said d'Artagnan.

"To London," said Porthos; "and what are you going to do there?"

"And that is what I cannot tell you, gentlemen; you must trust to me."

"But, to go to London money is necessary, and I have none," said Porthos.

"Nor I," said Aramis.

"Nor I," said Athos.

"I have," said d'Artagnan, lugging his treasure out of his pocket and laying it on the table. "There are in that bag three hundred pistoles; let each of us take seventy-five, which is quite enough to go to London and to return. Besides, be easy; we shall not all reach London."

"And why not?"

"Because, according to all probability, some of us will be left on the road."

"Is it a campaign, then, that we are about to undertake?"

"Yes, and a most dangerous one, I forewarn you."

"Ah! but, since we risk our lives, I, at least, would rather know the object," said Porthos.

"That will do you a mighty deal of good," replied Athos.

"Nevertheless," said Aramis, "I am of the same opinion as Porthos."

"Pray," said d'Artagnan, "does the king usually give you his reasons? He tells you bluntly—gentlemen, they are fighting in Gascony, or in Flanders; go, and fight; and you go. As for any reasons—you do not trouble your heads about them."

"D'Artagnan is right," said Athos. "Behold our three leaves of absence, which come from M. de Treville;

and here are three hundred pistoles, which come from I know not where. Let us go and be killed where we are told to go. Is life worth so many questions? D'Artagnan, I am ready to follow you."

"And I also," said Porthos.

"And I also," said Aramis. "I shall not be sorry to leave Paris, after all. I need distractions."

"Well, you will have quite enough of them, gentlemen, depend upon it!" said d'Artagnan.

"And, now, when must we set off?" inquired Athos.

"Directly," said d'Artagnan; "not a minute must be lost."

"Hollo, Grimaud, Planchet, Mousqueton, Bazin!" bawled out the four young men, calling their servants: "polish our boots, and fetch our horses from the hotel."

In fact, each musketeer left at the general hotel, as at a barrack, his own horse and that of his servant.

Planchet, Mousqueton, Grimaud, and Bazin, departed in the utmost haste.

"Now, let us arrange the plan of the campaign," said Porthos. "Where are we to go first?"

"To Calais," said d'Artagnan; "it is the most direct line to London."

"Well," said Porthos, "my advice is as follows——"

"Speak! What is it?"

"Four men travelling together will be suspected. D'Artagnan must therefore give his instructions to each of us. I will go first, by way of Boulogne, to clear the road; Athos shall set out, two hours after, by that of Amiens; Aramis will follow us by that of Noyou; and as for d'Artagnan, he will travel by that which he likes best, in Planchet's clothes; whilst Planchet himself shall follow, in the uniform of the guards, to pass for d'Artagnan."

"Gentlemen," said Athos, "my advice is not to include the servants in anything of this kind; a secret may, *perchance*, be betrayed by gentlemen; but is almost always sold by servants."

"The plan of Porthos appears to me to be impracticable," said d'Artagnan, "as I do not myself know what instructions I could give you. I am the bearer of a letter — that is all. I have not, and I cannot make, three copies of this letter, since it is sealed. We must, therefore, in my opinion, travel in company. This letter is here, in this pocket;" and he pointed out the pocket which contained the letter. "If I am killed, one of you will take it, and will continue the journey; if he is killed, it will be another's turn; and so on. Provided only one should arrive, it is all that is necessary."

"Bravo, d'Artagnan! Your advice is also mine," said Athos. "Nevertheless, we must be consistent. I am going to take the waters, and you will accompany me; but instead of going to Forges, I am going to the seaside: I may take my choice. If anybody wants to arrest us, I show M. de Treville's letter, and you will show your leaves of absence: if they attack us, we will defend ourselves; if they interrogate us, we must maintain sharply that we had no other intention than to dip ourselves a certain number of times in the sea. They would have too easy a conquest over four separate men; whilst four men united make a troop. We will arm our four servants with musquetoons and pistols; and if they send an army against us, we will give battle, and the survivor, as d'Artagnan has said, will deliver the letter."

"Well done," said Aramis: "you do not speak often, Athos; but when you do speak, it is like St. John with the golden mouth. I adopt the plan of Athos."

"And you, Porthos?"

"And I also," said Porthos, "if it suits d'Artagnan. As the bearer of the letter, he is naturally the leader of the enterprise. Let him decide, and we will execute."

"Well, then," said d'Artagnan, "I decide that we adopt the plan of Athos, and that we set out in half an hour."

"Agreed!" exclaimed the three musketeers, in chorus.

And each, plunging his hand into the bag, took from it seventy-five pistoles, and made his preparations to depart at the appointed time.

CHAPTER XX.

THE JOURNEY.

At two o'clock in the morning our four adventurers left Paris, by the Porte St. Denis. Whilst the darkness lasted they continued silent. In spite of themselves, they felt the influence of the obscurity, and suspected an ambuscade at every step.

With the first streak of day, their tongues became unbound, and gaiety returned with the sun. It was as on the eve of battle: the heart beat, and the eyes sparkled; and they felt that the life which they were, perhaps, about to leave, was, after all, a pleasant and a precious thing.

The appearance of the cavalcade was of the most formidable character: the black horses of the musketeers, their martial bearing, and that military custom which made these noble chargers march in rank, were all indications of their calling, which would have betrayed the strictest incognito.

The valets followed, armed to the teeth.

All went on well as far as Chantilly, where they arrived at about eight in the morning, and where they were obliged to breakfast. They dismounted at a tavern, which was recommended by the sign of St. Martin, giving half his cloak to a beggar. They ordered their servants not to unsaddle their horses, and to be ready to depart at a moment's notice.

They entered the common room of the inn, and placed themselves at table. A gentleman, who had arrived by the Dampmartin road, was seated at the table, breakfasting. He entered into conversation, concerning the rain and the fine weather. The travellers replied: he drank to their healths, and they returned his politeness. But at the moment when Mousqueton came to announce that the horses were ready, and as they arose from table, the stranger proposed to Porthos, to drink the cardinal's health. Porthos replied, that he desired nothing better, provided the stranger would, in turn, drink the health of the king. The stranger exclaimed, that he knew no other king than his eminence. On this, Porthos told him he must be drunk, and the stranger drew his sword.

"You have done a foolish thing," said Athos; "but never mind; you cannot draw back now: kill the fellow, and come after us as fast as you can."

And all three mounted their horses and departed at full speed; whilst Porthos promised his adversary to perforate him in all the fashions known to the fencing school.

"There goes one of us," said Athos, after they had travelled five hundred paces.

"But why did that man attack Porthos, rather than the others?" said Aramis.

"Because, from Porthos speaking louder than the rest of us, he took him for the leader of the party," said d'Artagnan.

"I always said," muttered Athos, "that the Gascon youth was a well of wisdom."

The travellers proceeded on their way.

At Beauvais they stopped two hours, as much to breathe their horses, as to wait for Porthos. At the end of that time, as neither Porthos nor any intelligence of him had arrived, they resumed their journey.

About a league from Beauvais, at a point where the way was narrowed between two banks, they met eight or ten men, who, taking advantage of the road being unpaved at this place, seemed to be engaged in digging holes, and making muddy ruts.

Aramis, fearing to dirty his boots in this artificial slough, apostrophised them rudely. Athos wished to restrain him, but it was too late. The workmen began to rail at the travellers; and, by their insolence, even ruffled the temper of the cool Athos, who urged his horse against one of them.

At this aggression, each of these men drew back to the ditch, and took from it a musket that was concealed there. The result was, that our seven travellers were literally riddled by shot. Aramis received a ball through the shoulder, and Mousqueton another in the fleshy part of the back, below the loins. But Mousqueton alone fell from his horse; not that he was seriously wounded, but that he could not see his wound, he no doubt thought it far more dangerous than it really was.

"This is an ambuscade," said d'Artagnan: "let us not burn priming, but away."

Aramis, wounded as he was, seized the mane of his horse, which carried him off with the others. That of Mousqueton had rejoined them, and galloped riderless by their side.

"That will give us a spare horse," said Athos.

"I should much prefer a hat," said d'Artagnan, "for mine has been carried off by a ball. It is very lucky, faith, that my letter was not within it."

"Ah! but they will kill poor Porthos, when he comes up," said Aramis.

"If Porthos were upon his legs, he would have rejoined us ere this," said Athos. "It is my opinion, that, in the combat, the drunkard grew sober."

They galloped on for two more hours, although the horses were so fatigued, that it was to be feared they would break down on the way.

The travellers had made a detour by cross-roads, hoping thereby to be less molested; but, at Crevecœur, Aramis declared that he could go no farther. In fact, it had required all the courage which he concealed beneath his elegant form and polished manners, to proceed so far. At each movement he grew paler; and they were at last obliged to support him on his horse. Putting him down at the door of a wine-shop, and leaving with him Bazin, who was more hindrance than help in a skirmish, they set off again, in hopes of reaching Amiens, and passing the night there.

"Zounds!" said Athos, when they found themselves once more upon the way, reduced to two masters, with Grimaud and Planchet, "Zounds! I will be their dupe no more. I promise you that they shall not make me open my mouth, or draw my sword, between here and Calais. I swear——"

"Don't swear," said d'Artagnan, "but gallop; that is, if our horses will consent to it."

And the travellers dug their spurs into the flanks of their horses, which, thus urged, recovered some degree of strength. They reached Amiens at midnight, and dismounted at the sign of the Golden Lily.

The innkeeper had the look of the most honest fellow upon earth. He received the travellers with a candle-stick in one hand, and his cotton nightcap in the other. He wished to lodge the two travellers, each in a charming chamber; but, unfortunately, these two chambers were at opposite extremities of the hotel. D'Artagnan and Athos declined them. The host objected, that he had no others worthy of their excellencies; but they declared that they would rather sleep in the common room, on mattresses, upon the floor. The host insisted, but the travellers were obstinate, and carried their point.

They had just arranged their beds, and barricaded the door, when some one knocked at the shutters. They inquired who was there, and, on recognising the voices of their servants, opened the window. It was indeed Planchet and Grimaud.

"Grimaud will be quite able to guard the horses," said Planchet, "and, if the gentlemen like, I will sleep across their door, by which means they will be certain that no one can get at them."

"And on what will you sleep?" asked d'Artagnan.

"This is my bed," replied Planchet, strewing a bundle of straw.

"Come, then," said d'Artagnan, "you are quite right: the countenance of our host does not at all please me; it is far too polite."

"Nor me, either," said Athos.

Planchet got in at the window, and laid himself across the doorway; whilst Grimaud shut himself up in the stable, promising that at five in the morning he and the four horses should be ready.

The night passed quickly enough. Some one attempted, about two o'clock, to open the door; but, as Planchet awoke with a start, and cried out, "Who is there?" he was answered that it was a mistake; and then the footsteps retreated.

At four in the morning a great noise was heard from the stables. Grimaud had endeavoured to awake the ostlers, and they had made an attack upon him. When the window was opened, they saw the poor fellow lying senseless, with his head split open by a blow from a broom handle.

Planchet went into the courtyard, and wanted to saddle the horses, but the horses were completely foundered. That of Grimaud, which had travelled for five or six hours with an empty saddle the evening before, might have continued its journey; but, by an inconceivable mistake, the veterinary surgeon, whom they had brought, as it appeared, to bleed the landlord's horse, had bled that of Grimaud instead.

This began to be vexatious. All these successive accidents were perhaps the result of chance; but they might also be the effect of design. Athos and d'Artagnan stepped out, whilst Planchet went to inquire whether there were three horses to be sold in the neighbourhood. At the door were two horses ready saddled, fresh, and vigorous. This was just the thing. He asked where their masters were; and was informed that they had passed the night there, and were now paying their bill.

Athos went down to settle their account, whilst d'Artagnan and Planchet remained at the door. The innkeeper was in a distant lower room, which Athos was requested to enter.

Athos went in confidently, and took out two pistoles to

pay. The host was alone, and seated at his desk, one of the drawers of which was partly open. He took the money which Athos gave him, turned it over in his hands, and suddenly exclaiming that the pieces were bad, declared that he would have him and his companion arrested as passers of false coin.

"You rascal," said Athos, as he went towards him, "I will cut off your ears."

But the host stooped down, and taking two pistoles from the drawer, presented them at Athos, vociferating, at the same time, for help.

At that very moment, four men, armed to the teeth, rushed in through the side doors, and fell upon Athos.

"I am seized!" bawled Athos, with the utmost strength of his lungs; "away with you, d'Artagnan; spur on! spur on!" and he fired off his two pistols.

D'Artagnan and Planchet did not wait to be twice warned. They unfastened the two horses which were standing at the door, jumped upon them, dug the spurs into their flanks, and went off at full gallop.

"Do you know what has become of Athos?" asked d'Artagnan, as they hurried on.

"Oh, sir," said Planchet, "I saw two men fall at his two shots, and it seemed to me, through the window, as if he were working away at the others with his sword."

"Brave Athos!" ejaculated d'Artagnan. "And then to know that I must abandon you! Well! the same thing awaits us, perhaps, at ten paces hence. Forward! Planchet, forward! You are a brave fellow."

"I told you so, sir," replied Planchet; "the Picards are only known by being used. Besides, I am in my own country here, and that stimulates me."

And both of them, spurring on as fast as possible, arrived at St. Omer without a moment's stay. At St. Omer they breathed their horses, with their bridles looped on their arms for fear of accident, and ate a morsel standing in the street; after which they again set off.

At a hundred paces from the gate of Calais, d'Artagnan's

horse fell, and could by no means be got up again; the blood gushed from his eyes and nose. That of Planchet still remained; but he had chosen to halt, and nothing could induce him to continue his exertions.

Fortunately, as we have said, they were only a hundred paces from the town. They therefore left the two steeds upon the high road, and ran to the harbour. Planchet made his master remark a gentleman who had just arrived with his lackey, and was not above fifty yards before them.

They hastily drew near this gentleman, who appeared to be exceedingly busy. His boots were covered with dust, and he inquired whether he could not pass over to England instantaneously.

"Nothing easier," replied the master of a vessel then ready for sailing, "but an order arrived this morning to let no one leave without permission from the cardinal."

"I have got that permission," said the gentleman, drawing a paper from his pocket; "there it is."

"Get it countersigned by the governor of the port," said the master of the vessel, "and give me the preference."

"Where thall I find the governor?"

"At his country house."

"And where is his country house situated?"

"At a quarter of a league from the town: see, you may distinguish it from here—yonder slated roof, at the foot of the little hill."

"Very well," said the gentleman; and, followed by his servant, he took the road to the governor's country house.

D'Artagnan and Planchet followed him, at the distance of five hundred yards.

Once out of the town, d'Artagnan hurried forwards, and made up on the gentleman as he entered a small wood.

"Sir," said d'Artagnan, "you appear in particular haste?"

"No one can be more so, sir."

"I am very sorry for it," said d'Artagnan, "for, as I am in a hurry also, I want you to render me a favour."

"What is it?"

"To let me pass the Straits before you."

"Impossible!" said the gentleman. "I have done sixty leagues in forty-four hours, and I must be in London by noon to-morrow."

"And I," said d'Artagnan, "have gone the same distance in forty hours, and must be in London by ten o'clock to-morrow."

"Sorry to disappoint you, sir; but I have got here first, and will not go over second."

"I am grieved also, sir," said d'Artagnan, "but I have got here second, and mean to go over first."

"The king's service!" said the gentleman.

"My own service!" replied d'Artagnan.

"But, it seems to me, that this is a poor quarrel which you are seeking to make?"

"Zounds! what would you have it?"

"What do you want?"

"Do you want to know?"

"Certainly."

"Very well! I want the order that you have in your pocket, as I have none, and must have one."

"I presume you are joking."

"I never joke!"

"Let me pass, sir."

"You shall not pass."

"My gallant, I will blow your brains out. Hollo! Lubin, my pistols."

"Planchet," said d'Artagnan, "take care of the man— I will manage the master."

Planchet, encouraged by what had already happened, rushed upon Lubin, and as he was strong and vigorous, laid him on his back, and put his knee upon his breast.

"Do your business, sir," said Planchet to his master, "I have settled mine."

Seeing this, the gentleman drew his sword, and fell on

d'Artagnan; but he had to do with rather a tough customer.

In three seconds d'Artagnan gave him three wounds, saying, at each thrust—

"One for Athos, one for Porthos, and one for Aramis."

At the third stroke the gentleman fell like a log.

D'Artagnan thought he was dead, or at least that he had fainted, and approached him to seize the order; but, at the moment that he stretched out his hand to search for it, the wounded man, who had not dropped his sword, stabbed him with it on the chest, saying—

"One for you!"

"And one more for you! and the best last!" cried d'Artagnan, furiously pinning him to the earth with a fourth wound through the body.

This time the gentleman closed his eyes and fainted.

D'Artagnan felt in the pocket where he had seen him place the order for his passage, and took it. It was in the name of the Count de Wardes.

Then, throwing a last glance on the handsome young man, who was scarcely twenty-five years old, and whom he left lying there senseless, and perhaps dead, he breathed a sigh at the strange destiny which leads men to destroy each other for the interests of those they scarcely know, and who often are not even aware of their existence.

But he was soon disturbed in these reflections by Lubin, who was howling with all his might, and crying for aid.

Planchet put his hand upon his throat, and squeezed it as hard as he could.

"Sir," said he, "as long as I hold him so, he will not cry out; but the moment I leave go, he will begin again. I can see he is a Norman, and the Normans are monstrously obstinate."

In fact, squeezed as he was, Lubin still endeavoured to sound his pipes.

"Stop!" said d'Artagnan; and, taking his handkerchief, he gagged him.

"Now," said Planchet, "let us bind him to a tree."

The thing was properly done. They then placed the Count de Wardes near his servant; and, as the night began to fall, and as both the bound man and the wounded one were some paces in the wood, it was clear that they must remain there till the next morning.

"And now," said d'Artagnan, "to the house of the governor."

"You are wounded, I fear?" said Planchet.

"It is nothing: let us now think of what is of the most consequence; we can attend to my wound afterwards; besides, it does not appear to be very dangerous."

And they both proceeded, with prodigious strides, towards the country house of the worthy functionary.

The Count de Wardes was announced.

D'Artagnan was introduced.

"Have you an order signed by the cardinal?" asked the governor.

"Yes, sir," said d'Artagnan, "here it is."

"Ah! ah! it is regular and explicit," said the governor.

"That is quite natural," answered d'Artagnan; "I am one of his most faithful servants."

"It appears that his eminence wishes to hinder some one from reaching England."

"Yes, a certain d'Artagnan, a Bearnese gentleman, who left Paris with three of his friends, intending to go to London."

"Do you know him personally?" inquired the governor.

"Whom?"

"This d'Artagnan."

"Perfectly well."

"Give me some description of him, then."

"Nothing is easier."

And then d'Artagnan gave, feature for feature, the exact description of the Count de Wardes.

"Has he any attendant?" demanded the governor.

"Yes, a servant named Lubin."

"We will watch for them, and, if we can lay hands upon them, his eminence may be assured that they shall be sent back to Paris, under a sufficient escort."

"In so doing, sir," said d'Artagnan, "you will merit the gratitude of the cardinal."

"Will you see him on your return, count?"

"Without doubt."

"Tell him, I beseech you," said the governor, "that I am his most humble servant."

"I will not fail to do so."

Delighted by this assurance, the governor countersigned the order, and returned it to d'Artagnan; who lost no time in useless compliments, but, having bowed to him and thanked him, took his leave.

Once out of the house, they took a circuitous path to avoid the wood, and entered the town by another gate.

The barque was still ready to sail, and the master waited on the quay.

"Well?" said he, seeing d'Artagnan.

"Here is my pass countersigned."

"And the other gentleman."

"He is not going over to-day," said d'Artagnan; "but make yourself easy, I will pay for the passage of both."

"In that case, let us be off," said the master.

"Away, then!" cried d'Artagnan; and he and Planchet springing into the boat, in five minutes they were on board the vessel.

It was full time, for when they were a half league out at sea, d'Artagnan saw a flash, and heard a detonation; it was the sound of the cannon that announced the closing of the port.

It was now time to think about his wound. Happily it was, as d'Artagnan had supposed, not at all dangerous; the point of the sword had struck against a rib, and glanced along the bone; and, as the shirt had stuck to the wound at once, scarcely a drop of blood had flowed.

D'Artagnan was overpowered with fatigue; and a

mattress being spread for him on the deck, he threw himself upon it and slept.

The next morning, at break of day, he found himself at not less than three or four leagues from the shores of England. The wind had been gentle during the night, and they had made but little progress.

At two o'clock they cast anchor in the harbour of Dover, and at half past two d'Artagnan landed in England, exclaiming—

"Here I am, at last."

But this was not enough; he must get to London. In England posting was pretty well regulated. D'Artagnan and Planchet took each a post-horse; a postillion galloped before them; and in a few hours they reached the gates of London.

The duke was hunting, at Windsor, with the king.

D'Artagnan knew nothing of London; he knew not one word of English; but he wrote the word *Buckingham* on a piece of paper, and every one could direct him to the mansion of the duke.

D'Artagnan inquired for the duke's confidential valet, who, having accompanied him in all his journeys, spoke French perfectly. He told him that he came from Paris on an affair of life and death, and that he must speak with his master without an instant's delay.

The confidence with which d'Artagnan spoke satisfied Patrick (for that was the name of the minister's minister). He ordered two horses to be saddled, and took upon himself the charge of guiding the young guardsman. As for poor Planchet, they had taken him off his horse as stiff as a stake. The poor fellow was quite exhausted; but d'Artagnan seemed to be made of iron.

They reached Windsor Castle, where they learned that the king and the duke were out hawking, in some marshes, two or three miles off.

In twenty minutes they reached the place. Patrick heard his master's voice, calling his hawk.

"Whom shall I announce to my lord?" said Patrick.

"The young man," said d'Artagnan, "who sought a quarrel with him one evening on the Pont Neuf, opposite the Samaritan."

"A strange recommendation," said Patrick.

"You will see that it is as good as any one could be."

Patrick gave his horse the rein, reached the duke, and told him, in the very words which we have just used, that a messenger awaited him.

Buckingham at once remembered d'Artagnan; and fearing that something had happened in France, of which information had been sent to him, he only gave himself time to ask where the messenger was; and having recognised the uniform of the guards at that distance, he rode at full speed straight up to d'Artagnan. Patrick judiciously kept himself in the background.

"No misfortune has befallen the queen?" cried Buckingham.

"I think not, sir; but I believe that she is in great danger, from which your grace alone can rescue her."

"I," said Buckingham; "and how shall I be sufficiently happy to render her any service? Speak! speak!"

"Take this letter," said d'Artagnan.

"This letter! and from whom comes this letter?"

"From her majesty, I believe."

"From her majesty," said Buckingham, growing so pale that d'Artagnan thought he was about to fall.

And he broke the seal.

"What is this rent?" asked he, showing d'Artagnan a place where it was pierced through.

"Ah!" said d'Artagnan, "I did not perceive it before: the sword of the Count de Wardes must have done that, when it was boring a hole in my chest."

"Are you wounded?" inquired Buckingham.

"Oh! a mere trifle," said d'Artagnan — "a mere scratch."

"Just Heaven! what have I read?" exclaimed Buckingham. "Patrick, remain here—or, rather, find the king, wherever he may be, and tell his majesty that I humbly beseech him to excuse me, but that an affair of the very greatest importance calls me to London. Come, sir, come."

And both took their way to the capital at full gallop.

CHAPTER XXI.

THE COUNTESS DE WINTER.

As they hurried on, the duke heard from d'Artagnan, not really all that had occurred, but all that d'Artagnan himself knew. By putting together what fell from the lips of the young man, and what was supplied by his own recollections, he was enabled to form a pretty exact idea of that position, of the seriousness of which the queen's letter, short as it was, afforded abundant proof. But what most astonished him was that the cardinal, interested as he was that this youth should not set foot in England, had not managed to stop him on his way. It was then, and on the expression of this astonishment, that d'Artagnan related to him the precautions which had been taken, and how, thanks to the devotion of his three friends, whom he had left bleeding here and there upon the road, he had managed to get off with merely the wound which had pierced the queen's letter, and which he had so terribly repaid to M. de Wardes. Whilst listening to this account, given with the greatest simplicity, the duke looked from time to time on the young man with astonishment, as if he could not comprehend how so much prudence, courage, and devotion, could be combined with a countenance which did not yet show the traces of twenty years.

The horses went like the wind, and they were soon at the gates of London. D'Artagnan had supposed that, on entering the town, the duke would slacken his pace; but he did not: he continued his course at the same rate, caring little for upsetting those who were in

his way. In fact, in passing through the city, two or
three accidents of this kind happened; but Buckingham
did not even turn his head to see what had become of
those he had knocked over. D'Artagnan followed him,
in the midst of cries which sounded very much like
maledictions.

On entering the courtyard of his mansion, Buckingham
jumped off his horse, and, without caring what became
of him, threw the bridle over his neck, and rushed
towards the staircase. D'Artagnan did the same, with
somewhat more uneasiness, nevertheless, for these noble
animals, whose merit he appreciated; but he had the
satisfaction of seeing three or four servants hurrying
from the kitchens and stables, and immediately laying
hold of the horses. The duke walked so quickly, that
d'Artagnan had some difficulty in following him. He
passed through many saloons, magnificent to a degree
which the most distinguished nobles of France could not
even imagine, and came at last to a bed-chamber, which
was at once a miracle of taste and splendour. In the
alcove of this chamber, there was a door in the tapestry,
which the duke opened by a small golden key, which he
carried suspended at his neck by a chain of the same
metal. Through politeness, d'Artagnan remained behind;
but at the moment that Buckingham stepped over the
threshold of this door, he turned, and perceiving the
hesitation of the young man—

"Come," said he, "and if you have the happiness of
being admitted into the presence of the queen of France,
tell her what you have beheld."

Encouraged by this invitation, d'Artagnan followed
the duke, who closed the door behind him.

They found themselves in a small chapel, splendidly
illuminated by a profusion of wax lights, and carpeted
with Persian silk carpets, embroidered with gold.
Above a kind of altar, and under a dais of blue velvet,
surmounted by red and white plumes, there was a
portrait, of the size of life, representing Anne of Austria,

and so perfectly resembling her, that d'Artagnan uttered a cry of surprise on seeing it: one would have believed that the queen was just about to speak.

On the altar, and under the portrait, was the casket which contained the diamond studs.

The duke approached the altar, and, after kneeling as a priest might do before the cross, opened the casket.

"Here," said he, drawing from the casket a large piece of blue riband, all glittering with diamonds—"here are those precious studs, with which I had made an oath to be buried. The queen gave them to me: she now takes them away: her commands, like those of Heaven, shall be obeyed in everything."

Then he began to kiss, one by one, the diamonds, from which he was about to part; but suddenly he uttered a terrible cry.

"What is the matter?" demanded d'Artagnan in alarm; "what has befallen you, my lord?"

"All is lost!" said Buckingham, becoming as pale as death. "Two of the studs are gone; there are but ten."

"Has your grace lost them, or do you suppose that they have been stolen?"

"Some one has stolen them," replied the duke; "and it is the cardinal who has managed it. See, the ribands which held them have been cut with scissors."

"Has your grace any suspicion as to who has committed the theft? Perhaps the person has still got them."

"Stop, stop!" said the duke. "The only time I have worn these studs was at a ball at Windsor, a week ago. The Countess de Winter, with whom I had been on cold terms, approached me during the ball. This appearance of reconciliation was really the vengeance of an offended woman. Since that day I have not seen her. That woman is an agent of the cardinal's."

"What! has he got agents, then, all over the world?" asked d'Artagnan.

"Oh, yes," replied Buckingham, grinding his teeth

with rage; "yes, he is a terrible adversary. But, yet, when will this ball take place?"

"Next Monday."

"Next Monday! Five more days; it is more time than we shall need. Patrick!" exclaimed the duke, opening the door of the chapel, "Patrick!"

His confidential valet appeared.

"My jeweller, and my secretary!"

The valet departed, with a silent promptitude, which proved the habit he had acquired of blind and dumb obedience.

But, although the jeweller had been the first sent for, it was the secretary who, as he resided in the mansion, came first. He found Buckingham seated before a table, and writing some orders with his own hand.

"Jackson," said he, "you will go to the Lord Chancellor, and tell him that I charge him with the execution of these orders. I desire them to be made public immediately."

"But, my lord duke, if the Lord Chancellor should question me about the motives which have induced your grace to adopt so extraordinary a measure, what am I to answer?"

"That such is my pleasure, and that I am not obliged to give to anybody an account of my motives."

"Is that to be the reply which he is to transmit to the king," replied the secretary, smiling, "if by chance his majesty should have the curiosity to inquire why no vessel must weigh anchor in a British port?"

"You are right, sir," answered Buckingham; "he will, in that case, tell the king that I have decided on war, and that this measure is my first act of hostility against France."

The secretary bowed and departed.

"There, we may be quite easy on that point," said Buckingham, turning towards d'Artagnan. "If the studs have not yet gone to France, they will not arrive till after you."

"How so?"

"I have just laid an embargo on the ships at present in his majesty's ports, and, without express permission, not one will dare to raise its anchor."

D'Artagnan looked with wonder at the man who thus employed, in the service of his love, the unlimited power with which he was entrusted by the king.

Buckingham saw, from the expression of his countenance, what was passing in the youth's mind, and smiled.

"Yes," said he, "yes, it is Anne of Austria who is my true queen: at her lightest word I would betray my country—my king—my God! She desired of me not to send to the Protestants of la Rochelle the aid that I had promised them, and she has been obeyed. I forfeited my word; but of what consequence was that, whilst her will was gratified? Say, was I not nobly recompensed for my obedience, since it was to that obedience that I owe her portrait?"

D'Artagnan marvelled at the fragile unseen threads on which the destinies of nations and the lives of men may sometimes be suspended.

He was immersed in these reflections, when the jeweller entered. He was an Irishman, but one who was most skilful in his calling, and who confessed that he gained a hundred thousand livres a year by the Duke of Buckingham.

"O'Reilly," said the duke, conducting him to the chapel, "look at these diamond studs, and tell me what they are worth a-piece."

The goldsmith glanced at the elegant manner in which they were mounted, calculated one by one the value of the diamonds, and without hesitation replied—

"Fifteen hundred pistoles each, my lord."

"How many days would be required to make two studs like those? You see that two are wanting."

"A week, my lord."

"I will pay three thousand pistoles each for them, but I must have them the day after to-morrow."

"Your grace shall have them."

"You are an invaluable man, O'Reilly, but this is not all : these studs must not be entrusted to any one ; it is necessary that some one should make them in this house."

"Impossible, my lord. I am the only person who can make them, so that no one could discover the difference between the new and the old studs."

"Therefore, my dear O'Reilly, you are my prisoner, and even if you wished to leave my palace now, you could not. Tell me which of your workmen you want, and describe the tools which they must bring you."

The jeweller knew the duke, and that all remonstrances would be useless. He therefore made up his mind at once.

"May I inform my wife?" said he.

"Oh! you may even see her, my dear O'Reilly," said the duke : "your captivity shall not be harsh, I assure you ; and, as every inconvenience should have its recompense, here is a present of a thousand pistoles, beyond the price of the two studs, to make you forget the annoyance you may experience."

D'Artagnan could not recover from the surprise which he felt at the minister, who made such a profuse use of men and millions.

As for the jeweller, he wrote to his wife, sending her the order for a thousand pistoles, and requesting her to send him in exchange his most skilful apprentice, and an assortment of diamonds, of which he sent her the weight and description, along with a list of the requisite tools.

Buckingham conducted the jeweller to the chamber prepared for him, which was, in half an hour, converted into a workshop. He then placed a sentinel at each door, with strict orders to allow no one to pass except his valet, Patrick. It need scarcely be added, that O'Reilly and his assistant were absolutely forbidden to go out, on any pretext whatever.

This being arranged, the duke turned to d'Artagnan.

"Now, my young friend," said he, "England belongs to us two. What do you desire?"

"A bed," answered d'Artagnan. "I confess that, at present, that is what I stand most in need of."

Buckingham allotted d'Artagnan a room which adjoined his own. He wished to keep the young man at his side; not that he distrusted him, but that he might have some one to whom he could constantly talk about the queen.

An hour afterwards the order was posted throughout London, that no ship would be permitted to leave the ports for France—not even the packet-boat with letters. In everybody's opinion, this was a declaration of war between the two kingdoms.

At eleven o'clock on the second day, the diamond studs were finished, and so exactly imitated, such perfect fac-similes, that Buckingham himself could not distinguish the new one from the old. Even the most skilful in such matters would have been deceived as he was.

He immediately summoned d'Artagnan.

"Here," said he, "are the diamond studs which you have come to fetch; and witness for me that I have done everything which human powers could accomplish."

"Rest assured, my lord, that I will truly represent what I have seen. But your grace gives me the studs without the casket."

"The casket would only encumber you. Besides, the box is the more precious to me, now that I have nothing else. You will say that I preserve it."

"I will perform your commission, my lord, to the letter."

"And now," said Buckingham, looking earnestly at the young man, "how can I ever repay my debt to you?"

D'Artagnan blushed, even to the white of his eyes. He saw that the duke wanted to find some means of making him a present; and the idea that his own blood, and that of his companions, should be paid for in English gold, was strangely repugnant to him.

"Let us understand one another, my lord," said d'Artagnan, "and state the case fairly, that there may be no misconception. I am in the service of the king and queen of France, and belong to the guards of M. des Essarts, who, as well as M. de Treville, is more particularly attached to their majesties. Everything that I have done has therefore been for the queen, and not at all for your grace. And more than that, perhaps I should not have taken a single step in the affair, if it had not been to please some one, who is as dear to me as the queen is to you."

"Yes," said the duke, "and I believe that I know who that person——"

"My lord, I have not named her," said d'Artagnan quickly.

"It is true," replied the duke. "I must therefore be grateful to that person for your devotion."

"Just so, my lord; for, now that we are about to go to war, I confess that I see nothing in your grace but an Englishman, and, consequently, an enemy, whom I should be still more delighted to meet on the field of battle, than in the park at Windsor, or in the galleries of the Louvre. This, however, will not prevent me from executing every particular of my mission, and welcoming death, if need be, in its accomplishment; but I repeat to your grace, that you have nothing more to thank me for, in this second interview, than for what I have already done for you in the first."

"We say, in our country, 'proud as a Scotchman,'" muttered Buckingham.

"And we," answered d'Artagnan, "say, 'proud as a Gascon.' The Gascons are the Scotchmen of France."

D'Artagnan bowed to the duke, and was about to take his leave.

"Well!" said the duke, "are you going in that manner! But what course will you take? How will you get off?"

"True."

"Egad! you Frenchmen stick at nothing."

"I had forgotten that England is an island, and that your grace is its king."

"Go to the port, ask for the brig *Sund*, and give this letter to the captain. He will take you to a small harbour, where you will certainly not be expected, and where few but fishing-boats go."

"And the name of this harbour is——"

"St. Valery. But listen:—when you are landed there, you will go to a wretched wine-shop, without either name or sign, a true sailor's boozing-ken; you cannot mistake it, for there is but one."

"And then?"

"You will ask for the host, and you will say to him, '*Forward*.'"

"What does that mean?"

"It is the watchword which commands him to assist you on your way. He will give you a horse ready saddled, and show you the road that you must take; and you will, in this manner, find four relays upon your road. If you please, at each of them, to give your address at Paris, the four horses will follow you there; you already know two of them, and appear to have estimated them as an amateur. They are those which we rode, and you may trust me that the others are not inferior. These four horses are equipped for the field. Proud as you are, you will not refuse to accept one, and to present the three others to your companions. Besides, they are to help you in fighting against us. The end justifies the means, as you French say—do you not?"

"Yes, my lord, I accept your presents," said d'Artagnan; "and, God willing, we shall make good use of them."

"Now, give me your hand, young man. Perhaps we may soon meet on the field of battle; but, in the meantime, I hope we part good friends."

"Yes, my lord, but with the hope of soon being enemies."

"Be contented; I give you my promise that we shall."

"I depend upon your grace's word."

D'Artagnan bowed to the duke, and hastened towards the port.

Opposite the Tower of London he found the vessel to which he had been directed, and gave his letter to the captain, who got it countersigned by the governor of the port, and then prepared to sail immediately.

Fifty vessels were waiting, in readiness to sail. On passing one of them, side by side, d'Artagnan thought he saw the woman of Meung—the same whom the unknown gentleman had called *my lady*, and whom he himself had thought so beautiful; but, thanks to the current and the favourable breeze, his vessel glided on so swiftly, that in a few minutes it had left the others far behind.

The next morning, about nine o'clock, he landed at St. Valery.

D'Artagnan immediately went to the appointed wine shop, which he recognised by the outcries from within. The war between France and England was spoken of as certain, and the joyous sailors were making merry.

D'Artagnan pushed through the crowd, approached the host, and pronounced the word '*forward.*' The host immediately made him a sign to follow him, went out by a door which led into the courtyard, conducted him to the stables, where there stood a horse, ready saddled, and then asked him whether he needed anything else.

"I want to know the road I am to take," said d'Artagnan.

"Go from this place to Blangy, and from Blangy to Neufchatel. At Neufchatel go to the tavern of the Golden Harrow; give the password to the innkeeper, and you will find, as here, a horse ready saddled."

"Have I anything to pay?" asked d'Artagnan.

"Everything is paid," said the host, "and most liberally. Go, then, and God protect you!"

"Amen!" said the young man, as he galloped off.

In four hours he was at Neufchatel.

Strictly following his instructions at Neufchatel, as at St. Valery, he found a saddled horse awaiting him; and when he was about to transfer the pistols from the one saddle to the other, he perceived that the holsters were already duly furnished.

"Your address at Paris?"

"D'Artagnan—Hotel des Gardes, company des Essarts."

"Very good," answered the innkeeper.

"What road am I to take?" demanded d'Artagnan.

"That of Rouen: but you will pass the town on your right. At the little village of Écouis you will halt. There is but one tavern, the French Crown. Do not judge of it from its looks; for it will have in its stables a horse of equal value with this."

"The same watchword?"

"Exactly."

"Adieu, master."

"A good journey, sir. Do you require anything else?"

D'Artagnan said no, by a shake of his head, and went off again at full speed. At Ecouis, the same scene was enacted. He found a host equally well prepared, a horse equally fresh and ready. He left his address as before, and departed in the same way for Pontoise. At Pontoise he changed his horse for the last time; and, at nine o'clock, he entered the courtyard of M. de Treville's hotel, at full gallop.

He had got over nearly sixty leagues in twelve hours.

M. de Treville received him just as though he had seen him the same morning, only pressing his hand a little more warmly than usual. He informed him that the company of M. des Essarts was on guard at the Louvre, and that he might repair to his post.

CHAPTER XXII.

THE BALLET OF "THE MERLAISON."

THE next morning nothing was talked of in Paris but the ball which the magistrates were to give to the king and queen, and in which their majesties were to dance the famous ballet of *The Merlaison,* which was the favourite ballet of the king.

For the last week every preparation had been in progress at the Hotel de Ville for this important entertainment. The city carpenter had erected scaffolding, on which the ladies who were invited were to be seated; the city chandler had furnished the rooms with two hundred wax lights, which was an unprecedented luxury at that time; and twenty violins had been engaged, at double the price usually paid, on the understanding that they were to play throughout the whole of the night.

At ten in the morning, the Sieur de la Coste, ensign of the king's guards, followed by two officers, and many archers of the guards, came to demand of Clement, the city-registrar, all the keys of the gates, chambers, and closets of the hotel. These keys were given to him immediately, each bearing a label indicating to what it belonged; and, from that moment, the Sieur de la Coste had the superintendence of all the doors and avenues.

Duhalier, the captain of the guards, came in his turn, at eleven o'clock, and brought with him fifty archers, who stationed themselves immediately at the respective doors which had been assigned to them in the Hotel de Ville.

At three o'clock, there arrived two companies of guards, one French, the other Swiss. The company of French guards was composed of equal numbers of the troops of M. Duhalier, and of M. des Essarts.

The company began to arrive at six o'clock, and were at once conducted to the places prepared for them in the grand saloon.

The lady of the first president arrived at nine o'clock. As she was, next to the queen, the most distinguished individual of the entertainment, she was received by the gentlemen of the city, and conducted to a box opposite to that of the queen.

At ten o'clock, a collation of sweetmeats was prepared for the king—in the small room on the side of the church of St. Jean—before the city's sideboard of silver, which was guarded by four archers.

At midnight, loud cries and multitudinous acclamations resounded through the streets. It was the king, who was proceeding from the Louvre to the Hotel de Ville, along thoroughfares illuminated throughout their length by coloured lamps.

The magistrates, clothed in their robes of cloth, and preceded by the sergeants, each holding a torch in his hand, hastened to receive the king, whom they met upon the steps, where the provost of the merchants complimented and welcomed him; to which his majesty replied by excuses for the lateness of his arrival, for which he blamed the cardinal, who had detained him till eleven o'clock, discoursing on affairs of state.

His majesty, in full dress, was accompanied by his royal highness the king's brother, the Count de Soissons, the Grand Prior, the Duke de Longueville, the Duke d'Elbeuf, the Count d'Harcourt, the Count de la Roche Guyon, M. de Liancourt, M. de Baradas, the Count de Cramail, and the Chevalier de Souveray.

Every one remarked that the king looked preoccupied and unhappy.

A closet had been prepared for the king, and a second one for his royal brother. In each of these closets were laid out masquerade dresses. A similar preparation had been made for the queen, and for the president's lady. The lords and ladies in their majesties' suite were to dress themselves, two by two, in apartments set aside for that purpose.

Before he entered his closet, the king desired to be

apprised of the cardinal's arrival as soon as it had taken place.

Half an hour after the arrival of the king, fresh acclamations resounded: these announced the arrival of the queen. The magistrates went through the same formalities as before, and, preceded by their sergeants, advanced to meet their illustrious guest.

The queen entered the room; and it was remarked that, like the king, she looked sad, and also weary.

The moment that she entered, the curtain of a small gallery, which had till then been closed, was opened, and the pale face of the cardinal appeared, clothed as a Spanish cavalier. His eyes fixed themselves on those of the queen, and a smile of terrible joy passed across his lips. The queen was there without her diamond studs.

Her majesty remained for a short time, receiving the compliments of the city gentlemen, and answering the salutations of the ladies.

Suddenly the king appeared, with the cardinal, at one of the doors of the saloon. The cardinal spoke to him in a low voice, and the king was very pale.

The king broke through the crowd, and without a mask, and with the ribands of his doublet scarcely tied, approached the queen, and, in an agitated voice, said—

"Madame, wherefore, I pray you, have you not on your diamond studs, when you knew that I wished to see them?"

The queen looked around her, and saw, behind the king, the cardinal, smiling with a satanic smile.

"Sire," replied the queen, in an agitated voice, "because, amidst this great crowd, I feared some accident might befall them."

"There you were wrong, madame. I made you this present in order that you might adorn yourself with it. I tell you that you were wrong."

The voice of the king trembled with anger. Every one looked, and listened with astonishment, not at all understanding this extraordinary scene.

"Sire," said the queen, "I can send for them from the Louvre, where they are; and thus the wishes of your majesty will be accomplished."

"Do so, madame, and that immediately; for in one hour the ballet will begin."

The queen bowed submissively, and followed the ladies who were to conduct her to her closet.

The king also retired to his.

There was a momentary excitement and confusion in the saloon. Every one could perceive that something had occurred between the king and queen; but both of them had spoken so low, that, as all had kept at a respectful distance, no one had heard anything. The violins played most strenuously, but no one attended to them.

The king left his closet first. He wore a most elegant hunting dress, and his brother and the other nobles were dressed in the same costume. This was the kind of dress most becoming to the king; and, thus habited, he truly seemed the first gentleman of his realm.

The cardinal approached the king, and gave him a box, in which his majesty found two diamond studs.

"What does this mean?" demanded the king.

"Nothing," answered the cardinal; "only, if the queen has the studs, which I must doubt, count them, sire, and if you only find ten, ask her majesty who can have robbed her of these two."

The king looked at the cardinal as if to ask what this meant; but he had not time to put any further questions. An exclamation of admiration burst from every lip. If the king appeared to be the first gentleman of his realm, the queen was indisputably the most beautiful woman in France.

It must be allowed, of course, that her costume of a huntress fitted her most charmingly. She wore a beaver hat with blue feathers, a robe of pearl gray velvet, fastened with diamond clasps, and a skirt of blue satin, embroidered with silver. Over her left shoulder glittered the studs, suspended by a bow of the same colour as the feathers and the skirt.

The king trembled with joy, and the cardinal with anger. Yet, distant as they were from the queen, they could not count the studs; and although the queen had them, the question was, were there ten or twelve?

At this moment the violins sounded the announcement of the ballet. The king advanced with the president's lady, with whom he was to dance; and his royal highness with the queen. They took their places, and the ballet began.

The king figured opposite the queen; and, as often as he passed her, he looked devouringly at the studs, which he could not manage to count. A cold moisture hung upon the cardinal's brow.

The ballet lasted an hour; there were sixteen figures. At its conclusion, amidst the applause of the whole assemblage, every one conducted his partner to her place; but the king profited by his privilege to leave his partner where she was, and advanced quickly towards the queen.

"I thank you, madame," said he, "for the deference you have paid to my wishes: but I believe you have lost two studs, and I bring them to you."

At these words, he offered her the two studs which he had received from the cardinal.

"What, sire," cried the queen, affecting surprise, "do you give me two more: why, that will make me have fourteen."

In fact, the king counted them, and found the twelve studs upon her majesty's shoulder.

The king summoned the cardinal.

"Well, what does all this mean, cardinal?" demanded the king, in a severe tone.

"It means, sire," answered the cardinal, "that I wished her majesty to accept these two studs; but, not daring myself to make her the offer, I have adopted this method."

F.C.TILNEY

"'What does this mean, Cardinal?'"

"And I am the more grateful to your eminence," replied the queen, with a smile that proved she was not the dupe of this ingenious gallantry, "as I am certain that these two studs have cost you more than the other twelve cost his majesty."

Then, having curtseyed to the king and the cardinal, the queen took her way to the chamber where she had dressed, and where she was now to remove her ball costume.

The attention which we have been obliged to bestow upon the illustrious personages introduced at the commencement of this chapter, has diverted us for a time from him to whom Anne of Austria was indebted for the unprecedented triumph which she had just gained over the cardinal, and who, obscure, unknown, and lost amidst the crowd at one of the doors, contemplated from that station a scene which was incomprehensible to all but four persons—the king, the queen, the cardinal, and himself.

The queen had returned to her apartment, and d'Artagnan was going to retire, when some one lightly touched his shoulder. He turned, and saw a young woman, who made a sign that he should follow her. This young woman wore a black velvet mask; but, in spite of that precaution, which, after all, was taken more against others than himself, he immediately recognised his ordinary guide, the gay and witty Madame Bonancieux.

They had met on the previous evening, but only for an instant, at the lodge of Germain, the Swiss, where d'Artagnan had inquired for her. The anxiety of the young woman to communicate the good news of her messenger's fortunate return to the queen, prevented the two lovers from exchanging more than a few words. On this account d'Artagnan followed Madame Bonancieux, influenced by the double sentiment of love and curiosity. During their progress, and as the corridors became more deserted, he endeavoured to stop the young woman, to touch her, and to gaze upon her, were it but for a moment; but, quick as a bird, she glided between his hands; and, when he wished to speak, she placed her finger on her lip, and, with a slight gesture of command which was full of grace, reminded him that he was under the dominion of a power which he must blindly obey, and which interdicted even the least complaint. After a few turns, Madame Bonancieux opened a door, and pushed the young man into a closet, which was quite dark. There she again enjoined silence, and opening a second door concealed in the tapestry, through which a brilliant light emanated, she disappeared.

D'Artagnan remained an instant motionless, and wondering where he was: but, shortly, a ray of light, which penetrated into this chamber, a warm and perfumed air, which reached him, and the conversation of two or three women, in language at once respectful and elegant, in which the word *majesty* was frequently repeated—clearly indicated to him that he was in a closet adjacent to the queen's apartment.

The young man kept himself in the shade, and listened.

The queen appeared gay and happy, which seemed greatly to astonish the ladies who surrounded her, who were accustomed to see her almost always full of care.

The queen attributed this joyous feeling to the beauty of the fête, and to the pleasure which she had experienced in the ballet; and as it is not allowable to contradict a queen, whether she smiles or weeps, every one expiated on the gallantry of these aldermen of the good city of Paris.

Although d'Artagnan did not know the queen, he soon distinguished her voice from those of the others—first, by a slight foreign accent, and then by that tone of command usually characteristic of the speech of sovereigns. He heard her approach and retire from that open door, and once or twice saw the shadow of her person intercept the light. Suddenly, however, a hand and arm, of an adorable form and colour, were passed through the tapestry. D'Artagnan comprehended that this was his reward : he threw himself upon his knees, seized this hand, respectfully pressed his lips upon it, and then it was withdrawn, leaving in his what he soon recognised to be a ring. The door was immediately shut, and d'Artagnan was again left in complete darkness.

He put the ring upon his finger, and once more waited. It was evident that all was not yet ended. After the recompense of his loyalty, should come the recompense of his love. Besides, although the ballet had been danced, the entertainment was scarcely yet begun. The supper was to take place at three, and the clock of St. John had, a short time before, already struck a quarter to three.

By degrees, in fact, the sound of voices diminished in the neighbouring chamber, and the ladies were then heard to leave it; after which, the door of the cabinet was opened, and Madame Bonancieux entered quickly.

"You come at last," cried d'Artagnan.

"Silence," said the young woman, putting her hand upon his lips; "get out again the same way you came."

"But where and when shall I see you?" cried d'Artagnan.

"A note, which you will find at your lodgings, will tell you. Go! go!"

And, at these words, she opened the door of the corridor, and pushed d'Artagnan out of the cabinet.

He obeyed like a child, without resistance or even objection, which proves that he was very positively in love.

CHAPTER XXIII.

THE APPOINTMENT.

D'ARTAGNAN ran the whole of the way home; and, although it was three in the morning, and he had to pass through the worst parts of Paris, he met with no misadventure. There is known to be a particular deity for drunkards and lovers.

He found the door in the passage open, ascended his stairs, and knocked gently, in a way agreed upon between him and his servant. Planchet, whom he had sent back two hours before, from the Hotel de Ville, to wait for him, came and opened the door.

"Has any one brought for me a letter?" eagerly inquired d'Artagnan.

"No one has brought a letter," said Planchet, "but there is one which came of itself."

"What do you mean, stupid?"

"I mean, that when I came in, although I had the key of your apartment in my pocket, and although this key had never been out of my possession, I found a letter on the green cover of the table in your bed-chamber."

"And where is that letter?"

"I left it where it was, sir. It is not natural for letters to enter gentlemen's rooms in this manner. If, indeed, the window had been found open, I should say nothing: but it was hermetically closed. Take care, sir, for there is certainly some magic in it."

In the meantime, the young man had rushed into his chamber, and opened the letter. It was from Madame Bonacieux, and expressed in these terms:—

"Warm thanks are to be given and transmitted to you. You must be at St. Cloud this evening, at ten o'clock, opposite the pavilion, which stands at the angle of M. d'Estrées' house.

"C. B."

On reading this letter, d'Artagnan felt his heart dilating and contracting in that delicious spasm which is the torture and delight of lovers.

It was the first note he had received—the first appointment that had been granted to him. His heart, expanding in the intoxication of his joy, felt as though it would faint at the portal of that terrestrial paradise which is denominated love.

"Well, sir," said Planchet, who had seen his master's colour come and go, "was I not right, and is not this some wicked transaction?"

"You are mistaken, Planchet; and the proof is, here is a crown for you to drink my health."

"I thank you, sir, and will strictly follow your directions; but it is not the less true, that letters which thus enter closed houses——"

"Fall from heaven, my friend—fall from heaven!"

"Then you are happy, sir?"

"My dear Planchet, I am the happiest of men."

"And I may take advantage of your happiness, and go to bed."

"Yes, go."

"May all Heaven's blessings fall upon you, sir; but it is not the less true, that this letter——"

And Planchet retired, shaking his head with an air of doubt, which all the liberality of d'Artagnan had not been able entirely to remove.

As soon as he was left alone, d'Artagnan read his note over and over again, and kissed, at least twenty times, these lines traced by the hand of his beautiful mistress. At length he retired to bed, and slept, and was visited by golden dreams.

At seven o'clock in the morning, d'Artagnan arose, and called Planchet, who at the second summons opened the door, his countenance yet bearing traces of his uneasiness on the previous evening.

"Planchet," said he, "I am going out, probably for the whole day; you are therefore free till seven o'clock in the evening; but you must be ready at that hour, with two horses."

"Well!" said Planchet, "I suppose we are going to have our skins pierced again in a few places."

"You will take your carbine and pistols."

"Well, then! did I not say so?" exclaimed Planchet. "There, I was sure of it—that cursed letter!"

"But be easy now, simpleton: it is only a party of pleasure."

"Yes, like that most delightful journey the other day, when it rained balls, and grew caltrops."

"If you are afraid, Planchet, I will go without you. I like better to travel alone, than with a timid companion."

"You insult me, sir," said Planchet. "I thought, however, that you had seen me at work."

"Yes, but I suppose that you expended all your courage on that one occasion."

"You shall see, at a fitting time, that some yet remains; only, I entreat you not to be too prodigal of it, if you wish it to last long."

"Do you think that you have got still sufficient to spend some this evening?"

"I hope so."

"Well then, I depend upon you."

"At the hour appointed I will be ready; but I thought there was only one horse in the guard stables."

"Perhaps there may be only one there at present; but, in the evening, there will be four."

"It seems as if our journey was an expedition to provide fresh horses for ourselves."

"Exactly so," said d'Artagnan; and, giving Planchet a last warning gesture, off he went.

M. Bonancieux was at his door, and d'Artagnan designed to pass by without speaking to the worthy mercer; but the latter accosted him so politely and kindly, that the tenant was obliged not only to bow in return, but also to enter into conversation with him.

How, indeed, was it possible not to display some slight complaisance towards the husband of a pretty woman who has just made an appointment with one at St. Cloud's, opposite the pavilion of M. d'Estrées, for that very evening? D'Artagnan approached him, therefore, with the most amiable manner that he was able to assume.

The conversation naturally turned on the poor man's imprisonment; and M. Bonancieux, not knowing that the young man had overheard his conversation with the man of Meung, related the persecutions of that monster, M. de Laffemas, whom he styled, throughout the whole of his narrative, the cardinal's executioner, and discoursed freely concerning the Bastile, the bolts, the dungeons, the air-holes, the grates, and instruments of torture.

D'Artagnan listened with the most exemplary attention: then, when he had ended—

"And Madame Bonancieux," said he—"do you know who carried her off? for I do not forget that it is to that vexatious occurrence that I owe the happiness of your acquaintance."

"Ah!" answered M. Bonancieux, "they took good care not to tell me that; and my wife, on her part, has sworn by all that's sacred that she did not know. But you, yourself," continued Bonancieux, in a tone of the most perfect good-fellowship, "what has become of you for the last few days? I have never seen either you or your friends; and it was not on the pavement of Paris, I should suppose, that you picked up all the dust which Planchet brushed off your boots last night."

"You are right, my dear M. Bonancieux: I and my friends have been making a little journey."

"Was it far from here?"

"Oh, lord, no! merely about forty leagues. We went to conduct M. Athos to the waters of Forges, where my friends have remained."

"And you have come back, have you?" resumed M.

Bonancieux, with the most spiteful look possible. "A handsome youth like you cannot get long leave of absence from his mistress. And you were impatiently expected at Paris, were you not? ha!"

"Faith," said the young man, laughing, "I confess it the more willingly, my dear M. Bonancieux, as I perceive that I can conceal nothing from you. Yes, I was expected, and most impatiently, I assure you."

A slight shade passed over Bonancieux's countenance, but it was so slight, that d'Artagnan did not perceive it.

"And you are about to be rewarded for your diligence?" continued the mercer, with a slight alteration of voice, which d'Artagnan did not perceive, any more than the cloud which had passed a moment before, over the face of the worthy man.

"I hope you may prove a true prophet!" exclaimed d'Artagnan, laughing.

"My reason for accosting you," continued Bonancieux, "is merely to learn whether you will return late."

"Why this question, my dear landlord?" asked d'Artagnan. "Is it because you intend to wait for me?"

"No, it is because, ever since my imprisonment, and the robbery which was committed on me, I am frightened every time I hear a door opened, and particularly at night. By our lady! I cannot help it: I am no soldier, truly!"

"Well do not be frightened if I enter at one, two, or three o'clock in the morning, or even if I do not enter at all."

Bonancieux became so pale at this that d'Artagnan could not but observe it, and asked him what was the matter.

"Nothing," replied Bonancieux, "nothing. Only, since my misfortunes, I am subject to these feelings, which seize me on a sudden, and make me shudder. Don't trouble yourself about that—you who have enough to occupy you in your approaching happiness."

"Oh, I am occupied in my present happiness."

"Not yet; wait a little: you said that it should be to-night."

"Well! the night will come, thank God! and perhaps you also may expect it as impatiently as me. Perhaps, this evening Madame Bonancieux intends to visit the conjugal home."

"Madame Bonancieux is not disengaged this evening," gravely replied Bonancieux; "she is detained at the Louvre, by her official duty."

"So much the worse for you, my dear landlord; so much the worse. When I am happy myself, I should like all the world to be so too: but that appears to be impossible."

And the young man went off, laughing loudly at the joke, which he alone, as he imagined, could comprehend.

"Laugh as you like," said Bonancieux, in a sepulchral tone.

But d'Artagnan was already too far off to hear him; and, if he had heard him, in the disposition of mind in which he then was, he would not have heeded him.

He went towards the hotel of M. de Treville; his visit of the evening before having been, as it may be remembered, very short, and very little explanatory.

He found M. de Treville in the heartiest joy. The king and queen had been most gracious to him at the ball. The cardinal, it is true, had been very ungracious. At one o'clock in the morning, he had retired, under the pretext of indisposition. As to their majesties, they had not returned to the Louvre till six in the morning.

"Now," said M. de Treville, lowering his voice, and looking cautiously around the room to be sure that they were alone—"now, my young friend, let us talk of yourself; for it is evident that your safe return is connected with the king's joy, the queen's triumph, and his eminence's humiliation. You must take care of yourself."

"What have I to fear," answered d'Artagnan, "so long as I have the good fortune to enjoy their majesties' favour?"

"Everything, believe me. The cardinal is not the man

to forget being made a fool of, at least until he has settled accounts with the person who has made a fool of him; and that person seems to me to be a certain youth of my acquaintance."

"Do you believe that the cardinal has got so far as you have, and knows that I am the individual who has been to London?"

"The devil! you have been to London! And is it from London you bring that beautiful diamond which glitters on your finger? Take care, my dear d'Artagnan; the present of an enemy is not a good thing. Is not there a certain Latin verse upon the subject? Stop a moment!"

"Yes, undoubtedly," said d'Artagnan, who had never been able to knock the first rule of the rudiments into his head, and who had driven his preceptor to despair by his ignorance. "Yes, undoubtedly, there must be one."

"Yes," said M. de Treville, who had a small amount of learning, "there is one certainly, and M. Benserade was quoting it to me the other day: wait a moment. Ah! here it is :—

Timeo Danaos et dona ferentes,

which means, 'Distrust the enemy with a present in his hand.'"

"This diamond does not come from an enemy, sir," replied d'Artagnan; "it comes from the queen."

"From the queen!" said M. de Treville. "Oh! oh! Truly, it is a complete royal jewel, which is worth a thousand pistoles, as fully as it is a single farthing. By whom did the queen send it to you?"

"She handed it to me herself."

"Where was that?"

"In the closet adjoining the apartment where she changed her dress."

"How?"

"In giving me her hand to kiss."

"And you have kissed the queen's hand," said M. de Treville, looking at d'Artagnan.

"Her majesty did me the honour to grant me that favour."

"And in the presence of witnesses? Imprudent! doubly imprudent!"

"No, sir; no one saw her," replied d'Artagnan; and he related to M. de Treville how everything had occurred.

"Oh! women, women!" cried the old soldier, "I recognise them well, by their romantic imaginations: everything which is at all mysterious charms them. Then you saw the arm, and that was all? You might meet the queen, and not recognise her? She might meet you, and not recognise you?"

"No; but thanks to this diamond——" replied the young man.

"Listen," said M. de Treville. "Will you allow me to give you some advice—some good advice—a friend's advice?"

"You will do me honour, sir," replied d'Artagnan.

"Well, then, go to the first jeweller's you can find, and sell this diamond for what he will give you for it. However great a miser he may be, you will get at least eight hundred pistoles. The pistoles have no name, young man; but this ring has a terrible one, which might destroy him who wears it."

"Sell this ring—a ring given me by my sovereign! Never!"

"Then turn the stone within, poor simpleton; for every one knows that a Gascon youth does not find such gems in his mother's jewel-case."

"You suspect, then, that I have some cause for fear?" said d'Artagnan.

"I mean to say, young man, that he who sleeps over a mine, when the match is lighted, ought to think himself in safety in comparison with you."

"The devil!" said d'Artagnan, whom M. de Treville's

serious tone began to disturb. "The devil! And what am I to do?"

"Above all things, be always on your guard. The cardinal has a tenacious memory and a long arm: believe me, he will play you some trick."

"But what?"

"Ah! has he not at his command all the wiles of Satan? The least that can happen to you will be an arrest?"

"What! Would they dare to arrest a man in his majesty's service?"

"Egad! they did not scruple much in the case of Athos? At any rate, young madcap, believe a man who has been thirty years at court: do not slumber in your security, or you are lost. On the contrary, I warn you to see enemies everywhere. If any one seeks to pick a quarrel with you, avoid it, even if it should be but a child of ten years of age: if you are attacked, by night or day, beat a retreat, without being ashamed of it: if you pass over a bridge, try the planks, for fear one should break beneath your feet: if you walk past a house which is being built, look up in the air, lest a stone should fall upon your head: if you come home late, let your servant follow you, and let him be armed, if, even, you can make sure of your servant. Distrust everybody—your friend, your brother, and your mistress —but your mistress most of all!"

D'Artagnan blushed.

"My mistress!" he mechanically repeated: "and why her, more than any one else?"

"Because a mistress is one of the favourite agents of the cardinal: he has no one more expeditious. A woman sells you for ten pistoles—witness Delilah. You know the scriptures, eh?"

D'Artagnan thought of the appointment which Madame Bonancieux had made for that very evening; but we must say, to the praise of our hero, that the bad opinion which M. de Treville entertained of women in general, did not inspire him with the slightest suspicion of his pretty landlady.

"But, apropos," resumed M. de Treville, "what has become of your three companions?"

"I was just going to inquire whether you had not received any tidings of them?"

"None whatever, sir."

"Well, I left them behind me on my way—Porthos, at Chantilly, with a duel on his hands; Aramis, at Crèvecœur, with a bullet in his shoulder; and Athos, at Amiens, under an accusation of passing bad money."

"Look there, now!" said M. de Treville. "And how did you escape yourself?"

"By a miracle, sir, I ought to confess: with a sword thrust in the chest, and by pinning the Count de Wardes on his back, on the road to Calais, as one might pin a butterfly upon the tapestry."

"There again! De Wardes—one of the cardinal's men, and a cousin of Rochefort's. Come, my dear friend, an idea has struck me."

"Speak, sir."

"In your shoes, there is one thing that I would do."

"What is it?"

"Whilst his eminence was seeking for me at Paris, I would take, without sound of drum or trumpet, the road to Picardy, and would endeavour to find out what had become of my three companions. Surely, in any case, they merit this slight attention on your part."

"The advice is good, sir, and to-morrow I will go."

"To-morrow! and why not this evening?"

"This evening, sir, I am detained at Paris by an affair of importance."

"Ah, young man! young man! some little love affair. Take care! I repeat it once more, it is woman who has always ruined us, even from the beginning, is ruining us, and will still ruin us to the end. Be advised by me, and depart this evening."

"Impossible, sir."

"Have you given your word?"

"Yes, sir."

"That is another matter; but promise me, that, if you are not killed to-night, you will set out to-morrow."

"I promise you."

"Do you want money?"

"I have fifty pistoles remaining: it is as much as I shall require, I think."

"But your companions?"

"I think that they can be in no want. We left Paris each with seventy-five pistoles in his pocket."

"Shall I see you again before your departure?"

"I think not, sir; unless anything new should occur."

"Well, a good journey to you!"

"Thanks, sir."

And D'Artagnan took his leave of M. de Treville, more than ever touched by his paternal solicitude for his musketeers.

He went successively to the homes of Athos, Porthos, and Aramis; but none of them had returned. Their servants were also absent, and nothing had been heard of either masters or lackeys.

He might possibly have gained some tidings of them from their mistresses, but he knew not those of Porthos and Aramis; and Athos had none.

In passing the hotel of the guards, he looked in at the stables. Three of the four horses were already there. Planchet, quite astounded, was busy currying them, and had already finished two out of the three.

"Ah, sir," said Planchet, "how glad I am to see you."

"And why so, Planchet?" demanded the young man.

"Can you depend on M. Bonancieux, our landlord?"

"I? not in the slightest degree."

"And you are quite right, too, sir."

"But why do you ask the question?"

"Because, whilst you were talking to him, I looked, without listening, sir; and his countenance changed colour two or three times."

"Bah!"

"You did not observe it, sir, preoccupied as you were by the letter you had just received; but I, on the contrary, who had been put on my guard by the strange manner in which this letter had got into the house, did not let one change of his countenance escape me."

"And what did you discover?"

"That he is a traitor."

"Really?"

"And, moreover, the moment you had turned the corner of the street, M. Bonancieux took his hat, shut his door, and began to run in an opposite direction."

"Upon my word, you are quite right, Planchet: all this looks suspicious enough; but be contented—we will not pay him one farthing of rent till all this is satisfactorily explained."

"You joke, sir, but you will see."

"What would you have, Planchet? That which will happen is written."

"Then, sir, you do not renounce your expedition this evening?"

"On the contrary, Planchet, the more I dislike M. Bonancieux, the more inclined am I to keep the appointment made in this letter, which disturbs you so much."

"Then it is your determination?"

"Immovably so, my friend; therefore, at seven o'clock, be ready here at the hotel, and I will come and find you."

Planchet, seeing there was no hope of making his master renounce his project, heaved a profound sigh, and set to work grooming the third horse.

As for d'Artagnan, who was fundamentally a young man of great economy, instead of going to his own home, he went and dined with the young Gascon priest, who, during the temporary distress of the four friends, had given them a breakfast of chocolate.

CHAPTER XXIV.

THE PAVILION.

At nine o'clock, d'Artagnan was at the Hotel des Gardes. He found Planchet under arms, and the fourth horse arrived. Planchet was armed with his carbine and pistol. D'Artagnan had provided himself with his sword, and placed two pistols in his belt. They each bestrode a horse, and went off quietly. It was a dark night, and none saw them depart. Planchet followed his master at the distance of ten paces.

D'Artagnan passed over the quays, went out by the gate of La Conference, and proceeded along the charming road—far more beautiful then than now—which leads to St. Cloud.

As long as they continued in the town, Planchet kept the respectful distance that he had fixed for himself; but, when the road became more lonely and obscure, he gradually drew nearer, so that, when they entered the Bois de Boulogne, he found himself quite naturally riding side by side with his master. In fact, we must not deny that the waving of the trees, and the reflection of the moon amongst the sombre copses, caused him much uneasiness. D'Artagnan perceived that something extraordinary was incommoding his lackey.

"Well, Planchet," demanded he, "what ails you, now?"

"Do you not find, sir, that woods are like churches?"

"And why, Planchet?"

"Because one is as much afraid of speaking loudly in the one as in the other."

"Why dare you not speak loudly, Planchet—because you are in fear?"

"Yes, sir; in fear of being heard."

"Fear of being heard! Our conversation is very proper, my dear Planchet, and no one would find anything in it to censure."

"Ah, sir," replied Planchet, returning to the ruling idea in his mind, "that M. Bonancieux has a sly gloom about the eyebrows, and something so unpleasant in the working of his lips!"

"What the plague makes you think so much of M. Bonancieux?"

"Sir, we think of what one must, and not of what one would."

"Because you are a coward, Planchet."

"Let us not confound prudence with cowardice, sir. Prudence is a virtue."

"And you are very virtuous, are you not, Planchet?"

"Is not that the barrel of a musket, sir, shining below there? Suppose we were to stoop our heads?"

"Really," muttered d'Artagnan, who remembered the advice of M. de Treville—"really, this animal will finish by making me afraid." And he put his horse at a trot.

Planchet followed his master's movements, precisely as if he had been his shadow, and soon found himself trotting by his side.

"Must we travel in this manner all the night, sir?" demanded he.

"No, Planchet, for you are at your journey's end."

"What! I am at my journey's end? And you, sir?"

"I shall go some little way farther."

"And leave me here alone, sir?"

"Are you afraid, Planchet?"

"No; but I will merely observe to you, sir, that the night will be very cold; that cold causes rheumatism; and that a lackey who has the rheumatism makes but a sorry servant, especially to such an active master as yourself!"

"Well, then, if you are cold, you can enter one of those wine shops which you see down there; but you must be waiting for me before the door, at six o'clock to-morrow morning."

"But, sir, I have most dutifully eaten and drunk the

crown that you gave me this morning; so that I have not got even a stray sou remaining, in case I should feel cold."

"There is a half-pistole. Good-bye till to-morrow morning."

D'Artagnan got off his horse, threw the bridle to Planchet, and hurried away, closely enveloped in his cloak.

"Good God! how cold I am!" exclaimed Planchet, as soon as he had lost sight of his master; and, eager as he was to warm himself, he hastened to rap at the door of a house, which had all the appearance of a suburban dram-shop.

In the meantime, d'Artagnan, who had taken a narrow cross-road, reached St. Cloud; but, instead of proceeding along the main street, he turned behind the castle, went down a narrow, unfrequented lane, and soon found himself opposite the appointed pavilion. It was situated in a perfect desert of a place. A long wall, at the corner of which was the pavilion, ran along one side of this lane; and, on the other a hedge hid from the wayfarer a small garden, at the bottom of which there stood a miserable cottage.

He had now reached the place of appointment; and as he had not been told to announce his presence by any signal, he waited.

Not a sound was heard: he might have fancied himself a hundred leagues from the capital. D'Artagnan cast a glance behind him, and then leaned his back against the hedge. Beyond this hedge, and garden, and cottage, a heavy mist enveloped in its shade that vast immensity where Paris slept—an immensity, void and open in which some luminous points glittered like the funereal stars of that vast pandemonium of suffering and sin.

But to d'Artagnan, all aspects indicated beauteous forms; all images were wreathed in smiles; all darkness was transparent light. The appointed hour was on the eve of striking.

In fact, at the end of a few minutes, the belfry of St. Cloud slowly emitted ten strokes from its broad sonorous jaws.

There was something melancholy in that voice of bronze, which thus breathed its lamentations in the night. But each of those sounds, which told the hour he sighed for, vibrated harmoniously in the heart of the young man.

His eyes were fixed on the pavilion, which stood at the corner of the wall, and of which all the windows were closed with shutters, except one upon the first floor.

From this window there shone a soft light, which silvered over the trembling foliage of two or three linden trees, which formed a group outside the park. Doubtless, behind that little window, which was so kindly lighted up, the pretty Madame Bonancieux awaited him. A lingering sentiment of diffidence restrained her; but, now that the hour had struck, the window would be opened, and d'Artagnan would at last receive from the hands of Love, the meed of his devotion.

Flattered by this sweet belief, d'Artagnan waited a half-hour, without any impatience, keeping his eyes fixed upon that charming little abode; and distinguishing, through the upper part of the window, a part of those gilded cornices of the ceiling which gave evidence of the elegance of the remainder of the apartment.

The belfry of St. Cloud proclaimed half-past ten

But, this time, without his knowing why, a shudder ran through the veins of d'Artagnan. Perhaps, also, the cold began to affect him, and he mistook for a moral impression what was in reality a sensation altogether physical.

Then the idea occurred to him, that he had mistaken the hour of appointment, and that it must have been at eleven, instead of ten.

He approached the window, placed himself under the ray of light, drew the letter from his pocket, and read it again. He was not mistaken: the appointment was really for ten o'clock.

He resumed his post, becoming uneasy at the silence and solitude.

It struck eleven.

D'Artagnan began to fear that something had really happened to Madame Bonancieux.

He clapped his hands three times—the usual signal of lovers—but nothing, not even echo, returned an answer. And then he thought, with some displeasure, that the young woman had perhaps fallen asleep whilst waiting for him.

He approached the wall, and attempted to climb it; but the wall was newly rough-cast, and he broke his nails to no purpose.

At this moment he thought of the trees, of which the leaves were still silvered over by the light; and, perceiving that one drooped over the road, he fancied that, from amidst its branches, he might be able to see into the pavilion.

The tree was easy to climb. Besides, d'Artagnan was scarcely twenty years of age, and, therefore, well remembered his school-boy habits. In an instant he was in the midst of its branches, and through the transparent windows, his eyes plunged into the interior of the pavilion.

Strange it was—and it made him shudder from the soles of his feet to the hair of his head—to find that that gentle flame, that quiet lamp, threw light upon a scene of frightful disarray: one of the panes of the window was demolished; the door of the room had been broken open, and hung, half-broken, on its hinges; a table, which must have been covered with an elegant supper, lay upon the ground; and glasses in fragments, and crushed fruits, were thickly spread upon the floor. Everything in the room indicated a violent and desperate struggle; and d'Artagnan believed that he could even detect, amidst this strange medley, some strips of clothes, and some stains of blood, congealed on the tablecloth and curtains.

With his heart beating horribly, he hastily descended to the ground, to examine if he could not find some further traces of violence.

The small and gentle light still shone amidst the calmness of the night. D'Artagnan then perceived—what had escaped him at first, when nothing prompted him to so close a scrutiny—that the ground was broken in one place, and dug up in another, and was marked by confused impressions of the footsteps of both men and horses. The wheels of a carriage, which seemed to have come from Paris, had, moreover, left upon the soft soil a deep rut, which proceeded no further than the pavilion, and then returned again towards Paris. And, last of all, in pursuing his researches, he found near the wall a woman's torn glove. But this glove, wherever it had not come in contact with the mud, was irreproachably fresh. It was one of those perfumed gloves which the lover likes to pull from a pretty hand.

As d'Artagnan pursued these investigations, at every fresh discovery, a more abundant and more icy moisture stood upon his brow; his heart was wrung with fearful anguish, and his respiration almost failed.

"And yet," said he to encourage himself, "perhaps this pavilion had nothing to do with Madame Bonancieux. Her appointment was *before* the pavilion, not *within* it. She has possibly been detained in Paris by her duties, or, probably, by her husband's jealousy."

But all these reflections were beaten down, destroyed, driven to flight, by that internal sentiment of grief, which, on some occasions, takes exclusive possession of our entire being, and announces, in an unmistakable language, that some great suffering hovers over our heads.

And then d'Artagnan became almost frantic. He ran upon the highway, hastened along the road he had come by, and advanced as far as the ferry-boat, and questioned the ferryman.

About seven o'clock in the evening, the ferryman had ferried over a woman, enveloped in a dark cloak, who

seemed to be exceedingly anxious to escape recognition;
but, precisely on account of her precautions, he had been
the more observant, and had discovered that she was
young and pretty.

There were then, as now, crowds of young and pretty
women, who came to St. Cloud, and who had reasons for
desiring to remain unseen; yet d'Artagnan doubted not
for an instant, that it was Madame Bonancieux whom
the ferryman had brought across.

D'Artagnan took advantage of the lamp in the ferryman's cottage, to read the note of Madame Bonancieux
once more, and to assure himself that he had made no
mistake—that the appointment was really at St. Cloud,
and not elsewhere, and before the pavilion of M. d'Estrees,
and not in another street.

Everything concurred to prove to d'Artagnan that his
presentiments were not groundless, and that some great
misfortune had actually occurred.

He ran back towards the castle, fancying that, during
his absence, something new might have taken place at
the pavilion, and that some fresh instructions might be
awaiting him there.

The lane was still deserted, and the same calm, soft
light streamed from the window.

D'Artagnan then remembered that dark and wretched
cottage, which doubtless had seen, and might perhaps
also speak.

The gate of the enclosure was shut, but he jumped over
the hedge, and, in spite of the barking of a chained dog,
approached the cottage.

At his first summons, no one answered. A death-like
silence prevailed here, as well as in the pavilion: yet, as
this cottage was his last resource, he persisted.

Now he fancied he heard a slight noise within—a timid
noise, which seemed itself to be afraid of being heard.

Then d'Artagnan ceased to knock, and made entreaties
in such a piteous accent of fear, mingled with flattery,
that his voice would have reassured the most timorous.

At length an old worm-eaten shutter was opened, or rather, half opened, and instantly shut again, as soon as the light of a miserable lamp, which was burning in a corner, had disclosed the belt, the hilt of the sword, and the pistols of d'Artagnan. And yet, quick as had been the movement, he had been able to see the head of an old man.

"In the name of Heaven!" said he, "listen to me. I expected some one who is not come. I am dying from anxiety. Has any misfortune happened in your neighbourhood? Speak!"

The window was again slowly opened, and the same countenance reappeared, only it was paler than before.

D'Artagnan told his story simply, merely withholding names: he stated that he had an appointment with a young woman, before this pavilion; and that, not seeing her come, he had climbed the linden tree, and had, by the light of the lamp, perceived the disorder of the room.

The old man listened attentively, with many signs of assent; and when d'Artagnan had ended, shook his head in a manner which was not encouraging.

"What do you mean?" exclaimed d'Artagnan; "in the name of Heaven, explain yourself!"

"Oh, sir!" said he, "do not ask me anything; for, if I should tell you what I have seen, most assuredly no good will befall me."

"You have seen something, then?" exclaimed d'Artagnan. "In that case, in Heaven's name," continued he, throwing him a pistole, "tell me what you have seen, and, on the honour of a gentleman, not one of your words shall pass my lips."

The old man read so much honesty and grief in d'Artagnan's countenance, that he made him a sign to listen, and said, in a low voice—

"It was about nine o'clock that I heard some noise in the street, and wishing to know what it was, I was going to my gate, when I saw some people trying to get in. As I am poor, and have no fear of being robbed, I went

to open it, and saw three men a few paces from me. In
the shade was a carriage, with horses harnessed to it,
and also some led horses. These led horses evidently
belonged to the three men, who were dressed for riding.

"'Ah, my good sirs,' I cried, 'what do you want?'

"'You ought to have a ladder,' said one, who
appeared to be the leader of the party.

"'Yes, sir, that with which I gather my fruit.'

"'Give it to us, and go back into your house; and
here is a crown for the trouble we give you. But,
remember, if you say one word about what you see or
hear—for, however we may threaten you, I am sure you
will both hear and see all that we do—you are a lost man.'

"At these words he threw me a crown, which I picked
up, and he took my ladder. In fact, having fastened the
gate in the hedge after them, I pretended to enter my
house; but I went out again by the back door, and,
gliding in the shade, I came to those alder bushes, from
the shelter of which I could see everything, without being
seen myself.

"The three men had brought up the carriage without
any noise: they pulled out of it a fat, short, gray little
man, shabbily dressed in a sad-coloured doublet, who
carefully mounted the ladder, looked sulkily into the
window, came down with a wolf's steps, and muttered in
a low voice—'It is she!'

"He who had spoken to me immediately went to the
door of the pavilion, which he opened with a key which
he had about him, and then shut the door after him, and
disappeared.

"The other two men mounted the ladder simultaneously.
The little old man remained at the carriage door, the
coachman took care of his horses, and a lackey of the
led ones. Suddenly great outcries resounded from the
pavilion, and a woman ran to the window, and opened it
as if to throw herself out. But, as soon as she saw the
two men, she threw herself back, and the two men rushed
into the chamber after her.

"Then I saw nothing more; but I heard the noise of breaking furniture. The woman screamed, and cried for help: but her cries were soon stifled. The three men returned to the window, carrying the woman in their arms; and two of them came down the ladder, and bore her to the carriage, into which the little old man entered with her. He who had remained in the pavilion shut the window, came out at the door directly after, and satisfied himself that the woman was in the carriage: his two companions were already on their horses waiting for him; he sprang into his saddle, and the groom took his place beside the coachman: the carriage, escorted by the three horsemen, departed at a gallop, and all was over. From that moment until your arrival I have neither seen nor heard anything."

D'Artagnan, overwhelmed by these terrible tidings, remained motionless and speechless, whilst the demons of jealousy and anger raged in his heart.

"But, my gentleman," said the old man, on whom this mute despair had more effect than cries and tears would have produced, "do not despond: they have not killed her; that is the great thing."

"Do you know, at all," said d'Artagnan, "who is the man who conducted this infernal expedition?"

"I do not know him."

"But, as he spoke to you, you could see him?"

"Ah! it is his appearance that you want to know?"

"Yes."

"A tall, lean, brown man, with black moustaches, a dark eye, and the look of a gentleman."

"That's it," cried d'Artagnan; "him again. The same man—always the same! It is my evil genius, apparently. And the other?"

"Which?"

"The little one."

"Oh, he was not a gentleman, I answer for it. Besides, he did not carry a sword, and the others treated him with no sort of respect."

"Some servant," muttered d'Artagnan. "Ah, poor woman! poor woman! what have they done with her?"

"You promised me to be secret," said the old man.

"And I renew my promise. Be satisfied! I am a gentleman: a gentleman has only his word, and I have given you mine."

D'Artagnan returned towards the ferry, almost heart-broken. Sometimes he could not believe that it was Madame Bonancieux, and hoped to find her the next day at the Louvre. Sometimes he fancied that she had an intrigue with another, and had been discovered and carried off by some third party who was jealous of him. He doubted, sorrowed, and despaired.

"Oh!" cried he, "if I had but my friends here! I should at any rate have some hopes of finding her; but who knows what is become of them also?"

Is was then nearly midnight, and he must at once find Planchet. D'Artagnan searched successively every wine-shop where he perceived a little light, but nowhere could he find his servant.

At length, after examining half a dozen, he began to reflect that the search was rather fortuitous. He had himself said six o'clock in the morning: therefore, wherever Planchet was, he was fully justified.

Besides, it occurred to the young man, that, by remaining in the neighbourhood of the place where this event had happened, he might gather some information. At the sixth wine-shop, as we have said, he therefore remained, and asking for a bottle of their best wine, placed himself in the darkest corner, and determined there to await the return of day. But this time, too, his hope was disappointed; and, although he opened his ears to every sound, he heard nothing—amidst the oaths, and gestures, and abuse which were exchanged by the workmen, lackeys, and cab-drivers, who composed the honourable society of which he was a part—that could put him at all upon the track of the poor ill-used woman.

He was obliged, therefore, after having emptied his bottle, and in order that he might avoid remark, to occupy himself in seeking for the easiest posture in which to sleep as best he could. It must be remembered that d'Artagnan was not twenty years old; and at that age sleep has undeniable rights, which must be submitted to, even by the most desolate hearts.

About six o'clock in the morning d'Artagnan awoke, with that feeling of discomfort which generally comes with the break of day after an uneasy night. His toilet did not occupy him long; and, having searched himself to see that no one had taken advantage of his sleep to rob him, and found his diamond on his finger, his purse in his pocket, and his pistols in his belt, he paid for his wine, and sallied forth to try whether he should be more fortunate in seeking for his servant in the morning than at night. And the first thing that he perceived, through the damp, gray fog, was honest Planchet who, with the two horses, was waiting for him at the door of a miserable little wine-shop, before which d'Artagnan had passed without even suspecting its existence.

CHAPTER XXV.

PORTHOS.

INSTEAD of returning directly home, d'Artagnan dismounted at M. de Treville's door, and rapidly ascended the staircase. He was determined to tell him, this time, all that had occurred. Doubtless the captain would give him good advice in this affair; and, as M. de Treville saw the queen almost daily, he might draw some information from her majesty concerning the poor woman, who was unquestionably being punished for her devotion to her mistress.

M. de Treville listened to the young man's recital with a gravity which proved that he saw something more in

this adventure than an amour; and, when d'Artagnan
had finished—

"Hum!" said he: "this savours of his eminence a
mile off."

"But what am I to do?" said d'Artagnan.

"Nothing, absolutely nothing, just now; but leave
Paris, as I have told you, as soon as possible. I will see
the queen, and tell her the details of the disappearance
of this poor woman, of which she is, doubtless, ignorant,
and these details will guide her, on her side; and, on your
return, I may possibly have some good news to give you.
Trust to me."

D'Artagnan knew, that, although a Gascon, M. de
Treville was not accustomed to make promises, and that,
when by chance he did make one, he always performed
it to the full and more. He therefore took his leave, full
of gratitude for the past and the future; and the worthy
captain, who, on his side, felt a lively interest for this
brave and resolute young man, affectionately pressed his
hand as he wished him a good journey.

Determined instantaneously to put M. de Treville's
advice into execution, d'Artagnan hastened towards the
Rue des Fossoyeurs, to look to the packing of his
portmanteau. On approaching No. 11, he perceived M.
Bonancieux, in morning costume, standing at his door.
Everything that the prudent Planchet had said the
evening before, about the sinister character of his landlord, now recurred to his mind, and he looked at him
more attentively than he had ever done before. In
fact, besides that yellow sickly paleness, which indicates
the infiltration of the bile into the blood, and which
might be only accidental, d'Artagnan remarked something gruffly perfidious in the wrinkles of his face. A
rascal does not laugh in the same manner as an honest
man; a hypocrite does not weep with the same kind
of tears as a sincere man. All imposture is a mask;
and, however well the mask may be made, it may always,
with a little attention, be distinguished from the true face.

Now, it seemed to d'Artagnan that M. Bonancieux wore a mask, and that this mask was a most disagreeable one.

He was going, therefore, from his repugnance to the man, to pass by him without speaking; when M. Bonancieux, as on the previous day, addressed him.

"Well, young man," said he, it seems that we are rather late of nights. Seven o'clock in the morning! Plague! It appears that you reverse customs, and return home when others emerge."

"No one could throw that in your teeth, M. Bonancieux," said the young man; "you are the model of regularity. It is true, that when one has a young and pretty wife, one need not run after happiness; happiness comes home to seek us, does it not, M. Bonancieux?"

Bonancieux became pale as death, and grinned a horrible smile.

"Ah, ah! you are a pleasant fellow. But where the plague have you been running this night, my young master? It appears as if the by-lanes were rather dirty."

D'Artagnan lowered his eyes to his own boots, which were covered with mud; but in doing this, he happened to look at the shoes and hose of the mercer: one would have said that they had been dipped in the same slough, for both were stained with spots of exactly the same appearance.

A sudden idea came across d'Artagnan's mind. That little, fat, gray, short man, like a lackey, clothed in a sad-coloured suit, and treated with no sort of respect by the swordsmen of the escort, was Bonancieux himself. The husband had assisted in the abduction of his wife.

A strong desire seized d'Artagnan to fly at the mercer's throat, and strangle him; but he was a prudent youth, as we have said, and he restrained himself. Nevertheless, his change of countenance was so visible, that Bonancieux was frightened, and endeavoured to retreat a step or two; but he was exactly before the half of the door that was closed, and the material obstacle which he thus encountered compelled him to keep the same place.

"Ah!" said d'Artagnan, "you who joke in this manner, my brave fellow—it appears to me, that if my boots need a rub of the sponge, your shoes also want a brush. And have you been rambling, too, Master Bonancieux? By my faith, it would be quite unpardonable in a man of your age, and who, moreover, has got a wife as pretty as yours is."

"Oh! mon Dieu, no," said Bonancieux; "but yesterday I went to St. Maude, to gain some information concerning a servant, whom I cannot do without; and, as the roads were dirty, I have collected all this mud, which I have not yet had time to get rid of."

The place which Bonancieux had mentioned, as the end of his journey, was a new proof in confirmation of the suspicions that d'Artagnan had formed. Bonancieux had said St. Maude, because St. Maude was in an exactly opposite direction to St. Cloud.

This probability was the first consolation he had found! If Bonancieux knew where his wife was, it would always be possible, by using extreme measures, to force the mercer to unclose his teeth and let out his secret. The great thing was, to change this probability into certainty.

"Pardon me, my dear M. Bonancieux," said d'Artagnan, "if I treat you without ceremony; but nothing makes me so thirsty as want of sleep: hence, I have a furious thirst. Allow me to beg a glass of water of you; you know you cannot refuse such a thing to a neighbour."

And without waiting for the permission of his landlord, d'Artagnan entered the house, and cast a hasty glance at the bed. The bed was undisturbed: Bonancieux had not slept in it. He had, therefore, only returned an hour or two before, having accompanied his wife to the place where they had conducted her, or, at any rate, for the first stage.

"Thank you, M. Bonancieux," said d'Artagnan,

emptying the glass; "that is all I wanted of you. Now I will go home: I am going to make Planchet brush my boots, and when he has finished them, I will send him, if you like, to brush your shoes."

He left the mercer quite stupefied by this singular adieu, and wondering whether he had not run his own neck into a noose.

At the top of the stairs he found Planchet, frightened out of his wits.

"Ah, sir," cried the lackey, as soon as he saw his master; "here, indeed, is something new; and how long you seemed to me in returning."

"What is the matter now?" demanded d'Artagnan.

"Ah! I will give you leave to guess a hundred, nay, a thousand times, before you find out the visitor I have received on your behalf during your absence."

"When was that?"

"About half an hour ago, whilst you were with M. de Treville."

"And who has been here? Come, speak!"

"M. de Cavois."

"M. de Cavois?"

"Yes, no other."

"The captain of his eminence's guards?"

"Yes, himself!"

"He came to arrest me?"

"I suspected so, sir, in spite of his wheedling way."

"He had a wheedling way, do you say?"

"That is to say, he was all honey, sir."

"Really!"

"He said he came from his eminence, who had the greatest goodwill towards you, to beg you to follow him to the Palais-Royal."

"And you answered him?"

"That the thing was impossible, seeing that you were from home, as he might perceive."

"And what did he say then?"

"That you must not fail to go there some time during

the day, and then he added, in a whisper: 'Tell your master that his eminence is perfectly well-disposed towards him, and that his fortune probably depends upon this interview.'"

"The snare is unskilful enough for the cardinal," said the young man, smiling.

"And, as I discovered the snare, I told him that you would be quite in despair on your return."

"'Where is he gone?' demanded M. de Cavois. 'To Troyes, in Champagne,' I answered. 'And when did he go?' says he. 'Yesterday evening!'"

"Planchet, my friend," interrupted d'Artagnan, "you are truly a valuable man."

"You understand, sir, I thought that there would be time enough, if you wished to see M. de Cavois, to give me the lie, by saying that you had not gone. It would then be me who had told the lie; and, as I am not a gentleman, I may tell lies, you know."

"Be easy, Planchet, you shall preserve your reputation as a man of truth: in one quarter of an hour we will be off."

"It was just the advice I was going to offer you, sir. And where are we going now, if it is not being too curious?"

"Egad! exactly the opposite way to that which you said I was gone. Besides, are you not in as much anxiety to know what has become of Grimaud, Mousqueton, and Bazin, as I to hear of Athos, Porthos, and Aramis?"

"Yes, indeed, sir," said Planchet, "and I will set off as soon as you please. The air of the country, I believe, will suit us both better than the air of Paris, just now. Therefore——"

"Therefore, prepare the baggage, Planchet, and let us be off. I will march off first, with my hands in my pockets, that there may be no suspicion. You will join me at the Hotel des Gardes. Apropos, Planchet, I believe that you are right regarding our landlord, and that he is decidedly a most horrible rascal."

"Ah! believe me, sir, when I tell you anything in future: I am a physiognomist!"

D'Artagnan descended first, as was agreed; and, that he might have nothing to reproach himself with, he went again to the lodgings of his three friends, but no intelligence of them had been received — only a perfumed letter, most elegantly addressed, had arrived for Aramis. D'Artagnan took charge of it. Ten minutes afterwards, Planchet rejoined him at the stables. D'Artagnan, that no time might be lost, had already saddled his own horse.

"That will do," said he to Planchet, when he had fastened on his valise. "Now saddle the other three, and let us be off."

"Do you believe we shall travel faster with two horses a-piece?" asked Planchet, with his sharp look.

"No, Mister Jester," replied d'Artagnan," "but, with our four horses, we may bring our three friends back— that is, if we can find them."

"Which would be a great chance," replied Planchet; "but we must not distrust the mercy of God."

"Amen!" said d'Artagnan, bestriding his horse.

They left the Hotel des Gardes by the opposite ends of the street, as the one was to quit Paris by the barrier of La Villette, the other by the barrier of Montmartre, to rejoin each other at St. Denis—a stratagetic manœuvre, which, being punctually executed, was crowned with the most fortunate results. Thus, d'Artagnan and Planchet entered Pierrefitte together.

Planchet, it must be confessed, was more courageous by day than by night. But yet his natural prudence did not forsake him for an instant: he had forgotten none of the incidents of the former journey, and took every one for an enemy whom he met upon the road. On this account, he always had his hat off, for which he was severely rebuked by d'Artagnan, who feared that this excess of politeness might cause Planchet to be taken for the valet of a man of little consequence.

Nevertheless, whether the passengers were really softened by Planchet's extreme urbanity, or whether no enemies were stationed on the young man's path, our two travellers arrived, without any accident, at Chantilly, and dismounted at the tavern of the Great St. Martin, the same at which they had stopped upon their last journey.

The landlord, seeing a young man, followed by a servant and two led horses, advanced respectfully to his door. Now, as he had already travelled eleven leagues, d'Artagnan judged that he had better stop here, whether Porthos were at the hotel or not. But it might not be prudent, at first, to make any inquiries about the musketeer. The result of these reflections was, that d'Artagnan, without asking any information from anybody, dismounted, recommended the horses to his servant's care, and entering a small room, reserved for those who wished to be alone, called for a bottle of the best wine, and as good a breakfast as the landlord could supply — a call which corroborated the high estimate that the innkeeper had already formed of his guest at first sight.

D'Artagnan was served with a celerity which was quite miraculous. The regiment of guards was composed of the first gentlemen in the realm; and d'Artagnan, travelling with a servant and four splendid horses, could not fail of creating a sensation, in spite of the simplicity of his uniform. The host wished to wait on him himself: seeing which, d'Artagnan made him bring two glasses, and began the following conversation :—

"By my faith, mine host," said d'Artagnan, filling two glasses, "I have asked for the best wine, and, if you have deceived me, your sin will bring its own punishment, since, as I hate to drink alone, you are going to drink with me. Take this glass, then, and let us drink. To what shall we drink, that we may wound no one's feelings? Let us drink to the prosperity of your establishment!"

"Your lordship does me great honour, and I sincerely thank you for your good wishes."

"But don't deceive yourself," said d'Artagnan; "there is more selfishness in my toast than you think for. It is only in prosperous houses that one gets well treated: in struggling inns everything runs to disorder, and the traveller is a victim to the landlord's embarrassment. Therefore, as I travel a great deal, and particularly on this road, I should like to see all the innkeepers making a fortune."

"In fact," said the landlord, "it appears to me that this is not the first time I have seen you, sir."

"Bah! I have passed through Chantilly perhaps ten times, and have stopped at least three or four times at your house. Yes, I was here about ten or twelve days ago, conducting three of my friends, musketeers; and one of them, by the bye, quarrelled with a stranger here—a man who sought a quarrel with him."

"Ah! yes, true!" said mine host; "I recollect it perfectly. Is it not of M. Porthos that your lordship speaks?"

"That is the very name of my travelling companion. Mon Dieu! my dear landlord, tell me, has any misfortune befallen him?"

"But your lordship must have remarked for yourself that he was not able to continue his journey."

"In fact, he promised to overtake us, but we saw no more of him."

"He has done us the honour to remain here."

"What! he has done you the honour to remain here?"

"Yes, sir, in this hotel; and we are somewhat uneasy over it."

"Why?"

"On account of certain expenses that he has incurred."

"Well, but the expenses he has incurred he will pay."

"Ah, sir, your words are a positive balm to my heart. We have been at considerable expense on his account; and only this morning the surgeon declared that, if

M. Porthos did not pay him, he should proceed against me, as it was I who sent for him."

"But is Porthos wounded, then?"

"I cannot tell you, sir."

"What! you cannot tell me? You ought at any rate to know better than anybody else."

"Yes; but, in our trade we do not tell all we know, sir—particularly when we have been warned that our ears shall answer for our tongue."

"Well! can I see Porthos?"

"Certainly, sir. Go to the first landing-place on the staircase, and knock at No. 1. Only, advise him that it is you!"

"What! advise him that it is me?"

"Yes; some accident might happen else."

"And what accident could happen to me?"

"M. Porthos might mistake you for somebody belonging to the house, and might, in a fit of passion, either run you through with his sword, or blow out your brains."

"Why, what have you been doing to him, then?"

"Oh! we asked him for money."

"Ah! I comprehend now. That is a kind of demand that Porthos always receives badly when he is not in cash: but I know that he ought to have plenty."

"So we thought also, sir. And, as the house is very regular, and our accounts are made up every week, on the eighth day we presented our little bill: but we seem to have hit upon an unlucky time, for, at the first word we dropped upon the subject, he sent us all to the very devil. It is true, he had been playing cards the evening before."

"What! playing the evening before? And with whom?"

"Oh! good Lord, who can tell that? With some nobleman who was travelling this way, and to whom he sent to propose a game at lansquenet."

"Just so: and the unlucky dog lost his all."

"Even to his horse, sir: for, when the stranger was

about to leave, we perceived that his servant was saddling M. Porthos's horse, and we remarked it to him; but he told us that we had better mind our own business, and that the horse was his own. So, we went immediately to let M. Porthos know what was going on; but he only answered, that we were scoundrels for doubting the word of a gentleman, and that, as this one had said that the horse belonged to him, it necessarily must be true."

"I recognise him there, exactly," muttered d'Artagnan.

"Then," continued the innkeeper, "I sent a message to him, that, as we did not seem likely to come to any understanding with one another about payment, I hoped that he would at least have the kindness to transfer the favour of his custom to my brother-landlord at *The Golden Eagle*, but M. Porthos replied that, as my hotel was the best, he desired to remain here. This answer was too complimentary for me to insist upon his leaving. I contented myself with begging him to resign his apartment, which is the most beautiful in the house, and to be satisfied with a pretty little room upon the third floor. But to this M. Porthos replied, that he was every moment expecting his mistress, who was one of the highest ladies at court: and that I ought to understand that the chamber which he did me the honour to occupy in my house, was scarcely good enough yet for such a visitor. Nevertheless, fully recognising the truth of what he said, I felt it my duty to insist; but, without condescending to enter into any discussion with me, he put a pistol on his night-table, and declared that at the first word which might be said to him about any moving whatsoever, either out of the house or in it, he would blow out the brains of the person who had been imprudent enough to interfere in what did not concern him. So, since that time, sir, nobody has once entered his room but his own servant."

"Oh! Mousqueton is here, is he?"

"Yes, sir. Five days after his departure, he came back in a very ill humour: it seems that he, also, had

met with some unpleasantry on his way. But he is, unfortunately, rather nimbler than his master, so that
he turns everything topsy-turvy, and, under the pretext
that we might refuse him what he asks for, takes anything he wants without asking at all."

"The fact is," replied d'Artagnan, "that I have always
remarked in Mousqueton a very superior intelligence and
zeal."

"Possibly so, sir; but if I should only find myself,
four times in a year in contact with a similar intelligence
and zeal, I should be a bankrupt."

"No! Porthos will pay you."

"Hum!" exclaimed the innkeeper, in a tone of doubt.

"He is the favourite of a lady of rank, who will not
allow him to remain in trouble on account of a trifle such
as he owes you."

"If I only dared to say what I think about that."

"What you think?"

"I might say more—what I know."

"What you know?"

"Or, even, what I am quite sure of!"

"And what are you so sure of? Come, say!"

"I should say that I know about this lady of rank."

"You?"

"Yes, me!"

"And how came you to know about her?"

"Oh! sir, if I thought I could depend on your
discretion."

"Speak; and, on the word of a gentleman, you shall
have no occasion to regret your confidence."

"Well! sir, you can understand that uneasiness makes
one do many things."

"What have you done?"

"Oh! nothing but what a creditor has a right
to do."

"Well?"

"M. Porthos had handed us a note for this duchess,
giving us orders to put it in the post. It was before his

own servant came; and, as he could not leave his room, he was obliged to employ us in his commissions."

"What next?"

"Instead of putting this letter in the post, which is uncertain, we took advantage of the occasion of one of our waiters going to Paris, and instructed him to deliver the letter to this duchess herself. That was fulfilling the intentions of M. Porthos, who had particularly enjoined us to be careful of the letter, was it not?"

"Nearly so."

"Well, sir, do you know what this lady of rank is?"

"No. I have heard Porthos speak of her: that is all."

"Do you know what this pretended duchess is?"

"I tell you again, I don't know her."

"She is an attorney's wife, sir; an elderly woman, called Madame Coquenard, who is at least fifty years of age, and yet takes it upon herself to be jealous. It seemed very strange to me, a princess living in the Rue aux Ours!"

"How do you know this?"

"Because she put herself in a great passion on receiving the letter, saying that M. Porthos was a fickle man, and that it was on account of some woman that he had received this sword wound."

"Then he has received a sword wound?" replied d'Artagnan.

"Ah, Mon Dieu! what have I said?" cried the innkeeper.

"You said that M. Porthos had received a wound from a sword."

"Yes; but he strongly enjoined me to say nothing about it."

"And why?"

"Plague, sir! because he boasted that he would perforate the stranger with whom you left him in a dispute; whilst, on the contrary, this stranger stretched him on the ground, in spite of his rhodomontades. Now, as M Porthos is a very vain-glorious man, except toward

his duchess, whom he thought to soften by an account of
his misadventure, he is not disposed to admit to anybody
that he is suffering from a wound."

"It is a sword wound, then, that keeps him in his
bed?"

"And a masterly one, I assure you. Your friend's
soul must be absolutely pinned to his body."

"Were you there, then?"

"I followed them, sir, from curiosity, so that I saw the
combat, myself invisible.

"And how did it happen?"

"Oh, the thing did not take long, I assure you. They
placed themselves on guard: the stranger made a feint,
and lunged, and that so rapidly, that, when M. Porthos
parried, he had already three inches of steel in his
chest. He fell back. The stranger put his sword to
his throat; and M. Porthos, seeing himself at the mercy
of his adversary, confessed himself vanquished. The
stranger then asked his name: and hearing that he was
M. Porthos, and not M. d'Artagnan, offered him his arm,
led him back to the hotel, mounted on horseback,
and disappeared."

"Then it was M. d'Artagnan that the stranger
wanted?"

"It appears so."

"And do you know what has become of him?"

"No, I had never seen him before that moment, and
we have not seen him since."

"Very well; I know all I want. And you say that
M. Porthos' chamber is on the first floor, No. 1?"

"Yes, sir, the handsomest in the house—a chamber
which I might have let ten or a dozen times."

"Bah! Cheer up!" said d'Artagnan, laughing:
"Porthos will pay you with the cash of the duchess
Coquenard."

"Oh! sir, attorney's wife or duchess would be no
matter to me, if she would only unloosen her purse-
strings; but she has positively said that she is tired out

by the inconstancies and exigencies of M. Porthos; and that she will not send him even a sou."

"And did you communicate this reply to your guest?"

"No; we were too careful for that. He would have found out the fashion in which we had executed our commission."

"Then he is still in expectation of the money?"

"Mon Dieu! yes. He wrote again yesterday: but his own servant this time took the letter to the post."

"You say the attorney's wife is old and ugly?"

"Fifty years old, at least, sir, and far from handsome, from what Pathand says."

"Be comforted, then. Her heart will melt towards him; and, at anyrate, Porthos cannot owe you much."

"What! not much? It is twenty pistoles already, without reckoning the surgeon. Oh! he denies himself nothing: it is plain that he has always been accustomed to live well!"

"Well, even if the duchess should fail him, he will find friends, I can assure you. So my dear landlord, do not disturb yourself, and continue to be most attentive to his comfort."

"You have promised me, sir, not to say a word about the attorney's wife, or the wound."

"That is agreed—you have my word."

"Oh! he would kill me, do you see!"

"Do not be afraid; he is not half such a devil as he seems!"

Saying these words, d'Artagnan mounted the stairs, leaving the landlord a little more encouraged concerning two things, of which he appeared to think a good deal—his money and his life.

At the top of the stairs, d'Artagnan found, on the most conspicuous door of the corridor, a gigantic No. 1 marked, with black ink. At this door he knocked, and, being invited from within, entered the room.

Porthos was lying down, and playing at lansquenet, with Mousqueton, to keep his hand in, whilst a spit burdened with partridges, was turning before the fire, and, at the two corners of an immense chimney, there were boiling, on two chafing-dishes, two saucepans, from which exhaled the double odour of a fricassee of fowls, and a hotch-potch of fish, which delighted the olfactory nerves. Besides, the top of a desk and the marble slab of a commode were covered with empty bottles.

At sight of his friend, Porthos uttered a loud and joyful cry; whilst Mousqueton, rising respectfully, gave up his place to him, and went to glance into the two saucepans, of which he appeared to have particular charge.

"Ah! egad! it is you!" said Porthos. "Welcome, welcome! Excuse me for not rising to meet you; but," added he, looking with some anxiety at d'Artagnan, "you know what has happened to me?"

"No."

"Has the innkeeper told you nothing?"

"I asked for you, and came up directly."

Porthos appeared to breathe more freely.

"And what has happened to you, then, my dear Porthos?" continued d'Artagnan.

"It happened that, in lunging at my adversary, to whom I had already given three sword wounds, and whom I wished to finish by a fourth, my foot caught against a stone, and I sprained my knee."

"Indeed!"

"Yes, upon my honour! Lucky it was for the rascal too, for I should otherwise have left him dead upon the spot, I assure you."

"And what became of him?"

"Oh, I know nothing about that; he had had quite enough of it, and went away without asking for the remainder. But you, my dear d'Artagnan, what happened to you?"

"So that," continued d'Artagnan, "it is this sprain that keeps you in bed, my dear Porthos?"

"Ah, Mon Dieu! yes; that is all; but in a few days I shall be on my legs again."

"But why did not you get yourself removed to Paris? You must have been sadly dull here?"

"It was my intention; but, my dear friend, I must confess one thing to you."

"And what is that?"

"It is, that as I became cruelly dull, as you say, and as I had in my pocket the seventy-five pistoles with which you provided me, I invited up a passing traveller, and proposed to him a game of dice. He agreed; and, faith, my seventy-five pistoles passed from my pocket into his, without reckoning my horse, which he carried off into the bargain. But you, my dear d'Artagnan."

"What would you have, my dear Porthos? You cannot be favoured in all your pursuits," said d'Artagnan. "You know the proverb—'lose at play, and win at love.' You are too fortunate in love, for play not to revenge itself. But what do these changes of fortune signify to you? Happy dog! have you not still got your duchess to assist you?"

"Nay! look, my dear d'Artagnan, how unlucky I am," replied Porthos, in the most unconcerned tone in the world. "I have written to her to send me some fifty louis, for which I have particular occasion in my present position."

"Well?"

"Well! She must be gone to her estate, for she has sent me no answer!"

"Really?"

"No; so I sent a second letter yesterday, rather more urgent than the first. But, my dear fellow, let us chat about your own affairs. I confess, I was beginning to feel some uneasiness on your account."

"But your host has behaved pretty well to you, apparently," said d'Artagnan, pointing to the teeming stewpans, and the empty bottles.

"So-so!" replied Porthos; "but it is only two or three days ago, now, since the impudent fellow brought me up his bill, and I showed them the door—both himself and his bill; so that I am now living here in something of the style of a conqueror. And, as you see, being somewhat afraid of being attacked in my redoubts, I am armed to the very teeth."

"Nevertheless," said d'Artagnan, laughing, "it seems that you sometimes make sorties."

And he pointed to the stewpans and the bottles.

"It is not me, unfortunately," said Porthos. "This miserable sprain keeps me in my bed; but Mousqueton, there, forages the country for supplies. Mousqueton, my friend," continued Porthos," "you see that a reinforcement has arrived: we shall want an addition to our rations."

"Mousqueton," said d'Artagnan, "there is a service you must do me."

"What is it, sir?"

"To give your recipe to Planchet! I may chance to be besieged myself hereafter, and I should not be at all sorry to enjoy all the advantages with which you gratify your master."

"Oh, sir," said Mousqueton modestly, "nothing is more easy. One must be a little adroit—that is all. I was brought up in the provinces, and my father, in his leisure moments, was something of a poacher."

"And how was he occupied in business hours?"

"He was engaged in a pursuit, sir, which I have always found a very happy one."

"What was that?"

"As it was in the time of the wars between the Catholics and Huguenots; and as he saw Catholics exterminating Huguenots, and Huguenots exterminating Catholics, all in the name of religion, he had made for himself a sort of mixed belief, which permitted him to be at one time a Catholic, and at another a Huguenot. He had a habit of walking out behind the hedges on the road side, with his carbine at his shoulder, and, when he saw a solitary Catholic coming, the Protestant religion immediately predominated in his mind, he lowered his carbine in the direction of the traveller, and then, when he was at ten paces from him, opened a conversation which almost always ended by the traveller relinquishing his purse to redeem his life. Of course, when he saw a Huguenot coming, he was seized with such an ardent Catholic zeal, that he could not comprehend how it had been possible for him, only a quarter of an hour before, to doubt the superiority of our most holy faith. For myself, sir, I am a Catholic; my father having, in conformity to his principles, made my elder brother a Huguenot."

"And what was the end of the worthy man?" asked d'Artagnan.

"Most unfortunate, sir. He found himself caught in a defile, between a Catholic and a Huguenot, with whom he had done some business previously, and they both recognised him; so they united against him, and hung him on a tree. And then they came and boasted of their foolish work in the very wine-shop, in the village, where my brother and I were drinking."

"And what did you do?" asked d'Artagnan.

"We let them talk," replied Mousqueton. "Then, as they went opposite roads when they left the wine-shop, my brother posted himself in the path of the Catholic, and I lay in wait for the Protestant. It was all settled two hours after: we had done the business of both of them—admiring the forethought of our poor father, who had taken the precaution to educate us each in a different faith."

"In fact—as you say, Mousqueton—your father seems to have been a very intelligent fellow. And you tell me, that the worthy man was, in his leisure moments, a poacher?"

"Yes, sir; and it was he who taught me to set a snare, and fix a night-line. The consequence was, that when I found our shabby landlord was feeding us on coarse meats, fit possibly for clowns, but not at all suitable to stomachs so delicate as ours, I had recourse again to my old trade. As I sauntered through the woods, I laid my snares in the paths; and, as I reclined beside the water, I slipped my lines into the ponds. In this way, thank God, we have experienced no scarcity, as you may be satisfied, sir, of patridges or rabbits, of carps or eels, and these are light and wholesome viands, highly suitable to sick persons."

"But wine," said d'Artagnan. "Your landlord furnishes the wine?"

"That is to say," answered Mousqueton, "yes and no!"

"What! yes and no?"

"He furnishes it, it is true; but he is unconscious of honour."

"Explain yourself, Mousqueton; your conversation is deep."

"This is the way of it; it chanced, that in my wanderings, I met with a Spaniard, who had seen many countries, and, amongst others, the New World."

"And what connexion can there be between the New World and those bottles on the desk and drawers?"

"Patience, sir, everything will come in its turn."

"That is fair, Mousqueton. I trust to you, and listen."

"This Spaniard had a servant, who had accompanied him on his voyage to Mexico. This servant was a compatriot of mine, and we became attached to one another the more quickly, as our characters were much alike. We were both particularly fond of hunting; and he related to me how, in the Pampas, the natives hunt tigers and bulls, simply with nooses of rope, which they throw over the necks of these terrible animals. At first, I would not believe that they could attain so great a degree of address, as to throw the end of a rope on what they wished, at the distance of twenty or thirty paces. But, with the proof before me, I was obliged to recognise the truth of his recital. My friend placed a bottle at thirty paces off, and, at each throw, caught it by the neck in a running noose. I practised this exercise; and, as nature has given me some capacity, I can now throw the lasso as well as any man in the world. Well! do you understand? Our landlord has a well-furnished cellar, of which he never loses sight of the key. But this cellar has an air-hole, and through that air-hole I throw the lasso; and as I now know the best corner, I always draw from thence. This is the connection, sir, between the New World and the bottles on the desk and drawers. And now will you taste our wine? and, without prejudice, you will tell us what you think of it."

"Thanks, my friend, thanks! But I have already breakfasted."

"Well!" said Porthos, "make all ready, Mousqueton; and whilst we breakfast, d'Artagnan will tell us what has happened to him during the ten days that he has been absent from us."

Whilst Porthos and Mousqueton breakfasted with all the appetite of convalescents, and that brotherly familiarity which draws men together in misfortune, d'Artagnan related that Aramis, being wounded, had been obliged to stop at Crevecœur; that he had left Athos fighting at Amiens, with four men, who accused him of being a coiner; and that he himself had been compelled to run the Count de Wardes through the body, in order to reach England.

But there the confidence of d'Artagnan ended: he merely announced that, on his return from England, he had brought four splendid horses with him, one for himself, and one for each of their companions; and he concluded by informing Porthos that the one destined for him was already in the stables of the hotel.

At this moment Planchet entered: he intimated to his master that the horses were sufficiently refreshed, and that it would be possible to go to Clermont in time to pass the night there.

As d'Artagnan was pretty well satisfied as to Porthos's state, and was anxious to gain some information concerning his two other friends, he gave his hand to the invalid, and told him that he should now proceed to continue his inquiries. And, as he expected to return by the same road, if Porthos, in seven or eight days, was still at the hotel of the Great Saint Martin, he would take him up upon his way.

Porthos answered, that in all probability his sprain would confine him till that time; and, moreover, he must wait at Chantilly for a reply from the duchess.

D'Artagnan wished him a speedy and favourable one; and, after having again commended him to the care of Mousqueton, and paid the landlord his own expenses, he once more took the road with Planchet, who was already relieved of one of the led horses.

CHAPTER XXVI.

THE THESIS OF ARAMIS.

D'ARTAGNAN had said nothing to Porthos, either about his wound, or about the attorney's wife. Young as he was, our Bearnese was very discreet. Consequently, he had pretended to believe everything that the boasting musketeer had told him, convinced that no friendship can support itself against a secret discovered, especially when that secret wounds the pride; since one always has a certain moral superiority over those with whose frailties we are acquainted. In his plans for the future, resolved as he was to make his three friends the instruments of his success, d'Artagnan was not sorry to collect in his hand those invisible threads by the aid of which he meant to lead them.

Nevertheless, throughout the whole of his journey, an overwhelming sadness hung upon his heart: he thought of that young and pretty Madame Bonancieux, who was to have bestowed upon him the reward of his devotion. Let us, however, at once declare, that the young man's melancholy was not so much a regret for his own lost enjoyment, as a dread that something unfortunate had befallen the missing woman. He had himself no doubt that she was a victim of the cardinal's vengeance; and it was well known that his eminence's revenge was always terrible. But how had he himself found pardon in the eyes of the minister? This was what he did not know, but what M. de Cavois, the captain of the guard, would undoubtedly have communicated to him, had he found him at home.

Nothing passes the time, or shortens the path, like a thought which engrosses all the faculties of an individual's organization. Our external existence is as a sleep, of which this thought is the dream; and, whilst we are subjected to its influence, time has no longer any measure, nor is there any distance in space: we leave one place, and arrive at another, and are conscious of nothing between. Of the intervening scenes, the only remembrance preserved, is somewhat akin to the idea of an indefinite mist, partially broken by obscure images of mountains, trees, and plains. It was under the dominion of this hallucination, that d'Artagnan at the pace that his horse pleased to take, passed over the six or eight leagues, which separated Chantilly from Crevecœur, without having, on his arrival at the latter village, any recollection of the things he had encountered on the road. But there memory returned to him: he shook his head, perceived the tavern where he had left Aramis, and, putting his horse into a trot, reined in at the door.

It was not a landlord this time, but a landlady, who received him. D'Artagnan, being somewhat of a physiognomist, examined, at a glance, the fat and good-humoured face of the mistress of the place; this glance satisfied him that dissimulation was not necessary with her, and that he had nothing to fear from such a happy-looking countenance.

"My good lady," demanded d'Artagnan, "can you tell me what has become of one of my friends, whom I was obliged to leave here about twelve days ago?"

"A handsome young man, of about twenty-three or twenty-four years of age, mild, amiable, and handsome?"

"Exactly so; and, moreover, wounded in the shoulder."

"Just so. Well, he is still here."

"Ah, my dear lady," said d'Artagnan, springing from his horse, and throwing the bridle to Planchet, "you give me life! Where is this dear Aramis? Let me embrace him, for I confess that I long to see him."

"Pardon me, sir, but I question whether he can see you at present."

"Why not? is there a lady with him?"

"Oh! dear me, sir, what a question! Poor youth! No, sir, there is not a woman with him."

"Who then?"

"The curate of Montdidier, and the superior of the Jesuits of Amiens."

"Good God!" exclaimed d'Artagnan, "is the poor young man so very ill?"

"No, sir, quite the contrary. But towards the end of his illness, he has been touched by grace, and has determined on taking holy orders."

"Ah, true!" said d'Artagnan; "I had forgotten that he was only a musketeer temporarily."

"Do you still insist on seeing him, sir?"

"Oh, yes, more than ever."

"Well, then, you have only to take the left-hand staircase in the courtyard, to No. 5, on the second floor."

D'Artagnan quickly followed this direction, and found one of those outside staircases which may still be sometimes seen in the courtyards of old-fashioned inns. But it was no such easy matter to get admission to the future abbé. The avenues of Aramis's chamber were as strictly guarded as the gardens of Armidus. Bazin was stationed in the corridor, and barred the passage against him with the more intrepidity, as, after many years of trial, he saw himself at length on the eve of acquiring that distinction, of which he had always been ambitious.

In fact, the dream of poor Bazin had ever been to serve a churchman, and he impatiently expected the so-long-anticipated moment, when Aramis would at last throw off his military uniform, and adopt the cassock. It had only been by the daily reiteration of this promise, that he had been induced to continue in the service of the musketeer, in which, as he said, he could not fail to forfeit his salvation.

Bazin was therefore at the very summit of happiness. There was every probability that his master would keep to his determination this time. The union of physical and moral pain, had produced the effect so long desired. Aramis, suffering at once in mind and body, had at length fixed his thoughts and eyes upon religion; and he had regarded, as a warning from heaven, the double accident which had befallen him—that is to say, the sudden disappearance of his mistress, and the wound in his shoulder.

In such a mood, it may be easily imagined that nothing could have been more disagreeable to Bazin, than the appearance of d'Artagnan, which might throw his master again into the whirlwind of those worldly ideas, of which he had been so long the sport.

He resolved, therefore, bravely to defend the door; and as, betrayed by the landlady, he could not say that Aramis was out, he attempted to prove to the newcomer, that it would be the height of impropriety to interrupt the pious conversation which his master had maintained since morning, and which, as Bazin added, could not be concluded before night.

But d'Artagnan paid no attention to the eloquent discourse of Bazin; not wishing to enter into a polemical discussion with his friend's valet, he simply put him aside with one hand, and turned the handle of the door of No. 5 with the other.

The door opened, and d'Artagnan entered the apartment.

Aramis, in a long black coat, and with his head encased in a kind of round flat cap, which was no bad representation of a skull cap, was seated at a long table, covered with rolls of paper, and enormous folios; on his right sat the superior of the Jesuits; and on his left, the curate of Montdidier. The curtains were half closed, giving entrance only to a subdued, mysterious light, appropriate to holy meditation. All those worldly objects which are apt to greet the eye in the chamber of a young man, and particularly when that young man is a musketeer, had disappeared, as though by enchantment; and, doubtless from a fear that the sight of them might recall his master's mundane inclinations, Bazin had laid hands upon the sword, the pistols, the plumed hat, and the embroidery and lace of every sort and kind.

But instead of these, d'Artagnan fancied he saw, in an obscure corner, something like a cord of discipline, hanging by a nail to the wall.

At the noise which d'Artagnan made on entering, Aramis raised his head, and recognised his friend. But, to the great surprise of the latter, this sight did not seem to produce much impression on the musketeer, so much was his mind detached from all terrestrial affairs.

"How are you, my dear d'Artagnan?" said Aramis. "Believe me, I am glad to see you."

"And I, also," said d'Artagnan; "although I am not yet quite sure that it is Aramis I am speaking to."

"The same, the same, my friend; but what could make you doubt it?"

"I thought I had mistaken the room, and entered the chamber of a churchman. And then another terror seized me, when I found you in the company of these gentlemen—I feared you were dangerously ill."

The two men in black launched a glance almost of menace at d'Artagnan, whose intention they perceived; but he did not on that account disturb himself.

"Perhaps I inconvenience you, my dear Aramis," continued d'Artagnan; "for, from what I see, I am led to suppose that you are confessing to these gentlemen."

Aramis coloured slightly.

"Oh, no, on the contrary, my dear friend; and, as a

proof of it, permit me to protest to you, that I rejoice at seeing you safe and sound !"

" Ah ! he is coming to himself again," thought d'Artagnan ; "this is fortunate !"

" This gentleman, who is my friend, has just escaped a serious danger," continued Aramis, addressing the two ecclesiastics, as he pointed to d'Artagnan with his hand.

" Praise God for it, sir," replied they, bowing their heads in concert.

" I have not failed to do so, reverend fathers," replied the young man, as he returned their salutation.

" You are come just in the nick of time, my dear d'Artagnan," continued Aramis, "and, by taking part in our discussion, you will enlighten it by your ability. M. the Principal of Amiens, M. the Curate of Montdidier, and myself, are arguing certain theological questions, which have long interested us, and on which I shall be delighted to have your opinion."

" The opinion of a soldier has but little weight," replied d'Artagnan, who began to be uneasy at the turn things were taking ; "you may rely upon the knowledge of these gentlemen."

The men in black bowed.

" On the contrary," replied Aramis, "your opinion will be of great value. The question is this : the Principal thinks that my thesis should be, above all things, dogmatic and didactic."

" Your thesis ! Are you preparing a thesis ?"

" Certainly," replied the Jesuit : "for the examination preceding ordination, a thesis is rigorously demanded."

" Ordination !" exclaimed d'Artagnan, who could scarcely believe what the landlady and Bazin had successively told him. " Ordination !" and his eyes wandered in astonishment over the three persons who were before him.

" Now," continued Aramis, disposing himself on his chair, in the same graceful manner as he would have done in the stall of a cathedral, and complacently examining his hand, which was as white and plump as that of a lady, and which he held up to make the blood flow out of it; "now, M. d'Artagnan, as you have heard, the Principal would have my thesis dogmatic, whilst, for my own part, I think it ought to be idealistic. It is on this account that the Principal has proposed to me the following subject, which has never yet been treated of, and in which I recognise matter susceptible of most magnificent developments :—

"*Utramque manum in benedicendo clericis inferioribus necessariae sit.*"

D'Artagnan, whose extent of erudition we are aware of, did not knit his brows at this citation, any more than at that which M. Treville had made to him on the occasion of the presents which he supposed d'Artagnan to have received from the Duke of Buckingham.

"Which means," resumed Aramis, in order to furnish him with every facility, "to the lower order of priests both hands are indispensable, when they give the benediction."

"Admirable and dogmatic," repeated the curate, whose knowledge of Latin was about equal to d'Artagnan's, and who carefully watched the Jesuit, in order to keep pace with him, and to reproduce his words like an echo.

As for our young Gascon, he was profoundly indifferent to the enthusiasm of the two men in black.

"Yes, admirable ! *prorsus admirabile !*" continued Aramis; "yet demanding a deep investigation of the writings of the fathers, and of the holy books. But I have owned to these learned ecclesiastics, and that in great humility, that the watches of the guards, and the service of the king, have made me to some extent negligent of study. I should therefore feel more at home, *facilius natans*, in some subject of my own selection, which would be, in relation to these difficult questions, what morals are to metaphysics in philosophy."

"See what an exordium!" exclaimed the Jesuit.

D'Artagnan was thoroughly tired; so, also, was the curate.

"*Exordium,*" repeated the curate, for the sake of saying something. "*Quem ad modum inter colœrum immensitatem.*"

Aramis glanced at d'Artagnan, and saw that his friend was gaping in a way to dislocate his jaws.

"Let us speak French, father," said he to the Jesuit. "M. d'Artagnan will more truly enjoy our discourse."

"Yes," said d'Artagnan, "I am fatigued by my journey, and all this Latin is beyond me."

"Agreed," said the Jesuit, somewhat piqued; whilst the delighted curate gave d'Artagnan a look of earnest gratitude. "Well! see the conclusion which might be drawn from this scholium.

"Moses, the servant of God—he is only the servant, do you observe?—Moses blessed with the hands: he had his two arms held forth, whilst the Hebrews battled with their foes; therefore, he blessed with the two hands. Besides, what says the Gospel? *Imposuite manus,* and not *manum*—lay on the hands, and not the hand."

"Lay on the hands," repeated the curate, performing at the same time the gesture.

"To St. Peter, again, of whom the popes are the successors," continued the Jesuit, "*porrige digitos*— stretch out the fingers: do you perceive now?"

"Certainly," said Aramis, in great delight; "but the point is subtle."

"The fingers," resumed the Jesuit — "Saint Peter blessed with the fingers. The pope, then, blesses also with the fingers. And with how many fingers does he bless? With three fingers: one for the Father, one for the Son, and one for the Holy Ghost."

They all crossed themselves at these words, and d'Artagnan thought it a duty to imitate the example.

"The pope is the successor of Saint Peter, and he represents the three divine powers — the remainder, *ordines inferiores*, of the ecclesiastical hierarchy, bless by the name of saints, archangels, and angels. The very humblest priests, such as our deacons and sacristans, bless with sprinklers, which simulate an indefinite number of blessing fingers. The subject is now simplified : *argumentum omni denudatum ornamento.* I could expand it," continued the Jesuit, "into two volumes of the size of this."

And, in his enthusiasm, he thumped the folio Saint Chrysostom, which made the table bend beneath its weight.

D'Artagnan trembled.

"Assuredly," said Aramis, "I render justice to the beauties of this thesis, but, at the same time, I feel that it would overwhelm me. I had chosen this text—tell me, dear d'Artagnan, if it is not to your taste :—'*non inutile est desiderium in oblatione*;' or, still better—'a small regret is not unbecoming in an offering to the Lord.'"

"Stop there !" vociferated the Jesuit, "for that thesis borders on heresy. There is a proposition almost identical in the *Augustinus* of the heresiarch Jansenius, for which, sooner or later, that book will be burned by the executioner's hands. Take care, my young friend : you incline towards false doctrines ; you will go astray, my young friend."

"You will go astray," said the curate, shaking his head in great concern.

"You are close upon the famous point of free-will, which is a fatal stumbling-block : you approach nearly the insinuations of the Pelagians and the semi-Pelagians."

"But, reverend sir——" resumed Aramis, somewhat stunned by the storm of arguments which descended on his head.

"How will you prove," continued the Jesuit, without allowing him time to speak, "that we ought to regret the world, when we offer ourselves to God? Listen to this dilemma: God is God, and the world is the devil; hence, to regret the world is to regret the devil. There is my reduction."

"It is mine also," said the curate.

"But, pray——" resumed Aramis.

"*Desideras diabolum!* unhappy man," exclaimed the Jesuit.

"He regrets the devil! Ah! my young friend," resumed the curate, with a groan, "do not regret the devil, I beseech you!"

D'Artagnan was beginning to lose his wits. He seemed to be in a company of madmen, and to be in danger himself of becoming as mad as those he was listening to. Only, he was necessitated to hold his tongue, from not understanding the language in which they talked.

"But, listen to me," interrupted Aramis, with a degree of politeness under which some impatience began to be perceptible; "I do not say that I regret. No; I never will pronounce that phrase, which would be unorthodox."

The Jesuit raised his arms towards heaven, and the curate did the same.

"No; but admit at least that it would be unbecoming merely to offer to the Lord that with which we are entirely disgusted. Am I right, d'Artagnan?"

"Quite so, I think, mon Dieu!" exclaimed the latter.

The curate and the Jesuit started from their seats.

"Now here is what I lay down—it is a syllogism. The world is not wanting in attractions: I quit the world: therefore, I make a sacrifice. Now, Scripture says positively, 'make a sacrifice unto the Lord.'"

"That is true," admitted the antagonists.

"Then," continued Aramis, pinching his ear to make it red, as he had before waved his hands to make them

white; "then, I have made a stanza upon this subject,
which I showed, last year, to M. Voiture, and on which
that great man highly complimented me."

"A stanza!" exclaimed the Jesuit scornfully.

"A stanza!" responded the curate mechanically.

"Recite it, recite it," vociferated d'Artagnan; "that
will be a little change."

"No change; for it is religious," replied Aramis; "it
is theology in verse."

"The devil!" exclaimed d'Artagnan.

"Here it is," said Aramis, with a gentle air of modesty,
which was not altogether exempt from hypocrisy :—

> "All you who mourn past happiness now flown,
>   And live through long and weary days of woe.
>   Your sorrows all a certain end shall know.
> When tears are offered to your God alone.
>   By you who mourn below!"

D'Artagnan and the curate seemed pleased. The
Jesuit persisted in his opinion.

"Be cautious of a profane taste in a theological style.
What, in fact, does St. Augustine say? '*Severus sit
clericorum sermo.*'"

"Yes, let the sermon be clear," said the curate.

"But," hastily interrupted the Jesuit, on seeing his
attendant blundering: "but, your thesis will please the
ladies, and that is all: it will have the popularity of
one of Maître Patru's pleadings."

"God grant it!" exclaimed Aramis, overjoyed.

"You say," resumed the Jesuit, "the world still speaks
within you, in a loud voice—*altissimâ voce.* You follow
the world, my young friend, and I fear that grace will
not prove efficacious."

"Doubt me not, reverend father; I answer for myself."

"Worldly presumption!"

"I know my own heart, father: my resolution is
irrevocable."

"Then, you persist in pursuing this thesis?"

"I feel myself called to treat that, and not any other one. I shall therefore continue it; and I trust that, to-morrow, you will be contented with the emendations which I shall have made in it, under your advice."

"Work slowly," said the curate; "we leave you in excellent dispositions."

"Yes, the ground is all sown," said the Jesuit, "and we have no reason to fear that some part of the seed has fallen in stony places, and some upon the highway, and that the birds of the air have eaten up the remainder: '*aves cæli comæderunt illam.*'"

"May the plague choke you with your Latin!" exclaimed d'Artagnan, whose patience would hold out no longer.

"Farewell, my son," said the curate: "farewell, till to-morrow."

"Adieu, till to-morrow, rash youth," said the Jesuit. "You promise to be one of the lights of the church: God grant that this light prove not a devouring flame!"

D'Artagnan, who had been gnawing his nails with impatience for an hour, was beginning to reach the flesh.

The two men in black bowed to Aramis and d'Artagnan, and proceeded towards the door. Bazin, who had kept standing, and had listened to this controversy with a pious jubilation, rushed towards them, seized the breviery of the curate, and the missal of the priest, and walked respectfully before them to clear their path.

Aramis himself conducted them to the bottom of the stairs, and came up again to d'Artagnan, who was still deep in meditation.

When they were left alone, the two friends at first maintained an embarrassed silence. Nevertheless, it was imperative that one of them should speak first, and d'Artagnan seemed determined to leave that honour to his friend.

"You see me," said Aramis, "return to my original ideas."

"Yes, as the gentleman said just now—efficacious grace has touched you."

"Oh, these plans of retirement have long been formed, and you, my friend, have often heard me speak of them, have you not?"

"Yes, certainly; but I confess that I always thought you were joking."

"What! about such things as these? Oh, d'Artagnan!"

"Why, we joke even in the face of death."

"And we are wrong to do so," said Aramis, "for death is the gate which leads to salvation or to condemnation."

"Agreed," said d'Artagnan. "But do not let *us* discuss theology: you must have had enough for the day; and, as for me, I confess I have almost forgotten the little Latin that I ever knew; and besides, to tell the truth, I have eaten nothing since ten o'clock this morning, and am as hungry as twenty devils."

"We will dine presently, my dear friend; only, you will remember, that this is Wednesday, and on that day I can neither eat meat, nor see any eaten. If you will be contented with my dinner, it is composed of boiled tetragones and fruit."

"What do you mean by tetragones!" anxiously inquired d'Artagnan.

"I mean spinach," replied Aramis; "but for you, I will add some eggs, although it is a grave infraction of rule, eggs being certainly meat, since they produce chickens."

"This feast is not very nourishing; but never mind: to remain with you, I will submit to it."

"I am grateful to you for the sacrifice," replied Aramis; "but, if it be not beneficial to your body, depend upon it, it will be so to your soul."

"So, Aramis, you decidedly entered the church? What will your friends say? What will M. de Treville say? They will look upon you as a deserter, I forewarn you."

"I do not enter the church—I re-enter it. It was the church that I deserted for the world; for you are aware that I did violence to my inclinations in taking the uniform of a musketeer."

"I know nothing about it."

"Are you ignorant, then, of my reasons for quitting the seminary?"

"Entirely so."

"Then listen to my history. Besides, the Scriptures say, 'confess yourselves to one another;' and I shall confess to you, d'Artagnan."

"And I give you absolution beforehand; you know that I am a good-hearted fellow."

"Do not jest with sacred things, my friend."

"Go on, then: I am listening."

"I had been at the seminary from the age of nine years until I was one-and-twenty: in three days more I was to be an abbé, and all would have been over. One evening, when I went, according to my custom, to a house which I frequented with pleasure—what can be expected from the young but weakness?—an officer, who was jealous because I often read the *Lives of the Saints* to the mistress of the house, suddenly came in unannounced. On that very evening I had been translating an episode of Judith into verse, and was communicating it to the lady, who was paying me all sorts of compliments, and was leaning on my shoulder to read the verses over with me. The attitude, which was, I confess, rather free, offended the officer: he said nothing at the time, but when I went out, he followed me and overtook me. 'M. l'Abbé,' said he, 'do you like canings?'—'I cannot tell, sir,' said I, 'no one having ever dared to give me any.'—'Well, then, hear me, M. l'Abbé: if you enter that house again, where I met you this evening, I will dare to do so.'

"I believe I was afraid: I became very pale; I perceived that my legs failed me; I sought for some answer, but found none; so I kept silent. The officer waited for my answer; but finding that it did not come, he began to laugh, turned upon his heel, and re-entered the house.

"I returned to the seminary. I am a gentleman born, and have a high spirit, as you have remarked, my dear d'Artagnan. The insult was terrible; and, entirely unknown as it was to the rest of the world, I felt it living and moving at my very heart's core. I declared to my superior, that I did not think myself sufficiently prepared for ordination, and at my request the ceremony was put off for a year. I sought out the best fencing-master in Paris; I engaged him for one lesson every day; and every day, throughout a whole year, I took that lesson. Then, on the very anniversary of the day on which I had been insulted, I hung my cassock on a peg; I took the complete costume of a cavalier, and went to a ball given by a lady of my acquaintance, where I knew that I should find my man. It was in the Rue des Frances-Bourgeois, very near La Force.

"My officer was indeed there. I went up to him, as he was singing a love ditty, and looking tenderly at a lady, and I interrupted him in the very middle of the second verse. 'Sir,' said I, 'are you still unwilling that I should enter a certain house in the Rue Payenne, and will you still give me a caning if I should take it into my head to disobey you?'"

"The officer looked at me with astonishment, and then said, 'What do you want, sir? I do not know you.'—'I am,' said I, 'the little abbé who was reading the lives of the saints, and who translated Judith into verse.'—'Ah, ah! I remember,' said the officer, merrily; 'and what do you want?'—'I would wish you to find leisure to take a walk with me.'—'To-morrow, with great pleasure, if you really wish it.'—'No, not to-morrow if you please, but immediately.'—'If you positively require it.'—'Yes, I do positively require it.'—'Come, then, let us go,' said he. 'Ladies, do not disturb yourselves; only give me time to kill this gentleman, and I will return and finish the second verse.'

"We went out. I led him to the Rue Payenne, to the exact spot where, a year before, and exactly at the same hour, he had complimented me as I have related to you. The moonlight was superb. We drew our swords; and, at the first pass, I struck him dead."

"The devil!" exclaimed d'Artagnan.

"Now, as the ladies did not perceive their singer return, and as he was found in the Rue Payenne, with a frightful sword wound right through his body, it was thought that it was I who had so accommodated him, and the affair caused some scandal. I was, therefore, obliged, for a time, to give up the cassock. Athos, with whom I made acquaintance about that period, and Porthos, who had taught me, in addition to my fencing lessons, some merry thrusts, determined me on demanding the uniform of a musketeer. The king had loved my father, who was killed at the siege of Arras, and this uniform was granted to me. Now, you will understand, that the day is now arrived for my return into the bosom of the church."

"And why to-day, more than yesterday or to-morrow? What has happened to you now, to give you such miserable ideas?"

"This wound, my dear d'Artagnan, has been to me a warning from Heaven."

"This wound—bah! it is almost healed. I am quite certain it is not that which causes the worst of your suffering."

"And what is it?" said Aramis, colouring.

"You have a deeper one in your heart, Aramis — one that bleeds more — a wound made by a woman."

The eye of Aramis sparkled involuntarily.

"Ah," said he, concealing his emotion under a feigned negligence; "do not speak of such things! Such thoughts are not for me; nor such solicitudes of love! *Vanitas vanitatum!* What, do you suppose then that my brain is turned? And for whom? Some pretty wench, some canon's daughter, to whom I might have paid my court in garrison? For shame!"

"Pardon, my dear Aramis, but I thought that you carried your aim a little higher."

"Higher? And what am I, that I should have so much ambition? A poor musketeer, unprovided for and obscure, who hates servitude, and feels himself an intruder in the turmoil of the world."

"Aramis! Aramis!" exclaimed d'Artagnan, looking on his friend with a glance of doubt.

"Dust," continued Aramis, "I return to dust. Life is full of sorrow and humiliation," continued he, in deep affliction: "all the threads which bind the woof of happiness break in our hands by turns: fragile, above all, are the threads of gold. Oh! my dear d'Artagnan," added Aramis, infusing into his tone a slight degree of bitterness, "believe me, you must conceal carefully whatever wounds you have. Silence is the last enjoyment of the unfortunate; let none know your grief; the curious would call up our tears, as insects suck the life-blood of a wounded deer."

"Alas! my dear Aramis," said d'Artagnan, sighing deeply in his turn, "it is my own history which you are unfolding."

"What?"

"Yes, a woman whom I loved, whom I adored, has just been carried away by force. I know not where she is, where she has been taken to: perhaps she is in prison —perhaps dead!"

"But you at least have the consolation of knowing that she did not quit you voluntarily, and that if you do not hear from her, it is because communication is prevented; whilst——"

"Whilst what?"

"Nothing," replied Aramis; "nothing."

"Then you renounce the world for ever? It is a settled choice—an irrevocable determination."

"Yes, for ever! You are my friend to-day; to-morrow

you will be only as a shadow, or rather you will no longer exist for me. As for the world, it is at best no better than a sepulchre."

"The plague! This is all very lamentable."

"What would you desire? My vocation summons me —it impels me onwards!"

D'Artagnan smiled, but made no reply. Aramis continued:—

"Nevertheless, whilst I am still belonging to the world, I would talk with you about yourself, and our friends."

"And I," said d'Artagnan, "would gladly have conferred with you about yourself, did I not see you so dissevered from all earthly things: at love, you cry shame; friends are shadows; and the world itself is but a sepulchre."

"Alas! you will, at last, yourself find it so!" exclaimed Aramis, with a sigh.

"Let us waste no more words about that," said d'Artagnan, "and let us burn this letter, which possibly announces to you some new infidelity of some pretty waiting-maid."

"What letter?" eagerly cried Aramis.

"A letter which came to your lodgings during your absence, and which I have taken charge of!"

"But from whom comes this letter?"

"Perhaps from some disconsolate wench, some waiting-maid of Madame de Chevreuse possibly, who was obliged to return to Tours with her mistress; and who, to make herself gaudy, has provided perfumed paper, and sealed the letter with a duchess's coronet!"

"What are you telling me?"

"I cannot surely have lost it," gravely remarked the young man, pretending to search for it. "But, happily, the world is a sepulchre—the men, and consequently the women, are shadows—and love is a sentiment at which you cry shame!"

"Ah! d'Artagnan! d'Artagnan! you kill me!" ejaculated Aramis.

"At last, here it is," said d'Artagnan, drawing the letter from his pocket.

Aramis made a bound, seized the letter, and read, or rather devoured it, whilst his countenance gleamed with joy.

"The waiting-maid seems to write in a good style," said the messenger carelessly.

"Thanks, d'Artagnan!" exclaimed the almost delirious Aramis. "She could not help it: she was compelled to return to Tours: she has not been unfaithful to me: she loves me still. Come, my friend, let me embrace you: my happiness suffocates me!"

And the two friends began dancing round the folios of the venerable St. Chrysostom, treading gallantly on the leaves of the thesis, which had fallen to the ground.

At this moment Bazin entered with the spinach and the omelette.

"Fly, wretch!" cried Aramis, throwing his skull-cap at Bazin's head. "Return whence you came; take away these horrible vegetables and those frightful eggs! Ask for a larded hare, a fat capon, a leg of mutton and garlic, and four bottles of old Burgundy!"

Bazin, who looked at his master, and could make nothing of this change, let the omelette fall, in his despair, upon the spinach, and the spinach upon the carpet.

"Now is the time," said d'Artagnan, "to consecrate your existence to the King of kings, if you desire to do Him homage: '*non in utile desirum in oblatione.*'"

"Go to the devil, with your Latin, my dear d'Artagnan. Let us drink! Egad! let us drink, and tell me a little of what has been going on in the world."

CHAPTER XXVII.

THE WIFE OF ATHOS.

"Now we must obtain some intelligence of Athos," said d'Artagnan to the joyous Aramis, after he had told him everything that had happened since their departure from Paris, and after an excellent dinner had made the one forget his thesis, and the other his fatigue.

"Do you believe, then, that any misfortune has befallen him?" demanded Aramis. "Athos is so cool, so brave, and wields his sword so skilfully!"

"Yes, doubtless, and no one knows better than I do the courage and address of Athos. But I like better the shock of lances on my sword, than the blows of sticks; and I fear that Athos may have been beaten by the rabble, who hit hard, and do not leave off quickly. It is, I confess, on this account that I should like to set out as soon as possible."

"I will endeavour to accompany you," said Aramis, "although I am scarcely in a fit state to mount a horse. Yesterday, I used the discipline, which you see on the wall; but the pain made me give up that pious exercise."

"My dear friend, none ever heard of endeavouring to cure the wounds of a carbine by the strokes of a cat-o'-nine-tails. But you were ill; and, as illness makes the head light, I excuse you."

"And when shall you set out?"

"To-morrow, at break of day. Rest as well as you can to-night, and to-morrow, if you are able, we will go together."

"Farewell, then, till to-morrow," said Aramis; "for, iron as you are, you must surely want some rest."

When d'Artagnan entered Aramis's room, the next morning, he found him looking out of the window.

"What are you looking at?" said he.

"Faith, I am admiring those three magnificent horses which the stable-boys are holding: it is a princely pleasure to travel on such animals."

"Well, then, my dear Aramis, you will give yourself that pleasure, for one of those horses belongs to you."

"Nonsense! and which?"

"Whichever you like, for I have no preference."

"And the rich caparison which covers him—is that, also, mine?"

"Certainly."

"You are laughing at me, d'Artagnan."

"I have left off laughing since you began to speak French again."

"And are those gilded holsters, that velvet housing, and that saddle, studded with silver, mine?"

"Yours! Just as that horse which steps so proudly is mine; and that other one, which caracoles so bravely, is for Athos."

"I'faith, they are superb animals."

"I am glad that they suit your taste."

"Is it the king, then, who has made you this present?"

"You may be quite sure that it was not the cardinal: but do not disturb yourself as to whence they came, only be satisfied that one of them is your own."

"I choose the one that the red-haired valet is holding."

"Well chosen."

"Thank God!" cried Aramis, "this drives away the last remnant of my pain. I would mount such a horse with thirty bullets in my body. Ah! upon my soul, what superb stirrups. Hallo! Bazin, come here this instant."

Bazin appeared, silent and melancholy, at the door.

"Polish up my sword, smarten my hat, brush my cloak, and load my pistols!" said Aramis.

"The last order is unnecessary," said d'Artagnan, "for there are loaded pistols in your holsters."

Bazin sighed deeply.

"Come, Master Bazin, console yourself," said

d'Artagnan; "the kingdom of heaven may be gained in any condition of life."

"But he was already such a good theologian," said Bazin, almost in tears; "he would have become a bishop —perhaps even a cardinal."

"Well! my poor Bazin, let us see, and reflect a little. What is the use of being a churchman, pray? You do not by that means avoid going to war; for you see that the cardinal is about to make his first campaign with a head-piece on, and a halbert in his hand; and M. de Nogaret de la Valette, what do you say to him? He is a cardinal too, and ask his lackey how often he has made lint for him."

"Alas!" sighed Bazin, "I know it, sir. The whole world is turned topsy-turvy, nowadays."

During this talk the two young men and the poor lackey had gone downstairs.

"Hold my stirrup for me, Bazin," said Aramis.

Aramis sprang into his saddle with his accustomed grace and activity; but, after some curvets and capers of the noble animal, the rider felt his pains so utterly insupportable, that he grew pale, and wavered in his seat. D'Artagnan, who, foreseeing such a misfortune, had kept his eye upon him, rushed towards him, caught him in his arms, and led him back again to his room.

"Never mind, my dear Aramis," said he; "take care of yourself. I will go alone in search of Athos."

"You are a man of steel," said Aramis.

"No," replied he, "I am fortunate—that is all. But what will you do whilst I am absent? No more theses; no more arguments on hands; no benedictions—hey!"

Aramis smiled.

"No, I shall make verses," said he.

"Yes! Verses with the same perfume as the note of Madame de Chevreuse's waiting-maid. Teach Bazin prosody: that will fill him with delight; and, as for the horse, ride him for a little while every day, and that will make you accustomed to the work."

"Oh! as for that, be satisfied that you shall find me ready to follow you."

They bade each other adieu; and in a few minutes d'Artagnan, having commended his friend to the care of Bazin and the landlady, was trotting onwards on his way towards Amiens.

And in what condition should he find Athos? Should he even find him at all?

The position in which he had left him was critical, and it was not improbable that Athos might have been destroyed.

This idea clouded the brow of d'Artagnan, and made him mutter many a vow of vengeance.

Of all his friends, Athos was the eldest, and apparently the least akin to him in sympathies and tastes. And yet he had a marked preference for this gentleman. The noble and distinguished air of Athos—those flashes of dignity, which, from time to time, shone forth from the cloud in which he had voluntarily enveloped himself—that unalterable equanimity of temper, which made him the best companion in the world—that forced yet ironic gaiety—that courage, which would have been denominated blind, had it not been the result of the rarest coolness;—so many excellent qualities attracted more than the esteem, more even than the friendship, of d'Artagnan: they attracted his admiration.

In fact, by the side even of the elegant and noble courtier, M. de Treville, Athos, in his bright days, might advantageously sustain comparison. He was of only medium height, but his figure was so admirably formed and proportioned, that, more than once, in his sportive contests with Porthos, he had subdued the giant, whose physical power had become proverbial amongst the musketeers. His countenance, with its piercing eyes, and aquiline nose, and a chin chiselled like that of Brutus, had an indescribable character of dignity and grace. His hands, of which he took no care, were the despair of Aramis, who cherished his at a great expense of almond paste and perfumed oil. The sound of his voice was penetrating and, at the same time, melodious. And then —a something altogether indefinable in Athos, who shrunk from all display—there was a delicate knowledge of the world, and of the customs of the most brilliant society, that was perceptible, apparently without his being conscious of it, in all his minutest actions.

If a banquet was to be prepared, Athos could preside better than anybody else, placing every guest in the precise rank and station to which his ancestry, or his own achievements, had entitled him. If heraldic science was required, Athos knew all the noble families in the kingdom, their genealogies, their alliances, their arms, and the origin of their arms. Etiquette had no minutiæ with which he was not well acquainted. He knew the various rights of the great landowners; and so thoroughly understood hunting and falconry, that one day, in talking of that art, he had astonished the king himself, who was a past-master of it. Like all the noblemen of the time, he rode and fenced to perfection. And, more than that, his education had been so well attended to, even on scholastic points, which were rarely introduced amongst gentlemen of that age, that he smiled at the scraps of Latin which Aramis let fall, and which Porthos pretended to understand; and two or three times even, to the great astonishment of his friends, when Aramis had made some mistake in the rudiments, Athos had put a verb into its proper tense, or a noun into its case. Besides all this, his probity was unimpeachable, at a time when military men made so light of their religion and conscience; lovers, of the rigorous delicacy of our own days; and the poor, of the seventh commandment of their God.

Athos was, therefore, a very extraordinary man. And yet, this nature so distinguished, this creature so beautiful, this essence so fine, was seen to turn insensibly towards a material life, as old men often tend to physical and moral imbecility. In his hours of privation—and these were frequent—Athos was extinguished as respected all his luminous nature, and all his brilliant qualities disappeared as in a dark night. Then, in place of the vanished demi-god, there remained scarcely a human being: his head drooped, his eye was dull, his voice heavy and languid; and he would look for hours at nothing but his bottle and his glass, or at Grimaud, who, accustomed to obey him by signs, read in his look the smallest wish, which he immediately gratified. If the four friends met by chance, during one of these intervals, a word, escaping as if by a violent effort, was all that Athos could contribute to the conversation; but, to compensate for this deficiency, Athos alone drank as much as all the rest, without any other apparent effect than a more manifest contraction of the eyebrows, and a more profound melancholy.

D'Artagnan, with whose inquisitive and penetrating mind we are already acquainted, whatever motive he might have for indulging his curiosity on the subject, had been unable hitherto to assign any cause for this melancholy, or for its frequent recurrence. Athos never received any letters, and never did anything which was not known to his three friends. It could not be said that this sadness was a result of wine; for, on the contrary, he only drank, in the hope of conquering that which this remedy did really increase. His despondency could not be attributed to play; for, unlike Porthos, who indicated, by songs and oaths, all the fluctuations of fortune, Athos maintained the same impassability, whether he had won or lost. In the circle of the musketeers, he had been seen to win three thousand pistoles in an evening, and to lose them again, as well as his horse, his arms, or even his gold-embroidered gala belt, and to win back the whole of these, and a hundred louis over, without his handsome black eyebrow having been depressed or raised by a hair's-breadth; without his hand having lost its pearly hue; and without his conversation, which was on that particular evening cheerful, having ceased for one instant to be agreeable and calm.

Nor was it, as in the case of our neighbours the English, an atmospheric influence which clouded over his countenance; for this sadness became more intense in the most brilliant seasons of the year: June and July were the bad months of Athos.

It was not about the present that he grieved; and he shrugged his shoulders when any one spoke to him of the future. His secret sorrow, then, had reference to the past, as had been vaguely told to d'Artagnan.

The mysterious complexion which was thus spread over him, only rendered more interesting the man who, neither by his eyes nor tongue, had ever, even in the most complete intoxication, revealed anything to the most skilfully conducted investigation.

"Well," mused d'Artagnan, "poor Athos may perhaps be now dead, and dead through my fault, for it was I who drew him into this affair, of which he knew neither the origin nor aim, and from which he could expect no benefit."

"Without reckoning, sir," said Planchet, "that we probably owe our lives to him. You remember how he cried out: 'Away, d'Artagnan! I am seized!' and, after having discharged his two pistols, what a terrible noise he made with his sword! One would have believed there were twenty men, or, rather, twenty mad devils!"

These words redoubled d'Artagnan's eagerness. He urged forward his horse, which, needing no urging, carried him on at a gallop.

Towards eleven in the morning they caught sight of Amiens; and at half-past eleven they were at the door of the fatal inn.

D'Artagnan had often meditated, against the treacherous host, one of those genuine acts of vengeance which give no satisfaction, except in the anticipation. He entered the hotel with his hat over his eyes, his left hand on the hilt of his sword, making his riding-whip whistle with his right.

"Do you know me?" said he to the landlord, who came forward to welcome him.

"I have not that honour, sir," replied the latter, his eyes dazzled by the splendid equipage with which d'Artagnan presented himself.

"Ah! you do not recognise me?"

"No, sir."

"Well, then, two words will restore your recollection. What have you done with that gentleman, against whom you had the audacity, about a fortnight ago, to bring an accusation of passing bad money."

The host turned pale, for d'Artagnan had assumed a most threatening attitude, and Planchet closely followed his master's example.

"Ah, sir, do not mention that," replied the host, in a most lamentable tone of voice; "ah, sir, how dearly have I paid for that fault! Alas! unfortunate has been my fate!"

"This gentleman, I ask—what has become of him?"

"Only deign to hear me, sir, and be merciful. Be seated, I beseech you!"

D'Artagnan, dumb from anger and anxiety, sat down, stern as a judge, and Planchet finally established himself behind his chair.

"This is the statement, sir," said the trembling landlord; "for now I recognise you. It was you who went away when I had that unhappy dispute with the gentleman of whom you speak."

"Yes, it was I; so you see that you have no mercy to expect, if you do not tell the whole truth."

"Condescend to listen, sir, and you shall hear everything."

"I hear you."

"I had been informed by the authorities that a celebrated coiner would arrive at my hotel, with several of his companions, all disguised under the uniform of guards or musketeers. Your horses, your servants, your features, gentlemen, were all exactly described."

"What next? what next?" cried d'Artagnan, who soon discerned the source of this precise description.

"Therefore, under the direction of the authorities, who sent me a reinforcement of six men, I took such measures as I considered indispensable to secure the persons of these alleged coiners."

"Well!" said d'Artagnan, whose ears were terribly wounded by this term *coiners*.

"Forgive me, sir, for speaking of such things, but they are truly my excuse. The authorities had frightened me; and you know that an innkeeper must respect the authorities."

"But, once more, where is this gentleman? What has become of him? Is he dead, or is he alive."

"Patience, sir, we have just come to that. Well, sir, you know what happened; and your hasty departure," added the innkeeper, with a cunning, which did not escape d'Artagnan, "seemed to justify my proceedings. The gentleman, your friend, defended himself desperately. His servant had, unfortunately, sought an unexpected quarrel with the officers of justice, who were disguised as stableboys."

"Ah! the wretches!" cried d'Artagnan. "You were all in the plot, and I know not why I should not exterminate you all!"

"Alas! no, sir, we were not all agreed, as you will soon perceive. The gentleman, your friend—pardon me for not giving him the honourable name which no doubt he bears, but we do not know that name—the gentleman, your friend, after having disabled two men by his two pistol-shots, beat a retreat, defending himself with his sword, with which he also maimed another of my men, and with the flat side of which he stunned me."

"But, hangman! will you make an end? Athos! what has become of Athos?"

"In beating his retreat, as I have told you, sir, he found behind him the cellar stairs, and, as the door was open, he rushed into it. Once there, he locked the door, and barricaded himself within; and, as we were sure of finding him there, we let him alone."

"Yes," said d'Artagnan, " it was not thought necessary to kill him, but only to imprison him."

"Good God! to imprison *him*, sir! He imprisoned himself, I swear! For, first, he had made a pretty severe business of it :—one man was killed outright, and two were grievously wounded. The dead man and the two wounded ones were carried off by their companions, and I have never since heard any more of either party. I myself, when I had recovered my senses, went to find the governor, to whom I related everything that had taken place, and of whom I inquired what I was to do with the prisoner. But the governor seemed as if he were entirely ignorant of the matter : he told me that he did not know what I was talking about; that the orders I had received did not come from him; and that, if I had the misfortune to tell any one whatever, that he had anything to do with this disturbance, he would have me hung. It appeared that I had made an error, sir; that I had arrested the wrong person; and that he who was to have been arrested had escaped."

"But Athos!" cried d'Artagnan, who became doubly bold when he found that the authorities disclaimed the affair: "what has become of him?"

"As I was in haste to repair the injury I had inflicted on the prisoner," replied the innkeeper, "I hurried to the cellar, to liberate him. Ah! sir, he was no longer a man —he was a devil! On proposing his liberation, he declared that it was a snare which was laid for him, and that before he came out he must impose conditions. I told him, with great humility—for I did not conceal from myself the awkward position in which I had placed myself by laying hands on one of his majesty's musketeers —I told him that I was ready to submit to his conditions."

"First," said he, "you must give me back my servant, completely armed."

"We hastened to obey this order; for, you understand, sir, that we were disposed to do everything that your friend wished. M. Grimaud—for he told us his name, although he speaks but little—M. Grimaud was sent down into ·the cellar, all wounded as he was; and his master having received him, barricaded the door again, and sent us about our business."

"But, after all," cried d'Artagnan, "where is he? Where is Athos?"

"In the cellar, sir."

"What, you rascal! have you kept him in the cellar all this time?"

"Good heavens! no, sir. We keep him in the cellar? You do not know, then, what he has been at there? Ah! if you could only persuade him to come out, sir, I should be for ever grateful to you—I would adore you as my patron saint!"

"Then he is there? I shall find him there?"

"Certainly, sir; he has obstinately persisted in remaining there. Every day we put through the air-hole some bread on the point of a pitchfork, and some meat too, when he asks for it; but, alas! it is not of bread and meat that he makes the greatest consumption. I endeavoured once to go down, with two of my servants; but he went into a terrible fury. I heard the click of his pistols, and of his servant's carbine. Then, when we asked what their intentions were, the master answered, that they had between them forty shots to fire, and that they would fire them all, even to the last, sooner than permit any one of us to put a foot in the cellar. Then, sir, I went and complained to the governor, who told me that I had only got what I deserved, and that this would teach me to insult honourable gentlemen who put up at my house."

"So that, since that time——" replied d'Artagnan, who was unable to refrain from laughing at the piteous face of the innkeeper.

"So that, from that time, sir," continued he, "we lead the saddest life that can be imagined; for, sir, you must know, that all our provisions are in the cellar. Our wine in bottles is there, and our wine in casks; beer, oil, spices, lard, and sausages; and, as we are forbidden to go down, we are obliged to refuse provisions and drink to the travellers who come here, so that we lose custom every day. Should your friend stop in my cellar one more week, we shall be utterly ruined."

"And serve you right, too, you knave! Could you not plainly see, by our appearance, that we were men of quality, and not coiners?"

"Yes, sir, yes; you are right," said mine host. "But, hark! hark! he is getting into a passion now."

"No doubt somebody has disturbed him," said d'Artagnan.

"But he needs must be disturbed," exclaimed the host. "Two English gentlemen have just come in."

"Well, what then?"

"Well, the English gentlemen love good wine, as you know, sir; and these gentlemen have called for the best. My wife has, no doubt, asked permission of M. Athos to enter, to satisfy these gentlemen, and he has refused, as usual. Ah, merciful goodness! listen how the row increases."

D'Artagnan did, in fact, hear a great noise proceeding from the cellar. He therefore arose, and, preceded by the landlord, who wrung his hands, and followed by Planchet, who carried his carbine ready cocked, he approached the scene of action. The two gentlemen were highly exasperated; they had travelled a long way, and were fainting with hunger and thirst.

"But it is positive tyranny," cried they, in very good French, although with a foreign accent, "that this down-right madman will not allow these good people the use of their own wine. We will break open the door, and, if he is too furious, we will kill him."

"Hold there, gentlemen!" exclaimed d'Artagnan, drawing his pistols from his belt; "you will not kill any one, if you please."

"Very good, very good," said the calm voice of Athos,

from behind the door ; "let these child-eaters enter, and we shall soon see."

Brave as they appeared to be, the two Englishmen looked at one another with some degree of hesitation. One would have said that the cellar contained one of those ravenous ogres—those gigantic heroes of popular legend—whose cavern none could enter with impunity.

There was a moment of silence ; but, at last, the two Englishmen were ashamed to retire, and the most impatient of them went down five or six steps of the staircase, and gave the door a kick, sufficient to break through a wall.

"Planchet," said d'Artagnan, cocking his pistols, "I will take the one that is up here ; you take charge of him who is below. Ah ! gentlemen, you wish for a fight, do you ? Well ! we will give you one !"

"My God !" cried the hollow voice of Athos, "I think I hear d'Artagnan's voice."

"Yes," said d'Artagnan, raising his voice in his turn ; "it is I myself, my friend."

"Good !" said Athos, "then we'll handle these door-breakers !"

The gentlemen had drawn their swords, but finding themselves caught between two fires, they hesitated again for a moment. As before, however, pride carried the day, and a second kick made the door crash from top to bottom.

"Step aside, d'Artagnan, step aside," cried Athos, "I am going to fire."

"Gentlemen," cried d'Artagnan, whose coolness never forsook him—"gentlemen, think better of it. Wait a moment, Athos. You are about to begin a bad business, gentlemen, and will be riddled with shot. Here are I and my servant, who will give you three shots ; you will receive the same number from the cellar ; and then we shall still have our swords, which I and my friend can handle pretty well, I assure you. Let me arrange the affair. You shall have something to drink directly, I give you my word."

"If there is any left," growled Athos, in a sneering tone.

The innkeeper felt a cold perspiration trickling down his spine.

"What! if there is any left!" muttered he.

"What the deuce!" replied d'Artagnan, "there must be some left; surely these two cannot have drunk out the cellar. Gentlemen, return your swords to their scabbards."

"Well! put your pistols back into your belts."

"Willingly."

D'Artagnan set the example. Then, turning to Planchet, he made him a sign to uncock his carbine.

The Englishmen were satisfied, yet grumbled as they sheathed their swords. D'Artagnan gave them an account of Athos's imprisonment, and, as they were men of honour, they blamed the innkeeper.

"Now, gentlemen," continued he, "return to your chamber, and I answer for it, that in ten minutes you shall have everything you want."

The Englishmen bowed and departed.

"Now that I am alone, my dear Athos," said d'Artagnan, "open the door to me, I implore you."

"Directly," said Athos.

Then was heard the sound of clashing fagots and groaning beams; these were the counterscarps and bastions of Athos, which the besieged was himself demolishing.

In another instant the door moved, and there was seen the pale face of Athos, who, with a rapid glance, surveyed the outworks.

D'Artagnan threw himself upon his neck, and embraced him tenderly. But, when he wished to lead him out of this humid habitation, he perceived that Athos staggered.

"You are wounded?" exclaimed he.

"Me? Not the least in the world. I am dead drunk, that's all; and never did man do more to become so.

Vive Dieu! landlord, I must have drunk, for my own share, at least one hundred and fifty bottles."

"Gracious heavens!" exclaimed the landlord; "if the servant has drunk only half as much as the master, I am ruined."

"Grimaud is too well-behaved a servant," said Athos, "to allow himself to live in the same manner as his master: he has therefore only drunk out of the cask. Hark! I verily believe that he has forgotten to put the spigot in. Do you hear? It is running."

D'Artagnan broke out into a roar of laughter, which changed the landlord's shivers into a raging fever.

At the same time Grimaud made his appearance, behind his master, with his carbine on his shoulder, and his head shaking, like the drunken Satyr in Rubens' pictures. He was soaked, both before and behind, with an unctuous liquid, which the landlord recognised as his best olive oil.

The little company crossed the large room, and installed itself in the best apartment of the inn, of which d'Artagnan took possession authoritatively.

In the meantime, the landlord and his wife hastened with lamps into the cellar, from which they had been so long excluded, and where a frightful spectacle awaited them.

Beyond the fortifications, in which Athos had made a breach to get out, and which were composed of fagots, planks, and empty casks, arranged according to the rules of strategic art, they saw here and there, floating amidst pools of oil and wine, the bones of all the hams that had been eaten; whilst a heap of broken bottles covered all the left-hand corner of the cellar; and a barrel, of which the tap had been left open, was losing through that opening the last drops of its blood. The image of devastation and death, as the poet of antiquity says, reigned there as on a battle-field.

Of fifty sausages, which had hung on the beams, scarcely ten remained.

The howlings of the landlord and his wife pierced through the vaulted ceiling of the cellar: d'Artagnan himself was affected by them; yet Athos did not even turn his head.

But rage succeeded grief. The innkeeper armed himself with a spit, and rushed, in a paroxysm of despair, into the room where the two friends were sitting.

"Some wine!" cried Athos, on seeing the landlord.

"Some wine!" exclaimed the astonished host. "Some wine! Why, you have drunk more than a hundred pistoles' worth; and I am a ruined man!— ruined! lost! annihilated!"

"Bah!" said Athos, "we were constantly thirsty."

"But, even if you had been contented with drinking— but you have broken all the bottles."

"Why, you pushed me on a heap, which rolled over. It was all your fault."

"All my oil is lost!"

"Oil is a sovereign balm for wounds, and it was necessary that poor Grimaud should bathe those you had inflicted."

"All my sausages are chewed away!"

"There is an enormous number of rats in that cellar!"

"You shall pay me for all this!" cried the exasperated landlord.

"Thrice-doomed knave!" exclaimed Athos. But he fell back immediately: he had exhausted all his strength. D'Artagnan hastened to shield him, by raising his riding-whip.

The host recoiled a step, and burst into tears.

"That will teach you," said d'Artagnan, "to behave with a little more politeness to the guests whom God sends you."

"God!—say the devil!"

"My dear friend," said d'Artagnan, "if you assail our ears in this way again, we will all four go and shut ourselves in your cellar, and see whether the destruction is as great as you pretend."

"Well, then, gentlemen," said the landlord, "I am wrong, I confess; but mercy is due to every sinner: you are noblemen, and I am only a poor innkeeper: you will have mercy on me."

"Ah, if you talk in that manner," said Athos, "you will pierce my heart, and the tears will flow from my eyes, as the wine ran from your casks. I am not so great a devil as I look. Come—come here—and let us talk it over."

The host approached, with some hesitation.

"Come here, I tell you, and do not be afraid," continued Athos. "At the moment I was about to pay you, I laid my purse upon the table."

"Yes, my lord."

"And that purse contained sixty pistoles: where is it?"

"Lodged at the register-office, my lord. It was said to be false money."

"Well, then! recover my purse, and keep the sixty pistoles."

"But your lordship well knows that the register-office never gives up what it has once got. If it was bad money, there might be some hope; but, unfortunately, it is all good coin."

"Let us see," said d'Artagnan: "where is Athos's old horse?"

"In the stables."

"How much is he worth?"

"Fifty pistoles, at the most."

"He is worth eighty: take him, and say no more about it."

"What! do you mean to sell my horse," said Athos—"my Bajazet! And on what shall I make the campaign? —on Grimaud's?"

"I have brought you another," said d'Artagnan.

"And a magnificent one," cried the landlord.

"Then," said Athos, "if there be another, younger and handsomer, take the old one. And now let us have something to drink."

"Of what sort?" said mine host, completely pacified.

"Of that which is at the bottom, near the laths: there are twenty-five bottles of it remaining; the others were broken by my fall. Bring up six."

"This man is a perfect tun!" said the landlord to himself. "If he should only remain here a fortnight, and pay for what he drinks, I should re-establish my affairs."

"Now," said Athos, "whilst we are waiting for the wine, tell me what has become of the others. Come, let me hear."

D'Artagnan recounted how he had found Porthos in bed with a sprain, and Aramis between two theologians. As he ended his narration, the landlord entered with the bottles which had been ordered, and a ham, which had been, fortunately, left outside the cellar.

"That's right," said Athos, filling his own glass and that of d'Artagnan; "here's to Porthos and Aramis. But, my friend, what is the matter with you? and what has happened to you yourself? I fancy that you are looking sad."

"Alas!" replied d'Artagnan, "I am the most unhappy of you all."

"You unhappy, d'Artagnan!" said Athos. "Let me hear how you can be unhappy? Tell me that."

"By and by," said d'Artagnan.

"By and by! And why by and by? Is it because you think that I am drunk, d'Artagnan? Just understand, then, that my ideas are never clearer that when I am in my cups. Speak, therefore; I am all attention."

D'Artagnan related his adventure with Madame Bonancieux. Athos heard him without even moving his eyebrow. Then, when he had ended—

"Those are all trifles," said Athos; "trifles."

This was the favourite word of Athos.

"You repeat the word *trifles*, my dear Athos," said d'Artagnan; "and it comes with a bad grace from you, who have never loved."

The dull eye of Athos lighted up suddenly; though it was but a momentary flash, and then it again became dull and wandering as before.

"It is true," he said quietly, "I *have* never loved."

"You see, then, stony heart," said d'Artagnan, "that you are wrong to be so hard on us who have more tender natures."

"Tender natures! wounded hearts!" exclaimed Athos. "What are you saying?"

"I say that love is a lottery, in which he who wins gains death! You are very fortunate to have lost, believe me, my dear d'Artagnan; and if I have any advice to give you, it is to lose always."

"She seemed to love me so much!"

"Of course, she *seemed*."

"Oh! She loved me!"

"Child! There is not a man who has not, like you, believed that his mistress loved him; and there is not a man who has not been deceived by his mistress!"

"Except you, Athos, who never had one."

"It is true," said Athos, after a moment's silence, "I never had one. Let us drink."

"But then," said d'Artagnan, "philosopher as you are, instruct and console me: I want instruction and consolation."

"Consolation—about what?"

"About my misfortune."

"Your misfortune makes me laugh," said Athos, shrugging his shoulders. "I should be curious to know what you would say if I were to tell you a love story."

"About yourself?"

"Or one of my friends—what does it signify?"

"Tell it me, Athos; tell it."

"Let us drink: that will be far better."

"Drink, and tell your story."

"Yes, I can do that," said Athos, emptying and again filling his glass; "the two things accompany one another admirably well."

"I am attentive," said d'Artagnan.

Athos collected himself; and, as he did so, d'Artagnan saw him grow more pale. He was at that point of intoxication at which vulgar tipplers fall down and sleep. As for him, he actually dreamed aloud, without sleeping. There was something awful in this somnambulism of intoxication.

"You absolutely wish it?" said he.

"I even entreat you," replied d'Artagnan.

"Well then, it shall be as you desire. One of my friends—one of my friends, you understand—not myself," said Athos, interrupting himself with a sombre smile— "one of the counts of my province, that is to say, of Berri, as noble as a Dandolo or a Montmorency, became enamoured, at twenty-five years of age, of a young girl of sixteen, who was as beautiful as love. Through the simplicity of her age, an ardent soul was perceptible; the soul, not of a woman, but of a poet. She did not merely please—she intoxicated the mind. Her home was in a small village, where she lived with her brother, who was a curate. They were new-comers into that part of the country. No one knew whence they came; and, on seeing her so beautiful, and her brother so pious, no one thought of inquiring. They were, moreover, said to belong to a good family. My friend, who was the great man of that neighbourhood, might have seduced her, or even seized upon her by force, if he had chosen. He was the master; and who would have thought of defending two unknown strangers? Unfortunately, he was a man of honour, and he married her. The fool! the ass! the idiot!"

"But why so, since he loved her?" said d'Artagnan.

"Wait a little," replied Athos. "He took her to his castle, and made her the first lady of the province, and, to do her justice, she filled her position admirably."

"Well?" said d'Artagnan.

"Well! one day, when she was out hunting with her husband," continued Athos, in a low voice, and speaking very quickly, "she fell from her horse, and fainted. The count hastened to her assistance, and, as she seemed half-suffocated by her clothes, cut them with his dagger, so that her shoulder was exposed. Guess what there was upon her shoulder, d'Artagnan?" said Athos, with a convulsive burst of laughter.

"How can I tell!" demanded d'Artagnan.

"A fleur-de-lis," said Athos. "She was branded!"— And at one draught he emptied the glass which was in his hand.

"Horrible! What are you telling me?" cried d'Artagnan.

"The truth, my dear fellow! The angel was a fiend —the simple young girl had been a thief!"

"And what did the count do?"

"The count was a powerful noble: he had the undisputed right of executing justice on his domain: he tore off the remainder of her clothes, tied her hands behind her back, and hung her on a tree!"

"Oh, heavens, Athos, a murder!" cried d'Artagnan.

"Yes, a murder—nothing else!" said Athos, pale as death. "But they leave me without wine, it seems."

And he seized the last bottle by its neck, put it to his mouth, and emptied it at a draught, as though it had been a glass.

His head then fell on his two hands; whilst d'Artagnan remained before him, overwhelmed with horror.

"That has cured me of women—beautiful, poetic, and fascinating women," said Athos, raising himself, and forgetting to preserve the mystery of an intervening count. "May God grant as much to you! Let us drink."

"And so she is dead?" stammered d'Artagnan.

"Egad!" said Athos—"hold your glass. Will you have some ham, you rogue? We cannot drink any more!"

"But her brother?" timidly added d'Artagnan.

"Her brother?" replied Athos.

" Yes, the priest."

" Ah! I sought him, to hang him also; but he was too quick for me—he had fled the evening before."

" And did any one ever discover who the wretch was?"

" It was the first lover and accomplice of the girl: a fine fellow, who had pretended to be a curate, that he might get his mistress married and provided for. He must have got quartered, I trust."

" Oh! my God! my God!" exclaimed d'Artagnan, astounded by this horrible adventure.

" Eat some of this ham, d'Artagnan; it is exquisite," said Athos, cutting a slice, which he put upon the young man's plate. " What a misfortune that there were not four such hams in the cellar. I should have drunk fifty bottles more."

D'Artagnan could no longer bear this conversation: it would have driven him mad. He let his head fall upon his hands, and pretended to sleep.

" The young men nowadays do not know how to stand their drink," said Athos, looking at him with pity; " and yet that is one of the best of them!"

CHAPTER XXVIII.

THE RETURN.

D'ARTAGNAN had not recovered from the consternation produced by the terrible communication of Athos. Many things yet appeared to him obscure in this semi-confession. In the first place, it had been made by a man who was quite drunk, to another man who was half drunk; and yet, in spite of that confusion of the brain which is produced by two or three bottles of Burgundy, d'Artagnan, on awaking the next morning, had each of Athos's words as thoroughly present in his mind, as though they had been stamped upon it as they fell from his companion's lips. His doubts made him only the more eager to arrive at certainty ; and he went to his friend's room with a determination to renew the conversation. But he found Athos quite himself again ; that is to say, the acutest and most impenetrable of men.

Moreover, the musketeer, after he had exchanged a smile, and shaken hands with him, anticipated his thought.

"I was very tipsy last night, my dear d'Artagnan," said he. "I perceived it this morning by my tongue, which was still heavy, and my pulse, which was still agitated. I would bet that I uttered a thousand extravagances."

And, as he said this, he looked at his friend with an earnestness which embarrassed him.

"No," said d'Artagnan ; "if I remember right, you said nothing out of the common."

"Ah! you astonish me. I thought that I had related some most lamentable story."

And he looked at the young man as if he would have read the very depths of his heart.

"Faith," replied d'Artagnan, "it appears that I was even more tipsy than you were, since I remember nothing."

Athos was not satisfied with this, and continued—

"You cannot fail to have observed, my dear friend, that each one has his own kind of drunkenness—sad or gay. Mine is of a melancholy sort ; and, when once I am tipsy, my mania is to narrate all the lugubrious tales with which my foolish nurse has filled my brain. It is my failing—a great fault, I confess ; but, barring that, I am an excellent drinker."

Athos said this in such a natural manner, that d'Artagnan was shaken in his conviction.

"Ah, then, that is it," said the young man, as if endeavouring to recall the truth ; "that is it. I remember, as one recollects a dream, that we talked of people being hung."

T M.—I.   M

"Ah! you see," said Athos, growing pale, but attempting to smile; "I was sure of it. People being hanged is quite my nightmare."

"Yes, yes," replied d'Artagnan; "and this is what I can recall to mind: yes, it was so; listen, then—it was something about a woman."

"See there," replied Athos, becoming almost livid; "it is my best story, the one of the woman with fair hair; and when I tell that, I am sure to be dead drunk."

"Yes, that is it," said d'Artagnan; "a story about a fair woman, tall and beautiful, with blue eyes."

"Yes, who was hanged."

"By her husband, who was a nobleman of your acquaintance," said d'Artagnan, looking earnestly at Athos.

"Well, now, see how a man might be compromised, when one no longer knows what he is saying," replied Athos, shrugging his shoulders, as if he pitied himself. "Positively, I will not get tipsy any more, d'Artagnan; it is a very bad habit."

D'Artagnan continued silent; and then, suddenly changing the conversation, Athos said—

"Apropos, I thank you for the horse you have brought me."

"Do you like him?"

"Yes; but he would not stand work."

"You are mistaken. I went ten leagues with him in less than an hour and a half, and he appeared as if he had only gone round the Place St. Sulpice."

"Ah, then, you make me regret him."

"Regret him?"

"Yes, for I have parted with him."

"How is that?"

"The fact is, this morning I got up at six. You were sleeping like a deaf man, and I did not know what to do, being still quite stupefied by last night's debauch. I therefore went down to the common room, and saw one of the Englishmen, who was buying a horse of a couper, his own having died the day before. I approached him, and, as I saw he was offering a hundred pistoles for a sorrel horse—'Egad, sir,' said I, 'I have also a horse to sell.'—' And a very handsome one, too,' said he; 'I saw him yesterday; your friend's servant was holding him.'—' Do you think he is worth a hundred pistoles?'—' Yes, will you sell him to me at that price?' —' No; but I will play you for him.'—' At what?'— ' At dice.'

"No sooner said than done; and I lost the horse. Ah! but, after all," continued Athos, "I won back his caparison."

D'Artagnan made a wry face.

"Does that annoy you?" asked Athos.

"Yes, indeed, I confess it does," replied d'Artagnan. "That horse ought to have led to our recognition on a battle-field: it was a pledge—a souvenir. Athos, you have done wrong."

"But, my dear fellow, put yourself in my place," replied the musketeer. "I was horribly tired of myself; and then, upon my honour, I do not like English horses. Besides, if it is of any consequence that we should be recognised by any one, the saddle will do well enough for that, for it is very remarkable. As for the horse, we will find some excuse, as a reason for its disappearance. What the plague! a horse is mortal. Let us say that mine has had the glanders, or the farcy."

But d'Artagnan did not laugh.

"I am sorry for this," continued Athos, "since you seem to set such a value on these animals, for I have not yet finished my tale."

"Why, what more have you done?"

"After having lost my horse—nine against ten, for that was the throw — the idea came into my head to stake yours."

"But you confined yourself to the mere idea, I hope?"

"No, I put it into execution instantaneously."

"Ah! was ever such a thing heard of?" exclaimed d'Artagnan anxiously.

"I staked him—and lost."

"My horse?"

"Yes; your horse — seven against eight, for I lost only by one point. You know the old proverb."

"Athos, you have lost your senses, I swear."

"My dear fellow, it was yesterday, when I was telling you those foolish stories, that you should have said that, and not this morning. I lost him, however, with all his ornaments and caparison."

"But this is quite frightful!"

"Listen, now; you have not heard the end of it yet. I should be a most excellent player if I did not get so infatuated; but I do get infatuated, just as I am when I drink. Well, accordingly, I obstinately persevered at the game."

"But what more could you stake? You had nothing left."

"Yes, yes, my friend; there remained that diamond, which now glitters on your finger, and which I had noticed yesterday."

"This diamond!" exclaimed d'Artagnan, putting his hand quickly on the ring.

"And, as I am a judge of these things, having had some few of my own, I valued it at a thousand pistoles."

"I hope," said d'Artagnan very seriously, whilst he was half dead with alarm, "that you did not make any mention of my diamond?"

"On the contrary, my dear friend, do you not see that this diamond became our last resource. I might, with that, win back our horses and their accoutrements; and, perhaps, money enough for our journey."

"Athos, you make me tremble," cried d'Artagnan.

"So I mentioned your diamond to my adversary, who had also remarked it. What the plague, my dear fellow!

would you carry a star of heaven on your finger, and wish no one to observe it? Impossible!"

"Go on, my dear fellow, go on," said d'Artagnan; "for, upon my honour, you horrify me with your calmness."

"We divided the diamond into ten parts, of a hundred pistoles each."

"Oh! you are joking, on purpose to try me," said d'Artagnan, whom anger began to catch by the hair, as Minerva caught Achilles, in the *Iliad*.

"No, I am not joking, by Heaven! I should like to have seen you in the same situation. For a whole fortnight I had not looked upon a human face, and had been brutalising myself in there by parleying only with bottles!"

"That was no reason why you should stake my diamond!" said d'Artagnan, closing his hand with a nervous contraction.

"Listen, then, to the end. Ten parts, of a hundred pistoles each, would be ten throws, without revenge. In thirteen throws I lost all—in thirteen throws! The number 13 has always been fatal to me. It was the 13th of July when——"

"Zounds!" cried d'Artagnan, arising from the table, the morning's narrative making him forget that of the night before.

"Patience," cried Athos. "I had formed a plan. The Englishman was an original. I had seen him in the morning talking to Grimaud; and Grimaud had informed me that he had made proposals to engage him in his service. I staked Grimaud—the silent Grimaud—divided into ten portions."

"Ah, well! was ever such a thing heard of!" said d'Artagnan, bursting out into a laugh.

"Grimaud himself—do you understand? And by these ten parts of Grimaud, who is not worth a ducat when entire, I won back the diamond. Tell me now if perseverance is not a virtue."

"Faith, it is all very droll," said the now comforted d'Artagnan, holding his sides with laughter.

"So, you understand, finding myself in the right vein, I began anew upon the diamond."

"Ah! the deuce!" said d'Artagnan, becoming again overclouded.

"I won back your trappings, then your horse, then my own trappings, then my own horse, and then lost them all again. In short, I ended by recovering your trappings and mine: and that is how we now stand. It was a superb throw, and therefore I left off."

D'Artagnan sighed as if the weight of the hotel had been taken off his breast.

"After all, my diamond is safe," he said timidly.

"Untouched, my dear friend—besides the trappings of your Bucephalus and mine."

"But what shall we do with our saddles, without horses?"

"I have an idea as to them."

"Athos, you make me tremble."

"Listen, d'Artagnan. You have not played for a long time."

"And I have no desire to play."

"Well, don't make a vow about it: you have not played for a long time. I should say, therefore, that you ought to be in luck."

"Well! and what then?"

"Well, the Englishman and his companion are still here. I observed that they regretted the trappings. You seem to value your horse; and, in your place, I would stake my trappings against my horse."

"But he would not wish for one set of trappings."

"Stake the two. Egad! I am not an egotist, like you."

"You would, would you?" said d'Artagnan, hesitating; for the confidence of Athos began to influence him unconsciously.

"Upon my honour, I would! on one throw."

"But, having lost the horses, I should very much like to keep the trappings at least."

"Then stake your diamond."

"Oh, that is quite another thing : never, never !"

"The devil ! I would propose to you to stake Planchet : but as that game has been tried once, the Englishman would not perhaps wish to try it again."

"Decidedly, my dear Athos," said d'Artagnan, "I would prefer risking nothing."

"It is a pity," said Athos coldly ; "the Englishman is well lined with pistoles. Egad ! do try one throw—a throw is soon made."

"And if I lose ? "

"You will gain."

"But if I lose ? "

"Well ! then you will surrender the trappings."

"Well, here goes for one throw," said d'Artagnan.

Athos went to look for the Englishman, and found him in the stables, where he was looking wistfully at the saddles. The opportunity was good. He made his conditions : the two sets of trappings against one horse, or a hundred pistoles, at choice. The Englishman calculated quickly ; the two sets of trappings were well worth three hundred pistoles ; so he agreed.

D'Artagnan trembled as he threw the dice, and only turned up the number three. His paleness quite frightened Athos, who contented himself with saying—

"That's a bad throw, comrade ; you will have the horses all caparisoned, sir."

The triumphant Englishman did not give himself the trouble even to shake the dice ; and, so sure was he of winning, that he threw the ivory on the table without looking. D'Artagnan turned away to hide his ill-humour.

"Well, well, well !" said Athos, in his usual calm voice, "this is a most extraordinary throw, and I have only seen it four times in my life :—two aces."

The Englishman looked, and was seized with astonishment. D'Artagnan looked, and coloured with joy.

"Yes," continued Athos, "only four times: once, at M. de Crequis's; once, at my own house in the country, in my castle of —— when I had a castle; a third time, at M. de Treville's, where it astonished us all; and a fourth time at a wine-shop, where it fell to me, and I lost by it a hundred louis, and a supper."

"Will the gentleman take back his horse?" said the Englishman.

"Certainly!" said d'Artagnan.

"Then, there is no revenge."

"Our conditions were: 'no revenge.' Do you remember?"

"True. The horse shall be delivered to your servant, sir."

"One moment," said Athos. "With your permission, sir, I desire to speak a private word with my friend."

"Speak."

Athos led d'Artagnan apart.

"Well!" said d'Artagnan, "what do you want with me now, tempter? You want me to play, do you not?"

"No, I want you to reflect."

"On what?"

"You are going to take back the horse?"

"Certainly."

"You are wrong. I would take the hundred pistoles. You know that you staked the trappings against the horse, or a hundred pistoles, at your choice."

"Yes!"

"I would take the hundred pistoles."

"Would you? But I shall take the horse."

"And you are wrong, I say again. What shall we do with one horse between us two? I cannot get up behind you: we shall have the appearance of the two sons of Aymon, who lost their brothers. And you would not mortify me by prancing about on this magnificent steed, close by my side. I would take the hundred pistoles without a moment's hesitation. We want money to return to Paris."

" I really have such a fancy for this horse, Athos."

" And you are wrong, my friend : a horse shies ; a horse stumbles and breaks his knees ; a horse eats at a rack where a glandered horse has eaten just before ; and thus you lose a horse, or rather a hundred pistoles. Then, it is necessary for the master to feed his horse ; when, on the contrary, a hundred pistoles feed the master."

" But how shall we return ?"

" On our servants' horses, to be sure. It will be evident enough, from our appearance, that we are people of consequence."

" A nice figure we shall cut on those hacks, whilst Aramis and Porthos are dashing about on their chargers."

" Aramis ! Porthos !" exclaimed Athos, and he began to laugh heartily.

" What now ?" demanded d'Artagnan, who did not understand the cause of his friend's merriment.

" Nothing, nothing. Go on," said Athos.

" And your advice is——"

" To take the hundred pistoles, d'Artagnan : with them we can feast till the end of the month. We have suffered much from fatigue, you know, and it will be well for us to repose ourselves for a time."

" I repose myself ? Oh, no ! Athos ; immediately on my return to Paris, I shall set out in search of that poor woman."

" Well, do you think your horse will be as useful to you for that purpose as the gold ? Take the hundred pistoles, my friend—take the hundred pistoles."

D'Artagnan only wanted a good reason for giving up ; and this appeared to him an excellent one. Besides, by resisting any longer, he feared that he should appear selfish. He therefore chose the hundred pistoles, which the Englishman immediately paid him.

Their only thought then was to set out. The peace, which they had finally sealed with the landlord, cost six pistoles, in addition to Athos's old horse. D'Artagnan and Athos took the horses of Planchet and Grimaud; and the two valets took to the road on foot, carrying the saddles on their heads.

Badly mounted as the two friends were, they soon left their servants behind them, and arrived at Crevecœur. At a distance they saw Aramis, leaning sorrowfully from the window, and, like Sister Anne, looking at the dust on the horizon.

"Hollo! hey! Aramis," shouted out the two friends, "what the plague are you doing there?"

"Ah, is it you, Athos? is it you, d'Artagnan?" said the young man. "I was just thinking how rapidly the things of this world disappear. My English horse, which was getting more and more distant, and has just disappeared amidst a cloud of dust, was to me a living image of the mutability of terrestrial things. Life itself may be resolved into three words—'Erat, est, fuit.'"

"And all this really means——" inquired d'Artagnan, who began to suspect the truth.

"It means that I have just been taken in in a bargain, and sold, for sixty louis, a horse, which, by the manner in which he moves, should be able to trot five leagues an hour."

D'Artagnan and Athos burst out into a laugh.

"My dear d'Artagnan," said Aramis, "do not be too much displeased with me, I entreat you: necessity knows no law. Besides, I am the person punished, since this infamous horse-dealer has cheated me out of fifty louis at least. Ah! you are thrifty managers; you come on your servants' horses, and make them lead your chargers slowly and by short stages."

At this moment a waggon, which for some minutes had been seen coming along the Amiens road, stopped, and out got Planchet and Grimaud, with their saddles on their heads. The waggon was going empty to Paris, and the two servants had engaged, as the price of their places, to keep the waggoner in drink throughout the journey.

"What does this mean?" said Aramis, as he saw them. "Nothing but the saddles?"

"Do you understand now?" said Athos.

"My friends, it is exactly like me. I too have kept the trappings by instinct. Hollo, Bazin! lay my trappings alongside of those belonging to these gentlemen."

"And what have you done with your doctors?" demanded d'Artagnan.

"I invited them to dinner the next day, my dear fellow," said Aramis. "There is some exquisite wine here, by the bye, and I made them both as drunk as I could. Then, the curate forbade me to abandon the coat, and the Jesuit entreated me to get him enrolled as a musketeer."

"Without any thesis," cried d'Artagnan—"without thesis! I demand, for my part, the suppression of the thesis!"

"Since that time I have lived very agreeably. I have begun a poem in one-syllable verse: it is rather difficult, but merit of every kind consists in conquering difficulty. It is gallant in character; and I will read to you the first canto. There are four hundred lines, and they only occupy a minute."

"Faith," said d'Artagnan, who detested verses almost as much as he did Latin, "add to the merit of the difficulty that of brevity, and you are, at least, sure that your poem will have two merits."

"Besides," continued Aramis, "it is pervaded by a virtuous passion. Well, my friends," added he, "and so we return to Paris? Bravo! I am ready. And we shall fall in with the simple Porthos, once more? So much the better: you could not believe how I have missed that great ninny. I like to see him, so self-complacent: it reconciles me to myself. Catch him selling his horse, even for a kingdom. I would I could see him on his horse, and in his saddle. He will have, I am sure, the look of the Great Mogul."

After they had halted an hour to rest their horses, Aramis paid his bill, placed Bazin in the waggon with his companions, and they then set out to rejoin Porthos.

They found him almost entirely cured, and, consequently, less pale than when d'Artagnan saw him at his first visit. He was seated at a table, on which, although he was alone, there was displayed a dinner for four persons. This dinner consisted of viands admirably dressed, of choice wines, and splendid fruit.

"Mon Dieu!" said he, rising, "you have come in the nick of time; I was just at the soup, and you will dine with me."

"Oh, oh!" said d'Artagnan, "it is not Mousqueton who has lassoed such bottles as these. Besides, here is a larded fricandeau, and a fillet of beef."

"I am recruiting my strength," said Porthos; "I am recruiting my strength. Nothing weakens one so much as these devilish sprains. Have you ever had any sprains, Athos?"

"Never," said Athos; "only I remember that in our skirmish in the Rue de Ferou, I received a sword-thrust, which, at the end of fifteen or twenty days, produced exactly the same consequences as a sprain."

"But this dinner was not for yourself alone, my dear Porthos?" said Aramis.

"No," said Porthos; "I expected some gentlemen from the neighbourhood, who have just sent word that they cannot come; but as you will take their places, I shall lose nothing by the exchange. Hollo, Mousqueton! bring chairs, and let the bottles be doubled!"

"Do you know what we are eating here?" asked Athos, after ten minutes had elapsed.

"Egad," replied d'Artagnan, "I am eating veal, larded with marrow.'

"And I, veal cutlets," said Porthos.

"And I, capon," said Aramis.

"You are all mistaken, gentlemen," gravely replied Athos; "you are eating horse."

"Come, come!" said d'Artagnan.

"The horse?" cried Aramis, making a horrible face.

Porthos alone was silent.

"Yes, the horse. Is it not so, Porthos? Are we not eating the horse, and perhaps the saddle with it?"

"No, gentleman, I have kept the caparison."

"Faith, we are all bad alike," said Aramis. "One would say that we had done it by agreement."

"What would you have?" said Porthos; "the horse shamed my visitors, and I did not wish to humiliate them."

"Then your duchess is still at the baths, is she not?" inquired d'Artagnan.

"Yes," replied Porthos. "Then the governor of the province, one of the gentlemen I expected here to-day, appeared to wish so much for him, that I gave him to him."

"Gave him!" exclaimed d'Artagnan.

"Oh, yes—zounds, yes—that is the expression," said Porthos, "for he was certainly worth a hundred and fifty louis, and the rascal would only pay me eighty."

"Without the saddle," said Aramis.

"Yes, without the saddle."

"You observe, gentlemen," said Athos, "that, after all, Porthos has made the best bargain of any of us."

There was then a perfect shout of laughter, at which poor Porthos was altogether astonished; but they soon explained to him the reason of this mirth, in which, as usual, he participated noisily.

"So we are all in cash now," said d'Artagnan.

"Not I for one," said Athos. "I found Aramis's Spanish wine so good, that I sent sixty bottles in the waggon with the servants, which has very much impoverished me."

"And I," said Aramis, "had given almost my last sou to the church of Montdidier, and the Jesuits of Amiens; and I had, besides, made engagements which I was compelled to keep—masses ordered for myself, and for you, gentlemen, which will surely be said, and by which I do not doubt we shall be greatly benefited."

"And do you believe that my sprain has cost me nothing?" said Porthos; "not to mention Mousqueton's wound, for which I was obliged to have a surgeon in attendance upon him twice a day."

"Well, well, I see," said Athos, exchanging a smile with Aramis and d'Artagnan, "that you have behaved nobly towards the poor lad. It is like a good master."

"In short," said Porthos, "when my bill is paid, I shall have about thirty crowns remaining."

"And I, about ten pistoles," said Aramis.

"It appears," said Athos, "that we are the Crœsuses of the party. How much remains of your hundred pistoles, d'Artagnan?"

"Of my hundred pistoles? In the first place, I gave you fifty."

"Did you really?"

"Most assuredly."

"Ah! it is true; I recollect it."

"Then I paid the landlord six!"

"What an animal that landlord was! Why did you give him six pistoles?"

"It was you who told me to give them to him."

"It is true; in fact, I am too generous!—and the balance?"

"Twenty-five louis," said d'Artagnan.

"And I," said Athos, pulling out a few small coins from his pocket—"see what I've got."

"You, nothing!"

"Faith! just so; or, at any rate, so little as to be not worth adding to the general store."

"Now, let us reckon up how much we have got :— Porthos?"

"Thirty crowns!"

"Aramis?"

"Ten pistoles."

"And you, d'Artagnan?"

"Twenty-five."

"That makes in all——" said Athos.

"Four hundred and seventy-five livres," said d'Artagnan, who calculated like Archimedes.

"When we reach Paris, we shall have four hundred," said Porthos, "besides the horse-trappings."

"But our regimental mounts?" said Aramis.

"Well! the four horses of our servants will procure two fit for their masters, which we must draw lots for. With the four hundred livres we can get half a horse for one of the dismounted ones; and then we will give the dregs of our pockets to d'Artagnan, who is in luck, and he shall go and stake them at the first tennis-court we come to. There, now!"

"Let us dine," said Porthos, "for the second course is getting cold."

And the four friends, now more at ease concerning the future, did honour to the repast, of which the remnants were abandoned to Mousqueton, Bazin, Planchet, and Grimaud.

On arriving in Paris, d'Artagnan found a note from M. des Essarts, announcing that, as his majesty had determined on opening the campaign on the first of May, he must immediately make ready his equipments.

He ran at once to his friends, whom he had only quitted half an hour before, and whom he found very melancholy, or, rather, very anxious. They were in grand consultation at Athos's, which always indicated a concern of some importance.

They had, in fact, each received a similar note from M. de Treville.

The four philosophers looked at one another in great amazement: M. de Treville never jested on a matter of discipline.

"And at what sum do you estimate these equipments?" asked d'Artagnan.

"Oh, one cannot say," replied Aramis; "we have just made our calculations with a Spartan economy, and fifteen hundred livres will be absolutely necessary for each."

"Four times fifteen make sixty; that is six thousand livres," said Athos.

"For my part," said d'Artagnan, "I think that a thousand livres would be sufficient for each. It is true that I speak, not as a Spartan, but as an attorney."

This word *attorney* awoke Porthos.

"Stop! I have an idea!" said he.

"That is something, however; as for myself," coolly observed Athos, "I have not even the shadow of one; but, as for d'Artagnan, he is mad, gentlemen. A thousand livres! why, for my part alone, I am certain that I shall require two thousand."

"Four times two make eight," said d'Artagnan; "so we shall want eight thousand livres for our accoutrements. It is true that we have already got the saddles."

"But besides that," said Athos, waiting till d'Artagnan, who was going to thank M. de Treville, had shut the door, before he brought to light his idea, so full of promise for the future—"more than that, there is the beautiful diamond which shines on the finger of our friend. By all the saints! d'Artagnan is too good a comrade to leave his brothers in difficulty, when he carries a king's ransom on his middle finger."

CHAPTER XXIX.

THE HUNT AFTER EQUIPMENTS.

THE most prudent of the four friends was certainly d'Artagnan, although, in his capacity of guardsman, it was much more easy to equip him than the musketeers, who were men of rank. But our Gascon youth was, as may have been seen, of a character not only economical, but almost parsimonious; yet, at the same time (explain the contradiction), almost as vain-glorious as Porthos.

To the thoughtfulness originating in his vanity, was now added a less selfish anxiety. Whatever inquiries he had made concerning Madame Bonancieux, he could obtain no tidings of her. M. de Treville had spoken of her to the queen; but the queen did not know what had become of her, and promised to have some investigations set on foot. This promise, however, was vague, and afforded little satisfaction to the troubled d'Artagnan.

Athos never quitted his own apartment: he was determined not to take a single step to equip himself.

"There are fifteen days remaining yet," said he to his friends. "Well, if at the end of those fifteen days I have found nothing, or, rather, if nothing has come to find me, as I am too good a Catholic to blow out my brains with a pistol, I will seek a good quarrel with four of his eminence's guards, or with eight Englishmen, and I will fight till one of them kills me; which, calculating the number, cannot fail to come to pass. It will then be said that I died in the king's service; so that I shall have served him, without needing to furnish myself with equipments."

Porthos continued to walk with his hands behind his back, saying, "I will pursue my idea."

Aramis, thoughtful and unadorned, said nothing.

It may be seen, from these disastrous details, that desolation reigned throughout the little community.

The servants, on their side, like the coursers of Hippolytus, partook of their masters' bitter grief. Mousqueton made a store of crusts; Bazin, who had always leaned towards devotion, haunted the churches; Planchet watched the flies buzzing about; and Grimaud, whom the general distress could not induce to break the silence which his master had imposed, sighed in a way to melt even the hearts of stones.

The three friends—for, as we have already said, Athos had sworn not to stir an inch in search of equipments—went out early, and came in late. They wandered through the streets, looking on every pavement to see if any passenger might not have dropped a purse. They might have been supposed to be pursuing a trail, so watchful were they at every step. And when they met, their desponding looks seemed to ask of one another— "Have you found anything?"

Nevertheless, as Porthos had been the first to find an idea, and as he had steadily pursued it, he was the first to act. He was a man of action, this worthy Porthos. D'Artagnan saw him one day going towards the church of St. Leun, and instinctively followed him. He entered the sacred edifice, after having raised his moustache, and pulled out his imperial, which operations always portended, on his part, the most irresistible intentions. As d'Artagnan took some precautions to conceal himself, Porthos fancied that he had not been perceived. D'Artagnan entered after him. Porthos went and ensconced himself on one side of a pillar, and d'Artagnan, still unseen, leaned himself against the other.

There was a sermon, and the church was therefore full. Porthos took advantage of this circumstance to ogle the ladies. Thanks to Mousqueton's good offices, the external appearance was far from announcing the internal distress. His hat was, indeed, rather napless, and his feather rather drooping; his embroidery was somewhat tarnished, and his lace a little frayed; but, in the subdued light, these trifles disappeared, and Porthos still looked the handsome Porthos.

D'Artagnan perceived on a pew, near the pillar against which Porthos and he were leaning, a sort of mature beauty, a little yellow, and slightly withered, but yet upright and haughty, under her black head-dress. The eyes of Porthos were furtively directed on this lady, and then fluttered vaguely over the other parts of the church.

On her part, the lady, from time to time, blushed, and, with the rapidity of lightning, cast a glance at the inconstant Porthos, whose eyes immediately fluttered away with greater activity than before. It was quite clear that this was a game which much piqued the lady in the dark hood; for she bit her lips till they bled, scratched her nose, and shifted desperately on her seat.

As soon as Porthos saw this, he once more curled his moustache, again elongated his imperial, and then began to make signals to a fair lady who was near the choir, and who was not only a fair lady, but undoubtedly a lady of some consequence; for she had behind her a little negro boy, who had carried the cushion on which she knelt, and a waiting-woman, who carried the coroneted bag in which she brought her mass-book.

The lady in the black hood slily observed all these glances of Porthos, and remarked that they were fixed upon the lady with the velvet cushion, the little negro boy and the waiting-woman.

In the meantime, Porthos was playing hard—winking his eyes, pressing a finger on his lips, and calling up little killing smiles, which really were assassinating the susceptible dame he scorned.

Thus it was, that, by way of *meâ culpâ*, and whilst beating her hand against her breast, she sent forth such a sonorous sigh, that everybody—even the lady with the red cushion—turned to look at her. Porthos was impenetrable. He had understood the sigh well, but he pretended to be deaf.

The lady with the red cushion produced a very striking effect, for she was extremely beautiful. She made a great impression on the lady in the black hood, who saw in her a truly formidable rival; a great impression upon Porthos, who thought her both much younger and much prettier than the lady in the black hood; and, lastly, a great impression upon d'Artagnan, who recognised in her the lady of Meung, whom his persecutor, the man with a scar, had addressed by the title of My Lady.

D'Artagnan, without losing sight of this lady with the velvet cushion, continued to watch Porthos's game, which amused him highly. He ventured to guess that this lady in the black hood was the solicitor's wife of the Rue aux

Ours; especially as that street was not far from the church of St. Leu.

He then, by inference, divined that Porthos wished to revenge his defeat at Chantilly, when the lady had shown herself so refractory in regard to her purse.

But, amidst all this, d'Artagnan thought he could remark that no sign responded to the gallantries of Porthos. It was all chimera and illusion: but, even for an actual love, and for a well-founded jealousy, what other reality is there than illusions and chimeras?

When the sermon was ended, the solicitor's wife went towards the vessel containing the holy water. Porthos hastened to it before her, and, instead of putting in only one finger, he immersed his whole hand. The lady smiled, in the belief that it was for her that Porthos had taken so much trouble. But she was quickly and cruelly undeceived. Whilst she was only about three paces from him, he turned aside his head, keeping his eyes invariably fixed upon the lady with the red cushion, who had arisen, and, followed by her negro boy and waiting-woman, was approaching the place where he stood.

When she had come near to Porthos, he drew his hand, all dripping with holy water, out of the vessel: the beautiful devotee touched with her slender fingers the enormous hand of Porthos, smiled as she made the sign of the cross, and left the church.

This was too much for the solicitor's wife, who no longer doubted that there was an understanding between this lady and Porthos. If she had been a lady of quality, she would have fainted, but, as she was only a solicitor's wife, she contented herself with saying in a concentrated rage.

"So, M. Porthos! you do not offer me any holy water?"

Porthos, at these words, started like a man just awakening from a sleep of a thousand years.

"Ah, madame!" exclaimed he, "is it indeed you?

How is your husband, that dear M. Coquenard? Is he still as miserly as ever? Where could my eyes have been, that I did not once perceive you during the two mortal hours that the sermon lasted?"

"I was only two paces from you, sir," responded the attorney's wife; "but you did not perceive me, because you had no eyes except for that beautiful lady, to whom you just now offered the holy water."

Porthos pretended to be abashed.

"Ah," said he, "you observed it, did you?"

"One must have been blind not to have observed it."

"Yes," said Porthos negligently, "it is one of my friends—a duchess—whom I have some difficulty in meeting, on account of the jealousy of her husband, and who apprised me that, for the sole purpose of seeing me, she would come to-day to this wretched church, in this abominable neighbourhood."

"M. Porthos," said the attorney's wife, "will you have the goodness to favour me with your arm for a few minutes? I should be glad to have some conversation with you."

"How is that, madame?" said Porthos, winking to himself, like a player, who laughs at the dupe whom he is about to ensnare.

Just at this moment d'Artagnan passed, in pursuit of the fair lady. He slily glanced at Porthos, and saw that triumphant wink.

"Ah," said he to himself, reasoning after the peculiarly easy morality of that age of gallantry, "there is one who might readily be equipped by the proper time."

Porthos, yielding to the pressure of the lady's arm, as a vessel yields to her helm, reached the cloister of St. Magloire, a retired spot, which was closed by a turnstile at either end. In the day-time, nobody was to be seen there, but beggars at their meals, or children at their play.

"Ah! M. Porthos," exclaimed the attorney's wife, when she was assured that none but the habitual population of the place could see or hear them: "ah! M. Porthos, you are a great conqueror, it appears."

"I, madame!" said Porthos bridling with his head: "how so?"

"Witness the signs just now, and the holy water. But she must be a princess, at the least, that lady, with her negro boy, and her waiting-woman!"

"You are mistaken. Mon Dieu! no; she is really only a duchess."

"And that courier who was waiting at the door, and that carriage, with the coachman in a magnificent livery?"

Porthos had seen neither courier nor carriage; but Madame Coquenard, with the glance of a jealous woman, had seen all.

Porthos regretted that he had not made the lady with the red cushion a princess when he was at it.

"Ah! you are the pet of all the most beautiful women, M. Porthos," resumed the attorney's wife, with a sigh.

"But," replied Porthos, "with such a figure as nature has bestowed on me, how should I avoid conquests?"

"Mon Dieu! how quickly you men forget!" exclaimed the attorney's wife, raising her eyes to heaven.

"Less quickly than women, I think," replied Porthos. "For, after all, I may say, madame, that I have been your victim, when, wounded and dying, I saw myself abandoned by the surgeons—I, the offspring of an illustrious family, who had depended on your friendship, was near dying of my wounds first, and of hunger afterwards, in a miserable wine-shop at Chantilly, and that without your deigning even to answer the burning epistles which I wrote to you."

"But, M. Porthos——" muttered the solicitor's wife, who felt that, if judged by the conduct of the noblest dames of the age, hers was very wrong.

"I," continued Porthos, "who for your sake had sacrificed the countess of Penaflor——"

"I know it well."

"The baroness of——"

"M. Porthos, do not overwhelm me!"

"The countess of——"

"M. Porthos, be generous!"

"You are right, madame; and I will not proceed."

"But it is my husband, who will not listen to a word about lending."

"Madame Coquenard," said Porthos, "do you remember the first letter which you wrote me, and which I cherish, engraven on my heart?"

The lady groaned.

"But," said she, "the sum which you proposed to borrow was, really, rather large."

"Madame Coquenard, I gave you the preference. I had only to write to the duchess of —— but I will not mention her name, for it has never been mine to compromise a woman; but this I know, that I had but to write to her, and she immediately sent me fifteen hundred."

The attorney's wife let fall a tear.

"M. Porthos," said she, "I swear to you that you have punished me sufficiently; and if, in future, you should ever again be so circumstanced, you have only to apply to me."

"Fie, madame!" said Porthos, as though disgusted; "do not let us allude to money: it is too humiliating!"

"Then you no longer esteem me!" said the attorney's wife, slowly and sorrowfully.

Porthos maintained a majestic silence.

"And is it thus you answer me? Alas! I understand."

"Think of the offence which you have given me, madame: it is indelible, here," said Porthos, putting his hand over his heart, and pressing it with force.

"But I will repair it, my dear Porthos."

"Besides, what did I ask of you?" continued Porthos, shrugging his shoulders with an air of the utmost simplicity, "a loan—nothing more. I know that you are not rich, Madame Coquenard, and that your husband is obliged to fleece his poor clients to gain a few pitiful crowns. Oh! if you had been a countess, a marchioness, or a duchess, it would have been another thing, and you would have been indeed unpardonable."

The solicitor's wife was piqued.

"Learn, M. Porthos," said she, "that my strong-box, although the strong-box of a solicitor's wife, is probably far better furnished than that of all those ruined minxes."

"Then you have doubly offended me, Madame Coquenard," said Porthos, disengaging the arm of the attorney's wife from his own; "for, if you are rich, your refusal is without excuse."

"When I say rich," replied the attorney's wife, who saw that she had gone too far, "you must not take my words literally. I am not precisely rich, but in comfortable circumstances."

"Come, madame," said Porthos, "let us say no more about it: you have misunderstood me, and all sympathy between us is destroyed."

"Ungrateful man!"

"Ah, I advise you to complain!" said Porthos.

"Go to your beautiful duchess? Let me no longer restrain you."

"Ah! she is not yet so shabby, I believe."

"Come, then, M. Porthos," said Madame Coquenard, "once more, and it is the last time—do you still love me?"

"Alas, madame," replied Porthos, in the most melancholy tone that he could assume, "when one is about to commence a campaign—and in this campaign my presentiments assure me that I shall be killed—"

"Oh, do not say such things!" exclaimed the attorney's wife, bursting out into sobs.

"Something tells me that it will be so," said Porthos, becoming more and more melancholy.

"Say, rather, that you have formed another love."

"No, I speak frankly to you. No new object has engaged my thoughts; and, indeed, I feel something at the bottom of my heart which pleads for you. But in a fortnight, as you do or do not know, this fatal campaign will open, and I shall be dreadfully busy about my equipment. Besides, I must go into Brittany, to my own family, to provide the funds necessary for my departure !"

Porthos observed a last struggle between love and avarice.

"And," continued he, "as the duchess, whom you saw just now, has an estate close to mine, we shall go down together. A journey, you know, appears much shorter when one travels in company."

"Have you no friends in Paris, M. Porthos?" asked the attorney's wife.

"I once believed I had," said Porthos, resuming his melancholy manner; "but I have clearly seen that I deceived myself."

"You have! you have! M. Porthos," exclaimed the attorney's wife, in a transport which inspired even herself. "Come to our house to-morrow. You are the son of my aunt, consequently my cousin; you come from Noyon, in Picardy, and you have several law-suits on your hands, and no attorney. Can you remember all this?"

"Perfectly, madame."

"Come at dinner-time."

"Very well."

"And be on your guard before my husband, who is a shrewd fellow, in spite of his seventy-six years."

"Seventy-six years! Plague take it! a fine age," replied Porthos.

"A great age, you mean to say, M. Porthos. So that the poor dear man might leave me a widow at any moment," added the lady, casting a significant glance at Porthos. "Fortunately, however, by our marriage contract, all the property reverts to the survivor."

"All?" said Porthos.

"Yes, all."

"You are a most provident woman, I perceive, my charming Madame Coquenard," said Porthos, tenderly pressing the lady's hand.

"Then we are completely reconciled, my dear M. Porthos?" said she, in a most insinuating tone.

"For life," replied Porthos, in the same tone.

"Farewell, then, till our next meeting, you traitor!"

"Till our next meeting, you forgetful one!"

"Till to-morrow, my angel!"

"Till to-morrow, light of my life!"

LONDON AND GLASGOW: COLLINS' CLEAR-TYPE PRESS

Collins'
Illustrated Pocket Classics

Cloth, **2/-** net   Leather, gilt top, **4/-** net

THIN PAPER EDITIONS AT POPULAR PRICES

Over 2,500 New Illustrations

LIST OF TITLES

Collins' Illustrated Pocket Classics

Collins' Illustrated Pocket Classics

Collins' Illustrated Pocket Classics

LONDON AND GLASGOW: COLLINS' CLEAR-TYPE PRESS